VAMPYRES OF HOLLYWOOD

ALSO BY ADRIENNE BARBEAU

There Are Worse Things I Could Do

ALSO BY MICHAEL SCOTT

The Alchemyst (The Secrets of the Immortal Nicholas Flamel)

VAMPYRES OF HOLLYWOOD

ADRIENNE BARBEAU

and

MICHAEL SCOTT

Thomas Dunne Books
St. Martin's Griffin
New York

THOMAS DUNNE BOOKS.
An imprint of St. Martin's Press.

VAMPYRES OF HOLLYWOOD. Copyright © 2008 by Adrienne Barbeau and Michael Scott. All rights reserved. Printed in the United States of America. For information, address St. Martin's Press, 175 Fifth Avenue, New York, N.Y. 10010.

www.thomasdunnebooks.com
www.stmartins.com

Book design by Spring Hoteling

The Library of Congress has catalogued the hardcover edition as follows:

Barbeau, Adrienne, 1949–
    Vampyres of Hollywood / Adrienne Barbeau and Michael Scott. — 1st ed.
      p. cm.
    ISBN 978-0-312-36722-0
    1. Motion picture producers and directors—Fiction. 2. Vampires—Fiction.
  3. Hollywood (Los Angeles, Calif.)—Fiction. I. Scott, Michael, 1959– II. Title.
PS3602.A759V36 2008
813'.6—dc22

2008015772

ISBN 978-0-312-56577-0 (trade paperback)

10 9 8 7 6 5 4 3 2

For my Armenian heroines: Aunty Ruby, Aunty Anna,
and Grandma on the Ranch; and to Jocelyn,
the best sister in the whole wide world.—AB

For Claudette, again.—MS

ACKNOWLEDGMENTS

There wouldn't be any *Vampyres of Hollywood* without the talent of Michael Scott. He is brilliant at what he does.

Thanks also and once again to Jane Dystel and Miriam Goderich at Dystel & Goderich Literary Management. And to Erin Brown, our editor at Thomas Dunne Books—working with you has been an absolute delight.

And as always, I couldn't have gotten these words on the page without my beloved Billy making the days easier, dearest Leti for keeping the house in order, and William and Walker and Cody filling our lives with joy.

—AB

The danger in even beginning a list of acknowledgments is that it is far too easy to forget someone—so if I have, I apologize in advance.

In particular order, they are:

My collaborator, the gracious and charming Adrienne Barbeau, who is a fount of knowledge about Hollywood and the Business.

Claudette Sutherland, who introduced me not only to Adrienne, but also to Jane Dystel of Dystel & Goderich Literary Mangement.

Erin Brown, our remarkable editor at Thomas Dunne Books, who kept us on the straight and narrow.

And of course, Barry Krost of BKM Management, who really started it all . . .

—MS

VAMPYRES OF HOLLYWOOD

PROLOGUE

It took an X-ray and an autopsy to confirm that Jason Eddings had been killed with the Oscar he'd won for Best Actor just six hours earlier.

He deserved it.

The Oscar, that is.

As for being murdered, well, he probably deserved that, too.

Jason Eddings was a great actor, all five feet, five inches of him. He was also one of the most ignorant, arrogant, and egotistical people I have ever known. And when you've been around as long as I have, that's a big pool to draw from. I'd like to think that good people, deserving people, hardworking people are the ones who succeed in this town but that's hardly the way it works. Jason Eddings was a prime example of a celebrity asshole who achieved stardom in spite of his nasty nature, or maybe even because of it.

And it shames me to admit it, but I helped him do it.

I'd been the first one to hire him; I'd discovered him, turned him from a bit player into a star. And more.

So I was there, three rows from the stage, during Tinseltown's annual exercise in self-adulation, when Eddings, eyes shining wetly, raised the Oscar above his head and repeated the threadbare sentiment: "I can't believe this is happening to me. Not with such incredible actors in this category."

What generosity.

What graciousness.

What bullshit.

Needless to say, no one believed him. Jason has been called a lot of things, and humble isn't one of them. Naturally, he didn't even deign to look in my direction.

I watched him walk offstage holding the Oscar like a sword above his head, trying for an impression of Russell Crowe in *The Gladiator*. That was a mistake. Jason was many things, but Russell Crowe he wasn't.

And six hours later he was dead.

He was found in the back of his complimentary limousine; the eight-and-a-half-pound statue he'd won for Best Actor stuffed— *Variety* said "rammed"—into the orifice by whose name he was often called.

It was the perfect Hollywood scandal: a superstar murdered at the height of his career—a legend in the making. The press went wild. Marcy Fisher from *Entertainment Tonight* broke her arm trying to climb over *Access Hollywood*'s Annie Lake to see inside the limousine where Jason's body was found.

The chauffeur, in true Hollywood style, made sure he had a deal in place with the highest bidder for his story before talking to the police. According to the report he gave *Star*, Eddings had been partying behind the limo's privacy screen with an almost-dressed young woman and a rather striking transvestite. By the time they reached their destination—the Spider Club—and the driver opened the back door to let them out, the girl and the tranny had disappeared and a naked Jason was laid out across the side seat with only the head of the Oscar visible.

The limo, a stretch Hummer naturally, along with the driver's uniform, is already up for auction on eBay—two separate lots of course—available for delivery as soon as the cops release them. Bidding on the uniform started at $20,000. The death car should reach six figures as long as they don't clean it. And there's a rumor that the Oscar will be sold by private auction.

Jason's death didn't bother me. My kind rarely cry. But this is Hollywood, land of make-believe: if you look at my picture in *People* magazine, you'll see a delicate track of tears on my cheek . . . thanks to my makeup artist and a menthol blower.

I didn't think too much of Eddings's death; an asshole like him—and I use the term deliberately—was bound to come to a messy end. But a week later Mai Goulart, the sweetheart who costarred in my last movie, *Vatican Vampyres,* was found dead in her refrigerator between the hummus and the slaw. Or rather, her head was. The rest of her showed up in various places across the city. Like both breasts in the trash bin behind Du-Par's.

Jason's murder I could understand. He had a lot of enemies and his friends weren't too fond of him, either. But Mai? She was twenty-three. She'd only been in town four years and her career had just started taking off. She still showed up for work on time, still came out of her trailer when the AD called places, still said "please" and "thank you" when a PA brought her water, and greeted the crew by name when she came on set. Mai didn't have enemies.

Jason and Mai had one thing in common, though, known only to me and a handful of others. I began to think there might be a connection.

Three days after that, Tommy Gordon, the macho star of FOX's latest Highway Patrol epic, *Cop Jocks,* was found dead in his Jacuzzi. The initial police report said the suction from a faulty drain held him down until he drowned. *In Touch Weekly,* sometimes a more reliable source than the Beverly Hills Police Department, suggested his manhood got caught in the filter. I knew from personal experience there wasn't much chance of that, unless it was a very, very small filter.

There's a theory in this town that whenever a star dies, two more follow within days. Those are natural deaths; these were anything but. It was Tommy's death, the third in less than fourteen days, that convinced me I had a problem.

A serious problem.

The police came to the logical conclusion: someone was picking off the Hollywood A-list. They were thinking deranged fan, celebrity stalker, pissed-off paparazzi. I knew better. Jason, Mai, and Tommy had one thing in common, and it wasn't their A-list status.

Eddings, Goulart, and Gordon were all vampyres.

Yes, vampyres. Undead, bloodsuckers, call them what you will: they were vampyres.

Most of the above-the-line names in Hollywood are. You see, it was the birth of the cinema that led the Undead to their true calling: movie stardom. The screen magnifies their presence. They're luminescent on film. You can't take your eyes off them. And you can forget everything you think is true about vampyres, including the garlic, mirrors, and silver allergies. Because everything you know about the race is informed by movies, and everything you know is wrong, because vampyres control the cinema.

I know.

Because I, too, am vampyre.

I am Ovsanna Hovannes Garabedian, Chatelaine of the Clan Dakhanavar of the First Bloodline. I am full born, not made, pureblood, able to create others in my image.

But you know me as Ovsanna Moore, writer and star of seventeen blockbuster horror films, several less than successful ones, and a few that went straight to DVD.

I love the irony: The horror movie scream queen is a real vampyre.

CHAPTER ONE

They don't call me the Scream Queen for nothing. "Where is he?" I shouted, and everyone who wasn't deaf, drunk, or dead heard me. "Where the fuck is Travis now?"

I did a hard twist in the air so I could scan the soundstage behind me. I was strapped into a safety harness forty feet up, desperate to go to the bathroom and royally pissed.

Yes, I *do* need to go to the bathroom occasionally, just not as often as the rest of you. And it isn't pretty. A diet of red blood and raw meat will do that to you.

No one answered me. Below me an entire crew, seventy people at least, hustled around like they knew what they were doing and, whatever it was, it was so important they hadn't heard me shout. Most of them had worked with me for a long time. They knew I rarely shouted, and when I did, someone was about to get his ass reamed. They also knew that my temper was legendary.

Finally, Candy, the 2nd. AD, raised her head and looked up at me.

I swear she should have been acting in this film instead of assistant directing—I've worked with stars who couldn't show as much fear in their face. She's an adorable little freckle-faced pixie with a featherweight boxer's body and macho attitude to match. The attitude was fast disappearing. And this was only her second week.

"I'm sorry, Ms. Moore. Mr. Travis said his blood sugar was low and he needed a protein bar from his trailer. I offered to send a PA, but he insisted he'd be right back."

"In the middle of a scene? This fucking scene! I'm hanging up here like Amish laundry flapping in the wind and he walks off the set! Is he fucking nuts?!" I spun in the harness. "Goddammit, Tony, get me out of this thing." Tony Tanner motioned to Jamie Long, and together my stunt co-coordinator and stunt double started lowering me down without a word.

I was halfway to the ground when Neville Travis, the boy-wonder director, object of my unmitigated rage, strolled casually back onto the soundstage, a cell phone pressed to his ear. Even at fifty feet, I could see the traces of white powder under the nail of his right pinkie finger. His eyes were dancing like Maria Tallchief in *Firebird*.

"Hey, Ovsanna, what are you coming down for, we've got two more setups in this scene." He was smiling, for God's sake. A lamb to the slaughter. A coked-up lamb . . . about to be spit and roasted.

"*I* may have two more setups, Neville, but you don't. In fact, *I* have the rest of this film to shoot, but you don't." Tony and Jamie dropped me gently to the floor. I unbuckled the harness and let it drop to the ground while I drew myself up to my full height—which, at five feet, six inches, is not very full. It still put me eye to eye with the little turd. I put my hands on my hips and pushed out my chest—and that brought him to a halt. "We are two days behind schedule. Two full days, Travis. Now I don't know what it's like in MTV-land, but losing two days on an Ovsanna Moore film is enough to send you back to whatever junior college you managed to get through. Nobody walks out on me in the middle of a take, do you understand that? *Nobody!*"

"What do you mean? What do you mean? You're firing me?" The coke was making him reckless and overconfident. He went for overfamiliarity, which I despise. "Ovsanna . . . hey, Ovsanna, sweetheart, baby, I wasn't walking out on you, I just needed a candy bar, you know, for my blood sugar."

"You needed candy, all right, but not for your blood sugar. Wipe your nose, Neville; you've got white stuff all over it. And don't ever call me baby." I turned and headed for my trailer. At a look from me, Shaheed, our 1st. AD, called lunch. I swear I never saw a set empty so quickly.

Travis trailed after me. One of the curses of my kind is a heightened sense of smell and hearing. Those senses served us well thousands of years ago, warning of intruders, keeping my Dakhanavar Clan alive. Normally I manage to filter out the extra input. But not today. Rage messes with my control. I could smell Neville Travis: the Abercrombie cologne, the failing deodorant, the fungus between his toes, and the dried blood in his septum. I didn't mind the blood so much but the fungus made me want to puke. And I can't do that; my kind has no gag reflex.

Neville's voice turned wheedling. "Listen, Ovsanna, you were wonderful in that take. You know that. I didn't think you even needed me there, you're so good. Hey, come on, we'll finish lunch and then speed through the day's schedule, maybe even grab a couple of shots we owe from yesterday."

I didn't look over my shoulder, didn't even raise my voice, but on the empty set it rang and echoed off the bare floor. "You finish your lunch, Neville. And enjoy it. Because it's the last one you're having around here." I walked up the steps of my trailer and closed the door behind me.

Maral McKenzie, my personal assistant, was at the desk in the back room. We'd converted it from a bedroom into an office when the production company bought the trailer for me three movies ago. I didn't like sleeping back there; I'd rather stretch out on the sofa in the living room so I can hear what's going on outside and know when the DGA trainee is coming to get me. That's the advantage of being Clan Dakhanavar—I can hear conversations all over the lot. I get a kick out of opening the door a fraction of a second before he knocks just to see the surprise on his face.

Maral was looking beautiful in a bizarrely cut black and white suit, Dolce & Gabbana probably. She's twenty-eight and she's been with me almost ten years. She's Warm, and one of the few outside the clan who knows the truth and still loves me in spite of it. Or maybe because of it. That's one of the few things she's never told me; maybe she doesn't know herself. She had her titanium Mac Pro up and running and I could see a version of my Web site on the screen. Probably answering letters posted to the guest book page or updating the "personal" blog I never write. She raised a razor-sharp eyebrow in a silent question.

"Get DeWitte on the phone. I want Travis out of here and off the set. I'll direct this damn movie myself if I have to."

"It may not be that easy." Maral's managed to lose most of her accent, which hails from somewhere between the Louisiana swamps and Jackson Square. A Cajun girl with a Scottish last name—go figure.

"Why not? What do you know that I don't?" I was having trouble with the zipper on my costume and she came over to help. I turned my back on her and raised my arms. The zipper hissed down and the leather and lace costume slid away. I stepped out of it and Maral draped a silk dressing gown over my shoulders.

"Travis is Thomas DeWitte's fair-haired boy. Mr. DeWitte thinks he can do no wrong."

"Yeah? Has he seen him on the set?" I turned to face Maral. "It's a wonder he hasn't caught his cock in the clapper. I doubt he's even looked at the budget for this movie."

"DeWitte's been championing him all over town. Word is that

Embassy is ready to hire him as soon as we wrap. You fire Travis and Thomas DeWitte's got shit on his hands."

"Oh, brother. Don't tell me. . . . Thomas is sleeping with him, isn't he?"

Maral shrugged. "Possibly." I was staring at her. "Probably." I raised my eyebrows. "Definitely."

"God damn it." I stretched out on the couch and closed my eyes. "Set up a meeting. We need to remind Thomas DeWitte just who calls the shots around here. Remind him that I'm the senior partner in Anticipation Studios, not him. He's still only head of development. I walk and he's finished."

"I'm not sure he'll see it that way."

"Well, he should. Besides, he needs to remember his history. If it weren't for me, he'd still be making porno down in Tijuana."

Maral had my costume in her hands, ready to hang it in the closet. She turned back to me and stared. "I didn't know he was a director."

"Actor, dear, actor. You've never seen *Going Down on the Titanic*? Check my video collection; I think I've got the uncut version."

She shook her head and laughed. "I didn't know he had it in him."

Score one for me. . . . I bit my tongue and didn't rise to the bait.

A half hour later the smell of Neville coming across the lot brought me back to consciousness. Usually I close my eyes for ten minutes, go into a deep sleep for five of those, and awaken refreshed and ready for the next scene. A half hour is a luxury I don't often get. Maral had helped me take advantage of this one.

She stood up from the couch, buttoned the sleeve of her suit, and handed me a Kleenex for my mouth. My relationship with Maral is discussed ad infinitum in the gossip rags, but no reporter has even come close to the truth. The tissue came away red. She took it from me, folded it, smiled and flushed it down the toilet.

Neville knocked. Maral looked to me for an answer.

"Let him in." I sat up on the couch, closed my robe and threw my boots on the chair across from me. He could come in, but he wasn't going to sit.

Neville's eyes were red. I couldn't tell if it was the coke or if he'd been crying. I didn't smell any weed, just his sweat. I stared at him, curious to see which approach he'd take. He'd already tried bonhomie and wheedling. My guess was he'd try for a straight-out apology and an excuse.

"Look, Ms. Moore, I, uh . . . I . . . well, I'm really sorry I ran out like that. I, uh, I just . . . wasn't feeling well and I needed some, you know, like a protein bar or something so I could concentrate."

"You're just not going to cop to the truth, are you, Neville?"

"The truth?" I watched his eyes widen and knew, before he opened his mouth, that he was about to lose it. Evidently attacking his veracity was enough to make him forget all he'd ever directed were music videos for mediocre bands. Suddenly he thought he was Tarantino. He put his balled fists on his hips. "The truth is you're being a fucking prima donna, and if I want to leave the set—"

I cut him off. "Let's not get into a pissing contest, Neville. You wanted to leave the set? Fine. You want to shove powder up your nose? That's fine, too. You can do it on your own time. Leave. I'm shutting down production for the rest of the day. It will give me the time I need to find your replacement."

His voice went up a notch, along with his arrogance. "I've got a contract, Ovsanna. Thomas DeWitte himself—"

Maral stepped in, her voice just this side of glacial. "Your contract is with Anticipation Studios . . . which Ms. Moore controls. Thomas DeWitte is the head of development and is answerable to Ms. Moore. As are you." She backed him out the door and closed it with a solid click, reminding me once again how much I'd like to Turn her. She has the potential for becoming one of my greatest creations. If only she weren't so valuable to me Warm. She looked at me, eyebrows raised in a silent question.

"Tell Shaheed to send everyone home. I'll absorb the cost. I can use the time to do some rewrites on the transformation scene, anyway. Did you manage to get Thomas on the phone?"

"He's got another new secretary—the third this month—and she said he left this morning for a creative meeting with some new talent."

"What does that mean, exactly?"

"Well, she was new enough and stupid enough to tell me where he was going."

"Did you trick her? Or bully her."

"I allowed her to *volunteer* that he was supposed to have breakfast at the Abbey and then look into a new S&M dungeon in Boys Town. He told her it was business, he was scouting locations."

"Any S&M movies in production that you can think of?"

"None that DeWitte has anything to do with. And nothing to do with Anticipation. I got the impression that this was personal rather than business."

"Shit. There go my rewrites." I finished dressing and pulled on my boots.

Maral looked at me quizzically.

"The last time DeWitte visited an S&M dungeon, he conducted meetings standing up for more than a week."

And in three days' time, on Saturday, a group of indecently wealthy Japanese investors were flying in to discuss a new project and a potential merger. I needed DeWitte focused. And seated. At the very least, he'd better be able to bow.

CHAPTER TWO

BEVERLY HILLS
10:30 A.M.

There are days when I hate being a cop.

I hate the petty bullshit. I despise the bureaucracy, the endless rules, the forms. And I have a real hard-on for psychological profiles. If you ask me, they're not worth the paper they're printed on. Like the one on the table in front of me.

"Obsessive . . . white male . . . probably collects movie memorabilia . . . lives alone . . . could be a movie extra or failed screenwriter."

Well, dammit: that could be me. Except for the screenwriting part. It could also be a good twenty percent of West Hollywood.

These profiles are useless. I once spent a full afternoon going over cases I'd closed, comparing the perps to the profiles the department's resident shrink presented me with when I first started the investigations. You know how many times she came anywhere close? Six out of eleven. And she got the sex wrong on one of those.

Not that she's a bad shrink, she's not—well, based on what little I know from seeing her when Jenny and I pulled the plug. No, it's the profiling system itself. I just don't buy it. And if I took it seriously, I'd never make a collar. It's just another example of Hollywood stretching the truth.

Don't get me wrong, I love watching B. D. Wong do his stuff on *SVU* and the girl with the blue eyes on the *Profiler* reruns and Robson Green in *Wire in the Blood* on BBC, but come on, real life ain't like that. Real detective work is slogging around in bad air and unhealthy temperatures, getting the truth out of people. Or getting lucky. The best detectives I know are just plain lucky.

I dropped the profile back on the table and added more sugar to my espresso. Across the counter, Reynaldo watched the white crystals dissolve in the brown sludge.

"Peter, do you want I should just give you the sugar jar, you can add a couple of drops of coffee and eat it with a spoon?" With a little weight on him he could have been Agador in *The Birdcage*.

"Get off my back, Reynaldo. You're lucky I come in here at all. If I didn't hate all that 'double-grande whipped non-fat-soy' B.S. over at Starbucks, I'd take my business to one of the three down the block."

"Ooo, sweetie. Not in a good mood today, I see. I'll just leave you to your detecting, Officer King." He started away and turned back. "I keep hoping you'll want to investigate *me*. You wouldn't need to add sugar."

"Are you propositioning an officer of the law, Reynaldo? Do I need to get my nightstick?"

"Oh, promises, promises." He went dancing to the other end of the counter to serve two thirty-somethings in sweats and ponytails. I couldn't tell if they were male or female. And I'm the detective.

I finished the coffee and left a dollar on the table for Reynaldo. He settles for that 'cause he knows damn well I'm not going to take him up on his offer. Ten years I've been drinking espresso in California

Coffee on Beverly Drive. Ten years Reynaldo's been making a pass. It's nice to have certain things you can count on.

Not that there's that much that changes in my job. Beverly Hills isn't exactly a hotbed of crime. Last year we had eighty-three larceny cases, nineteen burglaries, a couple of vehicle thefts, robberies, aggravated assaults, and one rape. No murders. I spend my time smuggling drunken starlets past the paparazzi and settling celebrity nightclub altercations without unwanted publicity. I'm good at that. I know how to keep my mouth shut. And I know how to do my job. After fifteen years with the Beverly Hills Police Force, I should. I even got asked to be a technical adviser on *L.A. Undercover*—a piece-of-shit series UPN ran for a season before they went under. "Real Cops, Really Undercover" was the tag. They should have put a tarp over it and covered it for good. But what the hell . . . . I got paid. Even better, I got my name on screen and on IMDb. That's what matters in this town.

I picked the profile off the table and headed for my car. One-thumb Manny keeps an eye on it for me, hiding it behind the Rolls and the Bentleys on the second level of the parking structure for the Regent Beverly Wilshire. I can't afford to tip him, but he knows he's got a friend on the force and he's happy to do it. It's a 1967 Jaguar XKE, which might be impressive if you didn't know my father was the original owner. Not something I mention in casual conversation. It did the trick when I was at UC Santa Barbara, pulling in chicks like the proverbial magnet. It does the trick now, making studio execs feel like I'm one of the gang. Plus, let's face it, it's a classic car. Maybe once a week, as I'm sitting at a stoplight, some kid who's just learned to shave will pull up alongside in his Lamborghini or Thunderbird and ask if it's for sale. Nope. My pop would turn over in his grave. And he's not even dead.

O'Brien's is an Irish bar on Pico, not far from 20th Century Fox. I needed to stop there before hitting the studio where two of the vics had got their start.

The first O'Brien's went up right after Zanuck and Schenck merged with Sidney Kent to form the Twentieth Century-Fox Film Corporation in 1935. Despite seventy years of earthquakes, floods, fires, and riots, it's managed to survive more or less intact. Never an art deco showpiece, it has an unwelcoming storefront that was probably beige at birth but gave in to age and pollution and is now closer to baby-shit brown. It has got one door and no windows. You go in there to drink; you come out drunk.

I pulled up outside the bar and parked in front of a fire hydrant. There isn't a meter maid in town who'll ticket the Jag. There was a bum camped out in the alcove between the bar and the trophy store next door, reading a crumpled, water-stained paperback of George R. R. Martin's *Fevre Dream*. The back cover was gone and it looked like the last twenty pages were also missing.

"Keep an eye on the car and I'll tell you how it ends."

He squinted up at me, and I realized he was a lot younger than he smelled. "I already knows how it ends. I read the end first. Had to use the pages for the crapper."

"Okay then, how about keep an eye on the car and I'll buy you a roll of toilet paper."

"How long you gonna be? I got rounds to make." He patted the grocery cart parked beside him. It was stacked with empty Gatorade bottles, plastic shopping bags, Krispy Kreme donut boxes, and a set of women's hot rollers.

"Shouldn't be too long. You on a schedule?"

"Gotta get to the Ralphs on Olympic before the trash truck makes its pickup, that's all. Tell you what, forget the t.p., bring a bottle out with ya and I can sit here all day. 'Sides, it's too hot to be movin' around." He was barefoot, in a heavy woolen jacket over an open plaid flannel shirt with a Metallica T-shirt underneath. I couldn't swear he was wearing pants.

"What're you drinking?"

"Anything. Everything."

"You got it."

The inside of O'Brien's isn't any more inviting than the outside. A long wooden bar on the right, O'Brien's office at the back. Five booths on the left, wounded leather banquettes patched with silver duct tape. A single bathroom behind the booths and a center hallway with a door leading out to the back alley. There's an air conditioner set into the wall above the back door and an old-fashioned ceiling fan in the center of the room, rotating in slow, solemn circles. There's no jukebox and the television set is a black-and-white, the type that came with a knob to dial up channels. The dial is long gone. The TV was turned to FOX News. It's always turned to FOX News; the O'Briens think Bill O'Reilly hung the moon. The sound was off, which is probably the best way to watch FOX News. There's no good way to watch Bill O'Reilly.

There was a time, back when Jenny and I were going through the worst of the breakup and I was drinking non-stop, when I used to see three men tending the bar, seven in the morning till four in the morning. Catch the gaffers and grips coming off a night shoot and the accountants and assistants getting ready to face the day. Those were the days before it became cheaper to film on location and L.A. lost out to Vancouver, Florida, Toronto, Prague, even Rhode Island. Those were the days before professional drinking bars went out of style. Now the young bartenders know they can make better tips at the sports bars and dance clubs where there's more eye candy on show.

These days only Young O'Brien works the bar. Young looks to be about seventy, give or take ten years. He was here the first day I stepped into this bar more than fifteen years ago and he's never changed. He's got an Irish accent that would make Barry Fitzgerald proud, but I doubt he's ever been to Ireland in his life. Just something he picked up from his dad, who ran the bar before him. He hadn't been to the Old Country, either. The customers love it.

O'Brien looked up and smiled when he saw me and moved

down the bar with that curious gliding motion that old-time bar-
keeps seem to perfect. "Heineken or Bud?"

I eased onto a bar stool that was more tape than leather. "How
about a Coke."

"Ah jeez, Peter, I don't see ya for months at a time and then ya
ask for a Coke? Don't tell me you're doin' the meetings now, will ya?"
He looked as if he was about to cry.

"No meetings, Young. Just common sense. Don't want one of
your sleazy customers calling the *Enquirer* to report Beverly Hills's
finest was drinking on the job."

"Ah, you've gone all holy on me. I'll be goddamned," he whispered, shaking his head. He popped the cap off a Coke and slid it
toward me, then moved down to the other end of the bar. The guy
sitting down there looked to be asleep. O'Brien put a bottle of Dos
Equis in front of him, added a whiskey chaser, and rang up the sale,
pulling a twenty from under the guy's fingers and placing the change
on the bar. He came back down to join me.

"So if you're not drinkin', then you must be here on business,
and if you're here on business, you don't even have to tell me: it's the
Cinema Slayer thing, right?"

I stopped the Coke halfway to my mouth. "The what?"

"The Cinema Slayer. That's what they're callin' it in the papers
this morning. Everything's got to have marquee value, don't y'know.
A logo. Son of Sam. Zodiac Killer. Helter Skelter."

I held up my hand before he listed every case from the past thirty
years. "How'd you know I was here about the murders?"

"It's elementary, my dear Watson. You're not here to drink,
you're here to talk. And the only thing anyone in law enforcement is
talkin' about these days is the Cinema Slayer. So . . . I figured it out,
just like Sherlock Holmes."

"You've watched too many movies, Young. You should go back
to the printed word. Holmes never said that in the books. He never
said 'Elementary, my dear Watson.' "

"Did he say 'Catch the local news at nine'?"

"They announced it? On the news?"

"Ah, you're such a fine detective. In fact, that's even what they said. 'One of our finest officers is in charge,' if I remember correctly. Then they showed that picture they always show, the one with you gettin' the medal."

That medal will follow me to my grave. I pulled a kid out of the Los Angeles River in the middle of the rainstorm and suddenly I'm the poster child for heroics. The kid was so scared he bit me on the butt before I could get a good hold on him. That's not water dripping off my face in the news pics; it's tears from clenching back a scream. I've still got the scars, two semi-circles of perfect teeth marks.

"So I'm glad it's you that's in charge, Detective, and I'm glad you know where to come for information. I was hopin' you'd get here. If you hadn't, I'd of called you myself." Young ran up a "no sale" on the cash register, opened it, and removed a business card from under the cash drawer. He pushed it over to me.

It was a black rectangle of cheap cardboard. Tiny twinkling stars dotted above a graveyard and a tilted cross. Embossed across the heavens was the legend "Death Star Maps. The Ultimate Guide to the Dead Stars."

"You remember Benny?" O'Brien said.

"Remind me?"

"Benzedrine Benny."

"I remember him. He still around?"

"Yeah. Only now it's Biblical Benny. He got religion. He sells these Star Maps over on the corner of Sunset and Rexford."

"Him and a hundred other guys."

"Benny specializes. Sells tickets to the Grave Line Tours and maps to the places where celebrities bought the farm. Tourists eat that stuff up. He's got himself a good spiel, a smart black suit, and a white clerical collar. He's doin' okay."

I didn't see where this was going, but I know enough to let Young tell his stories his way. "Yeah?"

"So Benny added the three Cinema Slayer stars to his collection, already had the maps printed up. He uses my nephew's one-hour print and copy shop over on Olympic."

"Well, he's up-to-the-minute; I'll give him that."

"He's up-to-the-minute, all right." Young leaned across the bar, enveloping me in a cologne that smelled like Jade West gone bad. That stuff must be thirty years old. My father wore it when I was a kid. "Benny had these maps printed up ten days ago."

"Ten days ago? You're sure?" I felt a little brain rush and it wasn't the Coke kicking in.

"Yep."

Ten days ago Benny printed maps showing the places where three top celebrities had died—that's no big deal, you'd think: a budding entrepreneur out to make a buck beating the competition. Nothing wrong with that.

Except Tommy Gordon died eight days ago.

The maps preceded the last death . . . by two days.

CHAPTER THREE

Maral always drives. I hate it.

Traffic in L.A. is . . . well, traffic in L.A. It reminds me of the last time I lived in Paris. In 1807 the streets of Paris were so gridlocked with carriages, drays, and vendors' stalls that it was quicker to walk. Of course, in those days, I was young enough that I still got a kick out of shape-shifting. If I had to be somewhere in a hurry, I'd just slip into something with wings. A hawk was always my favorite, but never a bat. Nothing so clichéd. These days, transitions like that take a real toll on my body. Even the simplest attempt leaves me screaming with effort. And afterwards, coming back to human form while my body readjusts, well, the muscle spasms are crippling. I need two hours of deep tissue massage, which Maral is happy to provide. Yet another reason she's more valuable to me Warm. My kind give lousy massages—we just don't know our own strength.

I've also noticed that I never quite return to my original shape. Something is always just ever so slightly out of whack. Last time, I was left with a few small feathers on my back. Try explaining that at the waxing salon.

I never liked Paris. Even back then, the French had an attitude. I love the language and the culture, but oh my God, when you're hypersensitive to scents like I am, you didn't want to be around Parisians, especially before Baron Haussmann began modernizing the city and Belgrand installed the sewers.

Besides, Europe in general was dangerous for my kind. The Church kept a stronger grip on its believers in Europe than it did in the Colonies. The existence of my race had passed into legend, but so recently that many in the Church still maintained they knew the truth that gave rise to it. Publicly, they dismissed my kind as demons and devils, but among themselves, they feared us. They believed we were fallen angels.

We're neither. Just another branch on the tree of evolution. Maybe not *Homo sapiens,* but. . . how about *Homo sanguineous?*

The Church made it hard for us when I was younger. The Jesuits, especially. They gave themselves a righteous title, Exorcists, but they were hunters, pure and simple. And there was nothing right about it. I can't tell you how many of my ancestors and kin fell to the axes, the fires, or the stakes of an exorcism. That's why I liked the Colonies. The earliest emigrants were too busy annihilating the natives to bring their superstitions with them. My kin in blood were free to roam the continent.

But these days, roaming in L.A. traffic makes me nuts. I've taken to scheduling 6:00 A.M. breakfast meetings at the Peninsula hotel or 10:00 P.M. dim sum at CHOW's. Nobody blinks an eye. This is Hollywood. There's nothing too odd for the natives to handle.

Maral handles the Lexus 470 SUV the way she does everything else: with grace and determination. Personally, I can't stand to drive it; I'm always sure I'm going to back into something short and concrete. But it was a gift from the Japanese conglomerate that's been wooing me and if I don't drive it they lose face. They even outfitted the headrests with 9" video monitors. So, it's comfortable, discreet, and fairly anonymous, and good for watching dailies while we're stuck in traffic. And it makes Maral happy.

She pulled out of my parking spot and drove slowly through the busy lot. I love seeing all the activity when we're shooting; let me tell you, there is nothing more depressing than a studio lot during hiatus season. Anticipation Studios, of which I own an 80 percent share, was currently shooting three movies, my own included. A sweet little MOW for Lifetime called *A Mother's Love;* a low-budget Power Ranger rip-off—which I believe may be a redundancy—for kids called *Ninja Cyber Warrior,* though it might be *Cyber Ninja Warrior* when we release it; and mine, *Hallowed Night,* a harrowing twist on the Christmas legend, which I'd both scripted and was starring in. I'd initially thought about directing it myself, but Thomas DeWitte had foisted Neville Travis on me again. I'd used him for second unit on *Vatican Vampyres* and hadn't been terribly impressed, but he'd made some semi-successful music videos since then and Thomas was championing him. His reputation would bring in the MTV audience, Thomas said. I should have checked him out more carefully, but I was deep in negotiations with the Japanese and I trusted DeWitte. Not anymore.

I've been working on the Japanese deal for about eighteen months now. A trio of Japanese industrialists has decided to invest in an American studio. A small studio, because they want to initiate their new digital technology and develop straight-to-computer, direct-to-cell-phone-and-PDA, low-bandwidth, high-def movies. I'm offering them 25 percent of my 80 percent of Anticipation. Their investment is worth close to $50 million in cash and technological investment, and this is the deal that will move Anticipation into the big league. It's that or get swallowed up by one of the majors. If that happens, I lose creative control, and that's not why I started this business.

"Where do you want to go?" Maral asked, jerking me from my musings.

"I want to go home, take a hot bath, and read Lee Child's latest Jack Reacher novel, but I don't think that's going to happen. Mr. DeWitte needs a talking-to."

Maral smiled. "He may still be out. You want me to call?"

"What, and give him the chance to put makeup on his bruises? Just drive."

She slowed as we neared the front gates. The guard recognized the car, raised the barrier, and waved us through.

I sighed; I'd mention it tomorrow. It's probably against human nature to confront the boss, but how does the guard know I'm not stealing company property in the back of the Lexus? He's supposed to stop all cars entering and exiting the lot, check the driver's license, and pop the trunk. He's also supposed to run a mirror under the chassis. Our version of homeland security. And now, especially with these three murders, we've got to be even more careful.

Maral caught my look and said, "I'll take care of it tomorrow. I'll re-emphasize the security measures and hire another guard for the daytime shift."

"Thanks. And make sure that Travis idiot is barred from the lot."

"Already done." Maral grinned. "Security escorted him to his trailer, watched him clear out his desk, walked him to his car, and waited for him to leave. The name on his parking spot has already been painted over. Took us thirty minutes tops."

"Stick with me," I told her, "and you'll end up running this studio." I was not entirely joking.

Maral gunned the engine and we shot out onto Stanford Avenue, heading for the freeway. On a good day at 5:00 A.M. the studio is fifty minutes from the office. At one o'clock in the afternoon, we were looking at an hour and a half. "Oh, I wouldn't want that," she said. She was serious.

"Why not?"

"I'd hate to end up fighting with you."

"I don't blame you. You'd lose." I ran my finger down her arm.

She glanced sidelong at me, her huge gray eyes hooded with what might have been lust. "You always win, don't you?"

"Always."

Chapter Four

BEVERLY HILLS
11:45 A.M.

Greed and stupidity.

That's how most criminals are caught. Forget the high-tech CSI/SVU stuff—Vincent D'Onofrio kneeling on the floor to chart the exact trajectory of a quarter-inch blood spatter on a burned-out halogen bulb found only in one corner of the Cloisters. That kind of stuff helps keep Dick Wolf's research staff busy, but it's not the truth.

The truth is, most criminals are stupid. Don't forget, *America's Dumbest Criminals* is a documentary.

You don't believe the story about the bank robber who called Triple A when he locked himself out of his getaway car? Or his compatriot who handed a teller his stickup note written on the back of an envelope with his return address on the front? They're true. Stupidity and greed. Criminals have it in spades.

So I wasn't surprised to hear that Benzedrine Benny, aka Biblical Benny, had had his new maps on the street before the killings hit the news. What bothered me is that he'd had them *printed* before the last killing took place. B.B. is stupid and greedy, but I've never known him to be psychic.

I knew he wasn't the killer. There's no way he could have gotten near any one of the victims. Benny doesn't have a close relationship with soap and water; his smell alone would have sent the vics screaming for bodyguards. These murders were up close and creative. Benny's thought processes are taxed making change for a ten.

But he knew something. Or he knew someone who knew something. Either way, it was more than I knew, and whatever it was, it would bring me one step closer to the killer and further out of the sinkhole this case was fast becoming.

Hollywood is a one-company town. Anything that screws with the company screws with the town. We've got three dead celebrities and suddenly nobody wants to show up for work. Productions are shutting down. Every talking head on every news channel has a theory, a comment, an observation, a quip, and a quote. Arnold is screaming up in Sacramento. We can't afford to lose more films to Canada or Australia or Europe.

And the celebs are absolutely freaked. Gavin de Becker can't hire enough staff to answer the phones at his security service. Homeboys from East L.A. are camping out at the Beverly Hills Hotel, standing guard outside the bungalows with their Ingrams. After the third murder, *Soldier of Fortune* magazine did a direct mailing to every member of S.A.G. with an ad offering "Bodyguard Specialists. European and Middle Eastern Trained." There was a discount if you hired in bulk.

The stars who can't afford to hire a shooter are buying the firepower themselves. Most of them can't operate a TV remote, you think they're going to know how to shoot a .50-caliber Desert Eagle? That's what they're buying, for Christ's sake. It's got to be in excess of .357 Magnum, and it's got to be nickel plated and ivory handled to boot. Either that or "the cute little one that will fit right in my purse. Does it come in platinum?" That's a direct quote from a well-known model-turned-singer to my brother-in-law who owns a gun shop in Venice. She wanted something to match her watch and her dog's collar.

No-Pants was waiting right where I'd left him. He'd put down *Fevre Dream* and had a copy of *Daily Variety* in his hands. This guy must have a library card. I handed him the six-pack of Corona I'd bought from Young.

"Mexie, huh? Good choice for a hot day."

"Enjoy it. Anything interesting in the trades?" You can't live in Beverly Hills as long as I have and not know the lingo.

"Nah, just more stuff on the murders. Buncha queens gettin' crazy 'bout their upcoming slates—ain't nobody above the line wants to leave the house to go to work." No ordinary bum then; this guy knew what he was talking about. On closer look, I thought I recognized him from a nighttime soap, maybe twenty years ago. *Dallas* or *Dynasty* or one of those *D* shows.

"Thanks for watching the car. And don't drink on an empty stomach." I handed him a five and got in the Jag.

I took Beverly Glen to Sunset and made a right, avoiding the traffic on Little Santa Monica through Beverly Hills. Benny had been working the same location for at least seven years.

I'd known him for ten. Since the first time he got busted. He grew up rich and white in Lenexa, Kansas, son of an entrepreneur who made it big in greeting cards and a mother who did charity work. All that business going on and nobody had much time for little Benny. Just plenty of weekly allowance and a lot of free time to spend it. Once he found out he could spend it on drugs, life got a whole lot better. By the time Mommy and Daddy figured out where their money was going, he'd fried his brain and pulverized a brand-new T-bird.

They sent him to Betty Ford, *the* place to go in the mid-eighties, and when he was released he took up running. Not exercising, just running. You know, walk into a mini-mart, pick up a couple of items, stand in line until you get to the register, and then start running. Simple, neat, and usually no one bothered to chase him. Until the day he hit Mr. Kim's on Western Boulevard near 6th. Mr. Kim must have run track back in Seoul, because by the time the uniforms got there he was seated on Benny's back, bouncing up and down like he was riding a bull, beating Benny around the body with a frozen dinner. Kim got his groceries returned and Benny got five days in County Medical—in a cast for his broken ribs.

Who knows what happened when he was inside, but when he got out he decided he'd follow in Daddy's entrepreneurial footsteps, and so he started a publishing company. This involved selling maps to the stars' homes from the side of the road. It wasn't quite the greeting card business, but it was—technically—publishing.

Why the hell anyone wants a map to a star's home is beyond me. There's not much to see. No one ever steps out of their house in Beverly Hills and when they do, they're so hidden by iron gates and bougainvillea they might as well be invisible. You think if you park a tour bus outside his home, George Clooney is going to come out and wave? He's a nice guy, but believe me, it's not going to happen. And you're not going to find Pamela Anderson with a pooper-scooper on her front lawn, either.

Nonetheless, it's a big business in L.A. And not just maps to a star's home or a star's former home or a former star's home. No. That's a little too common. How about the gas station where the son of Michael Ansara and Barbara Eden was found dead in his pickup truck? Or the cemetery where Robert Blake's attorney committed suicide? Or the mobile home where Lani O'Grady's life came to an end?

This is where Benny comes in. Dead stars. Maps and tours. Not just tours to their homes, oh no, Benny does the graveyard tours where they're buried and the "Check-Out Tours" where they took their final breath. I'd heard he'd once tried selling sheets that he swore Bob Hope had died in; someone got suspicious when they realized the sheets were polyester. Bob had much more class than that. I suppose if he could, Benny would walk the folks from Omaha down the halls of Cedars-Sinai to point out the hospitalized almost deads, too.

According to O'Brien, he's raking in the bucks.

I made a right on Rexford. Halfway up the block I could see Biblical Benny lounging in a lawn chair on the curb, a metal sign reading "Death Star Maps" staked into the grass between the street and the sidewalk. Leaning against his lawn chair was a hand-written sign with the legend "BIBAL STUDIES" in shaky capitals. Obviously this man of the Lord had no access to a dictionary. Or a Bible.

Benny's younger than I am, but you'd never know it by looking at him. He's got pasty red skin and long gray hair, yellowed from a lifetime of nicotine, with teeth and nails to match. His hairline's receding, so his head looks like a skullcap with a ponytail attached. He'd grown a beard since the last time I'd seen him, as in "Biblical Benny, the Christian Prophet," and I swear to God he looked like he was wearing a priest's cassock. I'd no doubt it had probably been stolen from the Good Shepherd Catholic Church on Bedford. It had to be 104 degrees outside and he was wringing sweat out of his beard.

He stared at me as I got out of the car, squinting into the sun.

"Can I help you, brother? You wanna see dead stars or share the Word of God? Jesus loves you, you know."

"I've always suspected that, Benny."

"Ah, a voice of authority. A voice of confidence." He shaded his eyes with his hands and tried to focus. "A hard man, an arrogant man." Recognition finally set in. "Ah, Detective Peter King, Beverly Hills's finest."

"Your brain may be toast, Benny, but your memory's still good." I squatted down beside him, upwind. This was one prophet who hadn't been cleansed. "I hear you've been saved."

Benny nodded vigorously. I moved a bit farther away in case something jumped from his beard to my suit. "I found Jesus," he said. "You can, too."

"I'm not looking for Him right now, Benny. Right now I'm just looking for information." I lifted one of the Death Star Maps from the cardboard box at his feet. "How's business?"

"Booming," he said gleefully. "Them recent killings are bringin' in a lot of tourists. They all wanna see where the murders took place." He glanced at a cheap Mickey Mouse watch on his arm. It was missing the minute hand. "I'm bookin' deluxe tours right and left."

"Deluxe, huh? What makes them deluxe?"

"Well, it's everything in the Regal tour, you know, the grave-yards, the homes, and the check-out spots, plus the top ten sex spots." He saw my blank look. "The places the stars go to get their rocks off. Man, don't you read the paper?"

"What about Jason Eddings, Mai Goulart, and Tommy Gordon? You've got their check-out spots on your tour?"

"Sure do," he announced proudly.

"And you've even got them on your map." I'd opened one and checked.

"Yes, sir. We're right up-to-date at Death Star Maps."

I folded the map over and slapped it down into Benny's lap with just enough force to make him jump. "A bit too up-to-date, Benny. You had these maps printed before Tommy Gordon died."

He started to shake his head.

"Don't talk," I said, "listen. I said I want information and you're going to give it to me. You don't want to lose your vendor's license, do you?" Then I realized he probably didn't have a vendor's license. "Or maybe this entire box of maps? Nice clean, newly printed maps."

"Hey, you can't do that—"

"I can do just about anything I want, Benny. Including ordering up a psych evaluation for a Jesus freak I happen to find stretched out in the road in the middle of Rexford Drive. Ten days in a psych ward: you don't want to do that again, do you?"

"Aw, man. Don't even talk about that." His eyes were rolling around his head like marbles in a pinball machine. "You don't want to know what they did to me the last time I was in there."

"It's your call, Benny. Nobody hears what you say except me. Where'd you hear about the dead stars?"

"I got a friend at Anticipation Studios."

"The horror film outfit?"

"Yeah, she works there. She told me about the dead stars. I just put them on the maps. I didn't realize until later that one of them wasn't dead when she told me."

"And you didn't think to bring this to the attention of the police?"

Benny looked at me as if I was mad. No one volunteered information to the police . . . not unless there was a reward.

"Who's your friend at the studio?" He started to shake his head. I sighed. I was hot and tired. I flipped out my handcuffs. "Okay, no problem, let's go downtown and continue the conversation. It shouldn't take more than a day or two. And when we're finished the IRS will want to talk to you. And they're mean bastards. They got Capone."

"Eva Casale, she's in the effects department. We do a little business together." He pulled out a box from under the lawn chair and opened it. Inside were tiny medicine bottles filled with what looked like . . . blood. I reached in and lifted one out to hold it to the light. The polluted L.A. sunlight turned the bottle crimson and black. It *was* blood!

"What the fuck are you doing, Benny?"

"No, it's not real blood, man. It's prop blood."

I opened the bottle and sniffed. It smelled familiar but I couldn't place it. It wasn't blood; real blood smells of copper and old meat—it's not an odor you ever forget. "Prop blood?"

"Yes, prop blood. As used in all the famous movies. This particular blood was used in *Bonnie and Clyde*. Eve gets it by the gallon and I rebottle it, slap a label on it, and sell it to the tourists. I make up stories about which actor used it in which flick. They eat it up. Somethin' to take home to the neighbors. Put it on the mantle, use it at Halloween to scare the kiddies."

I held up the bottle between thumb and forefinger. "How much?"

"Ten bucks a bottle. Split fifty-fifty with my special effects girl."

"This Eva Casale. How well do you know her?"

"Oh, I know her. In the biblical sense, too, if you know what I mean." He gave me a slow wink, just to make sure that I did.

"You're shitting me. She sleeps with you?"

"We don't do a lot of sleeping, if you get my drift."

I got his drift and the image that popped into my head came straight from Rob Zombie.

"Benny—no offense now—but why would anyone want to sleep with you? Or do anything intimate with you?"

Benny had the grace to look embarrassed. "Well, the thought did cross my mind. But she's a religious person. And she knows I spread the word of God, and the Good Book says that you should love your neighbor . . . so that's what she does. She does a lot of loving."

There's someone for everyone, right? Sounded like Benny had found himself a whack job who just happened to be working in a studio where at least one of the vics was a regular player. If this woman was nuts enough to sleep with Benny, she could have done the murders herself. If nothing else, she knew about a murder before it happened. And she didn't know enough to keep it to herself. So, at the very least, she was an accessory.

"You got a cell phone, Benny?"

"Of course, man. I'm an entrepreneur. How you think I'm gonna do business without a phone, sittin' here in the street." He pulled it out and I grabbed it. It was the latest model, picture phone, MP3, movies, the works.

"You're not doing business for the next hour or so," I told him, pocketing the cell. "I'm heading over to Anticipation and I don't want your lady friend to know I'm coming. So you sit tight, sell some maps, save some souls, and I'll give this little toy back to you when I'm done." I handed Benny the Bible he had propped up against the curb. "Do a little more studying. Learn how to spell 'Bible.' And have a look at the section that talks about bathing. I think it's in Revelations."

CHAPTER FIVE

The first offices I rented for Anticipation Studios were on Robertson above Michel Richard. The former tenant warned me about the dangers of working above a patisserie. I don't know what she looked like when she moved in, but when she took her name off the door she weighed at least 250 pounds. I wasn't worried. I can enjoy the taste of food if the smell isn't too overwhelming, but I don't eat. Not unless I absolutely have to, to guard my secret. And in this town, no one blinks an eye if you're starving yourself. It's become the chic way to get press coverage.

DeWitte, on the other hand, has a cholesterol problem and self-control issues, so when I took him on as a partner, he insisted we move. He claimed he'd put on twenty pounds just breathing in the sticky-sweet, cinnamon bread–scented air. I was still a little in love with him at the time so I agreed, and suddenly found myself paying a fortune for a beautiful suite of offices on South Beverly Drive. After *Tell Me What You've Seen* broke the 50-million mark, I bought the building. I like it because it's very old-world: weathered brick and stone, three stories, with dark paneling and a cherrywood circular staircase leading up to the second floor. It's unexpectedly grand in the midst of the modern bank buildings on the corner and across the street. The only trade-off is no parking garage. We use a valet to take our cars.

It was 1:30 by the time Maral pulled up in front of the building. She handed the keys to Jesus the valet and I hopped out, strode across the sidewalk, and pulled opened the huge wooden door.

The lobby of my building is designed to put you in mind of a very exclusive European hotel. It reminds me of happy days long ago in Vienna and Turin when I was singing and dancing to Johann's music. In the center of the room, bounded on either side by the circular staircases and right below a magnificent two-story crystal chandelier, is the receptionists' desk, where Ilona Anderson greets visitors and Sveta Tunyova offers them refreshments. Both girls have been with me since I took over these offices.

Neither was in sight.

Instead, standing in front of their desk with his arms folded over his chest and his feet planted wide apart was some bald-headed, tattooed steroid freak. He had a wispy white goatee and an earring in one ear and was wearing army surplus combat pants and fourteen-hole Doc Martens. He looked like an ad for Mr. Clean in Iraq.

"Yeah? Can I help you? Empty your pocketbooks." He must be a Jersey boy, I thought. Who else says "pocketbook" in L.A.? His voice sounded like his testicles had already shrunk from the 'roids.

"Who the hell are you? And where're Sveta and Ilona?" If Thomas had dragged this guy over from his morning activities at the S&M club, heads were going to roll. Literally. I can do that when I'm angry. And the way this day was shaping up, I was headed in that direction.

I wasn't waiting for an answer. As I started up the stairs, the guy moved in front of me to block my way. "Listen, lady, I don't know who you are . . ."

"That's your first mistake . . ."

". . . but you're not getting past me without some ID and a search."

He put his hands on my chest and pushed. I freaked. No one touches me without my permission. "And that's your second."

I grabbed his left wrist with my left hand, spun him around, pinned his arm against his back, and squeezed the pressure points on his right shoulder with my right hand. Mr. Spock would have been proud of me. Mr. Clean went down hard on his knees—I heard them pop on the marble floor—and started screaming.

"Now look . . . ," I said, fairly calmly.

"Anthony! I'm Anthony!" His voice had gone up an octave. "Mr. DeWitte hired me to be his bodyguard. Please, lady, let go!"

I loosened my grip but kept him on his knees facing away from me. Maral was staring at me like a kindergarten teacher whose class has gotten out of hand. She thought she knew what I was capable of; in truth, she didn't have a clue. I've never had to demonstrate in front of her.

"Now, Anthony. I don't take kindly to being strong-armed. Mr. DeWitte didn't do you any favors, turning you loose without giving you a scorecard. I'm one of the key players. In fact, I am *the* key player and you should have known that."

"Hey, all I know is Mr. DeWitte said don't let nobody upstairs without seeing some ID." He'd stopped struggling and was just sitting on his knees. "You're hurting my arm, lady."

"You're lucky I don't snap it off. Do you see the pictures on the walls, Anthony?" I caught his jaw in my free hand and twisted it to face the framed posters on the wall. "That's my ID. I'm Ovsanna Moore. I own this building. I own Anticipation Studios. That means I own Thomas DeWitte, too. Now, I'm basically a nice person, Anthony, and I'm sorry his paranoia has put you in this position, but if you're going to stay on, you're going to have to learn some manners. I'm very big on good manners, Anthony. That should have been in the job description." I jerked him to his feet and straightened his rumpled jacket; then I started up the stairs to save him any more embarrassment. "Maral, stay with Mr. Anthony, would you please. Maybe you can give him a crash course on how to make nice and keep us all safe at the same time. Either that or take him out and buy him some antiperspirant."

I walked into Thomas's outer office and slammed the door, restraining myself at the last minute so I didn't rip it out of its frame.

CHAPTER SIX

SANTA CLARITA
1:30 P.M.

I left Benny in his lounge chair and made a U on Rexford. I'd take Coldwater over the hill and then the 405 to Magic Mountain. Anticipation Studios are in Santa Clarita. At least at this time of day, I was going against the traffic.

Driving away, I realized that Benny is probably making more with his roadside scam than I am as a BHPD detective. And if I can believe his rap, he's getting laid more, too.

You'd think I'd have better luck with women, between the Jag and the badge and the publicity that came with the medal. According to the *L.A. Times* profile that I have stuck to the inside of my locker, I'm "just short of movie star handsome, with black wavy hair, hazel eyes and a nose that goes a little awry." Getting it broken twice in one year will do that to you; I'm lucky I can still breathe. And the description is more or less correct, even if it doesn't mention my winning personality, ready wit, and charm. But I'm clean, I make sure I smell good, and I read GQ before I go clothes shopping, so it's not the externals that have me sleeping alone. I'm pretty sure I've got some underlying ambivalence going on.

My friend SuzieQ says if I don't figure out why I'm only attracted to women who are unattainable I'll never get married again. When I told SuzieQ I thought I was "once bitten, twice shy," she said everyone's entitled to one mistake. Calling my marriage to Jenny a mistake is like calling the Vietnam War a minor error in judgment. Neither needs repeating.

SuzieQ is my tenant. She lives in the guesthouse on my property along with a seven-foot diamondback boa and a fifteen-foot albino python that she uses in her act. I always make it a point to knock. She keeps track of my comings and goings without a trace of embarrassment at invading my privacy. I just wish I were doing something I didn't want her to invade.

The truth is I'm not that interested in just getting laid for the sake of getting laid. It's been eight months since my last serious relationship, and I wouldn't mind meeting someone to do the deed with, but not just short-term; I'm too busy on the job to waste my energy.

But it would be Christmas in a couple of weeks, and the thought of spending Christmas alone was beginning to bother me. There's nothing lonelier than waking up on Christmas morning in an empty bed. Well, there is actually: waking up on New Year's Day in an empty bed. I've done both and neither is fun.

As soon as I hit the Valley the temp in the Jag spiked another ten degrees. That's the only problem with classic cars; they lack all the luxuries of the new ones. My AC was working overtime. The Santa Anas were blowing and the sky was a pale, clear blue instead of the usual layer of brown. I could see homes forty miles away in the mountain range ahead of me, separated by acres of scrub. I always wonder about people who live isolated like that. Why? What are their lives like? Do they know their neighbors? How often do they drive into the city? I couldn't live way out in the boonies like that. I'm a city boy.

I love L.A. I love the way the smog turns the sky outrageous shades of orange and pink and purple right before the sun sets. I love the fact that I can find anything I want in some part of town and that on Wednesday evenings I can put my recyclables out and they're gone Thursday morning, that the fruit in my twenty-four-hour grocery store is so amazingly gorgeous I take visitors there to gawk at it, that the hardware store is open 5:00 A.M. to 11:00 P.M. and the bookstore is open 8:00 A.M. to midnight . . . and that there are always people there. I can buy an Alka-Seltzer or an assault rifle—often in the same store—at any time of the day or night.

Which is why I've got to catch this Cinema Slayer fast. I blow this and the closest I'll get to L.A. is patrolling cow pastures in Bakersfield.

My cell phone rang. Caller ID said it was the Captain, calling on his private line. For one moment I thought about ignoring it, but I knew if I wanted to stay in L.A., I'd better answer. "This is Detective King." I don't like reminding people I've got caller ID, so I never use anyone's name when I answer.

"Captain Barton."

Captain Philip Barton's voice sounded even tighter and more clipped on the phone than in person. He had a habit of stating the obvious, speaking in little spurts and pursing his lips between sentences. "Cinema Slayer: update?"

"I'm heading out to Santa Clarita. Ovsanna Moore is shooting at Anticipation out there and there's someone there I need to talk to."

I could hear paper rustling. "Anticipation. The second vic, Mai Goulart, just finished a movie for them."

"I know, Captain. That's why I'm going out there." I wasn't ready to give him details, not till I'd had a face-to-face with Benny's blood-making bed buddy.

There was a long exasperated sigh down the line. "This case is a pain in my ass, Peter. I've got actors, agents, and lawyers freaking out all over town. I need some action."

"I know, Captain. There's movement, believe me."

The Captain's voice dropped a notch. "I had a call a while ago. The sharks are already sniffing around, talking about movie rights to the investigation." Coming from the reticent Captain, this was positively loquacious.

"Oh yeah?" Of course. Laci Peterson's film was on the air before the jury was chosen. I caught my own reflection in the rearview mirror. "Maybe they'll offer me a role." I always wanted to play myself in a movie—nothing big, just a bit part, something sexy and heroic.

"Never happen. You're not good-looking enough." Said without a trace of irony; the bastard was serious. Damn. Evidently he'd forgotten my news clippings from the L.A. River rescue. He resorted to stating the obvious. "Find this guy. He kills again and the whole town shuts down. You know the suits won't blame the killer—you'll take the fall."

I'll take the fall. Not the Captain, not the department. Me. Peter King, Ace Detective. It won't sound as good with an "ex" in front of it.

I've got a gold shield in my wallet, a police scanner in my car, and a Glock 17L strapped to my waist. I've got tickets to the Police Benevolent Fund under my visor. You'd think I could have gotten through the gate at Anticipation Studios in less than twenty minutes. Nope. The guard had to check my driver's license, call the Anticipation production offices, get a "drive-on," and write out a form with my name, car license, and temporarily assigned parking spot. Except for having to sit there while my engine overheated, I didn't mind. It told me no one was getting in or out of the studio without being spotted, videoed, and tagged. Might make my life easier later on.

"Everyone get this treatment?" The security guard's name tag read: "Oliver Gant." He looked old enough to have worked for D. W. Griffith.

"Well, it used to be if you had a permanent parking sticker on your windshield, I'd just open up the gate. But since 9/11 my instructions are to check the licenses, pop the trunk, and look under the car." He'd rolled out a dolly that looked like a carpet sweeper with a mirror on its flat surface, sort of a reverse periscope. "I'm supposed to do everyone, and I do. 'Cepting Miss Moore, of course, and Mr. DeWitte. She don't mind if I stop her, but he gets mighty cranky. I keep telling him, someone could plant a bomb under his car and he'd never know it, but he just barrels on through. Doesn't make Miss Moore any too happy when she sees it."

"Any reason you'd think that? About Mr. DeWitte and a car bomb, I mean? He have many enemies?"

Gant was running the mirror under the car. "Looks like you'll be needing a new exhaust."

I got out of the car to take a look. Reflected in the mirror were patches of rust dappling the exhaust pipe. Shit.

"Too many enemies," Gant said abruptly. It took me a second to come back to him. I was thinking about a studio exec I knew over at Disney. The guy was a jerk, but he had good taste in cars—and the same year XKE as mine. Maybe I could get someone in traffic to impound his car; it'd only take me a couple of hours to switch exhausts. He was working for the mouse; he could afford a new one quicker than I could.

Gant was still talking, "He thinks he's a throwback to Louis B. Mayer. Doesn't treat people too nice."

He finally had my attention. "Any examples?"

"Well, when Miss Goulart was killed, for instance. Miss Moore was really cut up about it. She runs the studio, you know, not DeWitte. She made a speech to the crew and everything, closed the set for two days. Not DeWitte. He started bitching about having to recast her part. And then he went golfing. Didn't show a lot of respect, if you ask me." He pulled the dolly out from under my car and pushed it back toward the gatehouse. "You're all done, Detective. Sorry to have delayed you."

"It's okay, Officer Gant. You've been more than helpful. Let me ask you another question. Any rumors about DeWitte and any of the ladies on the set? Mai Goulart, for instance, or Ovsanna Moore?"

He chuckled. "No sir, no siree, Detective. Mr. DeWitte's interests lay in a different direction, if you know what I mean." He paused and added, "His boyfriend, though, the one directing *Hallowed Night* over on Stage Three, Neville Travis, he fancied Miss Goulart like mad. He's a switch-hitter, if you know what I mean."

I scribbled a quick note in my notebook. The names were beginning to mount up. And all of them linked to Anticipation. "Is Travis on the set today?"

"He was, until a couple of hours ago." He wheezed a quick laugh. "Miss Moore had him thrown out, lock, stock, and barrel. Shut down the set for the rest of the day. Actually, I got you parking in his space. That Miss Moore's a pistol. Just like her mother."

"You knew her mother?" I was right when I said D. W. Griffith.

"Worked for her. That was a long time ago. Her daughter's just like her. Both of 'em powerhouses. Opinionated. Talented. Beautiful. They could have been twins."

"And this director, Travis, you say he had a thing for Mai Goulart?"

Gant nodded. "They met on the set of *Vatican Vampyres*. I'm not so sure she had a thing for him, though. But it's tough for a young star to say no to a director, even a jerk like Travis. She used to come to me in tears, sometimes, asking me to make sure she got out of the parking lot way ahead of him so he couldn't follow her."

"Follow her? Was she afraid of him? Was he stalking her?"

"Naw, I think she was more afraid of what might happen if DeWitte found out."

I made a few more notes. "You think DeWitte knew?"

"Go see the movie, son. It's up there on the screen. The kid was directing the second unit: He never took his camera off her face. Even when it was supposed to be just long shots and stunts and stuff. Everyone knew. Travis tailed after her like a puppy dog. Only way DeWitte would have missed it was if he slept through the movie."

"I need addresses for all the principals: Moore, DeWitte, Travis."

"You'll get those in the office. After you park, walk down past the barbecue and the catering truck, cross through the honey wagons, and go around to the other side of Studio One. The offices are there."

He handed me a map of the parking lot with an x on the spot he'd assigned me. When I reached it, I discovered it was two spaces away from Thomas DeWitte's. DeWitte's was empty. So was Ovsanna Moore's.

Fine with me. I wanted to ask questions without having to answer any, and I've found people are a little more open when the boss isn't around.

Chapter Seven

I pushed the door open with a little more strength than I intended and sent the anemic woman who had her head pressed to the other side flying flat onto her bony ass. A Marc Jacobs knockoff shoe skittered across the floor.

"What's the matter, I wasn't loud enough for you?" I growled, then snapped my lips closed; I could feel the prickling of suddenly sharp points against my tongue.

"I . . . I'm sorry. . . . I . . . can I help you?" The woman scrambled to her feet and limped around her desk, trying to put a barrier of some sort between us. She looked about fifteen—and was probably seventeen—flat chested, with short spiky hair and a half-dozen studs running up along the curve of her right ear. A pair of low-cut jeans had me giving thanks to whoever did her waxing, and three inches of taut, tanned belly showed beneath a cropped white shirt and a minuscule brown sweater. If she looked any more boyish, Thomas would have been on top of her as soon as she hit the floor.

I took another look: maybe she was a boy; it's hard to tell sometimes. I breathed deeply, inhaling a mixture of pheromones, N.V. Perricone's Lip Plumper, and a floral perfume that screamed $12.99 from CVS/pharmacy. No, definitely a girl. The boys tended to use a better cologne.

"Can I help you?"

Her voice was a little stronger now, but I could see from the way the muscle twitched in her left forearm that she was desperately pressing a button concealed under the desk. No doubt trying to call the rent-a-muscle downstairs.

"You can stop that: you're wasting your time. Anthony is busy at the moment." I smiled without parting my lips, which must have frightened her even more. Her eyes looked liked those candy buckeyes they sell in Ohio before the college football games—big peanut butter balls surrounded by dark chocolate. "No. I don't need any help. But you do. I think you need to go down to the kitchen and get yourself a cup of coffee. Or a glass of milk. Whatever someone your age drinks these days."

"But Mr. DeWitte—"

"I'll take care of Mr. DeWitte. I'm his boss. Ergo, I'm your boss." I watched her eyes flicker to the framed posters on the wall and saw them widen as recognition set in.

"You're—"

"I know who I am. Now move!"

She scrambled past me, scooped her shoe off the floor, and hopped out on one foot. I could hear a single heel stumbling down the stairs. I closed the door behind me, then turned the key in the lock. What sounded like a dozen dead bolts clunked into place. That was new; DeWitte was taking his security very seriously indeed.

The smell in Thomas's outer office almost put me back in the hall. He'd insisted on black leather sofas and glass-topped tables with limestone bases. He'd sourced the limestone from the same quarry the Getty Museum was built from. I love the museum; I hate the stench. It smells like hundreds of people with bad body odor. It's the stink of the limestone. Personally, I think it's only fit for mausoleums. Thomas's outer office smells only slightly less offensive than a cemetery in New Orleans, which is why we generally hold our meetings in mine.

I caught a glimpse of myself in the reflection of the glass over his Lichtenstein. Don't believe everything you read about vampyres. Of course we reflect in mirrors and glass; it would defy all the laws of physics if we didn't. But it makes a great movie effect, always did, right from the moment Lugosi strapped on the cape.

Right then I wasn't too happy with what I saw. My black curly hair was no longer cascading down my back in Christophe-styled ringlets. It was frizzed out about a foot in all directions, reacting to the change in my aura. I leaned forward and pulled down my lower eyelid. The whites of my eyes were filled out with tiny threadlike veins. Soon the entire white of my eye would turn red. I could feel my lower teeth pushing out of their sheaths and my incisors growing to meet them. Forget the Hollywood image of two nice, neat Christopher Lee fangs; think tiger canines instead, top and bottom. Plus—and this really pissed me off because I'd just had a manicure— my nails were elongating, flakes of coral nail polish spiraling to the floor.

I closed my eyes and concentrated on my breathing, using techniques that would have made a yogi proud, techniques I'd perfected over half a millennium of existence.

I opened my eyes and stared at the Lichtenstein, not seeing the art, just my reflection in the glass. The whites of my eyes were pink again and I could smile without showing teeth. My nails were a mess and my hair still looked like shit, but that could be explained.

I pushed open the door and strode into Thomas's office.

Thomas was standing in front of the Warhol, talking on the phone, with his back to me. He had on black Dolce & Gabbana jeans, a white XOXO T-shirt and a black Armani silk jacket, black

Kenneth Cole loafers, no socks. I may have been pissed, but I know my designers. I'd also lay money that he was wearing the Patek Philippe watch I'd given him in a moment of weakness and was carrying a quintet of platinum cards in the alligator wallet that just slightly disturbed the line of his jeans. There was the faintest hint of blood in the air; obviously his little session in the dungeon in Boys Town had gone well. I've been whipped and beaten, burned, branded, stabbed, shot, and poisoned. Every one of them hurt like a bitch and I've no intention of repeating any of them, so I simply cannot understand people like DeWitte who pay to have someone beat on them. And it's only the human race that does it.

Thomas and I had been lovers when I was going through my "wouldn't it be nice to have someone to take care of me for a change" stage. That lasted about four minutes. Beneath his aging Tom Selleck exterior—complete with moustache—was a weasely little Mickey Rourke with welts on his ass. Once I realized I wasn't the one making them, I kissed him good-bye. But I didn't kiss him off. He managed to be both a remarkably inventive lover—for a man—and a sexual slime at the same time. He was also a good exec; I think it had something to do with being a sleazy ass-kissing ego-maniac. I offered him 20 percent of Anticipation Studios and a seven-year contract. He bought the limestone tables.

He also bought some really good art. Two Hockneys, a Sam Francis, an Edward Ruscha, and the Warhol I coveted. Dear Andy, I had wanted so badly to Turn him. Something I rarely do. I wanted that talent to be immortal. But once I saw the pain he was in, I couldn't perpetuate it. He never knew, of course.

I made it across the room in two strides and ripped the phone cord out of the wall. Thomas spun around, something foul bubbling across his face, then dying when he saw it was me. Watching his lips curl from spite to smile was like watching a sidewinder curl across the desert.

"Ovsanna, what the hell . . . ? That was an important call—"

"Why are you standing, Thomas? Something wrong with your ass?"

Confirmation flickered in his widening pupils. "What are you talking about? You just hung up on Rodrigo Garcia. You know how hard I've been trying to get him to direct *Satan's Prayer*—you hung up on him!"

"Yeah? Then you'd better make sure you're still here when he calls back. Sitting down. That's what I pay you for. And you'd better teach Miss Von Dutch logo out there not to rat you out when you leave work in the middle of the day to get your rocks off. Better yet, save your S&M scene for after business hours." I poked him in the chest, allowing a tiny tendril of my strength to show through, emphasizing each word with another poke. It was going to leave a bruise. "But you are just one stupid prick."

DeWitte tried for bluster. "Oh, get off it, Ovsanna. You can't threaten me. You need me."

"I need you? For what? To hire your coked-up little lover boy to screw up my movie? I'm here to tell you that he's off the set, Thomas. And if I have my way, I'll see he's off every set in Hollywood. And get rid of that brainless piece of beef you've got standing guard out there. What if the Japanese had come in? What was he going to do, open fire?"

"He's a bodyguard, Ovsanna. And he's licensed to carry. People are getting killed all over town. We're in danger and I'm not taking any chances."

"The only person you're in danger from is me, Thomas. Fuck up one more time and you're gone. Gone and never coming back. I want this merger to happen and you're not going to screw it up because you're thinking with your cock instead of your brain. Get Travis out of the picture and replace Anthony with someone who can think and talk at the same time. And while you're at it, get a real secretary." I turned and walked out.

The tomboy must have kept an extra key downstairs because she was back at her desk when I went through the outer office. Her cheeks were bright pink and it wasn't makeup. She'd heard the whole thing. I ran my tongue over my teeth to make sure I didn't frighten her any more than I already had.

"I am a real secretary," she whispered, then cleared her throat and tried again. "I am a real secretary. I've got a certificate."

She had guts; I admired that. Maybe she would survive in this business. "Well then, start secretarying. And welcome to the Wonderful World of Movies."

CHAPTER EIGHT

SANTA CLARITA
2:00 P.M.

If I hadn't become a cop, I'd have worked in the movies.

My mother is the only person I know who knew the business from the inside and still wanted her kid to be an actor. She loves movies. She grew up in Hollywood during the glory days of the studio system and had dreams of being a contract player but never got that far. She appeared in a couple of movies in the fifties, though: in the crowd in the café in *Summertime,* in the crowd in the store in *The Long, Hot Summer,* and in the crowd in the hospital in *Suddenly Last Summer.*

Then television came along and she had a bit more success: she did Merv Griffin's series *Summer Holiday.* I'm not kidding. Then she played the "girl in the bar" in *Rawhide,* the "woman in the bar" in *Bonanza,* and the "woman behind bars" in *The Untouchables.* We still tease her about being typecast.

Whenever she wasn't working, she was going to the movies. She loved them and she wanted me to love them, too. As soon as I was old enough to stay still for two hours, she sat me down in front of the TV and showed me her pirated ¾" copy of *The Sound of Music* on our Sony Beta machine. Maybe she thought I'd grow up to be another Christopher Plummer. I didn't care about the von Trapp kids, though. It was the German soldiers with their smart gray uniforms—shiny belts and boots and guns—that captured my attention. The one thing my mom didn't want—that I'd follow in my dad's footsteps and be a cop—and the first movie she shows me gets me hooked on the trappings of law enforcement.

After I came along she gave up acting and went into on-set catering. "I've eaten so much bad food on a set—I know what actors want," she said. She was right. And she could cook! My dad's people are Welsh, but my mom's are Italian, so cooking's in her blood. She was so good, stars started requesting her, and within a couple of years they had clauses inserted into their contracts that King's Catering, The King of Caterers would do the food. By the mid-seventies, Mom had seven trucks working and she floated from one movie set to another, overseeing the ragu and the outdoor barbecues. She knew Clint's preferences, always kept a special aside for Meryl. Pacino and De Niro gave her hugs when she showed up, and Shirley MacLaine once gave her a gift certificate for a psychic reading.

My mom kept mementos from every movie and TV show she appeared in: scripts they gave her, costumes she bought at discount, photos she got signed, and props she walked off with. In her catering years, she made sure she got several scripts from each film signed by the entire cast. And if production was tossing out the personalized chair backs because the stars didn't want them, she grabbed those, too.

When eBay came along, she turned the catering company over to my brother and two sisters and started selling movie memorabilia. Last year she cleared close to six hundred thousand dollars and my parents bought their second condo in Miami.

My dad just retired from the LAPD and his father and grandfather walked a beat in New York. Before that, though, things got a little iffy. My great-great-grandfather was part of the Tweed Ring, taking bribes for Boss Tweed to grease the way for the Erie Railroad because, according to the family legend, "it was better to receive the bribes than to pay them."

My dad's proudest boast is that he'd spent nearly thirty years on the force and never fired his weapon at another human being. I don't remember the last time I've fired my weapon off the range. I love watching cop shows: guns fired in practically every episode . . . and no one ever does paperwork! Fire a shot in anger in this city and you drown under the form filling.

There are three boys in the King family and four girls. My older brother and two older sisters run The King of Caterers now; they've branched out into celebrity functions, births, bar mitzvahs, and weddings, and I hear they're developing a range of celebrity sauces. I'm the only cop in the family. I reckon I only became a cop to do something—just one thing—to make my dad proud.

And I've never regretted it.

But there are moments, like when I drive into a studio complex, or step onto a stage, or wander through a set, when I really do think, What if . . . ? How different would my life have been if I'd gone down the path my mom had so carefully laid out for me? She really wanted me to get into the business and she had the contacts then to get me a foot in the door. I might have been a movie star.

I moved through Anticipation's backlots, keeping to the shadows so I wouldn't sweat. December in L.A. and it was eighty-seven degrees. I've heard people grumble about the weather in L.A., but I've been in New York in December and, believe me, I know which I prefer.

I knew very little about Anticipation Studios, but that was hardly surprising. Beyond the biggies—Warners, Paramount, Universal, 20th Century Fox—there are dozens of small studios scattered across the city. Well, someone has to fill the gaping maw that is TV-land. All I knew about Anticipation was that it started out making low-budget horror films for the DVD market. It was owned by the horror queen, Ovsanna Moore, daughter of the equally famous Anna Moore. I knew what Ovsanna looked like—I think I may have even had a poster of her, or her mother, on my wall when I was a kid—but I'm damned if I could remember the name of her latest movie. Or any movie for that matter. But she's had a long career in Hollywood and done dozens of movies, and in a city where careers are often measured in single features or spans of months that was quite an achievement.

I stepped out of the blinding December sunshine into the dark of an empty soundstage. I stood and waited for my eyes to adjust before moving—a cop trick my father taught me—and then looked around. Directly ahead of me was a series of sets: the one on the left a young girl's bedroom complete with a pink chintz–canopied bed and white wicker furniture, the one on the right a cozy living room with Christmas tree, presents, and twinkling decorations. An enormous bloodstain dappled the ceiling and dripped down the walls, and instead of a star on top of the tree there was a remarkably realistic severed head. I guessed this wasn't your average Hallmark Channel Christmas movie.

The set was practically deserted: a couple of carpenters fixing a door, an electrician checking meters, and someone from set dressing comparing Polaroids to the set, rearranging props. Somewhere in the distance, someone was whistling "Havah Nagila" off-key.

I picked my way through the rats' nest of cables and I'd almost reached the set dresser before she turned and caught sight of me. Her jaw was working overtime on a double wad of pink gum. I edged my coat back, revealing my badge and gun clipped to my belt, ready to get some fast cooperation.

"Next door," she snapped.

I looked at her blankly.

"You deaf as well as lost?" she asked, chew, chew, chew. "*A Mother's Love* is shooting in Studio Two." She blew a huge pink bubble . . .

. . . which I burst with the end of my pen.

Snotty little twenty-year-old. Probably talks on her cell phone in restaurants, too. I hate to admit it, but my age is showing.

"The gun is real. The badge is real. Which means I'm a real cop. And you are?" I demanded.

She picked pink gum off the end of her nose and peeled it off her cheeks. "Tiny," she mumbled. She was a short, pinched-face redhead with troweled-on makeup and those startling turquoise eyes that only come from colored contacts.

"Excuse me?"

"Tiny . . . well, Tina really, but everyone calls me Tiny because I'm—"

"Tiny. I can see that."

"I'm looking for Eva Casale. She works in special effects."

Tiny rolled the burst bubble back into a ball and shoved it back in her mouth. I couldn't believe it, the thing had her face makeup all over it. "Go through the door marked 'No Exit,' past the honey wagons, and you'll see what looks like an old army Nissan hut. Actually, it *is* an old army Nissan hut. That's the prop department. She's probably there." I nodded my thanks and was turning away when she asked, "Is she in trouble?" She was unable to keep the note of eagerness out of her voice.

I turned back and put on my best smile. "Should she be?"

"Well, gee, I don't know," Tiny began, then continued quickly when she saw I was about to walk away. "It's about that man, isn't it?"

"You're very good," I said non-committedly.

"Watched him sneaking around," she said, glancing around in her best conspiratorial pose. "He gave me the creeps." She shuddered dramatically.

I nodded. It's hard to miss Benny, though how he got past security is another question; maybe I'd have another chat with the guard, or with Benny. "When did you last see him? Was he with anyone?"

"He was here a couple of days ago. It was early. We had a five A.M. call and I couldn't figure out why anyone would be on the lot at that hour if they didn't have to be. Sun wasn't even up yet." She shuddered again. "I thought he was a ghost with that white skin."

"Early riser" and "white skin": two phrases I don't associate with Benny. "Describe him."

Tiny chewed and considered and then chewed some more. She was about to blow another bubble and then thought better of it. "He was thin," she said finally. "Thin and ugly."

She wasn't giving me a lot to go on. "What about his beard?"

"Oh, no beard. And you know something else," she added. "He smelled. Just like he'd been dipped in shit."

"Thin. Ugly. Smelly." I wrote it down, just in case I forgot the detailed description.

"And he was bald."

"Bald?" Benny was many things—including thin, ugly, and smelly—but bald he was not.

"Bald and white," Tiny added.

"A Caucasian male," I added to my notes.

"No, white. I mean really white, white skin, no color. An Albanian."

"An albino?"

"No, no, a white guy. Only really white, like that guy in *Powder*. Did you see that flick? Boy, that director did a great job."

"Thanks, Tiny," I said, "you've been a real help." I turned and headed for the No Exit door, leaving Tiny to get back to the set. First Biblical Benny and now a bald albino; Eva Casale keeps very strange company.

The Nissan hut was set apart from the main studio, a slightly battered long metal rectangle that wouldn't have looked out of place in any

WW II movie. If Ovsanna Moore was putting money back into the company, she wasn't spending it on the facilities. Maybe the hut had once been green, but decades of L.A. sunshine and Santa Anas had scoured it to that peculiar color men's magazines like to call taupe. I've a pair of jeans in that color: I never wear them. The original tin structure had never been painted, but it was covered with Magic-Markered autographs from actors who'd filmed on the lot. My mother would have a field day on eBay if they ever demo'd the place and she got her hands on the pieces. I had a sudden image of her slicing it into irregular little chunks with a jigsaw.

The door was open and I could feel the frigid air blowing from massive air conditioners positioned on metal girders above the huge expanse. I stepped into a nine-year-old's dream come true. The long rectangular building was crammed with dozens of monsters in various stages of construction. Bits of human bodies, really good work, hung on the walls, alongside an assortment of bladed weapons that would have made Kurosawa drool.

My mother would have been in eBay heaven.

There was a large, chest-high worktable in the center of the room, probably ten feet wide by twenty long. It had been divided into four sections with three-inch black tape and each section was covered with what looked like prosthetics and effects items from different movies. A mangled Santa torso lay on its back, sliced almost in half by the chef's knife stuck in its liver. There was even an accompanying odor, sort of sweet and cloying. I didn't know effects wizards went to such trouble; maybe it was a joke for their own enjoyment. Except the odor wasn't coming from Santa. Crucified to the end wall of the hut was the amazingly lifelike body of a young woman. Her throat had been cut so deeply that her face was resting against her shoulder; she had a hole clear through her stomach right to the knotted white of her spine. A heap of offal on the ground represented the internal organs and that's where they'd spilled whatever stench they were using to represent death. This Casale woman was good!

I took a step closer and the smell got stronger. And more recognizable.

Then I saw the flies.

And then I heard the sticky dripping of bloody fluids.

This wasn't a special effect I was looking at. I had a good guess it was Eva Casale. Someone had just cast her in her own horror movie.

Chapter Nine

We were standing on the sidewalk outside my office, waiting for Jesus to bring the car around, when Maral's phone rang. My kind don't have premonitions—well, no more than humans do, I suppose. But when you've lived as long as I have you do develop your sixth sense: I knew it was trouble. Maral slipped her Bluetooth receiver over her ear as she glanced at her phone screen. "It's the production office," she murmured, "Bobby Wise's line." Bobby is the unit manager on *Hallowed Night*. "This is Maral, Bobby, what's up?"

The last time I'd seen the color drain from someone's face like that was when I was feeding and lost track of time. I love the description, though; it's so apt. At moments of stress blood is drawn away from the non-essential parts of the body and pushed to the extremities, readying to fight or flight. The face pales. Maral's face turned waxen, her eyes and lips bruise purple. She pulled the receiver off her ear and closed the phone.

"Eva Casale was found dead in the effects hut," she said.

"Murdered?"

"She was nailed to the wall, partially decapitated, and her insides scooped out."

"That's murder, all right," I said grimly. Maral didn't respond; she knows my gallows humor.

We didn't speak again until we were in the car. Without asking me, Maral headed back towards the studio. We drove in silence for a few minutes; then, sitting at the light at Sunset and Coldwater, she finally said, "I think we need to talk about this."

"About Eva?" I asked, though I knew that was not what she was talking about.

"About Jason and Mai and Tommy. And now Eva." A frown creased her unlined forehead. "But Eva's different, isn't she? She's not part of the pattern, is she?"

"The pattern?"

"Jason, Mai, and Tommy were your . . . *creations*," Maral said flatly. It wasn't a question.

"They were."

Maral knows what I am, and accepts it. But she's never questioned my past; what she knows about me and my kind she's picked up over the past ten years of our association. We don't discuss it. Maybe that's why we've been together for so long. She knows that I have what might be called *Creations*. I call them kin—though never children—but she's never exhibited any desire to be one of them or enquired into the actual process of creating one. She also knows that everything she's seen on the screen or read about my race is just so much bullshit.

"Eve was not one of yours." Again it was a statement, not a question.

"No, not one of my kind." Most of my kind are in front of the camera, although I make it a rule never to have more than two in any one movie. For purely selfish reasons. If I'm starring, I want the audience looking at me.

The light changed and we pulled away.

"So why was she killed?"

"Two possibilities—accident or design," I said quickly.

"This was no accident. You don't get nailed to a wall by accident."

"So it was planned. Again, we're down to two choices: is this murder a coincidence or somehow connected to the other deaths?"

Maral glanced sharply at me. "It has to be connected."

I nodded, absently picking strips of polish off my abused nails. I knew damn well it wasn't a coincidence.

"Maybe someone mistook her for one of your . . . kin," Maral suggested.

"Unlikely. Whoever picked off the other three knew what they were and knew the tried and trusted methods of killing them: impalement, decapitation, dismemberment, and drowning. We don't die easy, you know." Something icy and old ran down along my back, a bitter memory of another place and another century.

"Well, her neck was cut almost clean through—that's close to decapitation. Maybe someone's trying to let you know they know what you are. Maybe Eva's death was meant to frighten you."

I laughed, a sharp barking sound. Even to my own ears, it sounded ugly. "Death does not frighten me. You would not believe the number of deaths I've witnessed," I said. "I've survived wars, famines, plagues, and persecutions. Even the Crusades—all sixteen of them. All death does is make me angry."

"So it has to be a warning."

"Oh, of that I am sure."

"But what does it mean?" Maral asked, as we turned into the studio.

"It means that there's a Vampyre Hunter in Hollywood," I said grimly, "and he's just made his first mistake."

We made the rest of the drive in silence until we got to the gate and Officer Gant waved us through. God damn it, you'd think with a murder on the lot, he'd learn his lesson and stop the car.

"What mistake?" Maral asked finally.

"I'm not the only vampyre in Hollywood, you know that, but I was the first to come here and that makes it my domain. I am the Chatelaine. A few others came after me, and went into the business. Charlie and Rudolph, of course, and Douglas and Mary and the outrageous and dangerous Theda Bara. We created very few kin. We were careful, very careful. Except for Theda. She nearly brought us down, taking chances like making *A Fool There Was.* She played herself, a vampyre, for God's sake. She delighted in the image and the notoriety. We were forced to destroy her entire clan one bloody night in 1919. She hated California anyway, so she was more than happy when we suggested she retire. By then I'd introduced her to one of mine, silent film director Charles Brabin, and they married and moved to New York. But the others still have kin in and around the city. What's interesting is that this killer has targeted only my Creations."

"And now your employee."

There was fear in her voice. I laid my hand on Maral's pale flesh and allowed a little of my energy to flow through my hand, bringing my fingers to glowing light. She moaned as the white energy coursed through her body. "I will allow no one and nothing to harm you," I said formally. "You may not be of my blood, but you are my family, and therefore under my protection."

As I got out of the car, I silently vowed to do a better job than I had with Tommy, Mai, and Jason.

I disliked the cop on sight.

A ninety-dollar haircut and designer jeans. Cocky and overconfident. He probably drove a Hummer to make up for the size of his cock. And I'll bet he watched reruns of *Miami Vice.* A Don Johnson wannabe.

He was standing outside the effects hut, making notes in a small spiral notebook, while white-suited CSIs moved in and out around him. Through the door I could see the flashes of a camera as some-one recorded the close-up details of Eva's butchery.

Even from outside the hut I could smell the meat and blood of her, and it was taking an enormous effort to keep my fangs in place. I didn't need to see her; I needed to get away. I saw the cop look up, hazel eyes widen as he recognized me just as I turned my back to leave.

I heard his footsteps behind me as I strode toward the set of *Hallowed Night*. I was going to have to shut the set down; I couldn't ask Eva's crew to keep working without some downtime, and I didn't even know if they could handle the rest of the film without her to run things. I'd have to meet with them immediately.

"Miss . . . Ma'am . . . Miss Moore."

"Yes, Officer." I struggled to keep my voice neutral.

"Detective Peter King, ma'am, BHPD."

He didn't offer his hand but I put mine out anyway, and after he'd surreptitiously wiped his palm on the leg of his trousers he reached for it. I try to avoid physical contact with strangers when-ever possible because I don't need to be bombarded with unwanted impressions, but this time I welcomed them. I wanted to know how to handle him. They were a jumble of visual and physical sensations . . .

. . . *curiosity . . . anxiety . . . a poster from one of my films . . . the merest hint of awe . . . a filthy man in a preacher's collar . . . anger and disgust . . . Eva's body crucified against the wall . . . a Jaguar XKE.*

Well, no Hummer, at least.

"Are you all right?" He was staring at me with concern. I ran my tongue over my teeth to make sure I wasn't losing control.

I nodded, saying nothing. I'm not sure what I'd learned from the contact—more than I anticipated certainly, and enough to revise my initial impression. Maybe he wasn't a complete asshole after all.

"Is there someplace we can talk?" he asked.

"We can go to my trailer."

We cut through the set of *Hallowed Night*. I saw King glance at it—and suddenly the severed head on top of the Christmas tree didn't seem like such a good idea.

"I thought it was a special effect," he said suddenly. "The body on the wall," he explained, catching my look. "When I first saw it, I thought it was just another special effect. It's so hard to tell what's real anymore."

"Especially in this city," I agreed.

Chapter Ten

SANTA CLARITA
3:30 P.M.

All I could think was she must use a great cinematographer or a really fine makeup artist because up close and personal, she was older than I expected. Still hot, but older.

She didn't look like she'd had any work done, either, which, in this town, almost puts her in a category by herself. Women don't get older in Hollywood; they get freakier. Between Botox, laser peels, liposuction, and that stuff they shoot into their lips, there's not a real face walking Rodeo Drive. And that's before the cheek implants and the lunchtime thread-lifts. My tenant, SuzieQ, is a *Nip/Tuck* fan— well, the first two seasons, at least—and she keeps me up-to-date on all the available procedures. Whatever happened to a good old-fashioned nose job like my sister had in the sixties? Although, come to think of it, that wasn't too successful, either.

And it's not just the women.

I've never been tempted to go under the knife myself, not yet anyway, but when the time comes and there's more gray than black in my hair, I'll get Enrique, my barber over in Los Filez, to start adding a little color. Not too much, though; there's nothing worse than an older man with jet-black hair. I had my eyes lasered a while back, but that was practical; I've got to be able to see. And I use those teeth-bleaching strips from the drugstore, but in this town that's also practical—nobody wants to see a Beverly Hills cop with yellow teeth. But that's where I draw the line. I don't want to end up looking like David Gest.

I couldn't guess Ovsanna Moore's age from looking at her. Could be at least a decade older than me. No doubt it was listed in IMDb; I'd check when I got back to the office. There were the faintest traces of lines on her forehead and around the edges of her eyes, but as far as I was concerned, that only enhanced the package; everything else looked real and natural, moving and swaying in all the right directions. Ovsanna Moore looked like she'd been a few places, seen a few things, and maybe even done a couple of them. I'd have said mid-forties, but I could have been off by ten years.

The girlfriend, however, had to be at least fifteen years her junior. I say "girlfriend," but no one introduced her that way. She was waiting in the trailer with the door opened as we approached, a cell phone in one hand, folded laptop under her arm.

"Allow me to introduce Maral McKenzie, my personal assistant and right hand. Maral, this is Detective King, from the BHPD."

The assistant looked at me as if I was something she'd scraped off her expensive shoe. She didn't extend her hand.

McKenzie was a knockout. Ash-blond hair tumbling down her back, gray eyes behind black-framed Buddy Holly glasses, not enough of a rack to draw attention, but no question she was a girl. She was wearing some sort of strangely cut black and white suit that looked like high-end Rodeo Drive.

As Ovsanna stepped into the trailer a look passed between them.

I knew immediately there was something going on between these two that was more than professional. You can't spend fifteen years on the force and not read between the lines. Maral McKenzie had a personal stake in protecting Ovsanna Moore. And something to be afraid of. At that moment, it seemed like it was me. As we stepped into her boss's trailer, I watched her insinuate herself between the movie star and me. She almost bristled as I deliberately moved farther into the room. Then she turned away from me, stared into Ovsanna's eyes for a beat too long, and without a word went to the fridge and pulled out a White Ginkgo Tea. Another look passed between them when she handed it to Ovsanna. And a touch, fleeting and if you blinked you missed it, but it was there, nonetheless. I wasn't sure what the deal was between this pair, but with "personal assistant" as Maral McKenzie's job title it was pretty obvious the accent was on "personal." I'll bet the job covered a lot of ground.

I had three dead movie stars, all of whom had worked for Ovsanna Moore; a dead special effects supervisor, also working for Ovsanna Moore; and a personal assistant with an agenda—maybe she didn't like anyone coming between her and her sweetheart, or maybe she had something bigger to hide. Whatever was going on, Maral McKenzie was involved.

My dad told me four things when I joined the force: never go out without your vest, make sure your underwear is clean, buy comfortable shoes (preferably with steel toe caps), and never get involved with another officer (but if you do, wear protection). So far I'm good on all four counts. He also said that there are lots of reasons for crime—social deprivation, rage, anger, fear, societal factors—but at the end of the day it usually comes down to sex and money. People who haven't got either, want one or the other, or both. I used to think it was a simplistic, even anachronistic, point of view. Then I started clocking up the years. Now I think he was right.

It comes down to sex and money.

Money hadn't raised its head in this case yet, but sex just made an entrance. Ovsanna Moore and Maral McKenzie reeked of it. I added Ms. McKenzie to my short list of suspects. I only had two names on it—McKenzie and Moore—but it was a start.

And hell hath no fury and all that. . . .

Moore sipped at the iced tea. "Detective King is investigating Eva's death. Although why you're involved, Detective, and not the local police, is a question I'd like answered," Ovsanna added, without missing a beat. She'd taken a seat in one of those tall director's chairs with the name Marilyn Monroe printed on the canvas back. It looked like Marilyn had signed it in black ink under her name. I'd seen enough copies of her distinctive signature in my mom's collection to believe it was real. My mom would love it.

The only other places to sit were the sofa and the two banquettes on either side of a built-in table. I stayed standing because I didn't want Ovsanna Moore towering over me while I tried to interrogate her without her realizing that's what I was doing.

"Actually," I said, "I found the body."

It took the girlfriend a moment or two to process what I'd just said, but Ms. Moore realized the implications immediately. She sat back in the chair and crossed her legs at the ankle, Citizen of Humanity jeans riding up to reveal python Tony Lamas. SuzieQ would shit. "So you came to talk to Eva," Ovsanna said.

"That's an interesting assumption. Any reason you'd say that?" Give people enough rope and they'll talk themselves into the noose.

"Why else would you be in the FX hut, Detective King? It's not on the beaten path. Something brought you here; what was it?"

"I'm an investigator, Ms. Moore. I investigate. It's my job to ask the questions, not answer them."

"And it's my job to run this studio and to know what's going on here every minute of every day. I'm not a fool, Detective, don't treat me like one." There was a fast shift to ice in her voice and genuine anger. "I listen to the news," she said. "You're the lead detective on the Cinema Slayer case. You drove out here because of that, didn't you? You were looking for Eva."

"You're right, ma'am."

"Call me Ovsanna. 'Ma'am' makes me sound old." Another shift in her attitude. She smiled, maybe attempting to lighten the atmosphere, but the smile didn't go anywhere near her eyes.

"Ms. Casale's name came up as part of our ongoing investigation."

The personal assistant leaned forward, offering me a glimpse down the gaping neckline of her expensive-looking suit. I appreciated the gesture, but it didn't work. Given the distraction of sex or the obsession of work, I take work almost every time. "You're not seriously suggesting that Eva was somehow involved in those terrible deaths, are you?" McKenzie went on the attack.

"I'm not suggesting anything," I said mildly. "Would she have worked with any of the deceased?"

Ms. McKenzie was about to snap a response, but Ovsanna reached out and laid a hand on her arm. I thought movie stars got their nails done, but Moore's were a mess. "Eva is—*was*—one of the best up-and-coming special effects artists in the business. Everyone wanted her. She trained with Rick Baker, Rob Bottin, and Stan Winston. And yes, she worked with all three of the deceased—Jason, Tommy, and Mai."

"I know all three did movies with this studio. Did you personally work with any of them?"

"Yes, I did," she said immediately. "I gave Jason his break in this business; he played the priest who gets butchered in the confessional in *Tell Me What You've Seen*. Mai was my co-star in *Vatican Vampyres* and Tommy played a cop in *Road Rage*."

I made my notes and wondered if Netflix carried copies.

"What else can you tell me about Eva?"

"She's worked for me for six years now. Started out as an FX assistant on *Tell Me What You've Heard,* the sequel to *Tell Me What You've*

Seen. She runs—*ran*—the department with a permanent staff of four and hired extra people as she needed them, depending on the demands of the film. Her strength was getting the best effects for the least amount of money. She was clever and inventive and stayed on budget. Take a look at *The Convent II* and you'll see what I mean. When Hurricane Katrina hit and production on *Blood on the Bayou* got held up because they couldn't get supplies, she used V8 juice mixed with Yoo-Hoo to simulate the blood they needed for the were-alligator's victims. Nobody knew the difference."

"Very inventive," I said, suddenly realizing what was in those bottles Biblical Benny was selling. Ms. Moore certainly knew a lot about her staff. I deal with Beverly Hills bigwigs every day; most of them don't even know their employees' full names. Ovsanna Moore was obviously a more hands-on type of boss. "Can you think of any reason—no matter how improbable—that someone would have wanted to kill her?" It's the standard question, and it always sounds ridiculous.

Ms. Moore shook her head, but I was watching the girlfriend. I saw the tiniest crinkling at the corner of her eyes and knew instantly that she knew something.

"And what about you, Ms. McKenzie?"

Her pupils dilated just before she lied to me. Doesn't make for a good poker player. She took a step back, her hands crossing her body in classic defensive-denial pose.

Years ago I'd dated a psychologist who taught me the basics of interpreting unconscious non-verbal communication. She had a dozen books on what we cops call body language. Ms. Shrink said mine showed unresolved oedipal issues—I enjoyed hanging out at my mom's. I said hers showed unresolved Esther Williams issues—I found her fucking my pool man, in the pool. She walked out with her tan and left her books. I always figured I got the best part of the deal. Took me ages to find a new pool man, though.

"I have no idea why Eva was killed," McKenzie said quickly.

I love it when people lie to me. Means I'm getting close.

"What about her private life? How much do you know about that? Was she seeing anyone?"

Maral shook her head. "There was someone she was sleeping with, off and on. I didn't get the feeling it was a big romance or anything. I think he was a Born Again or a preacher or something. Every time she came back from screwing him she'd talk about God's love and blessings."

Flipping my notebook shut, I looked from Ovsanna Moore to Maral McKenzie. "I think that's all for the moment. I apologize in advance if this is inconvenient, but I hope neither of you has plans to leave the city in the immediate future."

"None, Detective," Ovsanna said shortly.

"And I'm going to have to declare the FX hut off-limits."

"For how long?"

"A couple of days, at least. I realize that this will cause a problem with your shooting schedule, but the CSIs need time to go over the entire building. We'll do our utmost to release it as quickly as possible. I'll also need your fingerprints, of course, and the fingerprints of all your crew."

Again a flare of anger from Ms. McKenzie, tinged now with what might have been alarm as her eyes found Ms. Moore. Moore reacted, too, her expression shifting to a blank mask. "Why?" she asked.

"For elimination purposes. We take your fingerprints and the fingerprints of everyone we know who had business there, we dust the building, we eliminate all the recognizable ones, and see if anything unusual pops up. It won't take long and we can do it here, rather than bringing you down to the station." I smiled my best professional smile to take the sting from the unspoken threat. Neither woman returned it. "Is there anything else you think might be relevant? Anything unusual or out of the ordinary happen recently, any strangers wandering around the set, fights on the set, differences of opinion, arguments?"

The two women were shaking their heads even before the questions were out of my mouth and I knew then that I wasn't going to get any more out of them. But I'd gotten enough.

"Well, thank you for your time. I'll leave you my card in case anything occurs to you." I was tempted to ask for a signed photo for my mother, but I resisted. I didn't want to look like some starstruck fan even though a part of me couldn't wait to call home and tell my mom whom I'd been grilling. Besides, I knew I'd be seeing both women again.

But before then, I needed to know a little more about them. Something I wouldn't find on IMDb or People.com.

Chapter Eleven

Maral stood by the door and watched the detective amble across the lot towards his car. Her voice was shaking with anger. "What do we do about him?"

"Well, we don't underestimate him. And we don't lie to him again. At least, *you* don't. He knows you lied."

"I didn't really lie. I don't know why Eva was killed. She wasn't one of you. Maybe her death isn't connected to the others at all." Her anger was giving way to wishful thinking. And fear. I could smell it overriding the Jo Malone Wild Fig and Cassis she must have bathed in.

"You're too genuine to carry off a lie, Maral. He picked up on it right away. You obviously know more about Eva than you volunteered."

She turned back to me slowly. Framed in the doorway, with the sunlight turning her blond hair into a white halo of fire while leaving her features in shadow, she was breathtaking. I had to concentrate on the conversation; lust was flushing through my system unbidden.

"Eva *was* seeing someone . . . well, more than one person actually," she said, coming back into the trailer and closing the door. She opened the fridge and took out a bottle of Xango and a bottle of Defense flavored Vitaminwater. Her hands were trembling as she measured a tablespoon of the Xango and followed it with the Defense chaser and suddenly I realized how hard this must be for her. It isn't every day a colleague turns up spectacularly dead. Nearly half a millennium wandering this earth has inured me to the sight of death. I've seen it in all its ugliness, from individual bodies to entire corpse-strewn fields. Now, only the death of a loved one still has the power to move me; it's one of the reasons I've avoided any close associations in the last few decades. Except for Maral. Eva Casale was an employee, and probably a nice person, but I wasn't going to get too emotional about her death, nor was I going to make any foolish promises about avenging it. I had to believe that her murder was a warning or a threat, a threat I had to take very seriously. The Vampyre Hunter was showing me that he knew how to kill my kind.

Maral lay back on the couch and stared at the ceiling. She pressed the cold bottled water to her forehead. "There was a time when Eva and I were . . . involved."

I'll be damned. I must be slipping in my old age; I'd never picked up on it. I kept my face expressionless.

"It was a couple of years ago. You were shooting *Elizabeta* at Cinecittà in Rome."

I remembered. Maral had stayed in L.A. to oversee production on our other films. The irony of shooting a movie based on the life of Elizabeth Bathory had rather appealed to me. She was born ten years after me, in 1560, but I never met her. I suppose today she'd be classified a serial killer—650 women, according to the register of names she kept. A thousand more according to the Hungarian emperor, when he finally imprisoned her. To my knowledge, she wasn't vampyre, just your garden-variety psycho like Vlad III, the Impaler. Evidently she took it into her head that bathing in the blood of young virgins would restore her youthful beauty. This was pre–plastic surgery; she didn't have a lot of alternatives. She strung them up by their ankles and bled them alive into a nice warm bath. I had a great time playing that scene. Even with fake blood.

"It didn't last long," Maral continued, "and when we broke up, we managed to remain friends. She told me recently that she was seeing a new man."

"'A new man' implies that there is an another man."

"She was having an off-and-on relationship with the preacher I told the cop about."

I sighed. Preachers, no matter what God they said they worshipped, were trouble. I didn't like the way the pieces of this puzzle were beginning to slot together. I've come close to death on several occasions over the centuries, and with only a few exceptions the Church and religion of one stripe or another had been involved. If it wasn't the Christians trying to burn me at the stake, it was the devil worshippers trying to sacrifice me to their horned god. I sent them all to their respective makers.

"Let's get out of here," I said suddenly. "We're going to need to get legal advice. I want to talk to Solgar and I can't do it over the phone." Maral looked at me blankly. "That detective is going to discover your connection to Eva. He's already suspicious of my connection to the three dead stars. And . . . he wants my fingerprints." I held up my hands. The pads of my fingers are smooth, without whorls or patterns. The anomaly is unique to my Dakhanavar Clan, and I knew with a chill certainty that my non-prints were going to turn up all over poor Eva's FX hut.

"We've got an alibi."

"Depends on the exact time of death. And we are one another's alibi. That's enough to make Detective King even more suspicious; then he'll really start digging. You know how vulnerable I am to a comprehensive investigation." Although I have extensive paperwork, the best money can buy—birth certificate, Social Security card, even SAT scores—no paper is infallible. There's an ancient Celtic saying that translates as "Happy the man who exists unknown to the law." For generations my race has survived in the shadows. Now technology is making that increasingly difficult. Where the Church and the crazed hunters had failed to eradicate us, twenty-first-century computerized record keeping might prove our downfall.

Warren Zevon's "Werewolves of London" howled from Maral's purse as we hurried across the lot. Her latest choice in ring tones. Just when I've forgotten how young she really is, her phone rings to remind me of her puerile sense of humor. It was Bobby Wise, the production manager. Officer Gant on the main gate had phoned in to report that the journalists and news vans had arrived. I was surprised it had taken them so long.

The December sun was beginning to dip in the sky and I pushed my Fendi Suns up into my hair to turn my face to the light, delighting in the heat. Start again from scratch and forget everything you know about vampyres: almost none of it is true. And none of it makes sense. An aversion to the cross—why? That wives' tale came about from the Christians who hunted us down in the Middle Ages. The crosses didn't do any harm; it was the guys bearing them. And what about Jewish and Muslim vampyres—what effect was a Christian symbol going to have on them? It would have to be a menorah or a crescent, wouldn't it? Believe me, those don't work, either.

Vampyre mythology was created mostly by the movies.

I know. I wrote a lot of it.

It's a mythology that has been informed by books, movies, and, more recently, TV. And most of that was a figment of some novelist's or screenwriter's imagination. And since everything they know is built upon a lie, they are simply perpetuating the lie.

I've been writing scripts for the past eighty years and rarely have I included any real truths about my kind. So contrary to what people believe, we don't burn in sunlight, though we are sensitive to the ultraviolet radiation, but that's to do with diet, we don't sleep in coffins lined with our own earth, and we don't crumble to dust when we die: rather, we dissolve into a particularly foul sludge.

Maral and I climbed into the Lexus and used the security code to drive out the back gate, successfully avoiding the media circus that was making Officer Gant work for his money at the front entrance.

"Tell me about this preacher and the new boyfriend," I said when we finally turned into traffic.

"I only met the preacher once. He came to the studio—"

I hissed in anger. This was pissing me off. I pride myself on knowing everything that's going on in my studio, and it was fast becoming clear I didn't. I'd taken my eye off the ball while negotiating the Japanese deal. It didn't take a genius to work out that Eva had found out about me from Maral and had revealed it to the preacher. A man of God had an obligation to cleanse this earth of the unclean, didn't he?

"I don't think he's involved," Maral said quickly. "I'm not even sure he's a real preacher, just one of those guys who puts on a white collar and calls himself a reverend. He also sells star maps as a sideline . . . ," she faltered, and added, "He conducts those tours that go to all the places where stars have died. . . ."

"Jesus. I'd think after you, Eva would have had better taste in men. So, not only was he a preacher, but he was a preacher obsessed with dead movie stars. Maybe he'd graduated from visiting them to making his own. What about the new one?"

"I never met him," Maral continued. "I got the impression she was a little in awe of him, maybe even frightened."

I picked more polish off my nails. "What does he do?"

"No idea. He must be in the business, though, 'cause he was always telling her stuff that hadn't even hit the trades. He sounded powerful."

"We need to find out." I had Peter King on my mind as I sorted through my options. This sudden police interest in the studio might frighten off the Japanese. I'd worked too long and too hard to allow that to happen. The Japanese arrived in three days; Anticipation had to be running smoothly by then. On a personal level, I needed to avoid having my fingerprints taken. I was going to need some subtle and expensive legal help. And I needed to aim the police in a different direction . . . away from me. For that, I was going to have to do their job for them. Time for *this* vampyre to hunt the hunter.

"Head over the hill. Phone Ernst Solgar and tell him I'm coming."

"Just like that?" Maral blinked. Solgar and Solari, Esquires, are the best entertainment lawyers in Century City.

"It's me, Maral. Solgar will always see me. He has to."

"Why?" Maral wondered.

"Because I am the Chatelaine of Hollywood."

Ernst Solgar has been my lawyer for years. He's also a vampyre. He's heard every bloodsucking lawyer joke ever told, and passes them on to me via e-mail every once in a while. He's a rather charming, affable man who could be anything from fifty to seventy—though he's close to a thousand as far as I know—with a wild head of hair he pays a fortune to keep groomed and old-fashioned circular wire-framed glasses. The glasses must be an affectation. I've never known any vampyre who has trouble with his vision.

Ernst is Clan Obour.

The Obour have a single nostril and are without fangs. They take sustenance through a sucker-like opening on the tip of their tongue, but they need an open wound to feed on; they don't have any way to puncture or slice their host. Not an effective design, if you ask me. Most of them carry a concealed *kirpan* to do the trick. Solgar has had the surgery that gives him a septum, but I make it a point of never allowing him to kiss my hand. Although he is much older than I am, he acknowledges my position as the Chatelaine of this city. In the *Liver Noir*, the vampyre bible, ownership of a city is clearly defined as belonging to the first to "inhabit, occupy or possess a township of greater than nine hundred and ninety-nine souls."

Hollywood is mine. I came here when it was nothing but orange groves. When Samuel Goldwyn was still Shmuel Gelbfisz and before he became Samuel Goldfish, and Hollywood was actually a city in its own right. I inhabited, occupied, and possessed it. When it consolidated with the "City of Angels" in 1910, I became the de facto Chatelaine of the entire L.A. basin. The few vampyres then living in the city acknowledged me as their ruler and swore fealty. Over the decades, the occasional rogue vampyre or mongrel clan has attempted to muscle in on the city. They forget most of us learned our statesmanship in Caesar's Imperium, the Borgias' Roma, or the Medicis' Florence. In my case it was the Paris Terror. I give them a little leeway in the beginning, but eventually those who don't assimilate we destroy or, perhaps more correctly, we allow the city to destroy. Hollywood can be as lethal to a vampyre as it is to the Warm.

I could tell Solgar's secretary was a fan from the way she jumped up to greet us. She led us down the long hallway where Ernst displayed his collection of Naïve art—he had two new pieces by Elke Sommer I hadn't seen before—and into his office, which always looks to me like Pierre Deux on speed.

Solgar came to his feet and scuttled around the French Provincial desk to greet me, both hands held out in front of him in the traditional greeting—a subtle way to show he wasn't holding a dagger in either hand.

"Ovsanna, Dakhanavar, a pleasure, a pleasure as always."

"Solgar, Obour," I acknowledged his name and clan.

I'm five foot six; Ernst Solgar is two inches shorter. Clan Obour didn't get the height gene. He was wearing a dark blue silk suit that had to be handmade, probably from Savile Row. His shirt was Charvez from Paris and the loafers were Italian, most likely hand-stitched in Rome. Like most of his clan, his feet are tiny. He bowed over my hand but didn't kiss it, and when he raised his head he nodded to Maral, who hovered by the doorway. She didn't like Solgar; I'd yet to find a Warm who did. They instinctively distrust both the Obour and Nosferatu Clans and not without reason. In this town, most of them are agents and lawyers. I glanced over at her. "Maral, why don't you give us a few moments here?" She nodded and slipped from the room without a backward glance.

Solgar & Solari had the penthouse suites at 9200 Sunset, the Luckman Building. Ernst's office took up the entire east side of the building. Three of the walls were glass and the view out over the city was spectacular, even with the smog touching everything a sulphurous yellow. I stood by the window, taking in the view. Across the street three men were covering the billboard of HBO's latest cancellation with an ad for a show that wouldn't last the season. I think they lost their touch when they canceled *Carnivàle*.

"I have a problem, Ernst," I said, reverting to the Armenian of my far-distant youth.

"I did not think this was social," he replied in the same language, though his accent was atrocious. It's hard to speak Armenian when you don't have a tip on your tongue. "I was wondering when I would see you. The three dead were yours." It wasn't a question.

"My Creations," I agreed.

"Killed in the old ways."

"There was another today." I filled him in on Eva's bloody death and the police investigation, headed up by King. As I spoke, I pressed the fingertips of my left hand on the window, then breathed on it. Four perfectly blank ovals appeared on the glass. To complete the set I pressed my thumb alongside them. "A detective wants my fingerprints for elimination purposes."

Solgar rubbed the glass clean with a gossamer-thin silk handkerchief as he bobbed his head quickly. "I can take care of that."

"His CSIs are working in my FX hut. I need the police off the lot as soon as possible. I have some potential investors coming in on Saturday."

Solgar's head bobbed again. "I can take care of that, too. We have friends on the force. I think the right words to the right people in the department will suffice."

"There may be issues with Maral . . . and her previous problem," I said.

"I will ensure there are no issues."

"Thank you, Ernst."

"Always a pleasure to be of assistance, Chatelaine." He came and stood alongside me and we looked out across our city in silence. There are perhaps two hundred vampyres in the city and between us we know them all, maybe ten times that number in the United States, not counting the new-made Creations. Probably twenty vampyres in L.A. were born, not made, and Solgar and I are two of those. The numbers of the vampyre clans have been gradually falling since the end of the First World War; there has not been a vampyre birth in eighty years, and even the number of Creations is down. As Chatelaine, I grant permission for Creations in this city. I'd authorized less than half a dozen this past year, and one of those was mine. To lose three Creations in less than three weeks could only mean one thing. . . .

"I believe there is a Hunter in town, Ernst."

His face twisted in an ugly mask, jaw briefly unhinging, tongue curling and uncoiling, flickering in the air. Blood flooded under the skin of the open tip and its color changed from pink to purple-red as it engorged. Hunters were abominations, vermin to be destroyed.

"And I think he's targeting me. Has anyone else lost a Creation recently?"

The Obour's face reassembled itself. He patted his damp chin with the handkerchief. "Rudy lost one of his to a drowning accident in a pool in Palm Springs a couple of months ago, but drink was a contributing factor, and Tod Browning lost another to a skiing accident in Big Sur. One of his newly mades went headlong into a tree and impaled himself on his Magfire 12s."

"Magfire 12s?"

"Slovakian skis. Very nice. Very fast. But it was an accident, I'm sure."

"Anyone we know with aspirations to rule Hollywood?"

"Everyone wants to rule Hollywood, you know that, but I do not believe that anyone is prepared to challenge you just yet. There are some Strigae newly arrived from Italy, but they're in New York and, from what I hear, may not survive there much longer. They've managed to irritate some of the Ch'Iang Shih."

New York belongs to the Chinese clan. The Italian Strigae have never gotten over the fact that they'd lost the city twenty years earlier. The Ch'lang Shih would have them for breakfast. Literally.

"Here's what I would like you to do for me, Ernst," I said, turning to face him. "Get the police off my back, give me some breathing space. I'm going to conduct my own investigation."

He bowed. "It will be done. But this detective you mentioned, Peter King, I know him by reputation. He got a commendation for bravery when he pulled a boy out of the river. I don't think he's the brightest, but he's tenacious and has an excellent arrest and prosecution record. If we back him off, he might get suspicious. And the last thing you need is a suspicious cop on your case."

"He's no fool, I know that. I *want* him to investigate. If he's as good as we think, he'll soon come to the conclusion that I'm innocent, but, more important, he might also discover the identity of the killer. And lead me to him."

"It's a dangerous game you're playing, Chatelaine. You know he might also discover your true self," Solgar suggested.

"I'll deal with that when the time comes. Police officers have accidents every day."

"Aaah, the famed Dakhanavar streak of brutality."

"There's nothing brutal about protecting my clan. Call it a mother's instincts."

CHAPTER TWELVE

VAN NUYS
5:00 P.M.

In the best tradition of inappropriate nicknames, John Trueblood is called Little John. He stands six foot eight. He claims he's a pure-blooded Chumash and I've never argued with him about it. He played basketball at Folsom State. Not the college, the prison. He got out with a G.E.D. and a body covered in permanent ink. Started riding with the Ventura chapter of the Hell's Angels, hitting the California tattoo conventions, and ended up on the extreme wrestling circuit fighting as Bloody Jack Baron, Kill Gore Trout, Doctor Savage, and Slippery Jim. He's got a tat for each name. When Hyam the Horrible crushed his testicles with a misplaced kick to the groin he changed careers and opened a tattoo parlor on Ventura Boulevard, where he specializes in bikers and servicemen. There's a sign on the window: "No Minors. No Women. No Musicians. No Exceptions." I've never asked him why.

Little John has a secret vice, which is how we met. And it's not what you think. He collects movie memorabilia, and he specializes in B movies. He's one of my mother's best customers; he even sends her Christmas cards.

They met at Rock & Shock in Worcester the year my mother decided to do the autograph convention circuit; that was the year she paid cash for her red Corvette, so I guess it was a good year. When she met him, Mom didn't see a six-foot-eight tattooed behemoth with the sides of his head shaved and the hair in the center gelled into six-inch spikes; she saw a comrade in arms, a fanboy who knew *Creature from the Black Lagoon*, *Them!*, and *Attack of the Killer Tomatoes!* And he saw a mother figure with great merchandise. Their friendship was sealed when Little John put the fear of God into a Goth who was questioning the authenticity of a signed Dwight Frye as Renfield in a *Dracula* photo. Whatever John said did the trick; the guy bought Frye as Renfield and as Fritz in *Frankenstein,* too. Little John knows everything there is to know about horror.

I figured if anyone could tell me what the deal was with Ovsanna Moore, it would be Little John.

I don't think I look like a cop. The gun isn't obvious, nor is the badge, and I don't wear rubber-soled shoes. But the moment I stepped into the darkened waiting room of Little John's tattoo parlor, I heard the murmur pass to every guy in the place. There were four bikers in full regalia, two marines, a wrestler whose name I couldn't remember, two blond-haired muscle-bound boys who screamed Aryan Brotherhood from whatever closet they were still in, and a trio of shaven-headed bodybuilders straight from Venice Beach who looked so much alike they might have been brothers but probably weren't. The men were sitting on hard plastic chairs staring intently at a TV set bolted to the wall behind a mesh screen. The bodybuilders high-fived each other every time Magnum punched out a bad guy on some beach in Hawaii.

Miss See was behind the counter. She's a tiny Asian woman of indeterminate heritage and equally indeterminate years who had managed Little John when he was wrestling. Word was she'd kept difficult wrestlers in line with a Taser. Her reputation alone was enough to keep the waiting room orderly. I once asked her if she knew any martial arts. "Of course," she said. "I protect myself. I have black belt in Mossberg." Then she pulled out a twelve-gauge pump-action Mossberg riot gun from under the desk.

"Detective King," she said loudly, just in case anyone in the room hadn't made me. The black unlit cigarette tucked in the corner of her lip didn't move.

"I need five minutes with Little John."

She glanced at the clock, then at the tiny TV monitor under the counter that allowed her to see into the back room where he worked. I leaned over to see what she was seeing. A skinny-shanked older man was climbing off the table; I wasn't sure, but it looked like he'd just had Dale Earnhardt tattooed on his butt. "He just finish."

"How have you been, Miss See?"

"You tell your mama stop sending my boy her catalogues. She getting lot of money out of him."

"I didn't know my mother produced catalogues."

"Every month," Miss See snapped. "And every month he buy." She leaned forward, enveloping me in her cloying perfume that made me think of rotten eggs. "This month he buy Lil Dagover's white nightgown, complete with certificate of authenticity."

I nodded blankly. I had no idea who Lil Dagover was.

A huge hand caught the back of my neck and turned me around. "She starred in the original 1919 version of *Das Kabinett des Doktor Caligari*." Little John's voice belonged to a pre-pubescent teenage boy, but there was no one sitting in that room who was going to make a joke of it. He was wearing his basic biker's costume—scuffed motorcycle boots with the toes showing metal underneath, leather trousers, and a leather vest over a completely hairless chest. Maybe there was some truth in his Indian heritage after all, with his high forehead, ridged cheekbones, and razor-thin lips. His Mohawk wasn't gelled this time, just pushed back off his forehead with a tribal head-band.

"How you doing, Little John?" I had to tip my head back to look in his face.

"Good. You tell your mama to keep sendin' the catalogues." He turned to the room where everyone had turned away from *Magnum* and was regarding us—well, me—suspiciously. "This here is Detective Peter King," he announced in his little-boy voice. "A good cop and a good man. He's the one pulled that kid out of the river a couple years ago. Now he's in charge of the Cinema Slayer case. He's a friend of mine."

The room warmed considerably. I got a couple of nods from the beach boys and one of the bikers stuck out his hand.

Little John motioned me into the back room and shut the door. He flicked off the camera, probably annoying Miss See no end. The walls were covered with drawings, transfers, and photographs of tattoos, ranging from the simple to the extraordinary, from the intricate to the excruciating. He had a gallery of the work he'd done on clients over the years. Shoulders, backs, ankles, biceps—all decorated with ink. It took me a few seconds to realize I was looking at a smiley face needled on someone's penis.

Little John bustled about, cleaning up after his last appointment, getting ready for the next. Every available inch of his skin was covered in tattoos, designs flowing into patterns, shapes morphing into letters, into animals, into creatures. Like that painting *Astral Circus* by Venosa. Some of it was crude and blotchy, but a lot was vivid and pristine. I briefly wondered what *his* penis looked like and then quickly shut that thought down.

"So I guess you're not here for some ink."

"Not this time. Looking for a little information—"

"Aw, Peter, I'm no stoolie—," he began, face falling.

"On a movie star."

He brightened up. "Well, that's different. My specialty. Who?"

"Ovsanna Moore."

Little John's face morphed into mush—I swear he was in love. "The Scream Queen. Third-generation Hollywood royalty," his high-pitched voice went higher. "I've got her grandmother's gloves from *Birth of a Nation*. I've got a letter her mother sent to Senator McCarthy refusing to attend a hearing, and I've got Ovsanna's costume from *Tell Me What You've Seen*." He stopped suddenly. "Why are you asking?" Then the color actually drained from his face. "Don't tell me . . . don't tell me something's happened to her?" This huge tattooed monster was on the verge of tears.

"She's fine," I said quickly. "Her name's popped up in an investigation. I just wanted a little background."

"Well, you won't find anything nasty. She's a sweetheart, does a lot of charity work, funds a couple of theatre scholarship programs. If you buy her signed photo online the money goes right to Paul Newman's Hole in the Wall Gang." He went over to his battered metal filing cabinet and produced a photograph. It showed Little John standing beside—well, towering over—the diminutive Ovsanna Moore. It was signed in silver ink: "To Little John, my 'biggest' friend." Her signature was an ornate loop.

"Very nice." I handed it back to him. This wasn't what I had come here to find. "Any scandal, any dark secrets, addictions, husbands, lovers?"

"Nah, not Ovsanna. She's blameless. No scandal, no addictions, no husbands. I think she's got some old boyfriends that she's still friendly with, even after they split."

My antenna went right up. No one—not even the Pope—is that blameless. "What's the story with her assistant?"

"Ah, now there's the secret! You discover that and the *National Enquirer* will give you a pension. No one knows. Maral McKenzie's been with her for about ten years. There's talk that they're gay or bi, but no one knows anything for a fact and they never say a word. There're some reporters who come right out and ask, too, but Ms. Moore just smiles and keeps her mouth shut. Part of the mystery."

In my job mysteries usually turn out to be nothing more than dirty little secrets. "Hmm, pity. I thought there might be some angle there."

The big man frowned. "Not your worst thought."

"Gee, thanks."

Little John went rooting through his cabinet again. "I've got something here. . . . You know about the guy her assistant killed, right? The one in the house on Mulholland: the Canyon Killings. It was just before she started working for Ovsanna. Girl woke up and found a guy standing over her with his pants around his ankles. She never gave him the chance to explain before she sliced him up real good."

Little John had his back to me, so he didn't see the look that must have crossed my face. I hadn't worked that case, but I'd read the file. Just never connected that McKenzie with this one. Some detective I was.

I kept my voice level. "Yeah. Vaguely. She did it with a knife, didn't she? Right in his gut." I love it when some piece of a puzzle clicks into place.

"Twelve-inch-long Sabatier kitchen knife. For some reason she had it in the bedroom with her. At least that's the story she gave you guys and you bought it." He turned away from the filing cabinet, holding a police evidence bag with the knife still in it. "The police finally released it and guess who sold it to me?"

"Someone *sold* it to you? Who?"

Little John's smile widened.

"Don't tell me it was . . . oh, *please* don't tell me—"

He told me. "Your mom."

CHAPTER THIRTEEN

"Take me to Bel Air, Maral. Please." I climbed into the back of the SUV, buckled myself in, closed my eyes, and stretched my legs out across the seat. A definite sign to Maral that I didn't want to talk. I needed to think. I needed to get home, sit in a tub, and listen to "Dead Can Dance" while my mind floated around with the bath bubbles. "I'm taking no calls," I added.

Maral nodded. She pulled the car out of the underground lot, turned left onto Sunset. "We'll be there in twenty minutes."

I have two homes in L.A., one in Bel Air and one at Point Dume. But I'm happiest at my home in Marin County—land of the Grateful Dead.

It was Catherine the Great, born Sophie Friederike Auguste but called Figchen by those of us she kept close, who taught me the value of owning real estate. We met when she arrived in St. Petersburg in 1744 and the Empress Elizabeth asked me to tutor the German-born princess in Russian before she was christened as

Yekaterina Alekseyevna and married the man who would become Peter III.

Officially, I was her Lady-in-Waiting, unofficially her body-guard, always her friend, and sometimes, when her frustration with Peter's impotence overcame her royal judgment, her lover. From Voltaire—gossip that he was—she learned my true nature, but she never wavered in her loyalty to me. Nor I to her. Twice, when I was stricken with the Thirst, she offered me her wrist. So you could say the blood of royalty runs in my veins. The blood of royalty and the wisdom to buy real estate.

Catherine acquired the Crimea, the Ukraine, Belarus, and Lithuania. Under a variety of names of individuals, companies, and corporations I own land in over twenty countries and have property in just about every state in the Union.

I own huge swaths of Hollywood and greater Los Angeles. When I came out here at the turn of the twentieth century it was possible to pick up land for dollars. I used the money I got from Thomas Hope, when I sold him the French Blue diamond in 1830, to buy as much land as I could, particularly in and around the canyons. It didn't take a genius to work out that the orange groves of the city of Hollywood and Los Angeles would prove an irresistible lure.

When I was younger, I drifted around the world, spending days or weeks on the various properties, but as I get older, I find myself traveling less and less. It's been decades since I was in France, a century since I visited Italy. I've not been back to Russia since Catherine died, even though I own a charming dacha on the Black Sea.

Catherine also taught me that once you have property, you don't sell it: you lease or rent it. Last year, the little hotel I own just off the Rue Perenelle, in Paris, earned me about $1.5 million in profit, the villa in Tuscany about the same, the house in Kensington in London nearly twice that. I have no idea what the L.A. properties earned. More than I could ever spend, certainly.

Vampyres move and travel to protect their secret. It was easier when I was younger. A century ago I could stay in one place for a number of years and then, before suspicions arose, I would take my leave or arrange for my death and burial and transport myself to a distant country where no one would question my appearance. Now, with jet planes and ocean liners and automobiles and news broadcasts, it's impossible to get away from people you know. Twice this century I've had to resort to "dying" and returning as my "daughter." Fortunately, L.A. today is so obsessed with staying attractive, no one questions how I manage to age so well. They just chalk it up to surgery and injections and non-stop Pilates. Little do they know it's nearly five hundred years of sucking blood. But living in Hollywood in the twenty-first century has allowed me to remain Ovsanna Moore a lot longer than I lived as her mother and grandmother. If Gloria Vanderbilt can look as good as she does at her age, I've got another twenty years before anyone gets suspicious . . . and by then, who knows what technology will have achieved?

I love the house in Bel Air almost as much as the one in Marin. They're completely different. Marin is all rough-hewn cedar and glass, built into the side of a mountain, surrounded by ancient oaks and redwoods. Bel Air is a Spanish hacienda, hidden from my neighbors by a two-foot-wide, twelve-foot-tall stucco wall.

My "grandmother" bought the property in the early twenties when Los Angeles was nothing but orange groves and avocado trees. She convinced Bertram Grosvenor Goodhue to draw up the original plans for the main house and the two guesthouses. Over the years I made changes, mostly for the sake of security. The windows are bulletproof glass, the massive carved wooden door has a steel core, and the grounds have the requisite cameras and sensor alerts. I didn't touch the original waterfall and running stream he created, just stocked the pond with ducks and geese. A lesson learned from Louis XVI—forget dogs; no one sounds an alarm better than waterfowl.

The house has its own well and I have diesel generators for

emergency power. This is Los Angeles, land of constant earth quaking. No one questions these things.

Lying on my back, I felt the car slow; then my sensitive hearing caught the whirr of the electric gates. The car moved forward and now gravel crunched under the wheels. I love this house.

I've lived here longer than anywhere else and it's filled with objects I've managed to keep with me through six centuries. Many of the vampyre collect; it is part of our nature. When life is so long, when memories crowd one atop the other and become confused with fantasy and dreams, then we need tangible objects to remind us of our past. A collection comes to represent something tangible in an otherwise ever-changing world.

For me, it's always been art. I'm particularly fond of the Impressionists and Postimpressionists, but only because I was so much a part of that culture. The art on the walls is all original: purchased, cajoled, bartered, or stolen from the original artists. The west wing is entirely devoted to van Gogh, whom I adored, Toulouse-Lautrec, whom I despised, and Gauguin, whom I was always ambivalent about. Didn't stop me from taking their work, though. Individually and collectively, they all called me their muse.

My insurance agent marvels at the money I must have spent to acquire such ancient artifacts when in fact most of them were trinkets I picked up at the time they were made. That Ming vase in the living room was a chamber pot I used in 1590 and the van Gogh in the bathroom was something Vincent was throwing away because he didn't like it.

Half my house in Point Dume is covered with Vincent's work. Vincent was special. We were never lovers; ours was a friendship that went deeper than that. I own more of his work than any other artist. I still miss him. When we left Paris for Arles together, I started the process of Turning him, but he grew terrified that becoming vampyre would destroy his talent. He refused to allow me to complete his creation. To this day I am convinced that his subsequent half-human, half-vampyre existence—what is called the *dhampir* stage—is what drove him mad. The evidence of his emerging vampyre senses is there on the canvas: the vibrant colors, the swirling energy, the sheer exuberance of life. To look at his work is to see the world through vampyre eyes.

"We're home." Maral turned off the engine and I straightened, opened the back door, and stepped out into the near darkness.

And immediately knew something was wrong.

I've no psychic abilities—only the Bobhan Sith possess those. But my instincts, honed by too many years of survival, were warning me that something was amiss. Leaning back into the car, I unsnapped the snub-nose .357 Magnum from its holster under the backseat and shoved it into the pocket of my coat. I kept my hand on it.

Maral's eyes flared when she saw the gun, but she didn't speak.

"Just a feeling," I whispered, leaning over to pat her face. "Maybe I'm just spooked—"

"You don't get spooked," Maral reminded me.

"Do you have your pepper spray?"

"Always." She patted her bag. Nothing discourages the over-eager, the rude, or the obnoxious better than a squirt of cayenne pepper spray.

"Get it ready. Take out your phone, pretend to answer a call, give us an excuse to linger here."

While Maral reached for her cell, I took the opportunity to look across the garden before finally settling to look at the house. Nothing seemed amiss. Doors were closed, windows locked. There was no movement in the undergrowth. Maybe it was just my imagination. I was turning back to Maral when I realized what had caught my peripheral attention. There was a series of regular indentations across the smooth gravel driveway. They came out of the hibiscus, crossed the turning circle, and finished at the doors to the screening room. Someone heavy had walked across the gravel.

I allowed my vampyre senses to flare.

Usually I keep them damped down: the additional stimuli are a lot to handle. Now I welcomed them. My pupils widened, contracted down to cat's eyes, then grew large again. The twilight brightened and jumped into sharp focus, and I followed the progress of the footprints across the grass, over the gravel, towards the house. Size elevens or twelves, I guessed. Breathing deeply, I sorted through the myriad odors in the garden, ignoring the sulfurous smog smells, identifying the camellias and the roses.

And then I caught it, faint, faint, faint . . . just at the very edges of perception: bitter spices and the tart iron of blood. Ancient blood. Familiar blood.

"Get back in the car!"

Maral opened her mouth to protest.

"Get back in the car!" My fangs began to unsheathe and that frightened her where my words hadn't. She scrambled back into the driver's seat. I pushed the door closed. "Get out of here. Wait for my call."

"Let me come with you."

"No," I snapped, with more venom than I intended. "No," I repeated gently. "I've a good idea what's inside and, trust me, you don't want to meet it."

"But—"

"I'll call you," I said firmly. "And if I don't contact you within the next thirty minutes, then phone Detective King and get him up here." I dug his business card out of my pocket and dropped it in her lap. "On no account are you to come into the house on your own."

"Ovsanna, I'm scared." Her gray eyes were huge behind her Buddy Holly frames.

"I can take care of myself," I assured her. But deep inside, I was experiencing an emotion I barely recognized: fear. I hadn't felt fear in a hundred years or more. I don't like it. It's not a comfortable feeling. And even the cold metal of the .357 and five hundred years of survival weren't offering much reassurance.

Chapter Fourteen

BEVERLY GLEN
6:15 P.M.

Not only had Maral McKenzie eviscerated a man with a top-quality twelve-inch-long Sabatier kitchen knife in a house on Mulholland, she'd almost beheaded him. The murder file read like an X-rated version of *Halloween*.

I'd broken a whole bunch of regulations and borrowed the file to bring it home with me. As a precaution, I requested a raft of files to disguise the one I really wanted. Too many inquiring eyes turn into "sources close to the investigation" when some scandal sheet flashes big bucks for the smallest snippet of information or nugget of gossip. Eva Casale's murder at Anticipation had already been tied to the Cinema Slayer by the media. The talking heads on FOX News and CNN had theories ranging from the ludicrous to the ridiculous. My favorite was the pet psychic from Animal Planet who claimed that an evil spirit manifested by Charlie Manson was inhabiting the body of a pissed-off capuchin monkey. According to the psychic, said simian had jumped its fence at the L.A. Zoo and was out wreaking havoc when no one noticed.

I was standing in the kitchen rereading the file and putting together the jug of sun tea I'd left sitting out all day when the door opened and SuzieQ, my tenant, appeared. SuzieQ stopped knocking about two days after she moved in. I have a nice little three-bedroom house in Beverly Glen that I bought with the fees I earned off *L.A. Undercover*. The best investment I ever made. It's got a hot tub with two settings, too hot and scalding; a black-bottom lap pool, which seems really cool until you realize it's hard to see the water moccasins lying in wait; and a separate guesthouse at the bottom of the garden. Renting out the guesthouse supplements my BHPD wages. SuzieQ—that's the name on her license and her checks and it's the only name she's ever given me—was my first and only tenant. She took it originally on a month-to-month lease. That was five years ago. She's an Amazon, taller than I am, blond, blue-eyed, and built— think Sandhal Bergman in *Conan*. She works out on Muscle Beach and earns her living as an exotic dancer. And they don't come any more exotic than SuzieQ: she dances with snakes—a nine-foot boa constrictor and a fifteen-foot albino python. She may have others, I don't know. I don't go visiting.

As usual, she got straight to the point. "Now listen, honey, I hear the Cinema Slayer's struck again; what are you gonna do?" Her Nashville twang turned "do" into two syllables. Folding perfectly sculpted forearms across her impressive chest, she leaned back against the fridge and regarded me with her baby blues. Last week, they were green. She wears colored contacts when she's dancing so her eyes won't clash with her snakes. In her V-neck sweater and cut-off jeans she probably hadn't caused too many accidents today, but then I don't think she'd left the house yet. She's usually just getting home at 4:00 A.M.

"We only found the body four hours ago. Which newsmonger did you hear that from?"

"Well, AOL has it on their welcome page and MSNBC.com just e-mailed me the headline and a link. I just love bein' signed up with them. Now I never miss the news."

"You didn't miss it when you didn't have it," I reminded her, but she didn't respond. When she wanted to ignore me, she could be as deaf as her snakes.

"The Slayer is still your case, ain't it, sugar? Only now you got a fourth body—ain't you just in a whole mess a trouble?"

"Actually not as much as you might think. I was the one who discovered the body. I was following a lead."

"Well, so tell me what happened? The news didn't have a whole lotta facts."

The sun tea looked plenty strong; I melted some brown sugar in the microwave, stirred it into the pitcher, and added a handful of ice cubes. Then I poured two glasses and handed one to SuzieQ. "We're trying to keep a lid on the details until we can contact the vic's family. Doesn't sound like we're doing a great job, does it? But so far there's nothing to say this is the Cinema Slayer. The vic was no movie star—she was a special effects artist at Anticipation."

"That's Ovsanna Moore's place. I worked for them a couple a years ago."

SuzieQ is always full of surprises. One of these days I was going to get around to asking how a convent-educated Catholic school girl ended up dancing with snakes and sporting a pentacle tattoo on the base of her spine.

"Dancing or wrangling?"

"Wrangling. You're such a good detective, ya know? It's amazin' how y'all do that. It was *Bride of the Snake God*. You remember that movie?"

I shook my head.

"I don't guess too many people saw that one. I'll lend you the DVD; it's got extras and everythin'. I used Spiro Agnew in that one and he was featured right nice. They even gave him a credit. And one for me, of course, as snake wrangler."

"Have you got a few minutes?"

SuzieQ grinned, teeth laser white and dentist perfect. "Sure. I'm teachin' a belly dance class to a bunch of Hadassah ladies but not till eight o'clock. And those ladies won't be on time for their funerals. I never seen such a bunch a talkers—even where I come from."

There's nothing between us, never has been, never will. SuzieQ's more like a big sister. I'm not sure if she's gay or straight or bi. I've seen her hanging around with people who fell into all three categories; personally I think the snakes put a lot of people off. She's also got a black belt in karate and has recently started kickboxing. Only last week one of the customers at the club where she dances grabbed her python's tail: she'd broken his jaw and four fingers before the bouncers pulled her off him. She was lucky: he was a televangelist from Idaho and naturally reluctant to press changes.

I headed into the living room and put my tea and the file down on the coffee table. The light was fading and there was a definite chill in the air. I piled a couple of white pine logs on the grate above the gas jet and lit the gas. Within seconds the dry wood was burning nicely and I settled onto the sofa. SuzieQ had already arranged herself in the lotus position on the rug in front of the fireplace. "Did you meet Ovsanna Moore?" I asked.

"I worked with her for three weeks. She was playing the snake god's bride and she was handlin' Spiro Agnew. She did pretty good, too." SuzieQ's snakes are named after politicians. She may sound like a backwoods hillbilly but she's smart as a whip, with a wicked sense of humor and a head for complete trivia. I took her to game night for a cop charity a year ago and we won two hundred dollars. Well, *she* won two hundred dollars. I only got one question right—I knew who won the race in the movie *Cannonball Run*.

"What did you think of Moore?"

"I liked her," she said. "And she's strong, too. Whoa, is that girl strong. She carried Spiro around like he was a little bit of a thing and he's getting to be a big boy now. He must weigh thirty pounds. That's a good size for a python." She whipped a flat silver PDA out of her shoulder bag and made a quick note. "Have to stop at the pet store for more mice."

"What about the assistant, Maral McKenzie?" I persisted. "Did you come across her?"

"Once or twice. I sure didn't like her. She's a real pain in the ass," she added dismissively.

"Any particular reason why?"

"Always hoverin' round Ovsanna, gettin' between her and ev'ryone else." SuzieQ's bright blue eyes snapped open. "Ooh, you think she done it, don't you? You think she killed that girl."

"I'm not thinking anything yet. I'm just asking questions. And I'm interested in her." The blue eyes got even bigger; pencil-thin eyebrows rose a fraction. "Not in that way."

"Well, you'd be wasting your time if you were, honey. That girl is gayer than an Apache dancer. She is definitely not interested in men."

"And what about Ovsanna?"

"Not sure. I saw her lookin' at men. She might go both ways. But I think she's interested in a lot of things. Not that I can say from personal experience, she was all business with me, but there was somethin' goin' on with her and that McKenzie woman. Maybe not fuckin' exactly, but somethin' . . ." She straightened one leg in front of her, crossed the other over it with her knee bent and did another yoga pose, the Twist. Her back cracked all the way up her spine. "So how come you think she did it?" she asked.

"I didn't say that, SuzieQ, I said I was interested in her."

"Oh fiddlesticks. It's damn near the same thing, sugar. Somethin's got you askin' questions. What is it?"

"In confidence . . . ?" I asked.

"Cross my heart!" She made an X over her impressive bosom.

I flipped open the file. "Miss McKenzie's got a jacket. Stabbed a man in the gut and damn near beheaded him."

"My kind of girl. He musta really pissed her off." She came to her feet and moved around to peer over my shoulder at the file. She smelled good, honeysuckle or something. She tapped the file photo with her fingertip. "Don't look like a killer." It showed a wide-eyed, wild-haired young teen, frightened, disheveled, with bruises darkening her cheek and jaw.

"They never do." I quickly flipped through the file. Most of it was public knowledge anyway and I couldn't let SuzieQ read any specifics, but over the years I've come to rely on her as a sounding board when I'm mulling over a case. "Not sure if you remember this case. Twelve years ago—"

"I've only been in L.A. six," SuzieQ reminded me.

"Well, twelve years ago we had a series of break-ins in expensive homes in the canyons and along Mulholland. The guy got off on getting past the alarm systems. It was like he deliberately chose houses with great security so he could laugh at us. Twice he found women at home and raped them, but neither of them could give us a description that was worth anything. He was on them before they even woke up and held a pillow over their faces while he was doing his business. Used a condom, so there was no DNA.

"Maral McKenzie was house-sitting for friends in a big home set off the road on Mulholland, sleeping in a guest room. She wakes up, finds the guy about to climb on top, grabs the knife and does him. She told the detectives she kept the knife on the night table because it was spooky staying in the big house alone."

"Sounds like one smart cookie to me. So she used it and saved herself a whole mess a trouble. What's your problem with it?"

"Ms. McKenzie claimed in her statement that she was lying in the bed when he walked in. Somehow she managed to eviscerate him and almost slice his head clean off. I'm not sure I could do that if I were standing in wait and the guy was immobile."

SuzieQ was smart. She got it. "Remind me again about the Cinema Slayer: how did the vics die?"

"Disembowelment, decapitation, impalement, and drowning."

"Wow, she's done two out of four. What do you think? I knew there was a reason I didn't like her."

"I don't know, Suze, it's all a bit too easy. Maral McKenzie kills three movie stars and a special effects artist in a way that vaguely mirrors her manslaughter beef a decade earlier?"

"She's an obsessive. She's killing anyone with an interest in Ovsanna," SuzieQ suggested.

"Too neat. Too obvious. What's her motive?"

"Who knows? Maybe she didn't like their work."

Chapter Fifteen

There were five rounds in the .357 with an empty chamber under the hammer. The gun was loaded with blue-tipped Glazer safety bullets; designed primarily for air marshals, they shatter upon entering a body and don't pass through—useful when you're on a plane. Once you get hit with one of these, you stay hit.

I wasn't sure how effective they would be against the vampyre in the house, though.

I'd recognized the scent: the unforgettable essence of old blood that only the very ancient exude. I haven't got it yet, but as vampyres go, I'm not exactly that old. Solgar has it, but he keeps it disguised with Old Spice. Stand too close to him and your eyes water; he must bathe in the stuff.

I moved towards the house, alert for any movement. I'd left all the doors locked and the alarm system on, but I wasn't surprised nothing had been tripped. Whoever had invaded the house had probably shape-shifted into something small enough to get through an open upstairs window or flown down the chimney, which was how I used to do it in my housebreaking days in Berlin. I thought about doing it now—taking on the shape of a bird or a bat and slipping into the house—but the effort would leave me in agony, wracked with muscle spasms and vulnerable to whatever waited within.

There was no point in trying for the element of surprise: the vampyre knew I was outside, in the same way that I knew it was inside. Standing outside the front door, I breathed deeply. The scent of old blood was stronger now, mingled with exotic spices and bitter herbs. I frowned; the scent was *too* strong.

Much too strong.

And I realized then that there was more than one vampyre inside.

Contrary to popular lore, vampyres do not run in packs.

There are many reasons, but primarily, I think it's because we don't like leftovers. Most of us are rather selfish and no one wants to share a meal. Second, we need to protect our anonymity and the likelihood of raising questions about our habits and idiosyncrasies increases if we're seen together. And our elders *must* stay out of sight; the physical changes that take place as we move into great age are almost impossible to conceal. Our skin thickens; our fingers harden and become clawlike. Some clans grow wings and their spines extend into tails. Now you know why Orson Welles wore capes towards the "end" of his life. I am convinced that the legends of devils and demons have their genesis in sightings of the Elders.

So smelling more than one vampyre inside my house added confusion to my fear.

Standing at the main entrance, I unlocked both locks, pressed the black iron thumb latch on the scrolled door handle, and pushed open the heavy wooden door. My alarm techs tried to sell me on biometrics—using fingerprints and retina scans to allow access to the house—but since I don't have any fingerprints to scan and my irises are subject to change I had to dissuade them. I'm sure they think I'm old-fashioned. Or cheap. Silently I keyed in the alarm combination—1550, the year of my birth—and watched the light change from red to green. With the gun held tightly in my right hand, I stepped farther into the cool foyer and listened.

The house was silent. But the smell of vampyre was stronger.

I'd kept the exterior of the house more or less as it was when "my mother" originally bought it. The foyer, library, music room, living room, and my office all open onto an outdoor courtyard and I'd replaced the floor-to-ceiling windows with UV bulletproof glass. The fountain in the middle of the courtyard was carved from stone I'd imported from the Tenochtitlán ruins. The interior walls are a pale buttercream, the floors are handmade terra-cotta pavers, the ceiling high and arched with exposed wooden beams. The wall directly to the right of the door is decorated with a selection of bladed weapons: knives, swords, axes, and halberds arranged in a pattern around the centerpiece, Hernando Cortés's original suite of armor. No, I didn't know him; he was dead before I was born. I just bought it in a junk shop in Tenochtitlán from a shopkeeper who didn't know what he had.

I ignored the swords—forget that rubbish about vampyres fighting with swords: give me a projectile weapon any day. Reaching into Cortés's armor, I pulled out the four-barreled derringer concealed there. Call me paranoid, but there are guns hidden all over the house. Paranoia has kept me alive. I'd have been happier with the AK-47, but that was upstairs under the bed.

A sound broke the silence. It took me a moment to make sense of what I was hearing: someone was playing my piano.

I slipped off my boots and socks and padded barefoot down the hall, making no sound on the tile. I had the silver Magnum in my right hand and the tiny derringer in my left. The music room is at the end of the west wing. That's where I keep the instruments I've collected over the years: Caruso's rehearsal piano, Glenn Miller's trombone, and one of Elvis's guitars. I've also got Bix Beiderbecke's cornet and two Stradivari—a mandolin Antonio gave me during his

Brescian period and a violin I bought on a London stall for ten shillings.

Stopping outside the door, I pressed my face against the smooth wood and listened. The smell of blood, of ancient power, was stronger now. There were at least three, possibly even more, Elders inside. They must have smelled me by now, but the strains of "Time Is on My Side" continued to emanate from the Steinway. There's only one vampyre I know who likes the Stones *and* has a sense of humor. I loosened my grip on the .357, pushed open the door, strode inside.

And stopped.

Here were the Vampyres of Hollywood.

Not only was Orson there but Olive Thomas and Mary and Douglas, Theda and her husband, Charles, and James Whale and Peter Lorre. Rudy Valentino was talking to Pola Negri. Ten of the most powerful vampyres in Hollywood and I'd never seen them all in one room together. The only ones missing were Tod and Charlie.

"God damn it, Orson. You scared the shit out of me."

He looked up from the piano. "Oh, I thought that was physically impossible, my dear, unless your clan has devolved in some way I'm not aware of. And really, Ovsanna, you've been in Hollywood too long. You've got the mouth of a guttersnipe."

I hadn't seen Orson since a month after his funeral. He'd been brilliant at arranging his death, using the conjuring tricks he'd learned as a child to deceive his mourners and choosing the same day Yul Brynner passed to diffuse the media attention. He even went so far as to have his ashes scattered at the famous Plaza de Toros de Ronda, in between bullfights. Ever the showman.

"You've lost weight, Orson. You look good." I'd never understood how he managed to consume two steaks, a half pint of scotch, and a pineapple every evening. The Strigoi Vui Clan are not solely blood drinkers, but still . . .

"I had no choice. I rarely venture out except in animal form; I can't take the chance of being recognized. The perils of being a celebrity," he sighed dramatically. "Even the young people pose a threat. They hear my voice and start screaming, 'Unicron! Unicron!'"

"Oh pish, Orson, stop bragging." Olive Thomas was seated on my sofa, looking as beautiful as when she'd taken the mercury bichloride tablets in 1920. Obviously her vocal cords had healed from the burns. I hadn't seen her since the night she invited Douglas and Mary and me to see *Beatrice Fairfax* on her home projector in 1916. Mary brought her dreadful brother along and the next thing we knew he and Olive were married. Four years later she used the pills he was taking for his syphilis to stage her "death." It was convenient but I always thought untimely. She could have continued acting for years and no one would have questioned her unfading beauty.

"It's not my fault, you sweet young thing," replied Orson. "They just rereleased the movie in some twentieth-anniversary edition and they've made a sequel to boot. That damn thing was a huge success. It still galls me to think my last work was some big-screen animated advertisement for Japanese toys. *Transformers: The Movie.* What was I thinking?"

"Don't worry, it's being remade. Your version will soon be forgotten," James Whale muttered. No one had dared remake James's original *Frankenstein* until years after he "drowned," but it still pained him that they had. He's never forgiven Mel Brooks.

"Ovsanna . . . ," Peter Lorre lisped. He came towards me with his arms outstretched and then they were all around me, enveloping me in the eye-watering taint of old blood. The fear I'd experienced out on the driveway gave way to a more subtle anxiety: only the gravest danger could entice these vampyres to come out of hiding.

We moved into the dining room. I don't entertain often. I don't want to deal with having to eat in front of people, but I have the requisite fifteen-foot-long dining table to keep up appearances. Orson sat at one end of the thick slab of macassar ebony and I sat at the other. Douglas and Mary stayed as far from each other as possible; he'd obviously not been forgiven for the affair with Lady Sylvia.

Pola draped herself over Rudy, voracious as ever. Peter Lorre wouldn't sit; he stalked the room back and forth behind Theda and Charles. James and Olive sat opposite them.

"This is madness," Peter said, his accent still terrible after all these years in the States, "so many of us together. Madness."

I was inclined to agree with him. "Who called this meeting?" I asked. As Chatelaine, it fell to me to call the Vampyres of Hollywood together, something I hadn't done since Sharon Tate was killed.

"I did," Douglas said gravely, in his wonderfully cultured accent. The room immediately fell silent. He brushed at his moustache with a forefinger, a sure sign that he was nervous. "You need our help, Ovsanna, and I didn't want to wait until you asked. Ernst called me as soon as you left his office and I reached the others. I hope you will forgive me."

I nodded and smiled. I could forgive Douglas Fairbanks anything; Mary glared at me.

"Tell us what is going on, Chatelaine," said James. "Douglas didn't have time to explain anything."

"I have lost three Creations," I said. "There was another killing today—one of my staff at the studio, not one of us."

"A mistake?" Olive asked.

"Not likely," Peter answered.

"I believe I am being deliberately targeted."

"Why?" Theda asked bluntly. "Who've you irritated this century?" She still resented me for wiping out her clan.

"I have no idea. The three deaths were all in the traditional ways. The death today was by disembowelment."

The Vampyres of Hollywood murmured together, a base animal sound.

I looked over at Rudy. I hadn't seen him since he'd re-created himself as Rolph Valenti and started a mid-level theatrical agency in London. He handled a couple of good Brits and an Irish actor who showed up as a regular on the BBC, some American expats, and that Scotsman I liked so much on *Murphy's Law* but no one else worth mentioning. Rudy was as dissolute as ever, skin pale and flawless, though there were deep bruise-colored circles under his eyes and his usually firm smile seemed loose, while an almost black tongue flickered between his lips. Creating him had been a mistake. Whenever I'd made mistakes before, I'd usually cleaned them up, but I'd let Rudy live and even I didn't know why . . . or maybe I did and just didn't want to admit it. "Rudy, Ernst said you lost someone. Could it be connected?"

Rudy sighed dramatically and brushed his overlong hair back off his high forehead. "One of my newly Turned drowned in a pool in Palm Springs in September. But he had drunk some tainted blood." His smile was ice. "I've no idea where he got it from." He stalked away from the table and struck a pose before the window.

I could only imagine; vampyres are immune to the effects of alcohol and drugs, but if we ingest blood recently tainted by either, we can get drunk or high. Some vampyres—and I suspected Rudy was amongst them—deliberately feed off drunken or drugged humans.

"I didn't authorize a Creation."

"I've been so busy." Rudy smiled, not even bothering to hide the lie. "I meant to get around to asking you."

It was a deliberate affront to my authority. Not his first, either. One of these days I was going to have to deal with it.

Mary smiled her sad little-girl smile—she was still using her own Mary Pickford line of cosmetics, for God's sake—and looked down the table at me. "I was talking to Tod Browning at a Sabbath night recently. One of his new Creations, just beyond *dhampir,* died in a skiing accident. He was very cut up about it."

Somehow I doubted it. I'd worked with Tod on *Dracula* in 1931, the movie that essentially created the modern vampyre legend. He was brilliant. And completely unsentimental.

James Whale stood up, his depression apparent still in the slump of his shoulders and the slowness with which he rose. "There have been whispers—nothing more," he said, a trace of his English accent still in his voice, "of some unusual activity in New York. An extraordinary number of Creations," he added.

"I've heard that," Theda said. Theda and Charles live in a penthouse on Central Park West with every room overlooking the park. She uses the name Theodosia de Coppet, which I've suggested she change, but as usual, she doesn't listen to me. The other residents in the building believe she was something in the cinema; they have no idea that she once *was* the cinema: the original femme fatale whose nickname was The Vamp. Yes, short for "vampyre." She was always putting us at risk. Fortunately, these days, without her signature eye makeup, she's unrecognizable. "There are so many young people wanting to become vampyres . . . or at least the cinema version of vampyres," she added with a sly smile.

"Everyone looks good in black," Pola agreed. "Even you, darling." Their enmity hadn't abated with the years. The original dueling divas.

Theda didn't even glance in her direction. "There are clubs which specialize in Goths and vampyres, all black leather and studs . . . ," she continued.

"Sounds like my type of place," said James archly.

"Why, James . . . finally out of the closet?" sneered Rudy. He should talk. He reveled in his bigamy conviction, but we all knew his first wife was a lesbian and his second was bi-sexual. Rudy was, too. I don't believe he ever intended to marry Pola, regardless of what she told the press. Why in hell did I Turn him? I was younger then, but that's really no excuse for the lapse in taste.

Theda ignored them both. "It's hard to tell the *dhampirs* and the newly created from the wannabes. Vampyre is a style now, a fashion, a culture." Theda and Charles own a chain of boutiques in the Village, New Orleans, San Francisco, L.A., and Tokyo. They have their own line of vampyre and Goth clothing and makeup.

"Well, what do you think?" I asked her. "Do we have a Rogue in L.A.?"

Theda looked at Charles and he shook his head. "We would know if there was a Rogue in the city," he said. "I might not, but Theda surely would. She's Azeman, after all."

Theda nodded in agreement. The Azeman transform into bats at night and spend hours scouring their cities. Rogue vampyres are arrogant, foolish, and dangerous. So very, very dangerous. Some have renounced their clans and the age-old principles that have kept us alive and hidden through the centuries. They believe that the vampyres are a superior race and that humans are cattle. They move indiscriminately through the human population, taking blood even when they do not need it, making Creations quickly and without thought. They are too careless to remain undiscovered. If a Rogue were operating, Theda would know and would have acted. It is the duty of every vampyre to destroy the Rogues.

"Not a Rogue then, a Hunter. We've been here before," I reminded them. "Some of you were with me in Paris during the Terror in '94 when Robespierre declared war on us."

Peter Lorre nodded. He had been instrumental in Robespierre's fall and subsequent execution. "If we wait, they'll make a mistake—they always do."

"I am not sure we can afford to wait," Douglas said gravely. "The world is different now. As celebrities, even dead celebrities, there are too many eyes on us, too many cameras. The Internet keeps track of everyone. We're all on IMDb; there are endless fan sites, thousands of photographs. All you have to do is type a name in Google and we're exposed. Not who we really are, of course, but our lives are laid out there."

I sensed a shift at the table, the tiniest ripple of nervous energy.

Rudy moved away from the window and crouched behind my chair. The smell of sour blood was stronger now and I had to fight hard to keep my teeth in place. "This Vampyre Hunter has targeted *your* Creations, Ovsanna. He's playing with *you;* eventually he will come for *you.*"

"I am flattered by your concern, Rudy." I doubt he heard the sarcasm in my voice; he's too self-involved to notice. Maybe that's what attracted me to him in the first place. He had all the attributes of a vampyre but without actually being one. He made the transition from Warm to vampyre without any effort or without experiencing the anguish others go through when their human body mutates into this vampyre form. That should have told me something right then. In the years of his phenomenal success, I lost him to his fans and his arrogance. When he *died,* we both attended the funeral; he moved through the crowd disguised and unnoticed, delighting in the adulation. And pissed off at Pola, who upstaged him by throwing herself in a faint across his casket, which she'd covered in flowers spelling *her* name. They deserved each other.

"I am concerned for all of us, Ovsanna. So far we've—*you've*—lost three minor actors." Everyone was minor in Rudy's eyes except Rudy. "But you're different. You're Hollywood royalty—or so it says in the *TV Times,*" he added bitchily. I'm sure he was still pissed at me for not casting one of his star clients, Andrea Goyan, in *Vatican Vampyres.* I'd used Mai Goulart instead. "If you are slain in some bloody and dramatic fashion, there will be endless media coverage and retrospectives, probably even a Biography Channel special. Who knows what an investigation might reveal?" He spun away from my chair and stamped to the other end of the room, making me wonder again what I had ever seen in him.

"You're right, Rudy. I know that. I knew it as soon as I talked to Ernst. We can't afford the attention."

I turned to look at Douglas. "Tell me you have a plan." Douglas always has a plan. He answered me with those beautiful, sensitive eyes. "What is it?" I asked, although I already had a very good idea. I wanted to hear him say it aloud.

"You really have only one course of action, Ovsanna," he said. "You must *die* again. Die and we will purge your remaining Creations. Disappear to some godforsaken place where no one has ever seen *Satan's Succubus* or *Thirst.* Come back in a century or two."

A growl of agreement rumbled around the table.

"I am at the peak of my career, Douglas. I have more work I want to do and I don't want to wait another couple of hundred years to do it. Besides, I am the Chatelaine. I will not allow a mere Vampyre Hunter to destroy what I have created."

"You yourself destroyed Theda's clan when she put us at risk, Ovsanna," Douglas reminded me. "You had Rudy die at the height of his fame to preserve his name and reputation. Yes, you are the Chatelaine, but you won't betray the rest of us for your own selfishness. I know you won't." He stood up and was already flowing into smoke, that most difficult and dramatic of transformations. Now I knew how they'd gotten into the house.

Orson watched Douglas disappear and then spoke. "I would never threaten you, my dear, but you know as well as I we cannot allow you to expose us. You must disappear, Ovsanna. Kill the Hunter or 'kill' yourself, those are your only choices." There was a flickering transformation—wings and tail and talons—and then he, too, curled into smoke.

One by one they all dissolved into gray and black smoke and disappeared up the chimney, leaving silence and the smell of old blood in their wake. Only Rudy stayed; he had to have the last word. "Make your decision soon, darling. You have a week, no more. And if you've not made a decision, then we will make it for you." And then, he, too, was gone.

I sat at the table for a long time, running the conversation over and over in my head. I may be the Chatelaine, but not even I could survive the wrath of the Vampyres of Hollywood. While I might call some of them friends, they would not hesitate to destroy me if they thought I was endangering their very existence.

Their message was clear.

I had a week. A week to prepare for my death or find the vampyre killer and prepare his.

Plenty of time for the first choice, but was it enough for the second? Either way, there would be a funeral.

CHAPTER SIXTEEN

BEVERLY GLEN
7:00 P.M.

I closed the file and looked at SuzieQ. "Time to visit Ms. McKenzie, I think."

"Get her away from Ovsanna," SuzieQ advised. "You'll have more success with her on her own. Even if their relationship isn't sexual, there's some sort of empowerment and validation thing going on."

"Very deep, SuzieQ, did you get that from Dr. Phil?"

"Nah. Dr. Patterson. She's my shrink and she's damn good."

My cell phone buzzed. I opened it and glanced at the screen, but I didn't recognize the number. "Yes?"

"Officer King?"

"Yes. Who is this?"

"Maral McKenzie. Ovsanna Moore's personal assistant," she added, just in case I didn't know who she was. She sounded upset.

"It's Detective King, Ms. McKenzie. Is there a problem?"

"I think Ovsanna is in danger. She went into her house with a gun because she thought someone had broken in. She wouldn't let me go with her, but she told me to call you if she didn't come out in thirty minutes. That was forty minutes ago. I haven't heard anything and I can't see anything. I'm frightened."

"Where are you? What's the address?"

"Nine twenty-two Stone Canyon Drive. North of Sunset. The gate is open and I'm hiding in the back by the car. Please hurry."

"Stay right where you are. Don't move. I'm on my way."

"Who was it?" SuzieQ demanded when I hung up.

"Maral McKenzie. Someone's broken into Ovsanna Moore's house."

"And she is phoning you why? And where is Ms. Moore?"

"Inside the house."

SuzieQ started trailing me through the house as I grabbed extra clips for the Glock from a shelf in the hall closet and strapped my backup piece, a snub-nose Smith & Wesson .32 revolver, on the left side of my belt. "Sugar, you're not goin' there alone, are ya?" SuzieQ's flawless brow creased in anger. "And is it at this point that you give me some macho bullshit reason why you're doing this?"

"No," I said, heading out the door.

"Peter!" Something in SuzieQ's voice made me turn back. She was standing in the center of the room, eyes huge behind unshed tears, looking almost lost.

I turned back and hugged her quickly. "Let me tell you how I think this goes," I said, walking her toward the front door. "McKenzie knows I'm getting close, so she sets up this crude trap: lure me to Moore's house in Bel Air and then kill me in some outrageous fashion. But what she doesn't know is that I'm already on to her and I know it's a trap. She'll try and kill me, but I'll subdue her, maybe wound her. When we search her apartment, we'll discover why she killed the others. Maybe we'll discover she was working with or for

Moore. Doesn't really matter, though. I'll have solved the case; I'll be the hero of Hollywood, sign a book deal and a movie deal and be famous for more than fifteen minutes." I pulled open the hall door and walked toward the car.

"Let me tell you how I see it," SuzieQ said. "You turn up at Moore's place. McKenzie and her accomplices kill you and frame you for the murders of the others."

Actually that sounded like a far more plausible scenario. "Here's the deal: if I don't call you within the hour, phone the department, tell them where I am."

I climbed into the car and SuzieQ leaned in to kiss me quickly on the top of the head. "But don't worry, Peter, if McKenzie or Moore kills you, I'll have Joe McCarthy avenge you."

It was only as I was driving away that I realized that Joe McCarthy was her eleven-foot-long Australian taipan.

Stone Canyon Drive is a winding road climbing from UCLA past the Bel Air Hotel on up to the Stone Canyon Reservoir and then Mulholland Drive. I took it doing sixty all the way, barely missing a ponytailed dog walker with five breeds on five leashes who flipped me off with her free hand. The address Maral McKenzie had given me was three-quarters up the hill, but none of these mansions could be bothered with numbers on them. If she hadn't been waiting in the middle of the road, I would have gone right past it. She waved me toward an open iron gate that looked like the Moors had designed it in Spain a couple of centuries ago. I parked beyond it so the Jag couldn't be seen from the driveway. I could see McKenzie running at me in the rearview mirror and I unsnapped the restraining strap on the Glock, just in case SuzieQ was right. But as soon as I got out of the car, I knew she wasn't the threat. The woman was wild-eyed with terror. She could barely get her words out.

"She went into the house and she told me to call you if she didn't come out and that was nearly an hour ago now and—"

"Slow down, slow down." I put my hands on both her arms to help her get a grip. "How far up the drive is the house?"

"A quarter mile."

"Okay, keep your voice down and get me up there."

We started walking while she filled me in on what had happened. Which didn't sound like much: In a nutshell, a spooked Ovsanna Moore had gone into her home and not phoned her assistant for an hour. McKenzie hadn't heard anything unusual, hadn't seen anyone who didn't belong. She was just spooked because her boss had been spooked. Thank God I hadn't called for backup. Ripping off the doors of a Hollywood mansion to find the owner taking an afternoon nap was not a good career move. Which reminded me . . . as we walked up the drive, I called SuzieQ on the cell and let her know I was okay. The last thing I needed was *her* calling up the department.

It was indeed a quarter of a mile from the gate to the house, and the walk gave me time to appreciate the Spanish-style hacienda Ovsanna had hidden away behind a wall that was at least twice my height. A whole lot of money and good taste—and in this city the two didn't necessarily go hand in hand—had gone into the house, which looked about as original as they come. No nude statues or Manneken Pis water fountains.

But a lot of security. She had cameras and sensors all over the place. And geese. Lots of geese. I stopped looking around and started watching the ground. I only own one pair of good shoes and I was wearing them.

"Tell me exactly what happened," I asked McKenzie.

"We pulled in around the back of the house in front of the garages." She pointed and I followed the directions. "When Ovsanna got out of the car, she got a strong feeling that something was wrong."

I felt my heart sink. In my book, celebrities with intuitions belonged on late-night chat shows. "She made me check I had my pepper spray, and then she took out the gun she keeps hidden under the backseat of the car."

"What caliber?" I asked automatically, knowing it would be something impressive. "And does she know how to use it?"

".357 Magnum. She trains every time she starts a new movie. She's shot a lot of guns, believe me."

Yeah, but at a real-life target? "Then what happened?"

"She told me to leave. And that if she wasn't in touch in thirty minutes I was to get in touch with you. She told me that on no account was I to enter the house on my own."

"Why me? Why not call 911?" I thought I knew the answer but I wanted to hear it from the assistant's mouth.

"She's a celebrity, Detective. A call to 911 from Ovsanna Moore ends up on CNN twenty minutes later. No one wants that kind of visibility unless they've got a movie to promote. Besides, maybe you're the only cop she knows."

I doubted that. Every celeb likes to have a cop in their BlackBerry, either for help researching a part or fixing a DUI. Though I have to admit, when I ran Moore through the system earlier, she came up squeaky clean. Not even a parking violation.

We were twenty feet from the front door when Maral pulled something out of her purse and closed her palm around it. I unholstered my Glock and held it pointing down at a pile of goose shit. Boy, does that stuff stink. "What's in your hand?"

"Don't worry, it's small enough to be legal." She flashed me a black and blue cylinder and I recognized the label, Pepper Shot pepper spray, the half-ounce size.

"Put that back in your purse and stay here. If there is someone dangerous inside, and he gets past my gun, that little spritzer isn't going to do you any good."

"I'm not staying here on my own. Besides, if Ovsanna reset the alarm, you'll need me to get in. I know the code." She moved with me toward the front door.

"Besides you and Ms. Moore, who else knows the code?"

"No one," McKenzie said, surprising me.

"What about maids, gardeners, cooks, people like that?"

"The gardeners and the housekeeper know the code to the front gate. The housekeeper only comes twice a week unless Ovsanna is entertaining, and Ovsanna just leaves the back door unlocked for her on those days. She doesn't have a cook, and the gardeners don't have reason to come in the house."

"Was today the housekeeper's day to show up?"

"No, she was here yesterday and she'll come again on Friday. Ovsanna doesn't like a lot of people around."

Not my impression of most celebrities. Usually they're surrounded by a crowd—the agent, the manager, the PR guy, the trainer, nutritionist, masseuse, acupuncturist, stylist, hairdresser, makeup artist, and any family members they can justify keeping on the payroll. My opinion of Ovsanna Moore just went up a notch.

None of the front windows were broken, no signs of forced entry. The front door looked solid—although it appeared to be wood, I was guessing a steel core, dead bolts, the whole nine yards. The rainbow refraction of the windows signaled bulletproofing. Ms. Moore took her security very seriously indeed. "Did Ovsanna have any enemies?" I asked.

Maral McKenzie took a heartbeat too long to respond. "She's an internationally famous movie star who runs a movie studio."

"What does that mean?"

"Means there are always weirdo fans or upset producers, aggrieved writers—"

"So a lot of enemies, then?"

"No more than anyone else in her position."

"Anyone in particular?"

McKenzie turned her key in the bottom lock and hesitated. "Well, there's no love lost between her and her head of development, Thomas DeWitte. He hates her."

"Senior partner?" I wondered, tiny pieces beginning to click and fall into place.

"Junior," Maral said with a sneer. "Very junior."

A junior business partner. That meant money, and in Hollywood money meant power. A whole slew of possibilities suddenly opened up.

Maral turned the key in the top lock and I grabbed her hand.

"How far inside the house is the alarm pad?" I asked.

"It's just inside the door on the right-hand wall."

"If the alarm is on when you open the door, I want you to hit the code and step back outside. Do not—I repeat, do not—follow me into the house. When it's clear I'll call you. Is that understood?"

"Yes," she said quietly.

"Open it."

McKenzie pressed the thumb latch and the door clicked open. She looked toward the wall on the right, shook her head no to tell me the system wasn't armed, and stepped back behind me. I took a two-handed grip on the Glock and nudged the door farther open with my foot. It swung silently inward.

I took a tentative step into the hall . . . spotted a shape first, and an instant later, the silver glitter of a gun.

CHAPTER SEVENTEEN

I was still in the dining room when I heard the voices outside. Darting down the hall, I reached the door just as it was opening. I saw a gun and let nature take control: my sheaths retracted to expose my fangs; my shitty-looking nails lengthened, hooked into cat's claws, and slashed at the hand holding the gun. Whoever belonged to the hand let out a curse, and the weapon clattered to the tiles.

"Shit!"

"Ovsanna! It's me!"

I recognized the voices simultaneously: Peter King and Maral. It took all my power to retract my claws while the last of the polish flaked to the floor, but I had my hands in the air when King darted through the door, a small revolver clutched in his left hand. He was brave; I'll give him that. Or stupid.

I pulled my fangs back in and bit down on the sheaths to keep them closed. "I'm alone. I'm okay. There's no one here."

King's right hand was balled into a fist and I could smell the blood before it even started dripping. I must have hurt him, but his face was a mask and his eyes didn't give anything away, and in that instant I reevaluated him. Maral came through the door after him and threw herself into my arms . . . and at the same time pressed a flat metal star into my hand.

"What in God's name happened?" King demanded. "What did you cut me with?"

He kept his small pistol in his hand and trained in my general direction while he retrieved what I identified as a Glock—not the snub-nose police issue but one of the military-style models with a barrel that was at least six inches long. I'd used one like it in *Highway to Hell*. He picked it up off the floor, checked the clip, and popped the round from the chamber before he put the revolver away. I held up the eight-pointed metal star Maral had slipped me. "I used this. When I saw the gun coming in through the door, I'm afraid I just lashed out. I'm sorry I cut you."

"A shuriken!" King held up his right hand. Three deep slashes began at his wrist and ran to his knuckles. "You damn nearly cut my hand off."

"It was a reflex reaction. I'm terribly sorry. Thank God I didn't shoot you." I smiled my best apologetic smile, but it didn't seem to work. He was suspicious and very, very on edge.

"Where's your gun? When I came through the door, I saw a gun."

I held out the weapon, muzzle pointed to the ground, then opened the cylinder and turned it so he could see the five copper cartridges and the one empty chamber. "It hasn't been fired."

"And of course you have a permit."

"Of course." I closed the cylinder, gently squeezing it into place—you only flip them on camera—and placed it on the table behind me. "I think we should take a look at your hand. I've got a first-aid kit in the bathroom. Maral, would you make some coffee, please. And maybe Detective King should have some cognac."

Maral didn't move. "You said if you weren't out in thirty minutes,

I was to contact Detective King." The fear in her eyes was giving way to hurt.

"I know I did. And I'm sorry." In truth, I'd actually forgotten that I'd given her that instruction until she burst through the door after King. I'd been distracted. Having ten of the most powerful creatures in North America gathered in your dining room threatening you with death—a True Death—will do that to you. "Make us some coffee, dear," I said, softening my voice, "while I tend to the detective's wounds."

"It's not a wound," he began, and for the first time took a look at the long cuts dripping blood across the Spanish tile and changed his mind. "Actually, it *is* a wound."

"Let's get you fixed up." I turned my back on him. Smelling his blood was seductive enough; having to stare at it really riled me up. It was the human equivalent of sitting down to the 18-ounce filet mignon at Ruth's Chris Steak House. And Peter King's blood was flooded with adrenalin and endorphins. That's like passing the béarnaise sauce at the table. It took a tremendous effort of will to control myself. If I Changed, I would have to kill him, and that would be a shame.

I once watched Peter Lorre make a full transformation into his real self—fangs, claws, bloodred eyes, tailed spine—just because they guillotined Robespierre faceup and Peter had a spectator's seat. Fortunately, there was such hysteria in the crowd, no one else noticed. Took all my strength to keep him from grabbing Maxie's head and lapping up his blood right from his neck.

"Follow me, please," I said, and started toward the bathroom. I concentrated on the artwork at the end of the hall, damping down my senses as best I could.

"Do you always carry a shuriken with you?" he asked. "What do you need with a Japanese throwing star?"

I didn't turn around. "I'm impressed," I said. "I wouldn't expect a Beverly Hills police officer to know what a shuriken is."

"Hey, I go to the movies," King said. "And I've seen the real thing. My mother buys and sells movie memorabilia. She's got a set signed by Chuck Norris. I think they were used in a movie called *The Octagon*. She's even sold a few of your own pieces," he added. "Which reminds me: Little John sends his regards."

"Big boy? Tiny voice? Tattooed?"

"That's him. With a major crush on you, by the way."

"He's actually very sweet. And harmless." Detective King was full of surprises. But in that tiny snippet of information I recognized the real danger that those of my kind now face in this modern world. There have always been collectors, but only in the last fifty years have the ordinary, the mundane, the trivial, and the disposable become collectable. I am convinced that it is the collectors, the gatherers of ephemera, who will finally bring down the vampyres. Someone will stumble upon something—something trivial which should have been disposed of centuries ago—that will blow our whole world wide open. It also revealed that King had been doing some research on me and that his contacts were a little out of the ordinary.

I led King into the largest of the downstairs bathrooms—which incidentally was the farthest away from the dining room. I wasn't sure if any of the vampyre odors still lingered, but with King's senses still heightened by adrenaline, I didn't want to arouse his suspicions further.

"You didn't answer my question," he said, crossing to the room-length mirror to look at the three long slashes in his flesh. "Why are you carrying a shuriken?"

Desperately trying to ignore the blood pooling into the sink—bright and red and so incredibly appealing—I kept my eyes fixed on the first-aid box. "I'm a bit paranoid about dangerous fans; I've had a couple in the last few years. I travel a lot and I can't carry a knife on the plane anymore, but I can stick the shuriken in with my jewelry and it passes unnoticed. I usually keep it on an Aztec silver chain and it looks like a necklace. When I heard the door opening, I grabbed it out of my purse." Not a word of truth in that story except for my purse lying open on the hallway table. I don't need bladed weapons—my nails and teeth are more than sufficient. While Detective King was staring at the wound on his fist, Maral had snatched the shuriken from its display on the wall and slipped it into my hand. It was that type of quick thinking that made her invaluable to me.

"I just saw the gun coming in through the door and lashed out," I said, repeating what I'd said earlier. It was a trick I'd learned from that wonderful charlatan Anton Mesmer before he was forced to leave Vienna in disgrace: emphasize positive reinforcement. All I had to do was to keep reminding King that I'd cut him with the shuriken and not allow him to consider any other possibility. If Mesmer were alive today, he'd make a fortune selling self-help books. "Take off your jacket."

King shrugged out of an unstructured Armani jacket that had to be ten years old at least, taking care not to get any blood on the sleeve as he pulled his arm through. Under the jacket he was wearing a black ribbed T-shirt, maybe Calvin Klein. The black was on its way to an indeterminate gray but the cut was still great on him. I took a quick glance at his left hand—no ring, no pale band of flesh, either. He was carrying two guns—the expensive Glock on his right hip and the snub-nose silver revolver on his left. I thought it an odd mixture of the ultramodern and the traditional that again revealed a little of the man: not afraid to embrace the new but still happy to utilize the tried and true in an emergency.

"Does this qualify as assaulting an officer? Are you going to charge me?" I asked, taking his large hand in both of mine and holding it under the tap. The water diluted the blood, making it a little easier for me to calm down.

King's laugh was genuine. "No, I'm not going to charge you. Not only would I be laughed out of the station, but I'd never work in this town again. I may ask you for a bribe, though." His eyes were smiling, but I wasn't sure where he was going with the conversation. I was disappointed. I consider myself a good judge of character and I didn't think King was the type of cop who would ask for a bribe, but maybe this was another sign that I was slipping up in my old age.

"What can I do for you, Detective King?"

"Could you sign one of your photos for my mother? She'd be thrilled."

The request was so unexpected that I spilled slightly more iodine onto the wounds than I'd planned. He yelped.

"Oh, don't be such a baby!"

"What is that: acid? First you try and cut my hand off, then you try and burn it." He was smiling as he said it, to take the sting from the words.

"You can take your pick from my photos. Is your mother a horror fan?"

"She's just a fan of the movies in general and of you in particular. Not the dangerous type of fan, though. No need for shuriken*s*." Now the smile had reached his eyes.

I rinsed the cuts clean and applied Neosporin as gently as I could—God knows what I'd had on my fingernails before I slashed him. The slashes were too long for simple Band-Aids, so I covered them with a gauze pad and secured it with surgical tape. It wasn't going to make drawing his gun any easier. He had good hands, with strong, long fingers, but his flesh was surprisingly soft, uncalloused, not at all what I expected. As I wrapped the tape, I caught a glimpse of him looking at me in the mirror. After nearly five hundred years on this earth, I know when I'm being checked out.

"I truly am sorry," I said, snapping him out of his reverie. He caught my eyes in the glass and knew he'd been caught.

"For what?"

"For nearly slicing your hand off."

He flexed his fingers. "I'll live. I'm just relieved I found *you* on the other side of the door and not the Cinema Slayer."

"Is that who you thought?"

"It seemed like a possibility. Given what happened today at the studio." He shook his head in exasperation. "What spooked you? Ms. McKenzie said something frightened you."

"When we pulled up earlier, I thought I saw movement inside the house," I lied. I helped King back into his coat.

His face tightened in exasperation. "So you took a gun and went inside to check it out. Hardly the smartest move. And why did you have your assistant call *me* anyway?"

"I didn't want the entire police force descending on my home and I certainly didn't want a 911 call recorded for any persistent reporter to get hold of—especially if I was overreacting. It doesn't look good in print, having the Scream Queen screaming in real life. Besides, we'd just met, you and I, and I had your business card in my pocket. At least you weren't a complete stranger." I walked out of the bathroom, forcing him to follow me, and down to the library in the east wing of the house. I wanted him away from the music room and I also wanted him to exit by the back door. If he ended up in the front hall, he'd be staring at the starburst display of shuriken hanging on the wall . . . minus one piece. "We'll have coffee in the library."

Beverly Hills real estate agents love announcing the home they're showing has a library. Of course it does—they make sure they stock the one room in the house that has built-in shelves with gilt-labeled, aged leather-bound sets of Shakespeare and Dickens and as soon as the house is sold move those crumbling masterpieces into storage to wait for the next listing that needs an impressive display. I've known decorators who buy classics by the carton or the length; in the antique book trade they are known as furniture. Every producer in this town has a library, and in my experience the more successful the producer, the less likely it is those books have been read. Movie people don't have time for the printed word in novel form. Or non-fiction, either, for that matter, unless it's the latest political exposé that might do box office like *All the President's Men* did in the seventies. Movie people read scripts. They read coverage of scripts. They read treatments. They do not read classics.

I, on the other hand, do. Or did. I've had a lot more time in my life than Jerry Bruckheimer or Joel Silver, and most of it hasn't been spent in Hollywood. So in my case, I can honestly call the room we entered a library: close to two thousand volumes surrounding us in floor-to-ceiling shelves. I only ever bought books that interested me, so it's an eclectic mix, history and geography, poetry and plays, and fiction: lots and lots of fiction. Everything from vellum-bound copies of Galileo's *Sidereus Nuncius* to Machiavelli's *Florentine Histories,* most of them dated and signed. My prize is a 1897 edition of *Dracula,* inscribed by Bram, "To Ovsanna . . . my Lucy."

Maral had already set out the coffee service and three snifters with a bottle of L'Esprit de Courvoisier. I was expecting Detective King to decline the cognac while on duty, but he didn't give me any indication one way or another, just started walking the room, head tilted slightly to read the titles.

I settled on the couch I'd stolen from Finca Vigia, Hemingway's farm outside Havana.

"I'm impressed," King said. "These don't look like they're for show. I like a lot of these myself." He was at the crime section. "I'm a big Connolly fan. And Crais and Sandford and Thomas Perry. You've even got Henning Mankel." He moved on down the wall. "Ah, Ed McBain. I read all the 87th Precinct."

I heard the doorbell ring in the distance and frowned, wondering who would arrive without calling first. Maral would get it.

"Are these all vampyre novels? There must be a hundred books in this section alone. These are guys I've never heard of."

"I use them for research. I'm not above purloining an idea now and then."

King smiled and stepped away from the shelves and sat down facing me. I was just opening the cognac when Maral stumbled through the door, spilling coffee from the sterling espresso pot she was carrying on a salver. Thomas DeWitte was right behind her, pushing her forward. I was on my feet instantly as Neville Travis and the bodyguard, Anthony, piled in behind him.

"I'm sorry, Ovsanna," Maral began. "We never closed the gate and they just barged in. I told them you were busy."

"I don't care how busy you are, you royal bitch, I've had it with you!" Thomas's face was livid. "Who the fuck do you think you are?"

Detective King stepped out from the coffee table and stood next to me. "Aren't you going to introduce me, Ovsanna?"

Whatever was surging through DeWitte's veins obviously gave him some misplaced bravado, or maybe it was just his usual arrogance. He got right into King's face and then poked him in the chest with a stubby forefinger. "I don't know who the fuck you are, which means you're nobody. So get the fuck out of my sight. I've got some business with the lady."

CHAPTER EIGHTEEN

BEL AIR
7:35 P.M.

I could have identified myself, flashed the badge and all, but my hand was throbbing and I didn't have the patience to deal with some coked-up queen, even one with good fashion sense. When he jabbed his fat finger into my chest and tried to push me out of the way, I grabbed his arm, spun him, and locked it behind his back, bringing him right up onto the balls of his feet.

"Manners, buddy. Where're your manners?" Keeping a grip on him wasn't helping the pain in my hand any but made me feel good nonetheless.

"What the fuck—"

The big bald guy in black fatigues, who was straight from central casting, reached behind him to the small of his back.

And stopped.

Facing a Glock 17L stops most people. There are some cute guns on the market, some that look like fashion accessories, nickel plated, ivory handled, all smooth and rounded. And then there's the Glock. It's big, black, and chunky and it holds seventeen rounds of 9mm.

"I'm Detective Peter King, BHPD. Let me see your hands." He raised his hands very slowly. "Good boy. Now, wanna tell me who you are?"

That stopped Baldy in his tracks. The one I was handling stopped struggling but kept shouting. "I'm Thomas DeWitte of Anticipation Studios and this is none of your goddamn business. Let go of me! You can't do this to me. I'll have your badge. I'll sue the department from here to kingdom come!"

"Are you threatening an officer of the law, Mr. DeWitte? Sounds like bad business practice to me." I twisted his arm a little higher. He was practically standing on his toes.

Ovsanna moved away from me to face DeWitte. She had a smile on her face. "You'd better calm down, Thomas. I don't think Detective King is someone to fuck with."

I had to hand it to her, she was one cool number. "You know these guys, I take it," I said.

She crossed over to her assistant, who was still holding the tray in her shaking hands, and took it from her. "Sit down, Maral," she said, "and pour yourself a glass of cognac. Everything's under control." Then she turned back to me and the jerk I still had a grip on. "Thomas is my business partner, the head of development at Anticipation. That's Neville Travis." She motioned to the skinny guy with an addict's sniff, standing just inside the doorway. "DeWitte's boyfriend and the *former* director of *Hallowed Night*. And the one with the arms and facial hair is what passes for Thomas's security. Anthony, right?"

Mr. Beefcake gave a short nod up and down.

"Okay, here's how we're going to do this," I said. "I'm going to let go of your arm, Mr. DeWitte, and you're going to keep your mouth shut until I check Anthony for weapons. If you say anything, if you move, I'll cuff you." I let him back down to the ground. "Good. Not a sound. Now you can have a seat if you want."

He kept quiet but stayed standing. I patted the bodyguard down and plucked a Skorpion vz.61 submachine pistol from his belt—a ten-round fully loaded Skorpion. He was also carrying a Taser, a NATO military switchblade, two extra ten-round clips for the Czech gun, a flat boot knife strapped to his right calf, and a brass knuckle-duster. No wonder he was wearing combat pants. He could have used a suitcase. I dropped them all on the couch beside me and slipped the knuckle-duster onto my left hand. It fit like a glove. "You looking to do a lot of jail time, Anthony?"

"Naw, man, that's a belt buckle. Look, it's got a screw and everything."

"Well, that's creative. I thought you were going to tell me it's a paperweight, like all the other muscles who shop the Web." I pocketed the knuckles and examined the Skorpion. It had been converted to full automatic—850 rounds per minute. Very illegal. "You got a license for the gun?"

DeWitte answered me. "It's *my* gun. I have the license in the car. Anthony just carries it for me for protection."

"Well, that's an interesting arrangement. Not sure how legal it is. What else do you carry to protect your boss, Anthony? Got a pocketful of Trojans?"

Ovsanna burst out laughing.

I put the gun on the desk behind me and turned back to DeWitte. I was on shaky legal ground, but DeWitte didn't seem to know it. The weapons cache and the illegal submachine gun gave me a little playing room.

"All right, Mr. DeWitte, you seem to be the one with the agenda. Seems to me, you and your friends are trespassing, maybe with intent to do harm. I'll give you a chance to correct that impression. Why are you here and what's going on?"

"I came to talk to Ovsanna."

"With your boyfriend and bodyguard. And an arsenal? Wasn't going to be a friendly chat, was it?"

"None of your damn business," he snapped.

"It is actually," I said mildly. "I'm investigating a murder at Anticipation Studios and here you are threatening Ovsanna Moore, who just happens to be the head of Anticipation Studios. Your boss. So tell me, where were you this morning between eleven o'clock and one?"

The question caught him completely off guard, and even through the coke—or maybe amphetamine—haze, I watched as the seriousness of the situation began to sink in. "I was in my office," he said eventually.

"No, you weren't," Maral said immediately. "I called your secretary before noon and she said you were having breakfast at the Abbey and then scouting locations in Boys Town. We got to the office at one thirty and Jesus hadn't even parked your car yet. You had to have just driven in."

Real old-fashioned hate blossomed in DeWitte's eyes. "I was out all morning on business."

"What sort of business?" I pulled out my notebook. "I'm going to need names and addresses."

"You cannot seriously think I had anything to do with—"

"You are the head of development in a studio that had connections with the three dead stars, then one of your own FX staff turns up dead, and a few hours later I find you threatening the head of the studio. With hired help carrying concealed weapons," I added. "I can think a lot of things."

"I didn't know he had those knuckles."

"Let's start with where you were this morning, and then we'll move on to why you're here."

He glanced quickly at Neville Travis and then away. "I was doing research for an upcoming movie," he said.

"Where?"

"In Hollywood."

"Where in Hollywood, Mr. DeWitte? Let's be a little more specific."

"A club on Santa Monica Boulevard."

"In the middle of the day? What kind of club? What's the name?" Another glance at Travis. "It's called Rough Trade."

"Tommy!" The cokehead Ovsanna had called Neville Travis spoke for the first time and stepped farther into the room. "You promised you wouldn't go there anymore!"

"Oh, grow up, Neville. And shut your mouth," DeWitte shot back.

Rough Trade. I turned to Ovsanna with an inquiring look.

"It's a private S&M club between La Jolla and Sweetzer. Hidden entrance, you wouldn't find it if you didn't know where to look. And no, there's nothing we're filming that needs that kind of location."

I turned back to DeWitte. "What time were you there?"

"I got there around ten A.M. and left about one."

Jesus. Almost three hours of sexual sado-masochism. I wondered if he was giving or receiving.

"So I'm assuming you weren't alone. Anybody there who can verify this?"

Neville looked like he was going to burst into tears. "Not Jeanne Paul, Thomas. Just say it wasn't Jeanne Paul!"

"You were at work, you silly little twat. What was I supposed to do? Nobody works me over like Ms. Marat. You should take some lessons from him."

"So you were with this what . . . guy? Girl? This Ms. Jeanne Paul Marat? Will he—she—remember you?" I was getting irritated.

"Of course he'll remember me. I am not unremarkable. And he'll certainly remember the three-hundred-dollar tip I gave him."

"You bitch!" Neville hissed.

"Besides, there were other people there and Anthony was waiting at the bar."

I turned to Anthony, who nodded. He was blushing. "People

asked me to beat them," he mumbled, sounding genuinely embarrassed. "Offered me money, too."

"Should have taken it. It's a better gig than the one you have
here," Ovsanna said quickly.

"Okay, well, all that will be easy to check. What are you doing
here now, Mr. DeWitte?"

Color touched his cheeks and flowed along his neck. This guy
had a temper problem, what Sheila Stein calls *control issues*. "Ovsanna
fired Neville off the set of *Hallowed Night* this morning!" He made
the announcement in that breathless voice newscasters reserve for
presidential resignations.

"Yeah?" I glanced at Ovsanna. "I presume that Ms. Moore, as
head of the studio, can do that?"

"She can't—," DeWitte began.

"She can," Ovsanna said. "I've got a health and safety issue with
directors doing coke on set. My health and safety." She frowned.
"But I told you this morning that Travis had been fired. Why are you
here now?"

"Neville went back to the set to pick up the rest of his things
and that geriatric guard wouldn't even let him on the lot. Said he
needed a drive-on from production. When he tried to get through
the gate, Gant pulled a gun on him, for Christ's sake! Told him he'd
shoot him for trespassing."

Good for Gant, I thought.

"Neville called me and I had to drive all the way out there to fire
him. A huge waste of my time."

"You fired Officer Gant!" Ovsanna snarled. The angles and
planes of her face subtly altered as the pleasant, innocuous mask fell
away. I suddenly realized how she had survived so long in Hollywood. This girl was a fighter. She looked over at Maral. "Sort it out.
Now." She looked back at DeWitte and I swear the whites of her
eyes turned red for a moment. "You work for me, Thomas. You do
not give orders and you do not fire my employees. How dare you!"

"God damn you, Ovsanna, you don't have the—"

I tried to regain some control of the situation. "Answer my question, Mr. DeWitte. You came here to . . . ?"

"To talk some sense into Ovsanna."

"Threaten her, you mean." I turned to Ovsanna and nodded toward the center courtyard. "You three—don't move. I don't want to have to pull my gun." I walked through the French doors and out into the cool night. Ovsanna followed me. She was smiling.

"I have to apologize, Detective Ki—may I call you Peter?"

That took me by surprise. I nodded.

"Peter. Thomas can be excitable. He reacts rather than thinks. But I don't think he's a killer."

"I agree. And I assume his alibi will check out. That's not one he's likely to be making up. And it's certainly one of the more interesting alibis I've gotten in my time." I glanced back inside. Travis and DeWitte were having a lovers' spat and it looked like Travis was winning. DeWitte must definitely be on the M side of his S and M proclivities. "What do you want to do?" I asked. "Press charges for trespass, unlawful entry, threatening behavior? Nothing's going to stick, but it will interrupt their plans for the evening."

"No. I've got to work with Thomas. In spite of his personality, he's good at what he does and I need him for the studio. I've got Japanese investors coming in three days' time. They're looking to put millions into Anticipation; I need the studio running smoothly. It's bad enough I had to fire my director in the middle of the shoot. I can't afford any more upsets and I can't afford any bad press. I'd prefer to keep this evening quiet." She turned to look at me, eyes huge and dark in her face. "Can you do that for me?"

I nodded. "I can do that."

"Thank you, Det—Peter."

"Okay then, I'll confiscate the weapons and let them go. And I'll check out DeWitte's alibi in the morning—just in case."

Ovsanna's smile was startling. She tipped her chin at DeWitte.

"Look at him; he's been standing since he walked in. His butt is probably raw from whipping. I'll bet it's too painful to sit. I think his alibi will hold, believe me."

"I'll get rid of them, and then I'll get out of your hair."

"You haven't had your coffee yet. Or your cognac. Would you mind staying a little longer? I'm sure Maral would appreciate the sense of security your presence offers."

She's a damn good actress. I couldn't tell if the invitation was a genuine plea for protection for her assistant or something a bit more personal for her. It was already nearly eight o'clock and there wasn't anything else I could do on the Cinema Slayer that night. Ovsanna reached out and touched the back of my hand. Something like static must have crackled between us because, for a moment, I thought she'd cut me again. "Are you in a rush?" she asked.

"No . . . no, not really."

"A girlfriend to go back to? Or a wife you're rushing home to?"

"No. Not anymore."

"Boyfriend?" she asked, but in a voice that suggested she didn't really mean it.

"No boyfriend." I laughed.

"Then stay for a while. We'd both feel more comfortable if you did."

Both of them? Was she coming on to me or was she telling me they were a couple? Or was she just asking me to stay a little longer? A real detective would know. Maybe if I stuck around, I could do some more detecting and figure it out.

"All right, I'll escort the boys off the premises and stay awhile. Put Ms. McKenzie's mind at rest."

"Good. We'll have coffee and cognac in the library."

Cognac with Ovsanna Moore in her library. Wait till my mother hears this.

CHAPTER NINETEEN

I liked him. He was smart and capable and not hard to look at.

I spend all my days in an industry populated by people who occasionally approach the complexity of two dimensions. I was beginning to discover that Detective Peter King was a fully rounded personality, and in truth, I've always been a collector of people.

And he was funny. That's always been the clincher for me.

As a rule, vampyres don't have a lot of humor in their lives. Hundreds of years of watching humanity suffer at its own hands tends to diminish one's capacity for fun. It's hard to stay in the moment when you've got an overview of nearly five hundred years of religious crusades, racial genocide, and garden-variety annihilation in your immediate memory—even when it's not your genus that's been suffering.

I've seen the research—usually in glossy magazines with single-word titles—that suggests women go for men who are physically attractive or ruggedly handsome, though in truth I've always been wary of a man who looks prettier than I do. There are certainly women who are attracted to the size of a man's assets—either physical or metaphorical. But if there is one defining factor that most women agree on, it is that they are attracted to men who make them laugh.

I have always loved laughter. And if I look back over my lovers through the centuries, they shared one thing in common: they managed to make me laugh, Daumier and Molière, Goldsmith and Sheridan, and even Melba. I've never been attracted to the stage comic or the movie comedy actor: they tend to be morose characters.

So I love to laugh. It takes me out of myself for brief flashes of time. That's why I stayed with Voltaire as long as I did. His lovemaking wasn't very satisfying—thin blood—but his wit was.

This life—this vampyre existence—is not a life that encourages relationships. As a rule, vampyres don't have a lot of romance in their lives, either. Desire, yes, passion and lust certainly, but not romance. Once I get aroused and the Change takes over, I could care less about candles and flowers. Or having a "relationship." It's all much baser than that, and that's fine with me.

Relationships are difficult for my kind. Vampyre couples do exist—look at Theda and Charles—but they are rare indeed. In the main we are solitary creatures. We take lovers from the human world, but these tend to be brief affairs, lacking in emotional attachment. They have to be. We're faced with two choices when it comes to humans: avoid relationships or Turn the ones we love.

I once thought it was easier to create another vampyre than it was to watch a human age and die. But the very act of creation often changes the nature of the person, and far too often the human I fell in love with was not the vampyre I created. Watching a loved one grow old is never easy; waiting while faculties fail and limbs weaken is extraordinarily difficult—especially when the passing decades have no effect on yourself. Ultimately, I have always told my human partners about my true nature and given them the choice. Surprisingly, many of them chose not to Turn. I've often wondered if they felt resentful as they aged and I remained untouched by time. Circumstances have often forced me to leave my human lovers as they aged, but I have always—with only one tragic exception—managed to return to be with them at the end.

There is a mythology that those of my race are without pity. It is not entirely untrue; there are many amongst the vampyre who believe that humankind are little better than slaves or food—or both. And it is also true that long life tends to give one a different perspective, a detachment that might be easily mistaken for indifference. Some of the world's greatest scientists, thinkers, and industrialists have been vampyre. They have used their extra-long lives to stunning effect, to change and better man's lot.

Loneliness is the curse of the vampyre.

I have heard stories of the incredibly old—those whose lives extend into millennia—who have simply chosen to end their lives. As vampyres age, they change, their physical bodies alter, skin hardens, spines extend into tails, nails harden into claws, teeth lock into position and do not retract. They become demonlike and gargoyle in appearance, and they are, I am convinced, the source of the demon legends. But this appearance guarantees a reclusive existence, and eventually these aged vampyres—the Ancients—grow lonely. Most simply stop feeding and starve to death, and drowning is not uncommon. In my lifetime, I've met three Ancients, each one two millennia old, and none were even vaguely human. But I've not encountered one in a long time. Solgar is now the oldest vampyre I know in America, and from conversations we've had I estimate him to be around one thousand years old. He claims to have ridden with Geoffrey Martel, who later became Geoffrey II, and I've no reason to doubt him. In all the years I've known him, first in Vienna, then Paris, London, Chicago, and now L.A., I've never known him to have a companion, a lover, catamite, or even close friend. And I've known him for nearly two hundred years.

I could not live like that.

Above all, I needed companionship . . . and laughter.

And Peter King made me laugh and that was intriguing. Somewhere at the back of my mind a tiny warning bell went off. I would have to be careful with this one.

"Detective King will be staying for coffee, Maral," I said as King escorted DeWitte, Travis, and Anthony out the back door. He handed each one of them a business card and then waited while they climbed into DeWitte's Rolls and watched them drive away. "Would you make a fresh pot, please?"

She bent over the table to pick up the coffeepot, her mouth pursed in anger. Maral doesn't like it when I make new friends.

I came and stood behind her, resting the palm of my hand on the back of her neck and allowing a little of my heat to flow through my flesh. I could feel a shudder run down her body. Bringing my mouth close to her ear, I whispered, "We need him. We can use him. We need to get to this killer before he strikes again." I brushed strands of blond hair off her forehead and turned to see Peter King standing in the open doorway. I knew what it looked like—he'd seen me caressing Maral, my lips against her face. No doubt he'd already heard the stories about the Scream Queen and her assistant and their quirky relationship. This would just add to the confusion.

It didn't help that Maral smirked at him as she waltzed away.

"Would you like me to check upstairs?" he asked.

"Please, sit. The alarm system will ping if anyone goes in or out up there." I resumed the position I'd been sitting in earlier, forcing him to sit down opposite me. "I want to thank you for the way you dealt with Thomas and Travis and the bodyguard. That could have gotten very messy."

"That's some business partner you've got there—"

"Junior partner. A position Thomas has trouble dealing with. But believe me, Detective, he's a pussycat compared to some of the bastards I work with in my business." I handed him the Courvoisier. "Will you do the honors?"

L'Esprit de Courvoisier is bottled in individually numbered, hand-cut Lalique crystal decanters. He handed it right back to me, clutching the base in both hands. "I'd rather handle a loaded gun with the safety off than run the risk of dropping that, ma'am. I'll stick with coffee."

Once again, I burst out laughing. I was still laughing when Maral walked in with the fresh pot and a pissed-off look that said I'd better make do with coffee because she wasn't going to be offering her wrist any time soon. I'd calm her down once we were alone.

She'd removed her suit jacket and her breasts were revealed in the black silk camisole she wore underneath. Bending over to pour the coffee brought them right down to Detective King's eye level. Ah, the jealousy of a twenty-eight-year-old. Whatever she was attempting didn't work, however; he glanced at them frankly—more of a courtesy really—and then turned his eyes back to me. That's when she splashed coffee on his bandaged hand. He hissed with pain.

"Maral—," I started.

"You ladies have it out for my right hand, I think," Peter said, dabbing at the coffee-stained bandage with a napkin.

"I'm sorry, Detective King," Maral said, without a trace of regret in her voice. "I'm still a little jumpy from the afternoon, I guess. I hope I didn't burn you."

I could tell she didn't hope anything of the sort and I suspect Peter could, too. Whatever companionable mood that had been growing between us disappeared. He checked his watch and I saw the tiniest ridges appear at the corners of his eyes. "I'm fine, Ms. McKenzie. Already bandaged, in fact. But while I'm here, I'd like to ask you some questions as well. Save us having to go to the station and make it official." He was smiling, but the threat was there.

Maral put the coffeepot down and poured herself a cognac. Then she moved beside me on the couch, her body rigid and close enough for me to feel her thigh against mine. Holding the snifter in both hands, she glared at King over the rim.

"What questions?" Maral asked, voice barely above a tight whisper, already guessing the type of questions King would be putting to her.

"I've seen your file, Ms. McKenzie. I'm sure it's hard for you to talk about, but sooner or later someone is going to make the same connection I did: Ovsanna Moore's personal assistant was responsible for killing a man, eviscerating him with a knife—not unlike one of the Cinema Slayer victims. I'm surprised Smoking Gun hasn't run that piece already. Especially given that you knew all four victims. Do you have an alibi for the nights of the murders?"

"You think I did it!" Maral began, her accent beginning to thicken. I saw the glass tremble in her hand and reached over to take it from her before she dropped it. I didn't need any more spilled blood from cut fingers to rile me up again. Replacing the antique Waterford crystal would be a bitch.

"That's not what I said. I just asked you a question," King said softly. "And I'm looking for something cast-iron and checkable."

"Maral was seated with me at the Oscars on the night Jason was murdered," I said. "There will be tape. *E! News* did a special on the clothes, and both Maral and I were interviewed on the red carpet. All of the news stations carried clips from the show and from the parties afterwards. We appear in a couple of them. You can't get more cast-iron than that. We were in Agoura when Mai was killed, shooting exteriors for the new movie. Maral was on the set from seven A.M. until we wrapped at nine that night. I know because we heard the news of her death on the drive home."

"And Tommy Gordon?" King asked, directing the question back to Maral.

She had herself back under control now. "I don't know, Officer," she said icily. "I don't know exactly when he was killed. But I've got a PDA that'll tell you everywhere I've been every day for the past five years. Today, while poor Eva was being butchered, I was with Ovsanna and Neville Travis in her trailer and then Ovsanna and I drove to see Thomas DeWitte at the office. I'm sure they'll all confirm that."

Although King made no move to write down the information we'd just given him, I had no doubts he'd check it out thoroughly. He reminded me of Dashiell Hammett, with that intense stare.

"I have to ask," the detective said, and I acknowledged that with a nod.

"Maral didn't kill anyone, Peter. Nor did I, in case that was your next thought," I said earnestly.

"I'm beginning to believe that," he said, surprising me. "Though I've a feeling that you may be next in line. All the dead are linked to Anticipation Studios. And you are Anticipation. The killings are coming closer to you." He frowned, head tilting to one side. "You knew this?"

"Suspected."

"And this doesn't frighten you?"

"I don't frighten easily, Detective."

"Maybe you should. You could be next."

"That sounds like a line from one of my movies. I appreciate your concern, but I don't share it. Besides, I've got guards at the studio and a state-of-the-art security system here in the house—"

"The guards didn't do Eva Casale any good and your security system didn't stop Thomas DeWitte and his friends from getting in, either."

"That was my fault," McKenzie said. "I left the gate open when I let you in. I never do that. I was just so rattled."

"Well, keep it closed from now on," King said. "And change all your access codes, too. Alter your patterns. If you have meetings planned for the next few days, reschedule them at the last minute. Talk to your publicity people and make sure no one releases anything about where you're supposed to be or when. I'd also think about some additional security, maybe someone a little higher caliber than Anthony." He stood up to leave. "Thanks for the coffee," he added without a trace of irony.

"I'll walk you out," I said, indicating the open door that led out into the garden.

The night was cold and I watched Peter King tighten up against it. I couldn't feel it—vampyres never do—but for the sake of verisimilitude I wrapped my arms around my body. Ever the actress.

"You'll catch your death," King said, which brought a slight smile to my face. "Go back inside. I can find my own way out."

"Good night, Peter. I'm sorry about your hand." I leaned up and brushed my lips across his cheek, tasting salt and sweat and a hint of my French roast coffee. "Oh, and I never gave you that signed photo for your mother."

"Save it for next time. Good night, Ms. Moore." He turned and walked down the driveway toward the street.

So . . . Peter King was planning on a "next time." Good. Maybe then I could get him to call me Ovsanna.

CHAPTER TWENTY

WEST HOLLYWOOD
5:30 A.M.

Ovsanna Moore was brushing my face with her lips. I turned my head to kiss her but she wouldn't stay still, so I reached out to take her chin in my hand . . .

And grabbed onto something long, thick, and muscular.

I opened my eyes . . . and found a handful of snake clutched in my fist. Black, beady eyes stared into mine and a tongue the color of old meat shot out to brush my lips.

I came out of bed as if someone had stuck a cattle prod in my butt. "Jesus Christ, it's a goddamned snake!" I heaved it across the room with enough force to kill it, but it went slithering into my open closet and disappeared. I grabbed my pants from the back of the chair and, with my eyes on the floor, I jumped on the chair to try to get them on.

The kitchen door banged. I had one pant leg up and was scrambling for my gun on the nightstand when SuzieQ walked in and turned on a light. She didn't even blink at the sight of me standing on a chair, hopping into my pants. "You're up early."

The sky had barely begun to lighten outside.

"I'm not up out of choice," I snarled. "I woke up with a snake in my bed. I was holding a goddam snake." I pulled the other leg of my pants up. "And what are you doing here?" I demanded, glancing at the clock radio. "It's five thirty in the morning." My alarm hadn't even gone off yet. "A goddamn monster snake." The phone started ringing. "Mean, ugly-looking fucker. It could have bit me. Or strangled me. Or whatever the hell those things do!"

"There's been another murder. I heard it on my police scanner on the way home from work."

"A murder . . . ?" That stopped me cold.

"Oh, I'll bet that's Dick Nixon." SuzieQ was more concerned about her snake. "He wouldn't strangle you, honey; he's just a Texas indigo. He was probably cold. He likes to climb up in bed and cuddle when he's cold. Where'd you put him?"

"He's in the goddamn closet!" I yelled as I picked up the phone.

Captain Barton's clipped, precise, slightly nasal tone whined down the phone. Five thirty in the morning and I just knew he was already wearing a tie. "You making homosexual jokes, King? I hope not. You know departmental policy," he said.

SuzieQ came out of the closet with the snake curled around her arm. "He's upset, Peter," she whispered. "What did you do to him?" She was flicking her tongue at the friggin' thing and it was flicking right back. Man, those things give me the creeps. This one was a blue-black color, about five feet long. A Texas indigo, Suzie called it. She'd never said if it was poisonous or not and I'd no inclination to find out. I just wanted to wash my hands and face, rinse out my mouth, and maybe get a rabies shot.

"What's in the closet? Who's in the closet?" Barton demanded.

"You wouldn't believe me if I told you," I muttered. "Nothing, Captain. It's nothing. What's going on?"

"We got a multiple homicide in a private club in West Hollywood. I want you there now."

"West Hollywood?" West Hollywood is not part of the BHPD beat, so there could only be one reason . . .

"Is this a Cinema—"

"Don't use that term. You know I don't approve of the tags the press use to glorify these monsters. All we know right now is that we have a multiple homicide . . . and that two of the vics had your cards on them. You've been busy," he added sarcastically.

"*Two* of the vics? How many were there?"

"I don't know. Ten or eleven maybe. They haven't finished putting all the pieces back together."

"I'm on my way."

I got the address from the Captain and hung up the phone. I threw on the rest of my clothes, and from my bathroom window as I brushed my teeth and gargled with mouthwash I watched SuzieQ walk back to her place with that damn snake wrapped around her neck. She was cooing at it, talking baby talk. Maybe it would strangle her and I could find a new tenant with goldfish instead. *Tiny goldfish who don't like to cuddle.*

At that hour of the morning it only took me twelve minutes to get to West Hollywood. I took Sunset to Doheny and as I turned left onto Santa Monica I fell in behind two CSI vans and a news truck from KCBS, all of us headed in the same direction.

It wasn't hard to find the crime scene. Eight police cruisers, a SWAT van, and nine more news trucks were parked in front of a building on the south side of Santa Monica, between La Jolla and Sweetzer. A private club, the Captain had said, between La Jolla and Sweetzer . . . and suddenly I knew where I was. I heard Ovsanna Moore's voice in my head: *A private S&M club between La Jolla and Sweetzer. Hidden entrance, you wouldn't find it if you didn't know where to look.*

Rough Trade.

She was right. I wouldn't have found it if I hadn't been looking, even with the LAPD chopper in the air above, fighting for space with two A STARS and a Jet Ranger from the local stations, lighting up the street with their high beams.

It was an anonymous brick rectangle with an unmarked metal door, lurking between a neon-lit condom store called All Things Rubber and a trendy sushi bar catering to upscale GLTB couples. No address, but a little metal plate above a keypad and speaker grille had the initials "RT" deeply etched into them.

I'd called the Captain back on the drive over and he'd given me more details. The club had only been open for a month and had a reputation as the pre-eminent S&M club in the city. I wasn't entirely sure what that meant and I didn't really care to find out. It had a mixed clientele, straights and gays. Entrée was by invitation only; there was a hefty fee to join and a monthly fee to let you keep coming back for more. More whips, more spankings, more bondage, whatever your pleasure.

I did wonder how the Captain knew so much about the club, but it didn't seem wise to ask. I hoped he was reading from a report and not reporting from experience.

I parked in front of the sign next door announcing "Custom-fit condoms in 70 sizes and colors" and climbed out of the car. Too bad I didn't have time to window-shop.

The cops on scene had set up a barrier at both ends of the block, but I was sure that wasn't keeping telephoto lenses at bay. There's nothing like knowing you're appearing on live TV all across the States to make you stand up a little straighter and suck in your gut.

Reporters were screaming at me from across the street. That's one of the few disadvantages to driving the Jag: I'm never anonymous. Seeing me, the media immediately made the connection to the Cinema Slayer case. And that, even without any more information, made it headline news. They started screaming like a pack of howler monkeys.

"King, King, is this a Cinema Slayer thing—?"

"Who's inside, Detective, another dead celebrity?"

"Come on, King, give us some facts . . . we have a right to know."

"Is SWAT going in?"

"How come BHPD is here?"

"It's gotta be the Cinema Slayer, right?"

"Has the Slayer struck again?"

I locked the car and approached Chris Miller, who was standing outside the door with a clipboard in his hand. Chris is a twenty-year veteran of the L.A. County Sheriff's Department; they handle police protection for West Hollywood. He was signing officers in as they entered the crime scene. His coffee-colored skin looked gray.

"Bad?" I asked, holding up my badge for Chris to copy the numbers.

"Real bad," he said, eyes meeting mine for a moment. "One of the worst I've seen." And that told me all I needed to know.

Before I even stepped inside the first door, I stopped to pull on my gloves and cover my shoes. The floor was flooded with blood. It looked like it had been hosed down by an open artery. I was standing in a long, narrow hallway leading to a second door that should have been on a submarine: three-inch-thick metal, studded with round-headed bolts, with a small circular porthole window at head height. Normally this door would have been the second line of defense against uninvited visitors, but now it hung off one hinge with a large indentation dimpling it just above the handle.

I studied the indentation for thirty seconds before I recognized the shape of what might have made it. Not a sledgehammer, not a battering ram. I closed my hand into a fist and shoved it into the hole. Without the bandage across my knuckles, it would have been a perfect fit.

The smell hit me before I even walked through the second door:

the unmistakable odor of blood, guts, vomit, urine, and feces. Not something I ever get used to. I snagged a face mask from a surprisingly verbose CSI tech who advised me that so far they thought they recognized a judge, a pro basketball player, two rappers, a TV weather girl, a fire-and-brimstone pastor . . . and a movie producer That's when they decided to call me in. I pulled on the face mask, grateful for its clean antiseptic odor. There were six other techs in the room and I recognized two other cops from the West Hollywood detail. No one was talking. You keep your mouth shut when there's that kind of foulness in the air. A taste of that filth stays with you for days.

Just like the hallway, there was blood on the floor. Only this floor was carpeted and the blood formed dozens of bubbles that popped with every step I took. It was harder to see the spatter patterns on the walls in this room because the walls had originally been black. Now they were red with tissue and gore.

This room must have been the reception area. There was a dark rosewood desk in the middle of the far wall with the lower torso of a body seated neatly in the chair behind it. The upper torso was sprawled face down across the desk, but it wasn't connected to the bottom. The skin where the body had been separated was shredded horizontally, as though something had hooked into the flesh and ripped the two parts apart. The upper part had long blond hair. Without moving it, I couldn't tell if it was a man or a woman.

To the right of the desk, on the side wall, was a small built-in bar, again dark rosewood. No bar stools, just a discreet service area where a bartender could mix chocolate martinis or dean martinis or SuzieQ's favorite, screaming orgasms. I'll bet that one had gone over big here at Rough Trade, that and slippery nipples and every other double-entendre drink they could think of.

The rest of the room was filled with overstuffed chairs, a sofa, and two chaise lounges, all upholstered in purple velvet and black and white animal skins. Blood and hunks of flesh made it hard to tell just what animals they'd come from.

A second body was draped across one of the chaise lounges. All across it. In pieces. Half the skull of a bald head had rolled underneath and the rest of the head, the part with a sparse goatee, lay atop a tattooed upper bicep at the foot of the chaise. I felt a flash of recognition but couldn't come up with a name. The heart and kidneys— giblets, as my mother would call them—were nestled in the seam of the chaise. That was a stain they were never going to get out.

The rest of the bodies were divided up into four smaller rooms that opened onto the reception area. And I mean divided. Human parts covered the floors. It looked like each of the rooms had been designed for a specific type of BDSM pleasure and the killer had put them all to good use. Body parts hung from a strappado; a cat-o'- nine-tails was wrapped around a severed leg; a woman's head and neck were still manacled to a wall while the rest of her lay in a heap below.

A cop I vaguely recognized from the West Hollywood Division came out of the room farthest from me.

"You're King, right?" he asked.

I nodded and he handed me a bloodstained business card.

"One of yours?"

Under the blood and what might have been a sliver of brain tissue, I saw my name and officer number. "It's mine."

"We found two of these. One on the couch out front amongst the meat. This one we found on the guy in the back. His license says Thomas DeWitte. Wanna take a look, see if you recognize him?"

I looked, but I didn't recognize him. Even though I'd been hassling him less than twelve hours ago, there was nothing about what I was looking at that was even slightly recognizable. But now I realized who was spread out on the chaise—DeWitte's brainless bodyguard, Anthony. Well, he'd lived up to the name. I wondered if Travis was here, also.

DeWitte was dangling from a cinder-block wall, pinned to it by a railroad spike that had been driven between his eyes and right into the stone behind. At first I thought his clothes had been ripped off in strips, but as the photographer lit up the scene with his strobe I realized I was looking at skin. Strips of skin somehow still attached to what was left of him. He'd been flayed from neck to waist, his ribs pulled apart, and there was a hole where his heart should have been. Then, just for good measure, he'd been set on fire. The smoke alarm activated the sprinkler system, but the water came way too late for Thomas DeWitte. Parts of the body were seared to the bone. The CSIs were talking about having to chip away the wall to release him.

The West Hollywood cop came up beside me. "Looks like a scene from a horror movie," he said. And he was right.

Someone was making the ultimate horror movie, with real blood and real corpses.

Chapter Twenty-One

I hadn't been able to settle down after Peter left. There was something about him. He interested me. He intrigued me. And yes, I'll admit it: he excited me.

It's a pattern of mine. It took me a century or two to recognize it, and I've a feeling I might have mentioned it to Sigmund in Vienna. No doubt he wrote a paper about it. Years can go by without my finding anyone attractive and then someone crosses my path with a certain look about them—man or woman—and I respond. If there is a response in return, a message in the eyes, an acknowledgment of mutual interest, then a connection is made and a subtle current of constant sexual arousal sets in. I start sleeping even less than my usual five hours. My skin gets hypersensitive to the touch. I have more trouble keeping my fangs in place, my nails from elongating, and it takes a very real act of concentration not to Change. The Thirst comes on me more often and with more insistence. I turn to Maral to slake it.

Blood and sex. The absolute truths.

Maral doesn't mind these . . . well, I can't call them romances . . . liaisons, maybe. Couplings. Passions. If she does, she's never let on. She has her own *affaires du coeur* and she knows what we share is something different. A symbiosis based on mutual need and respect and comfort. Do I love her? Yes. Is she the great love of my life? No. Once, I thought it might be Rudy. Well, we all make mistakes.

I could feel the energy burning through my body and I needed to get out of the house. I didn't want to face the papparazzi in Beverly Hills or Hollywood, so we drove downtown to Club 740 instead. I like the Beaux Arts architecture. It doesn't hurt that the fog machine on the dance floor helps maintain anonymity and the music—primal and pulsing, like a heartbeat—always distracts me. Is it any wonder that many of my kind were drawn to music, that we became composers or musicians? Every vampyre is driven by the beat of blood, by the rhythmic pulse. When Bela talked about the children of the night and the music they made, I've no doubts that every vampyre in the audience nodded in recognition. I think I'm most proud of that line.

I watched Maral dance and felt lust slowly spreading through my body. And Thirst. We didn't stay long.

At midnight, we were in my bedroom.

Maral knows when I need her. And how I need her. This wasn't one of those times when her wrist would suffice. She stood still in the middle of the room with her back to me and undid the button at the back of her skirt. I unzipped the zipper and slid the skirt down over her black lace boyshorts. She had on black thigh-high hose. The bare, vanilla-colored skin between them and her briefs was so smooth and soft, I never got as far as removing her jacket. I turned her around and knelt down to pierce her upper thigh with my teeth, finding the rich femoral artery. She stayed bent over my shoulder, her tongue licking the skin on my back, while I drank my fill.

The taste was warm and salty on my lips, and the room came to brilliant—almost painful—light. Every sensation was intensified and I was acutely aware of my surroundings: the softness of Maral's flesh, the scent of her arousal, the thickness of the liquid in my mouth. But when I raised my face from Maral's bloody flesh and looked up, it was Peter King's hazel eyes that floated before my face.

I wonder what Sigmund would have made of that?

Afterwards, I slept.

Alone. Like the rest of my kind.

Perhaps that is the true curse of the vampyre: to sleep forever alone.

Maral knows it's dangerous to stay by my side while I'm sleeping. I've awakened too many times to find myself in the middle of the Change; I have no control over the transformation and there are moments when the beast is truly in control. Too many of my kin have awakened and found they have destroyed their lovers in their sleep. I sleep at night, just like everyone else. Just not *with* anyone else. And not as long, of course.

I collect vampyre lore. I particularly love the folklore that my kind cannot walk during the day, that we are creatures of the night. The Irishman Stoker had a lot to do with our mythology, though he wasn't the first. Dr. Polidori started it; his Lord Ruthven character in *The Vampyre* preceded Bram. Poor Polidori—*New Monthly Magazine* mistakenly credited his patient and friend, Lord Byron, with authorship. Polidori was furious, and Byron was none too pleased, either. I knew them both; I had a liaison with Byron briefly while he stayed in the Villa Diodati in Switzerland. Le Fanu had published his vampyre novella *Carmilla* years before Stoker came to work for him as a theatre reviewer. Before that, Rhymer's Varney had been around in the Penny Dreadfuls for years. But Stoker was responsible for making it work, for taking all the mismatched myths and knotting them together—even when they made no sense. He rescued poor

Vlad III from obscurity and turned him into a monster, a genuine horror franchise. Then later, when Tod Browning and I were deliberately adding to the confusion, we took everything Stoker had written, added in all the Penny Dreadful material, lumped together the conflicting vampyre and werewolf stories, borrowed from Murnau's masterpiece *Nosferatu,* and created our own mythology with his film *Dracula.* Thus, in the Age of the Cinema, the cult of the vampyre was created. Some of the classic vampyre myths—like not casting a reflection—we threw in simply because we had just worked out how to do that particular special effect on camera.

I never dream when I sleep. Or if I do, I don't remember. Maybe my subconscious has nothing to work out. Or maybe it's a protective mechanism, designed to keep my race from going mad. Too many years . . . far too many memories.

An intermittent buzzing sound pulled me out of the depths of my blood-sated sleep. It took me a moment to identify it as the buzzer on the main gate, sounding in the kitchen intercom downstairs. A normal human would never have heard it . . . but I've never been a normal human. Whatever that is. I was not made a vampyre; I was born one, the only child of a Dakhanavar Clan father and a *strega* mother. I've never known what it's like to be human, to be frail, to feel the touch of age with every passing day, to sniffle and cough and ache. It's not something I miss.

Throwing back the single cover, I swung my legs over the edge of the bed and glanced at the digital clock—7:20 A.M. Who the hell was calling at this hour? And where was Maral? Why hadn't she answered the door?

My bedroom connects to a second, even larger room that I use as an office and study. I keep the overflow from my library there, my research books and those not for public viewing—the lurid romance novels and Japanese erotica. Framed one-sheets from all my movies take up two walls, along with posters of my *mother's* and *grandmother's* movies, all signed by the actors and directors "we'd" worked with: a who's who of the Golden Age of Hollywood. They're probably worth as much as the house itself. My computer sits on a huge amber-inlaid desk that I smuggled out of the Russian court in the weeks following the October Revolution. Poor Nicholas, I begged him to allow me to take the children with me, but he refused, confident that the people still loved him and that the family would come to no harm. He discovered how wrong he was in that cellar in Yekaterinburg in July 1918.

Padding naked into the study, I tapped the space bar on the Mac keyboard and brought the enormous widescreen to life. The house's security system's high-resolution cameras have a direct feed to a terabyte server in the basement, which stores both stills and video from every camera in the house and throughout the grounds. I accessed the drive and brought up the live images from the camera on the gate.

Detective Peter King.

And not with good news.

He was wearing almost the same clothes he'd been wearing last night—the T-shirt was a darker black—but his face had changed. Deep, bruiselike shadows under his eyes stood out against pale skin and his lips were drawn so tight I could barely see them through the high-res image. I watched him lean on the buzzer again and once again heard the insistent buzzing in the kitchen.

Where was Maral?

A sudden thought struck me and I darted away from the computer and out into the hallway. Maral. Where was Maral? Usually she was up before me. I ran down the hallway toward her room. There was no reason for King to be here at this hour unless . . .

Unless there had been another killing.

And why was he calling on me . . . unless it had something to do with . . . unless something had happened to . . .

I stopped outside her door, my fingers resting on the smoothly polished wood.

Maral.

If anything had happened to her I would . . . I would what? I would rage and I would grieve and I would mourn . . . and then I would get over it. And I would do as I have always done—swear never to get involved with a human being again. I would live a solitary and celibate life for a number of years, and then I would get lonely again.

That is the great curse of the vampyre: loneliness. I believe that's what kills us all eventually. When I was still young, I encountered a vampyre in North Africa who claimed he had been a Centurion at the time of Caesar Augustus. I wanted to ask him about the things he'd seen; he only wanted to talk about the loves he'd lost.

Maral was eighteen when I first met her. There was a manslaughter charge hanging over her head for the killing in the house on Mulholland and the cops weren't completely buying her story. They fully accepted that a guy had broken into the house and had intended to rape her. He'd done it before. And she might have been able to claim justifiable homicide when she stabbed him in the gut, but as far as the cops were concerned she'd crossed over the line when she nearly cut off his head. They were trying to hang a murder charge on her.

Maral needed a lawyer, a good lawyer, and she didn't have the money to pay for one. She had a job offer, though. A porn producer, with enough wit to call his company Chicken Sheet Productions but not enough talent to make a living at anything but exploitation films, wanted to capitalize on her moment of fame and use her to star in a straight-to-video "mockumentary" about the killing. *The Real Killer Commits the Real Kill!!* It probably wouldn't have helped her case much, but Maral wasn't thinking that far ahead. She needed money to hire a lawyer. Mr. Chicken Sheet promised said money and failed to explain the net profit element of the contract. Maral showed up for work.

I got there just before she did.

Chicken Sheet Productions had just finished filming a knockoff porno version of my movie *I Scream*. Without my permission, of course. They'd titled it *I Scream with Pleasure* and the "star" was a pneumatic young actress whose screen name was Oval More and whose face, in the few seconds the camera was on it instead of the rest of her—*all* the rest of her—bore a slight resemblance to mine.

Needless to say, I wasn't happy. I didn't think Mr. Chicken Sheet would respond to lawyers and lawsuits, so I showed up in Van Nuys at the two-bedroom fixer-upper he used for a studio and proceeded to convince him to shelve the project by kicking his ass across the set.

Maral arrived just as her new boss was cowering under his desk, scrabbling in a top drawer for a piece-of-shit Saturday night special. He tried aiming it at me from his crouching vantage point, but his hand was trembling so hard he couldn't hold it straight. I wasn't worried about the gun; it was a tiny .22 that might smart a bit if he actually hit me but it wasn't going to kill me. Especially not with the safety on. But Maral didn't know that. She saw a weasel-faced little runt holding his rug on his head and a gun on a woman and so she blasted him with the fire extinguisher. I started laughing and couldn't stop.

We walked out of Chicken Sheet Productions together. I bought her breakfast, listened to her story, hired her on the spot, and had Solgar represent her. There was something about her willingness to do whatever she had to that reminded me of myself. We've been inseparable ever since.

So if anything had happened to her . . . yes, I would rage and I would grieve. And then I would tear this town apart.

The door jerked open and Maral appeared, tousle haired and sleepy eyed. "There's someone at the gate," she mumbled as she shuffled past, a striped WCW referee's shirt hanging down to her knees. She paused at the top of the stairs and looked back at me, frowning as she realized that I was naked and standing outside her door. "Were you looking for something?"

"You," I said truthfully. A flush of pleasure touched her neck and chin and she smiled lazily. I watched her pupils dilate. "But not right now. Detective King is at the gate."

Maral's smile faded. "Trouble?"

"At this hour, it seems likely. I'm sure he's not here to chat. Let him in, give him coffee, and keep him in the library. I'll get dressed and be right down."

Maral made Hawaiian Kona. Even through the rich aroma of the freshly ground beans I could smell the blood on him as soon as I stepped into the library.

There were traces of it under his fingernails, a splash on the edge of his shoes, more ingrained in the leather of the soles. I felt my nostrils flare and I ran my tongue across my teeth, ensuring they were flat. What I wanted to do was walk over and kiss him, not a good idea under the circumstances. I didn't smell cordite so I didn't think he'd come from a gunfight, and I didn't smell antiseptic so that ruled out a hospital visit. Just blood. Lots of it. It permeated his hair and his skin and his clothes. Detective King had been to a murder scene . . . or a slaughterhouse.

King had taken up the same seat he'd occupied the night before. He came to his feet as I walked into the room.

"You look tired," I said, by way of greeting.

"I got an early call."

"Not good news, I take it . . . by the look of you."

"No."

"And it brings you here. Why?"

"There's been another killing. It has all the hallmarks of a Cinema Slayer murder."

He was expecting a response, but I had nothing I was ready to say.

"Did you go out last night after I left?" he asked.

I knew where he was going with this. "Yes, we went out to a club. I needed to relax a bit and I didn't want to stay in the house."

"*We?*" he asked.

"Maral," I said.

"Have you any proof, an alibi?" he said, without a trace of a smile.

"We have one another."

King's lips thinned to a barely visible line. "That's not going to be good enough. Not this time."

"Who was killed last night, Detective?"

"Thomas DeWitte."

"Thomas! Thomas?" I hadn't seen that coming. King must have believed the shock on my face because I saw him relax slightly. I wasn't acting. I was stunned. "How?"

"You really don't want to know."

It took me a second to find my voice. "He was my business partner, Detective King, and, believe it or not, a man I cared for at one time in my life. I *need* to know how he died. Believe me, I do."

"Evidently he went back to Rough Trade last night after he left here. He and his bodyguard, Anthony. We found both their bodies mutilated and the club set ablaze early this morning."

"Mutilated how? What does that mean?"

"A railroad spike had been driven into his skull with enough force to pin him to a brick wall. Much of the skin had been flayed from his body, his ribs pulled apart, heart torn out, and then he'd been set on fire. There may have been other atrocities committed on the body, but the corpse is so torn apart I'm not even sure an autopsy will tell. He and Anthony weren't the only ones murdered, but we haven't got all the bodies identified yet. I don't know what happened to his boyfriend; nothing I saw in that charnel house resembled Neville Travis." King stopped suddenly. "I'm sorry," he said, "but you wanted to know."

I nodded. "You're right. I did." And the hunter wanted me to know, too, needed me to know. Impalement through the skull, removal of the heart, fire: all good and traditional ways to kill a vampyre. Except Thomas had not been a vampyre.

"Have you anything to say?" he wondered.

"That poor boy, Anthony, he didn't deserve to die like that."

"And DeWitte did?"

"No, of course not. No one deserves to die that way. But Thomas lived on the edge. He enjoyed all the darkest corners Hollywood had to offer, delighted in pain and suffering—mainly his own—and more than once placed himself in situations that were dangerous, to say the least. Put it this way: it's rather like the three-hundred-pound man dropping dead of a heart attack: we're shocked when it happens, but not completely surprised."

I turned and walked out of the room before he could ask me any more questions about what I knew. I didn't want to lie to him and I couldn't tell the truth.

"Have you nothing else to say?" he called after me.

"I'd ask God to have mercy on his soul," I said, "if I thought he had one." And if I believed in God.

CHAPTER TWENTY-TWO

BEL AIR
7:40 A.M.

I couldn't figure her out and I was beginning to mistrust my judgment. Twelve hours ago I was imagining what she might be like in bed, thinking I'd like to spend some time with her and find out. I was even starting to worry about her, feeling more protective than even my normal cop mode. And getting some response . . . I thought. Her hand lingering a little too long on mine, standing a fraction too close, her eyes saying something more than her words. Oh yes, a definite connection. I didn't need to be a detective to know that Ovsanna Moore was interested in me.

This morning she was an ice princess, barely reacting to the death of her business partner. Normally I get a pretty strong conviction about someone's innocence or lack thereof when I tell them a murder's taken place. For all the reaction she gave me, she could have known DeWitte was dead when I told her. There had been the briefest moment of surprise, which certainly looked genuine, but I would have expected more, much more, when I described in unnecessary detail the method of his death. All she'd said was that she was sorry about the bodyguard. The fucking bodyguard! No word about her business partner, who also happened to be the guy who'd burst into this very room and threatened her with his gun-wielding bodyguard a couple of hours earlier.

And now both had turned up dead.

Moore was definitely in control, I'll give her that. Seven thirty in the morning and she was dressed for a publicity shoot. Tight black leather pants over black snakeskin spike-heeled boots with a deep burgundy cashmere sweater cut just low enough to be distracting without being disrespectful to the dead. I'd given instructions that none of the deceaseds' names were to be released to the press—hell, we still didn't know who some of them were—but murder is big business in Hollywood; the bigger the name, the bigger the price an ambulance driver, a CSI tech, a doctor or nurse, even a cop, could command from the bloodthirsty press. DeWitte was an executive, which put him on the lower end of the scale, but his name was still worth a few grand of some editor's money. I was sure the press was gathering for a feeding frenzy, and Ovsanna Moore looked like she was ready for them.

The evidence was mounting that she was somehow connected to the Cinema Slayer killings. As I followed her out into the hall, I started wondering if I had enough cause to get a search warrant for the house and her offices.

"Our conversation isn't over, Ms. Moore. I'd prefer it if you didn't walk away."

"And I'd prefer it if you called me Ovsanna and stopped speaking to me as though I'm a suspect. I've done nothing wrong, Peter." She'd stopped on the stairs and was posed like Gloria Swanson in *Sunset Boulevard*. I couldn't tell where the woman left off and the actress began.

"I am conducting a murder investigation, Ms. Moore. I have questions that need answers. And I know you have some."

"I have no answers for you."

"Last night I told you the killings were coming closer. First it was actors you worked with, then it was one of your staff, and now it's your business partner. Who's next, Ovsanna? Who's next?"

She fixed me with a stare that could freeze water. "Is that a question or an accusation? Are you going to arrest me, Detective?"

I hesitated just long enough for her to continue.

"If so, you can ask your questions through my lawyer." She turned and continued up the stairs.

She was either guilty or she was frightened. I didn't want her to be guilty, unbiased detective that I am, so I went with option two and played my last card. "I don't want to have to make a statement to the press," I said quietly, just before she disappeared at the end of the landing. I watched her slow, and knew she was listening. I turned my back on her, leaned against the banister, and folded my arms. It wasn't until that moment that I realized how many antique weapons she had displayed on her walls. They all looked genuine . . . and lethal. I wondered if they were a personal choice or some Hollywood interior designer's idea of chic. "I wanted to keep DeWitte's name quiet until I'd spoken to you, but I'd guess by now it's public knowledge. The press will be all over this. And all over you. You were his business partner. You were ex-lovers. I would imagine when I drive out your front gate, there'll be thirty reporters clamoring for sound bites. I'm going to have to make a statement. And that can go one of two ways. Either I've come here to bring you the sad news of your business partner's death . . . or I've come here to inform you that you're currently under investigation."

"But I'm not."

I jumped. She'd moved right behind me and I hadn't heard her come down the stairs. I turned. She was standing on the second step, which meant that her eyes were level with mine. I'd never realized it before, but her eyes were so dark they were almost black, her pupils indistinguishable from their surrounds. "Not at the moment. But a police investigation and a press investigation are two entirely different things. If the press think you're involved, they'll shine a spotlight on you so bright, nothing will be secret. You think Michael Jackson had press for his trial? Wait till they get the details about the scene at Rough Trade. Bobby Blake and O.J. pale in comparison. Think Anna Nicole. You won't be able to turn on the TV without seeing yourself: E! News, Access Hollywood, Extra!, The View, the morning shows—you name it. And not just CNN and FOX, every news station nationwide—worldwide—will be running clips and looking for a comment. You won't be able to move without being hounded and photographed." Even as I was speaking, a helicopter clattered overhead, right on cue. I nodded my chin upward. "Sounds too light to be a police chopper; that's probably the news."

A door slammed upstairs and Maral McKenzie came running down the hallway. "Turn on Channel Five," she shouted.

Without a word, Ovsanna turned and strode back into the library. She hit a button and a section of the bookcase slid aside to reveal a 60-inch flat plasma screen suspended on the wall behind it. Fishing a large remote control out from behind a cushion, she fiddled with the buttons.

"Let me," Maral said slightly breathlessly, hurrying into the room, taking the square box from Ovsanna's hands. It had more buttons than my TV has channels. She flicked past FOX and CNN to the local high-def news channel, where an older man with unnaturally red hair was staring somberly into the camera and intoning gravely.

"Another savage killing rocks Hollywood. The Cinema Slayer strikes again. More after this break."

We stood in silence as the commercial rolled and a doctor detailed the gravity of restless legs syndrome while a vacuous blonde enumerated all that could go wrong if you took the medication they were selling without advice from your doctor. Tuberculosis, lymphoma. The list of side effects from the drug was longer than the ad copy extolling its benefits.

Rather than coming back to the studio after the commercial break, the screen showed an overhead view of a sprawling hacienda-style house.

"That's us," Maral whispered.

"These pictures coming to you live this morning from our news chopper. This is the Bel-Air home of legendary Scream Queen and horror meister Ovsanna Moore." Ovsanna's picture—looking improbably glamorous—flickered up on the top left-hand corner of the screen. *"Last night her business partner, Thomas DeWitte, became the latest victim of the brutal killer dubbed the Cinema Slayer."* DeWitte's picture, looking considerably more handsome than he had been in real life, appeared on the right of the screen, and then the images cut away to show a series of bodies being stretchered out of Rough Trade. *"Thomas DeWitte was killed in an upscale private club in West Hollywood. The specific details of the murder are being withheld by the police at the moment, but we do know this is a multiple murder scene. Thus far, police are refusing to speculate about the identity of the killer, but sources say the crime scene bore similarities to earlier Cinema Slayer murders."* A slightly fuzzy image of me appeared, trailing the last of the bodies out of the club. I brushed past reporters and climbed into the Jag. *"The detective in charge of the case, decorated BHPD hero Peter King, drove to the home of Miss Moore this morning to personally bring her the news of the tragedy. We are awaiting a comment from Detective King, and we'll bring that to you live as it happens. Now, in other news—"*

I took the control from Maral's hand and turned off the TV. In the silence that followed, the thumping of the helicopter overhead seemed very loud.

"You've made your point, Detective."

"So what do I tell the press?"

Ovsanna's smile was cool. "Whatever you have to. Just get them away from this house." She reached out and touched my arm. "Then if you want to talk, we'll talk."

I stared into her black eyes, unable to read what was behind them. Maybe I was being played, but there was only one way to find out. "Let me go make a statement. I'll tell them you're devastated and going away for a few days. That should pull them away from the house."

Ovsanna nodded. "Then come back and have some breakfast. We'll talk. I'll tell you all that I know."

I didn't believe her.

Ovsanna Moore was a woman with a lot of secrets.

CHAPTER TWENTY-THREE

"He's good on television," Maral admitted grudgingly.

"Very good," I agreed.

Peter King was confident and self-assured; he looked directly into the camera when he answered, made sure he used the reporter's name, and didn't dodge any questions. He considered each question and answered it as frankly as possible—with one lie after another. He was one of the most convincing liars I'd ever come across. It was worth remembering that.

"We have no evidence at this time that Mr. DeWitte's murder is connected to the Cinema Slayer killings," he began. "His was just one of several bodies we took out of the club on Santa Monica. At the moment this has all the hallmarks of a drug-related crime."

"Why are you involved, Detective?"

"This is a West Hollywood Division case. I was called in as a courtesy because one of the victims was connected with the entertainment industry."

"So are you saying this is *not* related to the other crimes?"

"I didn't say that. This murder is a few hours old. We are pursuing several definite lines of inquiry."

"Why did you bring the news of DeWitte's murder to Ovsanna Moore yourself, Detective?"

"It was just a courtesy. I thought it would be better if she heard it from the police, rather than any other source. I also wanted to assure her that we are doing everything in our power to apprehend the murderer of her business partner. She asked the same questions you did, and let me reiterate, I have no evidence at this time that this murder is related to the murders that have been dubbed the Cinema Slayer killings. This is a multiple murder—the other killings were all single slayings. Mr. DeWitte was not a movie star—the other victims were. I think Mr. DeWitte was simply in the wrong place at the wrong time."

"How did Ovsanna take the news?"

"She was obviously upset. Mr. DeWitte has been a junior partner in her studio for a number of years."

"Does she have a statement for the press?"

"No. Ms. Moore was just about to leave town for the holidays, and I have encouraged her to do that. There is no reason for her to stay here."

"What about the death at Anticipation Studios yesterday? That's two people working for Anticipation. You're saying there's no connection?"

"Yesterday's killing was a crime of passion," King said firmly. "We have a suspect in custody."

I looked at Maral. She shook her head, obviously as surprised as I was. King had said nothing about having a suspect in custody. Maral's cell phone warbled "Werewolves of London," which suddenly didn't seem so funny anymore. "I'll change the ring tone," she muttered, glancing at the screen. "No caller ID. Hello?" Then she handed me the phone. "Solgar," she whispered, lips curling in distaste.

Solgar's voice sounded even more inhuman than usual on the phone. Again he spoke in the archaic Armenian of my youth, which ensured privacy; we were probably the only two people on the planet who still spoke it.

"You are watching the news?"

"Yes."

"Do you know how that pervert DeWitte was slain?"

"Spike through the skull, heart ripped out, body burned," I said tightly.

"An unsubtle message."

"It seems likely I'm next, Ernst."

"Do not be so sure, Chatelaine. This Hunter is making a point. Displaying the kill, revealing his familiarity with the traditional ways. I believe if this Hunter wanted you dead, then you would be dead."

Something ancient and savage must have shown on my face, because Maral involuntarily took a step away from me. "I'm not that easy to kill."

Solgar ignored me. "No, but you're easy to destroy. This latest death brings far too much attention to you." There was a long pause and I could almost hear the Obour Vampyre collect his thoughts. "I understand the Vampyres of Hollywood called on you yesterday. A singular honor indeed."

"They gave me a week to sort out the mess."

Solgar coughed, a peculiar sucking sound. "Yesterday they gave you a week. This latest killing changes things. They've asked me to inform you they want a resolution within forty-eight hours."

I watched King's press conference come to an end. As he turned and walked back toward the house Maral pressed a button on the remote control and the gates swung closed behind him. The camera lingered on his retreating form and then cut back to the news anchor for a wrap-up. I motioned to Maral to turn the TV off.

"Do you hear me, Chatelaine?"

Solgar's rasp brought me back to him. "I hear you, Solgar. Forty-eight hours. Then what happens?"

"Your clan will be destroyed and you will be asked to move on for a century or two."

"And if I don't want to move on?"

"You know what the Vampyres of Hollywood are capable of. It would be a mistake to fight them."

"Whose side are you on?" I asked.

"The Clan Obour do not take sides," he said immediately. "We are merely messengers, observers, bystanders."

"Yes, I know. Like the Swiss. Would you truly stand by and watch my clan destroyed, see me killed?" I really was curious what his answer would be.

"There is a way to avoid this," Solgar said.

Ah, he sidestepped me. Ever the lawyer. "How?" I demanded, but even as I was asking the question, I knew the answer.

"Find the hunter. Stop the killings."

Maral had gone back to my office and I was waiting for Peter alone when he stepped inside the door. "You didn't tell me you have someone for Eva's murder."

"We don't," he said mildly.

"But you just said you have someone in custody," I said, confused.

"A bone to throw to the media dogs," King admitted with a shrug. "We're holding someone but he's not the killer."

"Very clever. Who's the unfortunate suspect?"

"Eva's sometime boyfriend. A part-time preacher, goes by the name of Biblical Benny. I had him picked up this morning when I realized DeWitte was dead. I knew we couldn't afford to have Eva's killing and DeWitte's murder both chalked up to the Cinema Slayer. All hell would break out."

I turned and walked back into the library. King followed me. "So you initiated a cover-up." I was unable to keep the disgust out of my voice. Somehow I'd imagined something a little better from King.

"We bought ourselves a little time, that's all. If people start believing the Cinema Slayer has killed twice more in the past twenty-four hours, this town will go crazier than it already is. We pulled in Benny for questioning on the Casale murder and right now we're stating that the Rough Trade hits are unrelated."

"But you believe they are related."

King suddenly looked very tired. "Eva Casale's murder definitely . . . DeWitte's I'm not so sure of." He slumped into a chair. "There were multiple murders, which is not the Slayer's M.O., but they were as gruesome in their execution as your three actor friends and your effects artist. It could be unrelated or not," he added, trying—and failing—to keep the fatigue out of his voice.

"And how long will it take the press to ferret out the details and make the connection?"

"A day, maybe two."

So Peter King and I both had a forty-eight-hour deadline. Mine was slightly more serious and deadly than his, however. "What happens then?"

The detective's smile was grim. "Someone else will take over the case. I'll be reassigned and the new team will have a mandate to close the case any way they can. I'm not saying they'll cut corners, but if someone looks good for the killings they may not investigate any further. I don't see you as having a motive, but your friend Maral isn't quite so clean. She's got that murder charge in her sheet; she's attached to you and Anticipation; I've heard rumors she was attached to Eva Casale. I don't know what her story is yet, but whoever takes over from me will find out pretty quick. There's too much pressure on the department to make this go away fast, and the time may come when they won't care if the suspect they've got is the real killer or not. If they decide to press charges, then they can issue a press release. You can imagine the headlines," he added.

Unfortunately, I could.

I couldn't let any more suspicion fall on Maral. And I didn't want Peter off the case. I bought myself a little time by crossing to the French doors and staring out into the garden. One of the news helicopters gave up hovering overhead and took off towards the beach—maybe they hoped to find me heading to the Malibu house. By the time it was out of sight, I knew what I was going to say. I turned back to Peter and fixed him with the most innocent, vulnerable look I could manage.

"We're innocent."

"I don't believe that," he said simply. "No one is ever entirely innocent."

"So you think one—or both—of us killed DeWitte?"

"No," he said, surprising me. "I saw what happened to DeWitte and the rest of the unfortunates in that club this morning. Neither of you is physically capable of doing that. Maybe someone shafted one of the South American cartels on a drug deal and the scene in Rough Trade was a warning to others. Maybe DeWitte was in the wrong place at the wrong time. Or maybe the same killer who butchered Eddings, Goulart, Gordon, and Casale is upping their game." King brushed his hair back from his forehead and leaned forward, forearms resting on his thighs. "I don't think you killed DeWitte, but you know something. I am convinced of it."

"You are no fool, Detective."

"Please. It doesn't take a genius to work out that Anticipation is somehow at the center of all this. In a roundabout way that—more than anything else—convinces me of your innocence. If you were guilty, I would imagine you'd hide your tracks more cleverly."

Solgar had been right; Detective King was not the brightest, but he was tenacious. When all of this was over—assuming I survived— I might have to do something about him. It would be regrettable but necessary.

"I didn't kill Thomas, Peter, I can prove that, but the fact is I may be responsible for his death. I think I know *why* he was killed."

He didn't say anything. Just stared at me, waiting for the story I was making up on the spot. I'm a writer and an actress, used to thinking on my feet, but this was no movie I was pitching; this was life and death: mine.

"I told you I am expecting a contingent of Japanese businessmen to arrive on Saturday?"

King nodded.

"They want to invest in Anticipation. They're offering close to fifty million dollars in cash and probably the same amount in technological investment. When that happens, Anticipation will join the big boys. We'll become a major player overnight."

King considered the news. He'd lived in Hollywood long enough to understand the ramifications. "Is this common knowledge?"

"No. Not at all. We've managed to keep it pretty quiet, which in this town is as much a coup as the deal itself. The Japanese aren't talking, and aside from Maral and Thomas and my attorney, no one else knows."

"And how does that tie in to DeWitte's murder?"

"About a year ago, just a month after the Japanese approached me, I got an offer through my lawyers for fifty-one percent of my company. I wasn't interested. I didn't even bother to get the details, just turned it down and didn't think about it again. The next offer came in on my private office line. A male voice, offering me top dollar for fifty-one percent of Anticipation. The guy said he thought maybe I'd misunderstood the level of their interest—that the people he represented really wanted to make a deal. Again, I refused. Three more calls came in, the last one on my home phone, each one a little more threatening. And then Jason was killed and I got a call the very next day and the caller mentioned the murder. Said he was sorry to hear about it and wondered if maybe I wasn't so upset I'd like to reconsider the offer and get out of the business. He called again after the police found Mai and Tommy. Each time the message was less ambiguous."

"What about yesterday?"

"Yesterday the message was real clear. I got the call shortly after you left, same voice, same offer: fifty-one percent of Anticipation. The voice asked if I wanted to end up like the special effects lady. Told me I'd better make the decision to sell or someone close to me would die for every day I refused."

As spur-of-the-moment lies went, I thought it was pretty good. I wished I could summon tears, because right then would have been a good place to shed them. "It's my fault," I said, dropping my voice to a whisper and turning my back to Peter so he couldn't see that my eyes were dry. "I killed him. I killed Thomas."

"No, you didn't," he said, right on cue. "But that's what had you so spooked yesterday when you thought someone had broken into the house."

I nodded.

He reached out and touched my right shoulder, the merest gossamer touch, but the heat of it flowed down my arm. "Why didn't you go to the police?"

"What could the police have done?" I said bitterly. "Up until yesterday, I had nothing concrete, an unidentified voice on a phone offering to buy a portion of my company. It's hardly extortion and it's only the vaguest sort of blackmail. The threat was so veiled in the beginning even I wasn't sure there was a connection."

"But yesterday," he said, and I could tell there was real concern in his voice, not just a professional reprimand, "you should have called me as soon as you hung up the phone. I was here, Ovsanna, this is *my* case. You've got to trust me to help you. And this is information I need."

"I've been in this business a long time, Peter, a very long time. I'm a genre actress and the kinds of films I do aren't going to get me nominated for an Oscar. I've got a star in front of Grauman's—which my studio paid for just like every other star there—and I get Fangoria awards and fantasy film festival awards and lifetime achievement awards for horror films, but I'm never going to be on Spielberg's short list to star in next year's A movie. Tarantino might rediscover me, but I doubt it. I'm getting older, so there aren't that many lead roles in any of the interesting independents that I might be right for anymore. This studio is my life, but the last few years have been tough and getting tougher. This deal with the Japanese guarantees us a future. If I'd gone to the police with unfounded suspicions, the news of the threats would have been on the street in hours and the Japanese wouldn't have stayed long enough to unpack their digital DVs."

Peter just stared at me. I couldn't tell if he bought my story or not, but he didn't say anything.

"I made a terrible mistake not telling you, and Thomas paid for it with his life. Oh God, Peter, what do I do now?"

He came around to stand in front of me, dangerously close. I could smell the blood on him, just hours old, mingling with his own heat, and I was starting to get aroused. There's nothing like giving a good performance to get my juices going. I averted my eyes and turned my head to the side, just in case the blood vessels in my eyes started to burst and give me away. "Will they strike again?" I asked, pitching my voice to little more than a whisper.

"Yes," he said finally, after a long pause. "On the face of what we've seen so far, I am afraid they will."

"What do we do?" I whispered.

"There are three things we do—right now," he said quickly. "First, we make sure that both your alibis are watertight, so even if I'm removed from the case, we know you're both safe from accusations. Second, we have to ensure your safety, because I'm afraid either you or Maral could be next on their list of victims."

"And third?"

"The third isn't 'we' Ovsanna. It's me, by myself. I've got to find the killer."

CHAPTER TWENTY-FOUR

BEVERLY HILLS
10:25 A.M.

I work in one of the all-time great office buildings in Beverly Hills, certainly the best piece of architecture housing any police department I've ever seen. Like every great building, it's got different moods and atmospheres—but for me, my favorite view is mid-morning, when the sun washes the blue, green, and gold tiles on the dome of City Hall. Then it looks incredibly dramatic, almost foreign to L.A. It reminds me of that turn on the 101 in the Bay Area where suddenly the entire San Francisco skyline is laid out in a dramatic vista. It's breathtaking and heart-stoppingly gorgeous. You'd have to be dead not to revel in the glory of it. Well, the Beverly Hills Civic Center isn't quite that glorious, but it's still great to look at.

It's a stunning example of Spanish Renaissance architecture, originally designed in 1932 by William Gage. But by the late seventies it was way too small and of course, it wasn't earthquake safe. Instead of letting it go, the city held a blind bid contest among the top six architects of the time, committing to a ten-year renovation for a hundred and ten million dollars. When people tell me that L.A. has no soul I remind them about that: one hundred and ten million dollars to preserve a building less than a hundred years old. Frank Gehry lost out to Charles Moore, who said he was going to build *"a place that is distinguishable in mind and memory from all other places."* It's one of my favorite quotes because, for me, he wasn't just talking about the building; he was describing L.A. in general and Hollywood in particular. I think he succeeded. The civic center with its cop shop is pure L.A. Quintessential Hollywood, and like the famous sign, it's even featured in the movies: *Beverly Hills Cop* and *Down and Out in Beverly Hills.*

The department lives up to the building. We've got first-class equipment, up-to-date technology; *damn,* even the beat cops' uniforms look good. It's a good place to work and it's not a job I want to jeopardize. I knew my father called in several favors just to get me this job and I knew, as I climbed the steps to the double doors, that I was dangerously close to blowing it. I wasn't getting results fast enough for the brass to appease the press and the politicians. That cracking sound I heard in the background was the thin ice I was skating on.

I'd had XM radio installed in the Jag, so I alternated listening to CNN and the local talk radio stations as I drove over from Bel Air. CNN had a piece on the morning's killings, but it was pretty straightforward reporting. The talk stations, however, were heavy with commentary. Most of the deejays were buying my suggestion that the latest multiple murders didn't fit the profile of the Cinema Slayer but were drug related instead. Rough Trade's specialty had been leaked to the media by *a source close to the investigation*—me, in other words— and its reputation bolstered that theory. Bloody death, drugs, multiple murder in an S&M club, it didn't sound like the Cinema Slayer. The three dead actors weren't mentioned, and no one was talking about Eva Casale. We hadn't released any specifics about her murder, but we had her ex-junkie lover in custody so, as far as the media was concerned, that case was old news. This was one of those times when the attention span of the MTV generation was a definite advantage.

It's a cliché that police captains are white haired or ruddy faced or Irish. Captain Barton isn't Irish. He's got a beautiful head of white hair, though, and enough red veins on his nose and cheeks to ensure a second career as Santa at Nordstrom if he wants it. Fortunately for the department, he hasn't wanted it yet. He's a good man to work for: bright, fair, driven, more politician than police, more bureaucrat than badge, with a Ph.D. in criminology, speaks six languages, and has been married to the same woman for twenty-five years. Two of his five kids are training to be cops.

He's second generation on the job—his dad and mine were rookies together back when the Two Tonys killed Bugsy Siegel on Linden Drive—and he's worked his way up from the beat to captain without making a lot of enemies. No one knows Hollywood politics better than Barton. He's a damn good administrator, but he can be a pain in my ass sometimes. I had a feeling, when I got the note on my desk saying he wanted to see me, that this was going to be one of them.

We met in his glass-walled office, with its window looking out onto Rexford. It's a fabulous view—if you like palm trees and traffic . . . and if you look closely you can see where the acid smog has pitted the bulletproof glass. A metaphor for something, I'm sure—maybe pollution will get us before firepower—but no one's paying attention. The Captain was concentrating on a series of printed e-mails spread out across his desk. I didn't even need to look at them as I sat down to know that they were from me. They changed colors ever so slightly as the lights on the miniature Christmas tree in the corner of the room twinkled on and off.

"Good work, Peter. Excellent work," he said in that peculiar clipped fashion of his. His praise took me by surprise, immediately putting me on guard. "Good, solid police work."

There was something coming.

"But it's not enough."

Barton pulled out a pair of rimless glasses from his top drawer—I glimpsed pens sorted by color—and glanced at the e-mailed reports.

"I've got the higher-ups breathing down my neck for results. You haven't got anything on the first three murders, we're no closer to solving the Casale case, and now we've got this mess from this morning. I can't go out there and talk to *anyone* with what little you've got. This isn't going to cut it."

"That's unfair, Captain. I think I've accomplished quite a bit, given that I was only assigned this case yesterday morning. I was promised a task force, resources, an office. I'm still filling in the requisition forms."

"These crimes were always a priority, but obviously the murder yesterday and the killings this morning have changed all that. Your team is being assembled now."

"I wanted to pick my own team," I mumbled.

"Don't be ridiculous," he snapped, sounding like a disapproving parent. "You'll take what we give you." He looked back at the report. "I made you lead on the Cinema Slayer trio, but the murder yesterday and the massacre this morning changes all that. You'll work with Milmore, Long, and Delaney."

I kept my face straight: Larry, Curly, and Moe. Well, at least he wasn't turning it over to Homicide Special yet. Actually, John Milmore, Jake Long, and Del Delaney are all good cops and I've worked with each one on other cases.

Barton opened the first murder book on his desk and started reading from it. "We have two separate murder scenes within the past twenty-four hours which, conceivably, could have been committed by the same person or persons unknown." Without lifting his head, he looked at me over the rim of his glasses. "Nine bodies were taken out of this Rough Trade club. Six men, three women," he added, as if it made a difference. "We seem to be missing some body parts, which suggests that the killer or killers took said parts away, maybe a trophy of their kill. The ME is having trouble making sense of the scene."

Our medical examiner is one of the best in the country. "I don't understand. What can't he figure out?"

"There were teeth marks on some of the bodies."

"Teeth marks?" I blinked, and then shrugged. Why was I even surprised? I'm not squeamish, but I could feel my stomach start to gurgle. "A cannibal killer . . . the press will love that."

"The ME doesn't think they're human. Said at first glance they look canine. Or maybe feline—but big. *Big*. If it's a cat, it's a zoo animal—jaguar, panther, tiger, something like that—definitely not a pussycat. He's making casts of the marks to identify them."

"What about the weapons used?"

"None, according to the coroner. No guns, knives, clubs . . . everyone was killed by hand." He moved a buff-colored envelope of photographs across the desk toward me. I'd seen everything up close that morning, but these photos showed the minutest details. I closed the envelope and pushed it away. These were images they wouldn't even use in *Saw III*. "Most of the traumatic injuries were made post-mortem. Except for the people who were ripped apart. ME says they were alive when that happened. Something to do with the spray of the arterial blood. Oh, and we got an ID on another one of the vics. Kid named Neville Travis. I think this is what's left of him." The Captain pulled the top photo out of the folder and handed it back to me. It showed an arm resting three feet away from a mangled torso. They'd been jaggedly severed at the shoulder. No wonder I hadn't recognized Travis at the scene; there was no flesh left on his face. "Are you suggesting an ordinary human did that—without any weapons?"

"Hardly an ordinary human," Barton said mildly. "But then, the people who frequent these clubs aren't exactly ordinary, are they? I mean I don't see my next-door neighbors walking in there. These are precisely the type of people who give this city a bad name. A TV weather girl—what was she doing in a place like that? I got my weather from her every morning, for God's sake!" He sounded personally affronted.

"We ID'd a judge and a pastor in there, too," I reminded him.

"Well, *that* I can believe," he said dismissively, and I wasn't sure if he was referring to the pastor or the judge or both. "A place like that, it wouldn't surprise me to find out that there were animals there. Bestiality, you know. Makes me think about Catherine the Great." Before I could ask the obvious question, he hurried on. "Did you know," he said, leaning forward, "that there are more big cats in private hands in the United States than there are in the rest of the wild? More tigers in America than in all of India?"

"I didn't know that, Captain." Captain Barton was a practicing Methodist. Where was he getting this stuff?

"Neither did I until this morning." He hit a couple of keys on his computer and I could see a garish Web site reflected on the window behind his desk. "According to HollywoodGossip.com, some sort of drug-fueled orgy was going on in that place. Men, women, and animals. Or at least one animal, maybe a gorilla. The party got out of hand; someone went berserk, starting killing people. The animal got excited and started chewing on the bones—"

"Whoa, Captain, I was there. That's just so much bull—"

"I guarantee you, Detective, that's what's going to be reported as honest-to-god truth on the noon news. There'll even be a gorilla sighting in Beverly Hills." His lips curled in what might have been a smile and I realized why he was probably going to be mayor someday.

"I'd believe a gorilla in Beverly Hills," I said.

"And this department will make no comment. None," he added for emphasis.

"I hear you. I'm not talking to anyone."

"This town has a short attention span. Let the news stations get excited and run with it. It buys us time. Let's move on for a moment."

He hit the wireless keyboard again and leaned over to look at the screen. Reflected in his glasses I saw a photo: Biblical Benny, aka Benzedrine Benny, aka a lot of other Bennys.

"This Benny character will be back on the streets in a couple of hours. He called his parents and they called Thomas Mesereau—you know, the guy who defended Michael Jackson? Mr. Mesereau is talking about filing against the city, citing harassment, false arrest . . . theft."

"Theft?"

"You took his cell phone," Barton said mildly.

"So that he could not communicate with the woman I was going to see . . . I gave it back to him when we picked him up this morning."

"Which brings me to his alibi for the time of the murder." Barton read in silence for a moment, then looked up at me. "He claims he was being interviewed by you at the time that Eva Casale was being killed."

I opened my mouth to respond, but the Captain held up his hand. He had a Darth Vader Band-Aid on the tip of his little finger. "I'm not going to be able to keep him in custody much longer. I can throw a few misdemeanors at him: trading without a license, vagrancy—"

"Littering," I suggested, "tax evasion . . ."

The Captain took me seriously and dutifully made a note of my suggestions; then he pushed the keyboard back under the desk and folded his hands together, interlacing his fingers. "But once the press finds out we've released him and we're without a suspect in custody . . ."

He didn't have to finish what he was saying. I was basically up shit creek without a paddle—in a canoe with a hole in the bottom.

"Talk to me about Ovsanna Moore and the girlfriend. Where do they fit into all this? How are they involved?"

"Well, there's no motive for any of the killings, and no opportunity as far as I can see. They've got alibis for two of the three previous murders and claim they have an alibi for last night, which I haven't had time to check. Ovsanna Moore just admitted she thinks the killings may be related to a blackmail threat she's been receiving over the past number of months."

The Captain straightened in his Aeron chair. "Did she report it?"

I shook my head. "I asked her; she said she hadn't because she didn't think we'd be able to do anything about it. It was too vague a threat, she said."

"Maybe there is no threat?" He noticed me looking at Darth Vader and pulled the Band-Aid off his pinkie, tossing it in the wastebasket under his desk.

"She says she has investors lined up willing to put something like fifty million into Anticipation. She was afraid that if news of the blackmail attempt got out, she'd lose the investment." The more I repeated Ovsanna's words, the less I was buying them. I was starting to think she'd been playing me.

"So what was the threat—'sell us the company or we kill people'?"

"Not quite . . . more like 'sell us a portion of the company or we kill people.'" The Captain sucked on the cut on his little finger and stared at me. I nodded. "It's thin, I know."

"It's not just thin, it's a size zero."

"She sprung this on me this morning, and it sort of made a vague sense at the time." I'd been puzzling over her bizarre statement as I drove over from Bel Air. And now, hearing it in my own words with a couple of cups of sludge from the department coffeemaker in me, it just didn't make a whole lot of sense. "But why look for fifty-one percent of the company and not a total buyout? Why kill people on the periphery of her life and not those closer to her? Someone who had meaning to her?" I'd been played, all right. There were more holes in her story than in one of the paper snowflakes the Captain's grandkids had cut out and taped to his wall.

The Captain rummaged through the bottom right drawer of his desk and came up with a roll of adhesive tape. As he talked, he tore off half an inch and wrapped it around his pinkie. He sat back in his chair and then did what everyone who wears suspenders does: hooked his thumbs under them and pulled them forward. "She's a movie star—which means she's a drama queen. She has to be at the center of everything. So this is all about her. And secondly, you're a cop. People lie to you."

The Captain was right. People see the badge and they start making up shit. It's an occupational hazard. You can ask someone the time and they'll lie to you or think it's some sort of trick question.

"This sounds like one of her movie scripts. We're moving into fantasyland here, Peter. Why is she feeding you this line of bull if she's not involved?"

I started to shake my head. "I don't know, Captain. But she just doesn't feel right for it. Her alibis, for the first murders, at least, are solid. And what's the motive? Except for Thomas DeWitte, she was barely connected to any of the vics. What does she stand to gain?"

"Here's what I'm thinking. We have the . . . the Cinema Slayer killings," he was flipping pages on one of the murder books as he talked, "and then we have the two recent murders." He pulled the other two murder books closer to him. "Three movie stars—not big stars, but stars nonetheless—killed. Even though the M.O.s were different, we're pretty certain it's one killer. And at some time or another they'd all worked for Ovsanna Moore. Then yesterday, Casale, the special effects woman, and this DeWitte character. These slayings look like they were made by the same hand—well, except for the teeth marks and who knows what the fuck that's about at this point. But the viciousness of the slaughter, the total annihilation of the bodies, suggests the same perp for both. Neither one of these vics were actors, but both of them worked for Ovsanna Moore. There's your connection right there."

"It's a small town, Captain. You know that. Moore has been around a long time; she's probably worked with half of Hollywood. Yes, there's a connection, but what's her motive? What does she stand to gain with these people gone?" I stood up and started pacing the room.

"She could be guilty," Captain Barton suggested.

I started to shake my head. "I didn't believe she is, but I've nothing to go on, other than my gut."

"Make sure that gut feeling is not just indigestion." He glanced down at the notes. "Did you know that Miss Moore and Thomas DeWitte were romantically involved for a time?"

"She said something about it, but I didn't get any details."

"And did you know that Eva Casale had an affair with Maral McKenzie?"

"Just rumors, nothing concrete," I muttered, as I lied. That one had slipped right by me.

"And the link is Miss Moore herself."

I remembered what my dad told me. At the end of the day it all came down to sex and money. I stopped pacing. "Who've you been talking to, Captain?"

He allowed himself a self-satisfied smile. "I've been a long time in this town. I've got my sources and I didn't always just drive a desk." He extracted a single sheet of paper from one of the murder books and pushed it toward me. "And of course, we have the witness statement."

"Witness statement?" I spun the page and scanned the dozen lines. Yesterday morning, Ovsanna Moore had threatened the life of Thomas DeWitte. A tiny little detail she'd forgotten to tell me. *The only person you're in danger from is me, Thomas. Fuck up one more time and you're gone. Gone and never coming back.*

Ovsanna Moore had issued the threat less than twelve hours before Thomas DeWitte was butchered.

The witness statement was made by Milla Taylor, the late Thomas DeWitte's secretary.

CHAPTER TWENTY-FIVE

Vampyres are physical creatures.

I dropped a sugar cube of L'Occitane Green Tea with Jasmine into the bathwater and watched it fizz up under the Jacuzzi jets, their rumble drowning out the noise of the lone news helicopter still circling over the house. Probably KABC with nothing else to report on. I stepped into the tub and let my body collapse.

We are a long-lived species, certainly, immune to many of the afflictions of *Homo sapiens,* not susceptible to colds and flus, allergies, or most diseases. Our metabolism is highly specialized, designed to metastasize blood, extract the nutrients needed to sustain our lives. Our hearts can be twice the size of human organs; our kidneys and livers are usually enlarged; our stomachs are tiny. We can eat and drink normal food, but it usually passes straight through the system. Less than half a pint of fresh human blood will sustain an adult vampyre for about a month. Some of the vampyre clans—the Nosferatu and Strigae—can live off animal blood; others, like the Bobhan

Sith, can only survive on human blood. I've never come across a veg-etarian vampyre, and although there have been a couple of attempts to synthesize blood, it just hasn't worked. If you're of a metaphysical frame of mind, you might think we need more than just the blood, we need the life essence. Over the years, I've become an expert on blood. I'm fascinated with this stuff that keeps us alive. I even spent time in the twenties working as a lab assistant to the legendary im-munologist Reuben Kahn and later, much later, I anonymously helped fund research into Draculin, the blood-thinning drug that was developed from vampire bat saliva. Because when you strip away the mythology and the weirdos and the foolish legends and movie special effects, it is the act of drinking blood—or the ability to drink and ex-tract nourishment from blood—that truly separates *Homo sanguineous* from *Homo sapiens*.

It is said that the devil thrives because no one believes in him anymore; well, the same might be said of my kind. Just as the Nean-derthal lived alongside the Cro-Magnon for a time, I think the vampyre probably shared the earliest cave fires with mankind. Man's oldest legends are full of references to my breed, and we certainly lived and worked alongside him sometime in the first millennium. There are stories from that time about entire religions built around blood.

And from the very beginning there have been hunters—usually self-appointed, self-righteous guardians of humanity. When the power of the Church became absolute, there was a concerted effort to wipe my race from the face of the earth. Vampyres were consid-ered demons' spawn, and the witch hunters went out armed with the *Malleus Maleficarum* in one hand and a stake in the other. Boun-ties were offered on vampyre kills by the most pious of parishes. Scores of unfortunate innocents were killed, their teeth knocked out and their decapitated heads presented for the bounty as vampyre skulls. I've heard similar stories of Apache hunters killing Mexican villagers and scalping them because their hair was sufficiently similar for it to be passed off as Indian scalps. Over the years, stories passing from one Hunter to another helped establish the certain methods of killing my race: impalement through only the heart or skull, decapitation, disembowelment, drowning, and, of course, burning.

True Vampyre Hunters are rare now. Oh, there's always some creative psychopath who will claim vampirism as a defense for murder—either he was one or he was killing one—but a real Hunter, a proper Hunter, well now, that's a dying breed. Dying, but not dead. Not yet.

I turned off the jets and took the box of matches from the shelf beside the tub to light a floating candle, then rested my head on the bath pillow and allowed the memories to come, moving back years, then decades, then centuries . . . to London.

1888.

Jack the Ripper was the last real Hunter I'd encountered. He was a vicious butcher, the way too many sadistic Warm can be. The Charlie Manson of his time. Jack was really after Mary Kelly, because he'd discovered that she'd been Turned by a mediocre French artist she'd posed for. The artist was a vampyre, but a Rogue who had abandoned his clan. He didn't have the two shillings he'd promised the woman for posing, so he gave her something he claimed was much more precious. And he got dinner in return.

I'm not sure if Mary completely Turned; from the stories I've heard, I don't believe she did. But she did infect at least a dozen men and half a dozen women with a mild strain of vampirism before she died, and indeed, if Jack hadn't killed her, we would have been forced to put her down ourselves. The last thing we needed was a plague of newly Turned vampyre trollops wandering the streets. I'm not old enough to remember the last time that happened, but the Vampyres of Stabiae destroyed Pompeii and Herculaneum to stop a similar plague.

Jack killed the other four women simply to discover the location of Mary's address. When he finally found Mary, he used one of the traditional methods, savage disembowelment, literally tearing her body apart, to ensure that there could be no regeneration. I arrived too late to stop him; the Vampyres of London had finally roused themselves from their torpor and descended on Whitechapel, drawn by the aroma of blood. They feasted on Mary's remains while I searched for Jack. I never did discover him and was convinced either they'd killed him or he'd thrown himself into the Thames. Later, much, much later, I learned that they had caught him. They'd imprisoned him in a Roman dungeon deep below London, then Turned him, made him a vampyre so that they could continue to practice their tortures on him. That's another part of our DNA: vampyres feel very little remorse and we thrive on revenge. They're probably still chewing on him, a little at a time. Vampyre flesh regenerates with remarkable resilience. There is an urban legend amongst the vampyre community that Jack is still alive, locked in a hidden room beneath the Tower of London.

Jack was the last of the great Hunters. There hasn't been a proper one since. Oh, there have been allegations of course, there are always rumors of an order within the Catholic Church dedicated to my kind, but I've never encountered them.

But this Hunter is different.

He's displaying his kills. Hunters don't display their kills; they don't want to alert other vampyres they're in the area and they don't want to run the risk of suffering the alleged fate of Jack the Ripper. This one doesn't seem to care.

It's almost as if this Hunter wants us to know he's working in Hollywood. As though he's sending a warning to the vampyre clans that he's coming for them.

No, not coming for them.

Coming for me.

I blew out the candle and rose slowly from the tub, letting the thoughts on the outskirts of my mind swirl into consciousness like the water in the drain.

Eddings. Goulart. Gordon. I'd worked with all of them. I'd

Turned all of them. They were of my clan. But Eva Casale wasn't. Nor was Thomas DeWitte. Neither Eva nor Thomas were even vampyres.

But the five dead represented both halves of my world: vampyre and human. Personal and professional. The Hunter knew that. And he knew Eva's death and Thomas's death—two Anticipation employees—would force the police to look at my connection to the three previous murders. And the combination of police attention and media attention would rouse the ire of the Vampyres of Hollywood, an ire I'd be hard-pressed to survive. The Hunter may not be able to do away with me himself, but he was setting me up to be destroyed by my own kind—the Vampyres of Hollywood.

How the hell did he know about us?

I toweled myself dry and grabbed my robe with so much force I ripped the hook from the wall. Hurrying from the bathroom, leaving tiny wet footprints on the Italian tile, I raced into my office. My heart was pounding . . . well, as much as a vampyre heart can pound.

Maral looked up from the huge Mac screen. There were at least half a dozen windows open—AnticipationStudios.com overlapped Ovsanna.com and my Gmail site. I caught a glimpse of my Web site guest book. "Just answering your fan mail. Lots of condolences on the death of Thomas." She stopped. "What's wrong?"

"Get the car. The SUV."

Maral's fingers rattled across the wireless keyboard, shutting each window faster than I could read the rest of the site names. If she was surprised, she said nothing. She knew I rarely drove the SUV.

"How soon can we leave without attracting attention?"

Maral swung back to the screen and called up the images from the cameras on the walls and the front gate. There were only two cars left, two photographers, cameras dangling around their necks, chatting idly together. "That's all that's left of the press. Want me to call the security patrol, see if they can get them away from the house?"

"No, that would only excite their interest."

I started for my bedroom, removing my robe as I strode into the walk-in closet. Maral was right behind me and she watched me from the doorway as I pulled on my jeans and bra and black turtleneck sweater. She likes seeing me naked. And normally I would have taken my time getting dressed, both of us enjoying her watching me. But not now. "I want you to take the SUV and leave. Make it look like you're heading for LAX." I pulled on my black calfskin boots. "If the photographers ask, don't hesitate to tell them."

"And where will you be?"

"Once the paparazzi leave, I'll follow in the Mercedes. Wait in front of the Airport Valet on Sepulveda and I'll meet you there. We'll give the Mercedes to the valet and continue the rest of the way in the SUV. Bring something warm; it could get cold later."

"Where are we going?"

"Palm Springs."

"Great . . . ," Maral said dubiously. "Should I pack a couple of bags? Do I need to make reservations?"

"No. There's no need. We'll be back tonight." Maral knew better than to ask too many questions.

"Thank God for that," Maral muttered. "And can I ask why we're going to Palm Springs?" Well, Maral usually knew better than to ask too many questions.

"To see an old friend of the family."

"I didn't know you had relatives in Palm Springs. Anyone I know?"

"No one you've ever met, thankfully. She doesn't like visitors."

"What does that mean, 'she doesn't like visitors'?"

"She eats them."

"Eats them?"

"Eats them. Raw."

Maral paled; she knew I wasn't joking.

"What about you? You're a friend, right?" Panic started creeping into her voice.

"She hates me."

"But—"

"Don't worry. I'm not very palatable."

CHAPTER TWENTY-SIX

STUDIO CITY
12:00 P.M.

Before I spoke another word to Ovsanna, I needed to talk to the witness who made the statement against her. Pissed that I'd been lied to, I tore up Coldwater, taking the corners too fast and only slowing when I almost drove the car straight through a curve onto that front lawn with the Statue of Liberty on it.

DeWitte's secretary lived in Studio City, just blocks from my parents' front door. I made it over the hill with a half hour to kill before our appointment. I hadn't talked to my mother in two days and hadn't seen her or my dad in a couple of weeks. I called to say I'd stop by for a minute.

"Good," my mother answered. "I've got steak pizzaiolla for lunch."

"I can't stay, Mom, I'm working. I've got to interview a witness."

"Steak pizzaiolla," she said, and hung up.

I turned left on Moorpark and right on Van Noord and I swear I could smell her sauce from halfway down the block. By the time I parked the car in the driveway under the pepper tree, my stomach was growling.

There was a bottle of Australian Shiraz sliding around my backseat, an early Christmas gift from the Captain's secretary, who still didn't know I was off the sauce. As I opened the door to get it, a car pulled away from the curb across the street, the driver giving me a big wave. Two young moms pushing strollers past the house both smiled and said hello. Mrs. Boesch was watering her lawn three doors down, and when she realized it was me she mouthed, *Happy holidays, Peter,* over the noise of the hose. Studio City is less than ten miles from Hollywood and Bel-Air, but it's like living in another country. It got its name in the twenties when Mack Sennett built a two-hundred-acre movie studio on a lettuce farm on Ventura Highway. He shot his Keystone Cops comedies there. I love it.

My mom never locks the door. Maybe living with a cop all her married life made her feel secure or maybe she just can't think badly about the human race, but whatever it is, all anyone ever needs to do is yell hello through the screen door and wait for her "Come on in, it's open" reply. I unlatched the screen and followed my nose.

"Anyone home?"

Mom came bustling out from the kitchen. She's Italian but the tall and rail-thin Northern Italian type, and looking at her now makes me wonder why she never got more movie or TV work in her youth. She's still striking and she was beautiful then. She was wearing the *Some Like It Hot* apron I got for her last Christmas, which reminded me that I still hadn't found her anything for this year.

"I saw you on TV this morning," she said by way of greeting, kissing me quickly on both cheeks. "You looked tired."

"I *was* tired."

"And you need a haircut."

"You're right."

"And some new clothes."

"Well, I don't know about that. What's wrong with my clothes?"

"Never mind. Christmas is coming. Maybe Santa can go shopping for you. Sit. Eat. You want soda or Snapple?" She took the wine out of my hand and headed back into the kitchen, leaving me to trail behind. I doubt she'd paused to draw a single breath during the entire exchange.

"I don't have a lot of time, Mom," I protested. "I've got to interview someone a couple blocks from here."

"So, you're still entitled to your lunch break. It's on the table in five minutes. Go say hello to your father; he's in his office." Although my mother is L.A. born and bred and raised a Catholic, I'd grown up hearing what I later identified as a New York Jewish accent. I've never had the courage to ask her why. I once thought it was something to do with a part she'd done. But I've seen everything—my older brother dubbed all her appearances from the fleeting two-second glimpses to the longer three-minutes-in-the-background pieces onto a DVD—and in none of her appearances does she speak with a New York accent. Most of her appearances were non-speaking.

This is not the house I'd grown up in. That was a tiny two-bedroom near the Warner lot. My mom and dad slept in one bedroom, the rest of us in the other. Lots of bunk beds. When the girls finally needed their own room, we moved farther into Burbank, and then once all the kids were out of the house my parents bought this one, which is big enough for most of us to move back in if we ever need to. And, believe me, nothing would please my mother more. The best part about it is the kitchen, a huge rectangle built around a center island, big enough to service a small restaurant—which is good, because my mother practically runs one in the house. Between my brothers and sisters, the grandkids, retired cop friends of my father's, the neighbors and their kids, and my mother's bunco buddies, there are always extra places set at the table for every meal.

My father's office was the converted double garage. I followed the sound of an electric sander to the back of the garden and stepped into my father's domain, which smelled of freshly sawn wood, turpentine, linseed oil, and paint. In the height of the summer it would also smell of citrus blossoms from the small grove of gnarled orange and grapefruit trees that shaded the building. Starting next month, Dad will be bombarded with fruit dropping onto the roof and rolling down the shingles.

My father was a cop all his life; his only hobbies were cleaning his gun and playing ball with us kids. When he retired two years ago, we all worried he was going to spend his days watching *Judge Judy,* shouting at the TV, and dying of boredom. Or at the hands of my mother, who wouldn't have been able to take having him underfoot. But he surprised us all. He spent ten thousand dollars from his retirement fund on every conceivable piece of woodworking equipment available and signed up for a twelve-week woodworking course. Now it's his passion, and he's getting quite a reputation at the craft fairs.

He had his back to me when I stepped in out of the early-afternoon sunshine. He was bent over a woodworking wheel, carefully holding a tiny piece of rosewood no bigger than his little finger against the garnet surface of the sander. I'm told I resemble him and, looking at him—tall, handsome, still with a full head of hair even if it is snow-white—I hope I look like him when I'm his age.

I stood back and waited for him to finish. Never disturb a man when he's working with anything noisy and electrical. He straightened up, the whine of the machine dying away to a murmur. Pushing goggles onto his forehead, he lifted the piece closer to his face to examine it, and then realized I was standing there.

"Saw you on TV this morning," he remarked.

"Looking tired apparently."

"Looking as if you were glad you hadn't eaten breakfast. Bad?"

"Very," I sighed. "Nine bodies: six men, three women. Bloody. Very bloody. Which I suppose is right for an S&M club," I added.

"It used to be a bakery in my day," my father said, handing me the tiny carving. It was a chess piece, a pawn, carved to look like Tony Montana from *Scarface,* complete with machine gun.

I held it to the light, admiring the detail. "This is amazing, Dad. You've really got a talent for this."

"I enjoy it: that's what makes the difference. People recognize passion." He took the piece from my hand and added it to a line of others on the shelf over his workbench. I looked closer; it was a chess set where each piece was a character from a movie, all hand-carved from different types of wood. "Your mother's idea, of course," he said, adding ruefully, "and she was right. She has orders for sixteen sets so far, at—get this!—three thousand dollars a set. I originally wanted to do a set of American presidents. I did a couple of samples and your mother advertised them. We had two inquiries. Then she advertised the movie set and I can't keep up with the orders."

"The workmanship is fabulous."

"It has nothing to do with the workmanship. It's because they're movie related. You can sell any old shit so long as it has a movie connection, you know that." Crossing to the sink, he started to scrub sawdust out of the creases of his palms. "How are you getting on with the Cinema Slayer case? This morning's killings related?"

I picked up the queen chess piece—Marilyn Monroe in her classic pose—and turned it over in my hand. "Dad, I just don't know. It's a multiple murder, all the rest were single killings, and that's throwing me, but one of the dead guys this morning was a movie exec from Anticipation Studios, which is tied to all four of the other vics."

"The effects girl, yesterday. That was Anticipation, wasn't it?"

"That's the fourth tie-in."

"When I heard you'd arrested her ex-boyfriend, I thought it was just a little too neat and far too quick."

"Nah, he's not good for it. Just a bone to throw to the press. We're going to have to street him real soon."

The little intercom set over the sink crackled with Mom's voice, coming from the kitchen. "Lunch is ready."

"Coming," we both called.

"So you got less than six degrees of separation between the five vics . . . sounds like you got one person pulling the trigger."

"Hey, it'd be a lot easier if there'd been a trigger involved. I've got five M.O.s, all a little alike and all a little different. I'm going around in circles."

"You'll figure it out; you've got great instincts. Just follow your gut. But right now you'd better follow it to the table—you know how your mother gets when the food's been served and we're not sitting down."

I'd forgotten how good home-cooked food was and especially how good my mother's was. I didn't get the cooking gene in our family, so I didn't eat as well as I should. The three of us ate in easy silence in the completely enclosed back garden. It was relatively peaceful, the roar of traffic on Coldwater reduced to a dull murmur by the thick grove of avocado, sapote, and persimmon trees the previous owners had put down. They'd matured into a nice, natural sound break. I forked down the last of the homemade cannoli and licked the crumbs up with my finger.

"That was fabulous."

Mom beamed. "You're not eating right. You've lost weight. Hasn't he lost weight, Seth?"

"The boy looks fine to me," my father said evenly. His people are Welsh and he's got that unflappable quality to him. "Besides, at his age he has to watch his weight. Puts on a few pounds now and he'll never get them off, head into middle age with a gut."

"Middle age? He's still a baby!"

I changed the topic before it got ugly. "I saw Little John, Mom, he sends his best."

"How is he? He keeps inviting me to stop by his tattoo parlor. He's even offered me a free tattoo."

My dad and I looked at each other and said nothing.

"He's such a nice boy."

"I think John Trueblood is many things, Mom, but nice is not one of them. I've seen his rap sheet."

"Well, he's always been very nice to me." She looked sidelong at me as she poured the espresso and then passed the plate of lemon peel to go with it. "He's not in any trouble, is he?"

"No, he's not. I had to talk to him yesterday about Ovsanna Moore."

"The Scream Queen?"

"You know her?"

"Peter! Of course I know her. I've never met her, but I used to see her mother around all the time when I was younger. She's one of my big sellers. I've sold a lot of Moore memorabilia over the years. I love those horror fans; they're my best customers. Very discerning. Very loyal."

"Very gullible," my father muttered.

"Listen, buster, are you implying my stuff isn't legit?" She was holding the paring knife she'd used to cut the lemon with and she playfully threatened him with it. "You know damn well, Seth King, that I authenticate every item I sell. And you shouldn't denigrate horror fans; collecting is their hobby just like woodworking is yours. Shame on you. You want any more food today you'd better watch your mouth."

My dad laughed and pushed away from the table. "Yeah," he said, "I'll watch it all right. I'll watch it right on your cheek." And with that he gave her a kiss on her cheek and took his plate into the kitchen.

"Well," I said, "I met with Ovsanna yesterday and then again this morning. I've asked her for a signed photo for you."

"You're a good boy, Peter. I'd love one for myself, but get a couple if you can, and ask her just to sign them, no dedication. Makes them easier to sell," she added.

"Do you have anything of hers or her mother's in stock at the moment?"

She nodded. "A few bits and pieces. Little John buys just about everything of hers as soon as I find it. And he has a lot of her mother's stuff and her grandmother's, too. They were all in the business. Let me go see what I have," she volunteered, and darted away.

I checked my watch. I was late for my appointment. "Hurry, Mom, I've got to go."

My father came back out with another cannoli in his hand. "I swear I've never seen her happier than when she's selling her stuff," he said. "Did she tell you Jack Nicholson himself phoned her last week, wondering if she had anything from *The Cry Baby Killer*? He wanted that and something for that skinny girl he used to date." He shook his head. "Only in Hollywood."

Mom returned with a couple of thick padded envelopes. "I knew I had something. . . ." She started to push the envelope across the table toward me, then suddenly pulled it back. "Are your hands clean?"

I held them up for inspection.

She passed me a pair of white cotton gloves, two sizes too small. "Use these anyway."

Slipping on the gloves as best I could, I pulled out an eight-by-ten black-and-white photo of Ovsanna Moore. The pose was a classic: she was wearing a pillbox hat and her face was half in shadow, a thread of gray smoke curling from a cigarette held between two gloved fingers. It was signed in a looping flowing signature across the bottom right-hand corner.

"For Ronald, with Love and Respect."

I glanced up at my mother. "Any idea who Ronald is?"

"Was, dear, was. Ronald Colman died in 1958."

It took me a second to put it together. "This is Ovsanna's mother?"

"That's Anna Moore. Surely you didn't think it was Ovsanna?"

I looked at the photo again, staring into those dark liquid eyes. I'd stood less than ten inches away from that face and looked into the same eyes just a couple of hours ago. The resemblance was astonishing; the mother's eyes were identical . . . in fact, I could have sworn I was looking at Ovsanna Moore.

The second envelope held a trio of color eight-by-tens. The first showed a partially clad Ovsanna wearing some sort of barbarian chain-mail costume. She was holding a bloody Japanese *katana* above her head in one hand and a thick leash in the other. Attached to the leash were two snarling white lionesses.

"Now *that's* Ovsanna, the daughter. They're from *Bride of the Snake God*," my mother said.

The name rang a bell. "My friend SuzieQ was the snake wrangler on that movie."

"Check out the next picture."

The second picture showed Ovsanna even less partially clad. This time it was some sort of art deco headdress and bra and bikini number made out of a shiny gold metallic fabric. She was standing on one leg, both hands pressed palms flat together over her head. A huge snake was coiled around her body.

"I think that's Spiro Agnew, SuzieQ's boa constrictor," I said. "All her snakes are named after asshole politicians," I added, forgetting to watch my language in front of my mother. She just gave me The Look.

"Yeah? Has she got a Nixon?" my father asked.

"That's the first one she named. A Texas indigo."

"Shoulda been a viper," he muttered. He despised Nixon.

The final image was from a movie I didn't recognize. It showed Ovsanna Moore clad in either black paint or a very sheer body stocking, holding aloft what looked like a bloody heart which she'd obviously just torn from the unfortunate stud lying on the slab before her. Tendrils of steam were coming off the heart.

"That's from *Satan's Succubus*."

I kept going back to the first image, the black-and-white of her mother. "What's this from, do you know? Any idea of the date?"

"It's a generic head shot. Not a studio head shot, though, which means it's something she had done herself. Probably late-thirties, around the time Colman was doing *Prisoner of Zenda* and *Lost Horizon*."

"You said you met Anna Moore when you were in the business . . . ," I prompted. "What was she like?"

"Very sweet, very down-to-earth. It was before you were born and I don't know how old she was then, but she looked amazing. She did a guest appearance on *The Twilight Zone* and I remember Rod Serling asking her how she kept so young. She said she used royal jelly. I thought it was some face cream she imported from England. It was years later when I discovered it's a nutritional supplement made by bees."

"What happened to her?"

"Died sometime in the mid-sixties, I believe. A few years later, Ovsanna appeared. She'd been in school in Europe. I heard she'd had a couple of proposals of marriage over there, including one from a royal, but she refused and came to Hollywood to do what her mother and grandmother had done and keep the dynasty alive."

I rubbed the surface of the picture with my white-gloved hands. "I don't suppose I could hold on to this, could I?"

"No! This is an eighty-dollar picture. But I'll make you a copy." She picked up the photographs and headed back into the house. The larger bedroom was entirely given over to my mother's office. She amazes me. I bought her an iMac for her fiftieth birthday and now she's a high-tech freak. Knows more about computers and scanners and Adobe Photoshop than I ever will. Maybe that's what I could get her for Christmas—a subscription to *MacLife*, or one of those huge widescreen monitors.

My father waited until she was out of earshot before he said, "Ovsanna Moore is tied up in all your murders, isn't she?"

I took a moment to answer. Then I nodded. "Yes . . . yes, she is."

"What does she have to say? Is she talking?"

"She spun me a yarn this morning that, no matter how I examine it, just doesn't hold up."

"Is there a boyfriend in the picture?"

"Girlfriend."

"And money?"

"Lots of money."

"Then she's involved. Or she knows who is. It all comes down to sex and money, Son. This town was built on it, thrives on it. It's the fuel for just about every crime committed here. Just ask yourself the basic question—who stands to benefit?"

CHAPTER TWENTY-SEVEN

Maral was driving, which might have been a mistake because she was obviously distracted, but at least she was keeping her eyes on the road. She talked to me over her shoulder. "This friend of the family . . . is she . . . related to you?" Maral still didn't know the right term to use.

"Yes. By blood."

"Is she one of your clan?"

"No, this woman belongs to no clan. But all my race are related by blood," I said, without a trace of irony. "You really don't understand much about me, do you?" She shook her head and I went on, "You've never asked. I've always gotten the feeling you were more comfortable not knowing."

I had stretched out on the backseat of the SUV and was staring up at the sky through the tinted sunroof. Wisps of high clouds were beginning to gather as we drove south. Now I sat up behind the driver's seat and leaned forward, my lips just inches from Maral's ear.

Adding to her distraction, I pulled her hair back and licked her neck in lazy circles with the tip of my tongue, ending with a gentle kiss before I spoke again. "Does it bother you? My . . . nature?"

"No, it never has. I'm sure you would know if it did. We both would."

"But why not?" I asked. I was genuinely curious. In all the years we'd been together, we'd never talked about it. "Most people would run screaming in terror once they knew the truth. Yet, you accepted me right from the start."

"Because I love you," she said simply.

"And the fact that I am . . . different. Vampyre. You can still love me in spite of that?"

"I love you for who you are, not what you are," she said simply.

The simple statement shocked me to silence. I am not celibate as some of my kind are. I have had lovers through the centuries—sometimes not so many as I wished and sometimes more than I wanted. Ultimately many of them came to know my true nature. A few left, terrified by what I was and what they might become, while those who remained proclaimed fervently that it didn't matter. But it did—in the end, it always mattered. Until just this moment. Looking over Maral's shoulder, watching the reflection of her face in the rearview mirror, hearing the truth in her voice, I knew that it truly did not matter to her: she did indeed love me.

The 10 freeway was at a standstill, not surprising for L.A. in the middle of the day. Maral kept her foot on the brake and drove past downtown doing twenty miles an hour. "I think I started loving you the day I met you—in that coffee shop in the Valley where you bought me breakfast and listened to my story and hired Solgar to defend me. You were so strong and in control and kind, and beautiful on top of that. I wanted to *be* you. I sure didn't wanna be me—poor white trash runaway tryin' to make it in the promised land. And facing a jail sentence just for doin' what I had to do to save my life." Maral's accent slipped when she got emotional.

"All I done was gut that fucker before he got my legs spread, but the cops wouldn't believe me—they didn't like it that I'd tried to slice his head off—and if you hadn't been in that crappy producer's house that morning, tryin' to beat him up—"

"And succeeding, if I remember correctly. Until he pulled the gun on me."

"Well . . . if we hadn't met and you hadn't offered to help, I'd probably still be in jail." Maral kept her eyes on the road, invisible behind her big D&G glasses, but her lips held back the emotion I heard in her voice. "I remember lookin' at you that morning and you were everything I wanted to be: strong and beautiful, confident and kind. I think that was the moment I fell in love with you. You didn't even know me and you did so much for me."

"I knew enough," I said softly. I kissed her lightly again, just behind her ear, feeling the thud of her heartbeat through her entire body.

"You didn't ask anything in return. Just gave me a job and watched over me."

"I'm glad I did."

"Me, too."

"When did you realize there was something different about me?"

"I knew fairly early on that something was amiss. . . ." Her voice trailed away as she remembered. "I think I thought you were a junkie. I remember being so disappointed with that. I very rarely saw you eat; you barely slept and yet were capable of incredible energy throughout the day. I'd seen a lot of that type of behavior when I was growing up. I was convinced you were doing speed or coke or E. When I discovered the truth, as hard as *that* was to believe, it was still a relief." She tilted her head to look sidelong at me. "And believe me, it *was* hard to believe. Remember?"

I nodded. Of course I remembered.

I was doing the damn banshee movie. That was a mistake right from the start.

I didn't want to shoot in L.A. because we didn't want to spend the money. Two million dollars goes a lot further with European crews, especially in the countries that offer tax breaks to lure in foreign production. And somehow I couldn't see banshees living in Simi Valley.

I could see them in Ireland, however, since that's where their legend originated.

In all my years of travel, I'd never been to Ireland; it was too small, too isolated, too Catholic for my tastes. Like my Armenian homeland, it was a country in touch with its folklore; tales of the *Sidhe, selkies, pookas,* and *dullahans* were as accepted as those of the more widely known leprechauns and banshees. The Irish knew my race and called us Bobhan Sith and Dearg Due. This was also Stoker's country, and although I may have shaped the vampyre myth, he was instrumental in creating it. I suppose I never went there for fear of being recognized for what I am.

When I thought of Ireland, I thought of *Ryan's Daughter* and the harsh magnificence of the vistas David Lean captured as his backdrop. That would work fabulously well for *Banshee,* my cheap little Celtic horror film. So when the Irish Film Board agreed to provide partial funding and let me claim their Section 481 tax breaks, we packed our bags and headed for Dublin.

I discovered then why Ireland is green. It rains there. A lot.

That year, Ireland was cold and miserable, struggling through the wettest summer in a decade, according to the weather forecasters, who seemed to take a particular delight in the reports of rain followed by more rain, with added rain. The unrelenting daily storms gave new meaning to the word "deluge." Forget getting any gorgeous Irish exteriors, we couldn't even shoot in the studio—you couldn't hear dialogue over the sleet pounding on the roof.

The studio just south of Dublin was grim beyond belief, with two inches of standing water on the floors. But that didn't matter because the road to the studio had been washed away and we couldn't get the equipment loaded in anyway.

I was almost ready to close the production and move to a drier climate—like the rain forest—when I remembered Roger Corman's studio in the west of Ireland. I'd worked with Roger before and called him, wondering if I could use the facilities. Roger had produced my first three screenplays and once again he came through like the sweetheart he is. I never got a chance to ask him how he ended up with a studio in the mainly Irish-speaking west of Ireland. I knew it was hard to get to, in the far west of the country, miles from any airport, rail line, or even a good road, but if I left Ireland, I'd lose my funding and have to shut down the production.

We started filming only two days later than scheduled. The facilities were perfect and the scenery was extraordinary: dramatic, breathtaking, and gothic. I immediately rewrote some of the interior scenes to shoot them as exteriors.

A few miles west of Roger's place was Achill Island, one of the most westerly points in Europe. Once I saw it I was determined to work it into the climax of the script. The view of the Atlantic Ocean from Achill is wondrous beyond belief and the island itself is spectacular, though technically I suppose it's not entirely an island. It is joined to the mainland by a bridge and is dominated by two mountains, Slieve Croaghaun and Slieve More.

And according to the locals, it's also banshee country.

I don't believe in portents and I never read my horoscope. Maral insists on reading mine to me every day. I keep reminding her that since astrology lost the Thirteenth House all astrology is fatally flawed. But when I learned that this part of the country was where banshees were regularly sighted and heard, I remember thinking that it boded well for the shoot.

I heard a banshee story the very first day I walked on set. The local crew was worried that the script was mocking one of the *Sidhe*. Banshee comes from the Gaelic *bean-sidhe,* woman of the *Sidhe,* a fairy woman. Irish fairy folk are not the cuddly three-wishes type Tinker Bells from children's stories. They're dark, savage creatures who share a lot in common with their East European and Nordic ancestors. As far as the crew was concerned, the banshees were responsible for the failure of the De Lorean car factory—the place where they'd made the *Back to the Future* car. Apparently its fate was doomed from the moment two ancient fairy thornbushes were uprooted from in front of the manufacturing plant. Maral did a little research and discovered that it was actually true: John De Lorean ended up bankrupt and the factory in Dunmurry had closed eighteen months after it opened.

I've never encountered a ghost or felt a presence, never seen a demon or a spirit. I've met plenty of people who have, and much of what they claimed they saw was either natural causes . . . or they'd had an encounter with my race or one of the other clans that walk the shadows of this earth. As Hamlet says, "There are more things . . ." and blood drinkers are not the only other evolution of man. Every myth and legend has its roots in a reality, and on that island in the west of Ireland I came to believe that perhaps the *Sidhe,* like the vampyre, really do exist. Maybe they are simply another evolutionary branch on mankind's tree.

We'd had production problems from the moment we arrived in Ireland, but once we started shooting on Achill they increased tenfold. Despite the best movie mythology, there are no such things as *cursed* sets. Put upwards of a hundred people together, with wires, electricity, machinery in unfamiliar surroundings, and you'll find that a few accidents happen.

But on the *Banshee* shoot, there were more than a few.

We lost one entire set to a fire . . . a fire that started at dead of night and the security cameras show nothing. The leading man drank himself into a stupor and sat down on a straight razor . . . which was open at the time. I'm told his scream would have done justice to the legendary banshee. Two stuntmen were injured in what should have been a simple car jump. The car flew farther than expected and ended up sinking in a chunk of bogland. The two men were dragged from the windows just moments before the car disappeared. My leading lady's husband turned up on set and discovered his wife in bed with a woman—his mistress. One accusation led to another, which led to the truth, and a three-way brawl. My star was so bruised I had to shoot his close-ups in the dark.

Anything—no, everything—that could go wrong did. Continuity went out the window—the weather never stayed the same long enough to complete an exterior scene. I'd be delivering my lines in a downpour and when we came in for coverage we'd have cloudless skies and blazing sun. The house we were using for exteriors lost all its roof tiles in a howling wind and we had to wait a week for matching tiles to come in from Shannon. The ones that arrived were the wrong color.

And then I had the accident.

In a life as long as mine, accidents occur. I've broken my left leg twice, my right arm twice, left wrist once, cracked my ribs innumerable times, been stretched on the rack, burned, scalded, and drowned. Luckily, my race is tough and our heightened metabolism ensures that we heal far more quickly than the human kind. That knowledge sometimes makes us arrogant . . . and foolish.

It was our day off, a Sunday morning. The location manager had told me about a spot he'd found halfway up Slieve More—which in English means "the Big Mountain"—and I wanted to see it for myself before I decided on using it for a scene we'd be shooting at the end of the week. He'd drawn me a map and said it was an easy climb once I got to the car park. The weather was perfect, the sky the palest of pale blues. I threw on some jeans, a thermal tee, and my hiking boots and drove to the base of the mountain.

By noon I'd climbed about a thousand feet, almost halfway to the peak. The view across the island towards the Atlantic was extraordinary. I could imagine the early Irish standing there looking out over the ocean and wondering what lay on the other side. Suddenly the stories of monks and sailors discovering America centuries before Columbus were credible.

And then the weather changed.

From brilliant cloudless sunshine without a breath of wind it turned cool, then cloudy, then cold. Then it started to rain. Not the fine misty "soft rain" that the Irish like to brag about, but cold, bitter, steel needles that beat on me like a carpenter's nail gun. In seconds I was as drenched as if I'd walked into the ocean fully clothed. And then the flesh-stinging hail began.

I should have stayed where I was. I should have hunkered down against one of the stone boulders and spent a miserable couple of hours wet and shivering. That's what I should have done.

But life is full of should-haves.

And most accidents are caused by should-haves and insteads.

I thought about shape-shifting. I wouldn't have had any trouble getting down the hill as a wolf or large dog, even with the downpour washing the path away down the side of the mountain. But the Change would have exhausted me, left me with muscles cramping and back spasms. I had to work the next day; I couldn't very well do a balls-out fight scene against my mythical celluloid banshees while I was bent over in pain. And the last time I'd taken on a lupine form, I'd had to wax a residual moustache twice in a week.

So I wrapped my arms around my body, dipped my head, and headed down the mountain. I'd taken maybe a dozen steps when it felt as though something pushed me from behind. I knew there was nothing there; my hearing is too acute, even over the sleet and rain, not to hear someone coming near. But when I turned to look behind me, I slipped.

And fell.

And continued to fall. Sixty feet down the side of the mountain. Rolling over and over again on scree and razor-sharp shale until I smashed against a huge boulder and landed ass over teakettle in a river of mud.

The lacerations were excruciating. My left arm was shattered, although strangely enough I didn't feel pain there. My left leg had snapped in two midway up my calf, the bone jutting out at an impossible angle. Two of my ribs were cracked, one had punctured a lung, and a third felt like it was lodged in my diaphragm. My collarbone was broken.

My body went to work immediately. Lying broken in a muddy grave, organs and flesh began to pulse and stretch, muscles blossoming, tendons coiling around pliable bones as they began to reconnect and my vampyre physiology attempted to heal itself. It was only seconds before the process started, but I swear, just like the movies, my life flashed in front of my eyes. Well, parts of it. Not all four hundred and fifty years. That frightened me more than the pain. I'd been wounded and hurt many times before, but I always knew instantly that I'd recover. Now, if I was seeing pieces of my life, what did that mean? Was this the time I wouldn't heal?

Cities flashed through my mind: Paris, Berlin, St. Petersburg, Istanbul, Marrakesh. All places I'd lived and been happy. And I immediately regretted the countries I'd never seen. Tibet, Peru, Chile, the Galápagos Islands, Argentina. Was I never going to see the turtles or ride the Pampas?

The healing process was more painful than the injuries. I would have screamed with the pain but I didn't have the strength. Then the cold set in and with that, no sensation at all. Brittle cold but no pain. I could hear flesh rend and meld, bones grind and knit, but I grew to realize I wasn't going to heal; the damage was too extensive. The last time I'd really fed had been weeks before, and I didn't have the nutrients I needed to sustain the healing process. The energy my body was expending trying to heal was so great, the effort alone was killing me.

Once I died, no one would know what had happened to me. The cliché that vampyres turn to dust is not so far from the truth. When those of us who live past our first century die, putrefaction sets in immediately. The same heightened metabolism that sustains us over hundreds of years breaks down with extraordinary rapidity.

Not into some dusty, desiccated form, but rather into a liquid, gelatinous sludge. If anyone came looking for me, they'd find nothing but an unexplainable luminescent goo slithering down the mud streams to the ocean.

I don't know how long I lay there retracing my past, every memory taking me closer to death. I sensed when the images reached the middle of the sixteenth century and my Armenian homeland I would die.

I was somewhere in the early seventeenth century, in Constantinople, when Maral found me.

She'd gone in search of me as soon as the skies opened up and had found my rental car in the car park at the bottom of Slieve More. There were several trails she could have taken, but knowing me as well as she did, she took the steepest, the one that went all the way to the peak. Later, she would say that as she started to climb the muddy track that meandered up the side of Slieve More, she heard what sounded like a young woman crying, the sound a cross between a piteous sob and a howl of triumph.

It was probably just the wind.

Lying on my back, staring up into the heavens, I saw her shape appear before me. I will remember the look on Maral's face until the day I die—a palette of horror, fear, love, and rage. I watched her mouth move, but her words were lost; my hearing was fading with the rest of me. She pulled off her coat and draped it across me as she frantically pulled out her cell phone. The last thing I wanted was to be examined by a doctor. With a tremendous effort of will I caught hold of the hand holding the phone and pulled it away from her face.

Don't, I mouthed.

Her lips moved and, although I was unable to hear her, I got the gist. She thought I was raving and was prepared to ignore me. I'm not sure what caught her attention, but suddenly she was no longer looking at my face: she was staring at my left arm. I couldn't move my head to see what she was seeing, but I had a good idea. The sleeves of my T-shirt had ripped away as I scraped down the shale in my fall. Maral was watching movement beneath my skin as my muscles and bones shifted and attempted to fuse back together. It would have looked like fat worms crawling beneath my skin. She looked into my face, then pressed two fingers of her right hand against my cheek. I was unaware until that moment that I had shattered my cheekbone. Maral could see—and feel—the delicate bones moving together, desperately trying to fit back into place. Together we both looked down at my leg, and Maral's face paled as the protrusion angled back toward the top of my tibia, cells reaching for cells to reconnect. She turned back to face me, staring at the twitch and curl of my broken ribs as they writhed beneath my skin. Then she leaned forward, her face inches from mine. I could see my eyes reflected in hers—the whites of mine were suffused with red. And although I still could not hear her words, I could trace them on her lips. "What are you?" she asked.

"Vampyre," I said eventually. "Dying," I added.

I was beginning to lose detail from my vision. My sight was darkening around the edges, so I knew the end was on me. I saw Maral lift a ragged triangle of scree—the same stone that had sliced my flesh—and slash it across her wrist. Even through my numbed senses, I caught the meaty-rich odor of fresh blood . . . and then Maral pressed her wrist to my mouth.

That moment, that sensation was indescribable. I will carry the vivid, indelible memory of it to my final grave.

I couldn't control myself; I started Changing. My fangs slipped into place, my red eyes disappeared into slits, my nails elongated into claws as the fresh blood coursed through me. The sight would have terrified a lesser person, driven them back, but Maral kept her hand pressed against my mouth . . . and later she told me that my fangs, both top and bottom, had locked into her flesh, so even if she had wanted to get away, she couldn't.

Deuteronomy 12:23 is right: blood is life. And Maral's blood healed me.

My highly specialized vampyre metabolism did what it was designed to do—extract the nutrients from the blood trickling from the cut in Maral's wrist, nutrients necessary to sustain and maintain my form. In less than twenty minutes, bones had healed, ribs knitted, torn flesh visibly melted shut, bruises faded away to leave pristine skin. Later, we worked out that I must have fed on close to two pints of blood—enough to leave Maral reeling with shock and dizziness, but by that time I was strong again, stronger than I'd been for a very long time, perhaps in half a century or more. I cradled her in my arms when she swayed and now our positions were reversed. I held her gently against me on the wet ground.

This time when she spoke, I heard every word. "You're a vampyre?"

"Yes." I took her coat from my shoulders and draped it over her, careful not to touch her wrist, which was bruised and swollen with my puncture and the ragged slash she'd inflicted on herself. I brought her hand to my lips and licked at the damage, the natural antiseptic in my saliva healing the wound.

"Another few moments," I said, "and I would have been gone. You saved me. How did you know what do to?"

Her skin was deathly pale, and for a moment I feared I had taken too much. "Everyone knows what an injured vampyre needs," she muttered, eyes flickering.

"How?"

"You see it in the movies all the time."

We've been inseparable ever since.

CHAPTER TWENTY-EIGHT

STUDIO CITY
1:00 P.M.

Her name was Milla Taylor.

It wasn't her real name, but that was to be expected; this was Hollywood, after all. Where Bernie Schwartz became Tony Curtis and Krekor Ohanian is Mike Connors and Reginald Keith Dwight is Sir Elton John. She'd been born Prudence Hotchkiss in Dillon, Montana, where there were more women than men in a population totaling less than four thousand and the average household income was $26,389. Working for Thomas DeWitte in Beverly Hills, California, making $1,500 a week, must have been like winning the lottery in comparison. She was twenty-three years old, looked about seventeen from her photo ID, and didn't have so much as a traffic ticket on record.

I sat outside the apartment on Chandler and scanned the brief statement she'd made. It was stark enough, written in that peculiar language people use when talking to officialdom. Watch *Judge Judy;* you'll see ordinary people turn into Perry Mason. Milla Taylor said that Ovsanna Moore had forced her way into the Anticipation offices, threatened Anthony, the bodyguard, pushed her way into DeWitte's office, called him a *stupid prick*—I couldn't argue with that—and then told him that if he fucked up one more time he was gone. "Gone and never coming back" was the direct quote. It was hardly a death threat, but unfortunately DeWitte *was* gone and never coming back and so now it took on a new significance.

Taylor's apartment building was a nondescript grey stucco two-story box with a brown Japanese pagoda-style roof. A double set of glass doors formed a security entrance, with the renters' names and apartment numbers in a metal frame on the side wall. You picked up an intercom, keyed in the apartment number, and the phone rang in the apartment so the tenant could buzz you in. At least that's what you were supposed to do if you wanted to gain access. The broken door-jamb on the interior door made it a moot point. I checked for Taylor's apartment number, grabbed the handle, and pulled the door open.

I was facing a central courtyard. Directly in front of me was a fountain in the shape of a Buddha, spitting water out of his smiling mouth into the little leaf-clogged moat around him. Behind him was a kidney-shaped swimming pool with a few nylon-webbed chaise lounges lined up, three on one side, two on the other. A bleached blonde with skin the color of old leather sat with her back to me on one of the lounges, copies of *Variety* and the *Reporter* spread out in front of her. Her hair was in curlers and she was wearing a lime green one-piece bathing suit and high-heeled mules. In December. Only in L.A.

Taylor's apartment was number 27, so I started up the staircase to my left. I'd taken four steps when the blonde stopped me with Selma Diamond's voice.

"Help you?" She was out of the chaise and at my back before I even turned around, standing at the foot of the stairs with her hand on the railing. She could have been doing movie trailers; this was a forty-cigarette, bottle of whiskey a day voice, and even from four feet away I got the yeasty odor of something malt and alcoholic.

I also got a better look at her . . . she must have been sixty-five if she was a day. From the back I'd placed her at forty, but the crêpelike skin on her arms and legs gave her away. That and the face that was slightly off-kilter.

"Police, ma'am."

"I can tell." She squinted at me. "Help you?" she asked again, peering at me in the way shortsighted people do when they don't wear their glasses.

"Yes, ma'am. . . ." I stepped back down to her level. "You live here?"

"Show me a badge first, Officer. I've lived here long enough to know you're not going up those stairs without some identification." Well, she may have had a few beers in her, but she sure wasn't out of it.

"Yes, ma'am." I badged her and she actually took the time to lean in and read it, something most people don't do. "I'm Detective King."

She smiled, a perfect, probably twenty-thousand–dollar smile in a ten-dollar face. "Peter King, Angela's boy? The one that pulled that kid out of the river?"

"Why, yes, ma'am. You know my mother?"

"Angie and I were in the business together, young man. You don't recognize me, do you?"

Even without the lift, I'd never seen her face before. But I needed her cooperation, no sense in hurting her feelings. "You know, I do. But I'm terrible with names. Unless I've got them writ-ten down in my notebook, I just can't remember. You were on that sitcom, weren't you?" If she was sixty-five, there had to have been some sitcom on the air when she was working.

"Oh, I did a couple a spots on *Gomer Pyle* and *Mr. Ed*, just under-five stuff, but you probably remember me from *Captain Kangaroo* or

Ben Casey. Those were guest star roles. Your mom and I did a couple of features together. How is she?"

"She's just fine, ma'am, thank you for asking. I've just had lunch with her."

"You be sure and tell her Marie Chilcote said hello."

I snapped my fingers. "Of course, I remember now. It's a pleasure to meet you, Ms. Chilcote." I pulled out my notebook. "Do you mind if I ask you a few questions?"

"Not at all. What do you need to know?"

"You live here, right?"

"I own the building, young man. My husband, Alfred, passed away six years ago and left me to manage it. I'm right there in Number One, facing the pool."

"I'm here to talk to one of your tenants, Milla Taylor in Twenty-seven, but maybe you can tell me a little about her first. I guess not a lot goes on here that you don't know about."

"You got that right. I keep my shades open and I can see out from my living room and my kitchen. I like to know what's going on."

"Do you mind if we sit down?" I followed her back to her chaise lounge and pulled up another one next to it. "What can you tell me about Ms. Taylor?"

"Well, when I first met her she'd just moved here from one of the cowboy states—Wyoming, Montana, one of those maybe . . . South Dakota? It was someplace she wanted to get away from, she said. Didn't know a soul in town. Came for the glitter, you know. Reminded me of myself. I'm originally from Cody, Wyoming, just west of Bighorn. I offered to cut her rent down a bit if she wanted to help me manage this place, but she wasn't interested. Wanted to work in the business. So I made a few calls, fixed her up with a friend of mine at the D.G.A. who uses temps to input data on the computer all day. Next thing I know she's got a good job working as Thomas DeWitte's secretary at Anticipation Studi—" She stopped, eyes widening. "That's what this is about," she said, in a voice they could hear down the block. Unless Milla Taylor was deaf, she'd know by now I was downstairs. "DeWitte turned up dead in that S&M place." She leaned forward and I buried my head in my notebook to stave off the reek of alcohol and old cigarettes. "Is she a suspect?"

"I'm just taking statements, Mrs. Chilcote."

"It's Kater. Chilcote was my maiden name and that's the one I worked under. Well, I wouldn't be surprised if she's a suspect. She sure changed once she got that job, and not for the better, let me tell you." Her voice got even louder. I was surprised Ms. Taylor hadn't stepped out on the balcony to shut her up.

"What do you mean?"

"Oh, the way she dresses, the way she looks. I think that Thomas DeWitte was a bad influence. And she went from not knowing anybody in town to knowing some pretty creepy-looking characters. Suddenly she wanted to be an actress. Got herself a manager." She turned the statement into an accusation. "We didn't have managers in my day. Most of us didn't even have agents. Now, even nobodies have managers, agents, and entertainment lawyers."

For my brief flirtation with fame, I'd once had all three. Did that make me a nobody? "Well, you did say she wanted to be an actress. Maybe she thought a manager would be able to get her some work. What about these disreputable looking people? Drug addicts, working girls, that type of person?"

"Oh no, hell no. Everything is aboveboard here . . . not like just down the road where they shoot porno in two of the upstairs apartments. You should raid that place."

"I'll make a note of it. What about Ms. Taylor?" I persisted. "What sort of people does she hang out with?"

"Well, there's one guy; he's real freaky. There's just something about him that bothers me. Every time he sees me watching him, he disappears. I don't know if he waits for her outside the building or what, but he's like a ghost the way he shows up and then he's gone. And it doesn't help that he's so white. Creeps me out."

"He's so white? You mean, he's conservative? Waspy? Republican?" She was pretty observant for a daytime drinker; I'll give her that. Maybe she'd like a job as a profiler.

"No, white. Skin. An albino."

Something cold gripped the pit of my stomach. "An albino. You're sure?"

"Yeah. Think *Da Vinci Code.* You know, the monk. White hair, red eyes. White skin. He was a good actor, that guy. Paul somebody. Married to that beautiful actress."

"Bettany. Paul Bettany, married to Jennifer Connolly," I said absently. "And this man you've seen with Milla Taylor is an albino?"

"You're not listening, Detective King. I haven't seen him with her; I've just seen him hanging around her apartment waiting for her."

I had my gun out and was moving before she finished her sentence. Eva Casale, the effects girl, had been seen with an albino, and now she was dead. . . .

Halfway along the second-floor balcony I knew I was too late. The door to Apartment 27 was open and the eye-watering stink of blood and feces fought with the Valley smog. I pressed my back against the wall to the left of the door and pushed it farther open with the barrel of my gun. A score of flies buzzed out, swirled in the air, and then flew back into the room again. I risked a quick darting look inside before I stepped in and cleared all three rooms.

Milla Taylor was waiting for me in the living room, but she wouldn't be giving me a statement. She wouldn't be going back to one of those cowboy states, either. At least, not in one piece. Her body was stretched out on one of three overstuffed chairs facing a chrome and glass entertainment center.

Her head, perched on top of the JVC 26-inch TV and dripping blood down its screen, was the entertainment. Well . . . Milla Taylor finally got her wish to appear on TV.

Chapter Twenty-Nine

Palm Springs.

Depending upon whom you believe, the area was originally named Agua Caliente by early Spanish explorers or Agua Caliente by the Agua Caliente Band of Cahuilla Indians. Either way, it translates into "Hot Water," and I was pretty sure that's what we were heading into. I tapped Maral on the shoulder as we passed Mr. Rex and Dinny, the Cabazon Dinosaurs Claude Bell built in the sixties. They started out as a roadside attraction and now they're a "museum" teaching Intelligent Design. Evidently Noah had the dinosaurs on his ark.

"You know why I hate Palm Springs?" I said softly.

"You're not gay?" Maral suggested.

"Very funny."

"Well, maybe not gay enough. I don't know . . . it's too hot? You don't play golf?"

I ignored her. "Starting in the thirties, the town was known as

'The Playground of the Stars.' The Hollywood elite came down here in droves to stay at the Desert Inn or El Mirador and party at the Palm House and the Mink and Manure Club. Any actor who didn't want the studio to know what he or she was doing escaped to Palm Springs. There was even a railway that ran right into town. They called it the 'Station from Hell' because its location was originally so isolated. Then, in the fifties, they opened the Spa Hotel with the hot-springs mineral baths and the town was booming. Sinatra bought here, Kirk Douglas, Cary Grant, Lucille Ball, Clark Gable. Bob Hope was honorary mayor."

"So what's not to like? Didn't you used to know some of these people?"

"I've always had friends here. Liberace and Dean and Jane Russell. I also have clan. And there are others who are like me that I don't control. They've been here since my 'mother' was alive. They came for the privacy, too. But not just to escape Louis B. or Hedda Hopper. They came to be themselves. I've always hated Palm Springs because it's where every vampyre in Hollywood came to hide out and . . . well . . . do what vampyres do: drink blood. This town had a reputation for debauchery that would have put Sodom and Gomorrah to shame . . . and no, I wasn't there for that," I added quickly. "I'm not that old."

"I know that."

"But there is one here who is," I said very softly. "She's the real reason my kind came here. To worship."

My left hand, resting lightly on Maral's shoulder, twitched and suddenly my claws appeared. If she noticed, she never reacted. I sat back on the soft leather and moved directly behind her so she wouldn't see my reflection in the mirror.

"When you say 'worship' . . . ?" Unconsciously she put her foot on the brake and our speed began to slow.

"I mean worship. As in pray to. Honor. Revere. As in, make sacrifices to."

Traffic was backed up most of the way. We stayed on the 10 to the 111 and Palm Canyon Drive, driving in a sudden silence while I watched the farm of wind turbines, wondering why some were rotating wildly and others were completely still. They looked like circus performers marching on stilts in a line across a barren dirt stage. The air was clean and crisp, and the colors the sun threw on San Gorgonio Mountain were enough to distract me for a minute.

Maral finally spoke. "Are you in danger?"

"Some." There was little point in lying.

"Can you tell me what's going on?"

"If I knew, I would," I said truthfully. "I'm really not certain. At the moment, I'm just following a hunch."

"Vampyre's intuition?"

"Something like that."

We finally came to the road I'd been looking for. What should have been a two-hour drive had taken four, and my mood wasn't improving. "Turn here."

"What's your hunch based on, can you tell me that?" I watched as she took one hand off the wheel and eased the little nickel-plated Colt out from under her seat and onto her lap.

"I lied to Peter King yesterday when you came in and found me alone in the house. I didn't just forget to call you for no reason; I forgot because I walked into a room full of my clan—all the Vampyres of Hollywood I'm supposed to control. I can't tell you how bizarre that was, all of them together at one time. That rarely happens. They came out of hiding because they were frightened for themselves. The killings, first of the vampyres and then of my staff, had convinced them that the police and press investigation were going to reveal my true nature. They gave me a choice: find the killer or destroy my clan and retire."

"Retire! You mean—"

"Officially, I would die. Unofficially, I would go into hiding for a century or two."

"And if you refused?"

"They would not allow me to refuse. The Vampyres of Hollywood will always protect themselves. We've done it before. We've destroyed clans, forced actors and actresses to die or retire in order to protect ourselves."

"But what is it about these deaths that's got them so terrified?" Maral wondered.

"It's the nature of this Hunter," I said, allowing the pieces to fall into place as I spoke. "The nature of the killings. They deliberately target the vampyre and human halves of my existence. Someone is determined to not only destroy me but destroy my world also. So, the vampyres gathered to give me my ultimatum."

"How can this hunter know so much about you?" Maral asked. She frowned and then her eyes flared in understanding. "You think it's another vampyre," Maral whispered, arriving at the same conclusion I had earlier.

I nodded. "It's a possibility. But if another vampyre has declared war on me, he would need permission from the most senior vampyre in North America. Vampyre wars are very carefully controlled now; previous wars in the Crimea and the Transvaal almost eliminated the race."

"But you are powerful . . . very powerful," she said, a note of doubt in her voice.

I shook my head. "Powerful by human standards, but not especially so as vampyres go. Remember, I'm not even that old. Solgar is twice my age. I have influence, though. I am Chatelaine of Hollywood and, inasmuch as Hollywood is one of the wealthiest cities in the world, that gives me extraordinary power. As Chatelaine I am entitled to take a tithe of all earnings of the vampyres under my protection."

I could hear Maral swallow. "Remind me to ask you for a raise."

"Hiding it from the IRS is the hardest part. But Solgar has had centuries of practice. He was the Medicis' banker."

We came into town and turned right on Via Escuelo. "When

this is over," I said brightly, "we'll come back here another day and I'll show you Albert Frey's Tramway Gas Station, the Neutra House, and my favorite, Bob Hope's flying saucer house."

"I'll look forward to it," Maral said, in a voice that suggested she didn't.

"Keep on this road. It'll take us into the foothills near the Agua Caliente reservation."

"And this 'friend of the family' we're going to see . . . this person who hates you—"

"Is no person."

"Is she the one your kind came to worship, to honor?"

"Oh yes, she is vampyre royalty. We are going to see a genuine legend and possibly the oldest creature on this planet: Lilith, the Night Hag."

CHAPTER THIRTY

BEL AIR
2:00 P.M.

I called the meat wagon and then cooled my heels waiting for Jake
Long to get to Milla Taylor's apartment. Mrs. Kater was pretty
concerned . . . about the room.

The CSI techs got there about the same time Jake did. I filled
them in with what I knew—but that didn't amount to much. The
ME was of the opinion that Milla Taylor's head had been ripped off,
very similar to a couple of the decapitations in Rough Trade.

"Ripped?" I asked.

"As in pulled," he said.

The rest of the apartment was clean and the door hadn't been
forced. Jake was booting up her computer when I left. I told him to
keep an eye out for an albino, or indeed any guy with pale skin, and
said I'd meet him back at the office. I had a call to make.

Milla Taylor's murder just didn't tie in to any of the other killings. She wasn't a movie star; she wasn't close to Ovsanna. She'd only worked for Thomas DeWitte a short time. The only person who had even the slightest motive to want her out of the way was Ovsanna.

It was so obvious it screamed setup.

Or maybe I just wanted it to seem that way.

And there was one other tiny factor . . . we already had Milla's statement and there was no way that Ovsanna even knew that she had come forward.

I tried Ovsanna's numbers, the house and the cell, and got voice mail on both. I'd come back over the hill on Beverly Glen, so it wasn't that much out of my way to drive back up Stone Canyon. Maybe she was holed up in the house, screening her calls.

There were no reporters outside the gates, which were firmly closed, and I guessed, even as I was pulling up, that Ovsanna would not be there. I was leaning across to hit the intercom when a shape detached itself from the bush and set my heart thumping. "Jesus, Eddie, I nearly shot you!" In truth, I'd been nowhere near my gun.

Steady Eddie lifted his Canon EOS Digital and I heard the motor whirr as it fired five quick shots. "Decorated police hero Detective Peter King arrives at the home of Ovsanna Moore with a search warrant," he intoned.

Steady Eddie Albert is one of this city's top paparazzi. If you've seen this month's hot starlet getting out of a limo sans underwear, you've seen Eddie's work. He was the one who got the close-up of the Oscar in Jason Eddings's ass as they pulled Eddings out of the limo. Must have made twenty-five thousand dollars off that one shot. He spends it all on food and suspenders. Eddie weighs 300 pounds if he's an ounce and he's got a collection of suspenders for every day of the year. He needs them to keep his size 50 pants up over his gut. Today they were red-and-white diagonal stripes with turquoise stones on the bronze clips. Steady Eddie is probably my age; he looks ten years older. He's completely bald but cultivates one of those long drooping moustaches that makes him look perpetually miserable.

"You're wasting your time, Detective; she's gone."

Something must have shown on my face, because Eddie took a quick step back and grabbed another couple of shots. "Frustration shows on the face of Detective Peter King—"

"Shut up, Eddie. I suppose you were here when she left? I suppose you got it all on film?"

"That's my job." He held up a second camera he had dangling around his neck. This one was a Nikon with a telephoto lens.

"Anyone else still inside? Her assistant?"

"Nope, her assistant left about twenty minutes before she did, driving the black SUV."

"What time was this?"

"Around noon. The other guys quit when they saw the SUV take off, but I guessed it was a ruse and stuck around."

"A *ruse*?"

"Yeah, a ruse. It's a good word, isn't it? I've been reading a lot of Dorothy L. Sayers. Lord Peter Wimsey. You got a lot of time on your hands with this job."

"Well, what was Ovsanna Moore driving when she perpetrated this ruse?"

"Silver Mercedes SLR McLaren. The $450,000 model. Sort of hard to keep a low profile in that one."

"Anyone else coming or going? Anyone still in the house?"

"There's been no movement, but I don't think they'll be gone long."

"How do you make that out?"

"No luggage." He grinned. I was guessing he hadn't seen a dentist's chair in years. "I got some images of them leaving the house." He called up a series of blurred shots. "Right at the limit of the zoom. But you can see that neither of them put cases in either car. They're either staying local or they're coming back."

"Shit!" I banged the steering wheel in frustration.

Eddie fiddled with the back of the camera and then said slyly, "We could go inside and check out the grounds, though. I've got the code to the gate."

"You've got what?" My blood started to boil. After everything I'd said to both those women about protecting themselves and someone goes and gives Steady Eddie access to the yard? What the hell were they thinking? "Who gave it to you?"

"Well, no one really gave it to me. I sort of took it." Eddie leaned in my car window and turned the back of the Canon toward me. Images flickered by on the large LCD and then stopped at one particular shot. What looked like a Lexus 470 was partially in frame, stopped outside the gates.

The next image showed a hand stretched out the open window, index finger pointed.

The next image was a close-up of the same finger pressing on the keypad. Eddie must have set the camera to burst mode. Each subsequent image showed the finger pressing a different button. I had him scroll back and forth through the images until I was reasonably sure of the sequence. "Very impressive," I said, taking the camera out of his hand, and turning it away from him. I hit the menu button, found FORMAT, and then waited while the gigabyte card reformatted. Without saying a word, I handed it back to him. "Now, beat it."

"Hey, I thought I could go inside with you, grab a few images of the gardens, maybe get a couple of shots through the windows—"

"Eddie. That would be trespassing."

"I could always cut you in—"

"Don't say another word! Even what you're thinking now is illegal. Now get outta here before I find something to arrest you for. Loitering, maybe. Move!" I shoved open my car door and that pushed him back onto the street. He looked like he was going to cry. I waited while he got into his car, a sixties Ford Fairlane with a new paint job, and drove down the street—giving me the finger as he passed—before I turned back to the keypad and hit the combination I'd memorized. One five five zero. It worked. The electric gates clicked and started to open. "Thanks, Eddie," I murmured, and jumped in the Jag and drove through. The gates closed behind me.

I wondered how long it was going to take him to discover I'd blanked his images.

The geese started cackling and calling as I drove up the driveway and parked outside the front door. I sat in the car for a moment, watching the windows, looking for signs of movement, but finding none. Finally, I climbed out of the car and walked around the house. There wasn't anyone on the property, and the house was sealed up tight. No back door left open for the housekeeper. I could see in through the windows. Everything was neat and tidy, much as it had been when I'd left this morning. Ovsanna had left a few lights on, which told me she didn't intend to return any time soon.

I needed to find her . . . either to keep her alive or to keep her from killing someone else.

I tried Ovsanna's cell again; it went to voice mail. As long as the phone was on I could track her location, but getting the phone company to help without a court order would take too long. I'd gotten the plates on the SUV when I'd interviewed Ovsanna at the studio and I'd seen the Mercedes parked outside the garage the night Maral had called me in a panic. It was brand-new, with the temporary registration taped on the front window and the dealer's ubiquitous logo on a business card beneath it. That made things easy for me. I called Auto Steigler in Encino and asked to speak to Ms. Schyjer.

"This is Renee."

"It's Peter, Renee, a voice from the past."

"Peter King? You son of a bitch, how are you? What's it been, three years? Saw you on the news this morning. You looked tired."

"Thanks. Look, I need a favor."

"Well, you haven't changed a bit, have you? Still get right to the point. Honest to God, Peter, I don't know how you get away with it."

"It's my enduring charm. And my long memory. What was it you said the last time I saw you . . . something about owing me big-time?"

"I do. You know I do. Kenny would still be on the streets if it weren't for you. So what can I do for you? Loan you a car to impress the next Mrs. King?"

"Something a lot simpler. For you, at least. I need the password for the Teletrac system on a car you just sold in the past couple of weeks. A Silver McLaren SLR."

"Jesus, Peter, that's Ovsanna Moore's car. She's got the only silver McLaren we've sold in the last six months. I processed the paperwork myself."

"Can you help me?"

"Is she in trouble?" I said nothing, and she filled in the rest herself. "This is about the Cinema Slayer, isn't it? You were at her house this morning." Anxiety flooded her voice and I knew Ovsanna had another hard-core fan. Made my job easier.

"I need to find her, Renee, and I need to find her fast. That's why I'm not going through channels. I need that password."

"Hold on."

She put me on hold and I listened to Weird Al Yankovic sing two verses of "Weasel Stomping Day" before she came back on the line. One of these days I've got to download that song.

"You still there, Peter? I've got the password."

"Go ahead."

"It's 'lifeeverlasting'. Lowercase, all one word, no spaces. Strange choice, huh?"

"There's a lot about Ovsanna Moore that's strange, Renee. This is the least of it."

Once I had the password, the rest was easy. I called Del Delaney and asked him get into the Teletrac system, and to do it on his personal laptop rather than the department computers. I was sailing into murky legal waters now. There was going to be a whole lot of explaining to do when this was over. But if I solved the case, then I was golden, and if I didn't . . . well, then nothing much mattered.

It took Del about six minutes: Ovsanna's Mercedes was parked at the Airport Valet on Sepulveda and 96th.

I sent Milmore over to brace the valet company and I headed back to the office to talk to the Captain. My cell buzzed just as I pulled into the lot. It was Milmore. "She didn't take a plane, pardner. No tickets in her name or the girlfriend's name, no one matching their description on any specified flight, commercial or private." Milmore went to the University of Wyoming in Laramie. He talks like an educated cowpoke. "It's a fancy car. The valet remembers that she didn't have any luggage. Left her car and drove off in a black SUV driven by a blonde. When the valet asked what time he should have the car ready for her, she said maybe later tonight. She's gonna call him."

"She didn't tell him where she was going, did she?"

"Nope. But she did tell the blonde. Valet heard her say it'd take 'em about two hours to get there. They're headin' to Palm Springs, pardner."

CHAPTER THIRTY-ONE

Almost every house in Palm Springs has some tenuous claim to fame: Einstein slept there or Zanuck died there or that's where Elvis shot up the TV with his gun. This house was originally owned by the King. At one time, he had four homes in Palm Springs—with a different girl in each of them. My "mother" had known Elvis in the fifties; he'd sung "Love Me Tender" to her at a birthday party in the Sands in Vegas once. I'd never been tempted to Turn him; he was just too damaged, and I'd learned by my mistake with Rudy.

This house was Elvis's hideaway. The one not even the Memphis Mafia knew about.

It's a fortress really. Three stories of rock and steel built into the side of a mountain, surrounded by a fifteen-foot stone wall with a moat on the other side. Elvis had kept an alligator in the moat. The last time I'd been here, it had been stocked with red-bellied piranhas.

The main two gates looked like the doors from a pueblo church; the distressed and sun-faded wood concealed the solid steel core. As far as I knew, it had been decades since the gates had last opened. To the left of the main gates, the stone wall had a single steel door opening onto a narrow rock bridge over the moat. The doorway was low, deliberately sized to allow only one person entry at a time, stooped over and vulnerable. I knew from previous visits that there would be guards, lots of guards . . . and none of them would be human. The creature I was going to see surrounded herself with the finest warriors in the vampyre world: the ferocious and exclusively female Dearg Due and Bobhan Sith. There would also be half-human *dhampirs* and maybe even some were-creatures.

I took my time climbing out of the car, knowing my every movement was being watched and recorded. I stepped up to the driver's door and leaned in. "Lock the doors and stay in the car. I'll be at least thirty minutes and no more than an hour. Do not get out under any circumstances. Do not talk to strangers—"

"I'm not a kid—," Maral began, smiling, but the smile faded when she realized I was serious.

"—no matter what they look like—punk kid, old lady, high school cheerleader, or flaming queen. They will be vampyre, Maral. And not mine. They won't want to cause a scene; the last thing they want is attention. But they may try and lure you out of the car. Ignore them; don't even look at them—some of the vampyre clans possess the power of mesmerism. Do not talk to them. If they tell you that I've asked you to come in, you'll know it's a lie: I'm telling you now, I would never ask you to do that. Never."

"Because this person eats people."

"Literally."

"Are you going to take the gun with you?"

"No point. You hang on to it. And if anyone does come near the car, shoot them in the throat: try and remove their head."

"What do I do if you're not back in an hour?" Maral asked, glancing at the watch I'd given her last Christmas. I suddenly wondered what I was going to get her for this one and then realized that depending how the next thirty minutes went, the whole question might be academic.

"If I'm not out in sixty minutes, then leave. Drive back to L.A. and tell Peter King that I got a call to come here. Let him handle it." I kept my face neutral and tried not to look at Maral's face as I spoke. "We're probably being watched right now, so do not react to what I'm about to say. If I'm not out within the hour, it probably means I'm not coming out. And there'll be no point in looking for a body, because there won't be one. In the bottom of the big wall safe behind the Dalí you'll find a padded buff envelope with an up-to-date version of my will. I just had it revised and I didn't use Solgar. It leaves just about everything to you. There's some cash in an envelope along with it. Take it, fly to Geneva, claim your inheritance. You'll find some names and numbers on a sheet of paper. They are men and women who specialize in creating new identities. Avail yourself of their services, Maral, but, whatever you do, do not come back to Hollywood. In fact, it would be better if you did not come back to America."

"You're scaring me, Ovsanna," Maral said shakily. In the gloom, her eyes were huge gray beads behind unshed tears.

"If the vampyre in there decides to destroy me, then she will kill you, too. She's spent millennia protecting her identity and the true existence of the vampyre clans. She cannot afford to allow you to live."

"Who is she? Who is this Lilith?"

"She is the mother of all vampyres."

Every vampyre knows the legend of Lilith.

And everything they know is wrong.

In her, legend, mythology, and religion come together to create a story that she took centuries and a great deal of delight in creating.

I walked across the quiet street, heading straight for the low arched door, well aware that I was possibly walking into a trap. As the most senior vampyre in this country, only she could have authorized an attack on me and my clan.

The Ancients called her Lilitu and the Night Hag, and she was certainly the oldest creature in North America and possibly the entire world. She claimed to have been the first wife of Adam—before Eve—and that she'd been cast out of the Garden because she refused to accede to Adam's somewhat primitive sexual urges. On the banks of the Bosphorus, she consorted with demons and in time gave birth to the first of the vampyre and the were races.

Most of that is bullshit.

She's ancient, all right. Solgar says she's thousands of years old. I know she was around before Christ, but as for being Adam's wife, I'll leave that to the theologians to decide. All I know for sure is she's not pure vampyre. She was part human once. Not Turned, either.

I've spent years quietly researching her history, sorting through the myriad legends and fragmentary stories associated with her name. I believe that she was possessed by an Akhkharu serpent demon in ancient Sumeria who left her pregnant with a *dhampir*. The earliest *dhampirs* were incredibly powerful, possessing the best attributes of both their human and vampyre parents. I am sure that Gilgamesh was probably one of her *dhampir* sons. And I've no doubts that she slept with him, as well. She bred with the earliest and most powerful of the vampyre ancestors, and she was never Turned. But she could not have lain with them, slept with them and had their children, without some of their vampyre traits rubbing off on her. In time, she gave birth to more vampyres and a hybrid race of were-creatures. And God knows what else.

Now . . . well, now no one knows what she is. Except quite mad and truly powerful. And capable of just about anything.

The steel door opened before I'd even crossed the street, and a red-haired, green-eyed young woman appeared smiling the vampyre smile: lips tightly closed. Her coloring suggested that she was either Greek Strigae or Irish Dearg Due. "We've been expecting you," she said in an accent that had never been heard in Ireland. "Follow me."

I'm not tall, but even I was forced to duck my head as I entered the arched gate. It's an incredibly vulnerable position and I bit down hard on the inside of my cheek, preventing myself from looking up to check for the blade or swordsman that could be hidden in the shadows above my head.

The grounds hadn't changed at all since the last time I'd been here. Spanish daggers, agaves, prickly pear cactus, and jumping chollas formed a barrier on the far side of the moat, just waiting to slice any intruder who survived the piranhas. Devil's Weed and Black Nightshade and Christmas Roses covered the ground up to the house, poisonous, hallucinogenic, and beautiful.

Not so beautiful were the *dhampirs* patrolling the grounds. Armed with automatic weapons, with wolves and dogs by their side, the animals were were-creatures, that peculiar offshoot of vampyre that can only change into a specific beast form. Usually, they feel more comfortable that way and as they get older, stop reverting to their human shape completely. They end their lives as animals. Who knows, maybe Lilith had given birth to these.

There was movement all around me, and I caught glimpses of nightmarish creatures that should have been carved in stone on Notre Dame. I managed to keep my face impassive as a creature Ray Harryhausen would have been proud of appeared at a window and stared at me. There was nothing even remotely human about it. It was joined by a second creature, which made the first look almost handsome. Their eyes, yellow and sulphurous, tracked my movement, and I swear I saw a forked tongue flicker.

But vampyres are solitary creatures, especially the ancient ones. What were they doing here?

I knew then that something was very wrong indeed: these were old vampyres—very old, the legendary Ancients. As vampyres age, they revert to something much more saurian looking, draconian even. Some turn completely black; others grow wings and tails; others shrink, hunch over, become troll-like. Mankind may have its roots in the great apes; perhaps ours lie in the great lizards. Whatever our genesis, in the end all of us become hideous to human eyes.

Except Lilith. Lilith is unchanging. Maybe her human blood, maybe the demon's possession, maybe bedding her own *dhampir* sons—who knows? She doesn't change.

The Dearg Due sashayed ahead of me, confident that I would follow her. Not that I had much choice. We crossed the bridge and entered the house through another steel door set into the main living area, which was on the second floor of the structure. I remembered the bedrooms being upstairs, seven of them, each with its own raised black marble tub and fireplace. Below, on what was actually the ground floor, were the kitchen, the gym, an office, and the maids' quarters. Because the entire house was built into the side of a mountain, there were no windows in the back. Floor-to-ceiling bullet-proof glass wrapped around the three-quarters of the house that faced the desert, but because of the surrounding fifteen-foot wall, the view was only visible from the top floor.

Lilith's foyer was bare save for a huge unlit Baccarat crystal chandelier. The lowering desert sun left the room in shadows and touched it with an icy chill.

"Wait here." The Dearg Due moved off into the dim light.

I ignored her and stepped into the living room. I wanted to see as much of the house as possible. At the other end of the foyer, I could see out in a side garden, complete with the requisite swimming pool. The creature that was swimming lengths of the pool looked like something out of the Cretaceous—a mosasaur maybe. Light was fading fast, and it would soon be night—which was not a problem for my race. But I was guessing that more Ancients would appear with nightfall, those who are particularly sensitive to sunlight. I'd already counted maybe ten Ancients here, along with assorted *dhampirs* and were-creatures. Along with the Vampyres of Hollywood, I'd seen more of my race in the last two days than I'd seen in the previous century.

Which begged the question, why was Lilith gathering so many vampyres together? And what did it have to do with me?

Two more Dearg Due came into the living room and stood silently by each door, making sure I didn't move any farther into the house. They were both beautiful in their way, and if I hadn't had my mind on Lilith and my possible demise, I might have found some way to enjoy looking at them. Instead I stared out the windows and waited.

And waited.

The bitch kept me there almost ten minutes—the oldest power ploy in the book. I had to fight my rage to keep from Changing.

And then something acrid drifted into the room, the scent of something long dead and mummified, of old blood and tainted meat, and I knew, even before she spoke, that Lilith was standing behind me.

"Ah, the legendary Ovsanna Moore, the Scream Queen." The voice was barely human, without cadence, without inflection or accent.

I turned and looked at Lilith, the mother of all vampyres, the oldest living human, responsible for the *dhampir* and were clans, the source of all the evil in the world.

She was the spitting image of Baby Jane Hudson in *What Ever Happened to Baby Jane?*

CHAPTER THIRTY-TWO

PALM SPRINGS
3:00 P.M.

Palm Springs.

That made sense. If she and Maral really are lovers, Palm Springs is the place to be.

I left the Jag in my spot, grabbed a squad car, and made the freeway doing eighty-five down La Cienega with my flashers on. I didn't know where I was going exactly, but I needed to get there before anyone else lost his head. Literally.

I reached Delaney at the office. "I need you to track down some property records for me, Del. Fast. In Palm Springs or maybe Palm Desert. See if Ovsanna Moore or Maral McKenzie owns anything down there."

"What about Rancho Mirage? Lady with Moore's kind of money oughta be in Rancho Mirage."

"That's good. And if that doesn't work, start calling the hotels. See if there's a reservation in either name for tonight. And put a BOLO into the system for Moore's black Lexus SUV. License number's in the Casale murder book. I'm heading down there and I've got to find them. I'll be on my cell."

He was halfway through telling me to be careful when I cut him off. I was past being careful now. My every instinct was telling me that this case was rolling toward the endgame . . . and that was going to mean bodies. Probably lots of them.

I made it to Banning in under an hour, probably some kind of record. The flashers come in handy. Del called back just as I passed the outlet stores. "Well, if either of those ladies owns property down there, it's not in her own name. I couldn't find a damn thing. And they're not sleepin' overnight in any of the big hotels, either. But I gotta tell you, the more I'm digging, the more I'm thinking something's really wrong here, Pete."

I hate being called Pete, and he knows that. "Tell me something I don't know," I snapped.

"Your Ms. Moore's so squeaky clean, she's suspicious."

"When did being innocent make you a suspect?" I asked.

"We're cops, Pete. We know that no one is entirely innocent or that clean. I mean there's too many loose ends and not enough paperwork. She was born in Rome, Italy, in '60, except there're no hospital records for the birth, just that it was registered with the American Embassy there. Her mother, Anna Moore, didn't spend much time with her and I can't find anything at all about a father. Looks like she went to a lot of boarding schools. She's registered with a dozen high-class ones all over Europe: London, Paris, Geneva, then back to Rome to start acting, then to London and RADA. Whatever that is," he muttered.

"Royal Academy of Dramatic Art. Upscale acting school."

"Studied there for three years, then came over here when her mother's increasing ill health forced her to give up acting."

"Sounds fine to me."

"If she was studying in RADA, why do they have a record of her finishing, and graduating with honors, but no record of her daily attendance? Where was she living in London? Where was her bank account? She must have taken public transport everywhere, because there is no evidence of a car registered in her name. I've no records of transatlantic calls to Mummy dearest, no evidence that Mummy ever sent her a dime. And if she came back here to look after a sick mother, why are there no hospital records?"

"She wasn't in a hospital?" I suggested.

"I'm talking about *no* medical records of any kind. No doctor bills, no prescriptions, no insurance payout. No record of what the mother died of or when."

"The rich pay for their privacy," I said.

"No one is this private! You can't move through the modern world without leaving a shitload of tracks and paperwork. There are big pieces missing from the Ovsanna Moore jigsaw. On the surface, it looks fine. She's got all the paper here she needs: passport, driver's license, Social Security, but when you start digging past twenty-five years ago, there's nothing there."

"So . . . more to Miss Moore than meets the eye," I said.

"Less, I'd say. Much less."

"What about Maral McKenzie?"

"Oh, she's legit. I've got everything on her, right down to her shoe size. Her story is real movie-of-the-week stuff."

"Anything else?"

"I checked on the Japanese connection: that turns out to be true. Three investors, ex-Sony, ex-Mitsubishi, ex-Toyota, with more money than sense, are deep in negotiations with Anticipation. It's very hush-hush, but it's legit."

"Thanks, Del. Keep digging. And patch me through if you get a hit on the BOLO."

Two minutes later, the phone rang again. I was reading the

marquee at the Morongo Casino and I flipped it open without even looking at it.

"That was fast, Delaney; did the car show up?"

"Detective King?"

"Yes?" It wasn't Delaney.

"This is Maral McKenzie."

"I've been trying to find you," I said, deliberately allowing the snap of anger to show in my voice.

"We're in Palm Springs."

Well, at least I knew she wasn't lying. And at least I knew now that I was driving in the right direction.

Her words tumbled out in a rush. "Ovsanna doesn't know I'm calling you—"

"Hold on," I said. "Where are you exactly? Where is she . . . ?"

"I don't know the address. I'm in the car on a private drive off West Chino Canyon, a road that runs right into the foothills. But you can't miss it—it's the only house for miles and it's built high up, right into the mountain. Ovsanna went inside to talk to someone about the murders. She wouldn't let me go with her. She said—"

Maral McKenzie never finished her sentence. I heard the shatter of safety glass and a truncated scream. Then the thud of the phone hitting the floor. A car door opened. Pressing my hand against my right ear, I concentrated intently on the sounds of fabric dragging against leather. A door slammed shut . . . and there was dead silence.

Palm Springs is basically a small town. The PSPD officer who answered the phone knew exactly which house I was talking about. He said he had two men in the vicinity and he'd call me back when they got there. I took down the directions and guessed it was no more than fifteen miles from my present positon.

Night falls fast in the desert, and it was almost dark by the time he got back to me. His men had found the phone and the SUV. The driver's window was broken and Maral wasn't in sight. So tell me something I didn't know.

I was on West Chino when an unmarked police cruiser flashed its lights. I pulled over to the side of the road and two plainclothes officers got out of their car and introduced themselves. Robert Montoya looked to be Native American and Robert Morales was Hispanic. With their black hair and desert tans, all I could see in the darkness were the whites of their eyes and their teeth when they talked. Which they didn't do much of. Neither was happy.

"What did you see beside the smashed window?"

"Glass on the road, key in the ignition, phone on the floor. No signs of a struggle, no signs of blood. House is so walled in you'd need a low-flying plane to see if anything was going on inside."

"What do we know about the neighborhood?"

"Closest neighbor is quite a ways away. Everybody's got at least a couple of acres up there. Old money mostly. Lots of it. Lots of the houses show up in architectural magazines. Lotta weird houses. Elvis spent his honeymoon in one of 'em."

I turned and headed back to the car, calling over my shoulder, "I'll follow you. Don't announce our arrival."

The two Bobs turned onto a dirt road and killed their lights as soon as they parked. I pulled in behind them and did the same. Turned the dome light off and got out of the car as quietly I could. Ovsanna's SUV was parked about fifty yards down on the right. In the dark, I could barely make out a huge stone wall surrounding a massive stone, steel, and glass structure that looked like it was growing out of the mountain. The top floor was lit, but the glass must have been electrochromic because I couldn't see a damn thing inside. Someone really wanted his privacy.

Morales had been driving the cruiser. He rolled down the front window and I leaned in. "You know anything about this place . . . who owns it? Local gossip?"

"Nada. House has been here a long time; I remember seeing it as a kid and thinking how cool it must be to live inside a mountain like that."

"What about the rest of the area? Ever been called out here for anything? Any neighbor complaints—loud parties, drug traffic?"

Montoya was reading his PDA. "Here's one. Six weeks ago—got a call from an Abigail Hilton. Address is Shangri-La, which is down here to the left, the last house we passed before the dirt road. It was midnight, Halloween. Said there was a party going on up here and she couldn't stand the noise. Officer came out to investigate, but by the time he got here everything was quiet. He didn't even enter the premises."

"Where was the party?"

"That house back there, almost opposite where the SUV is parked. It's called Eden."

Abigail Hilton took an inordinate amount of time opening the door, and when I saw her I understood why. She was ninety if she was a day. Maybe five feet tall to begin with, age had hunched her over to even less. I think if I'd taken her cane she would have collapsed on the floor. Her voice, however, was razor sharp, her diction pure Boston Brahmin.

"You're investigating what? My complaint? That was six weeks ago, young man, and why is a Beverly Hills police officer investigating a crime in Palm Springs at all?"

"It's intra-agency policy, ma'am, helping out our neighboring departments."

"Well, that's a bullshit answer if I ever heard one. Let me see some identification, young man."

She took my badge and closed the door in my face. The two Bobs sat in the car and watched me, their faces expressionless; I was guessing they both wore mirrored shades during the day. I knew the producer of *Reno 911;* maybe I'd pass on his number.

Mrs. Hilton returned to the door, opened it, and handed me back my badge. "Okay, young man, what do you want to know?"

"You called in a complaint on Halloween night. A loud party, I understand."

"Loud. And I'm partially deaf, so the noise must have been very loud indeed."

"What did you hear, ma'am?"

"Screams, shouts, howling."

"Howling? When you say 'howling'——"

"Animal howling. We get a lot of coyotes around here, but it didn't sound like that. More like dogs or wolves. It was disturbing."

"And this was close to midnight."

"It started about ten, but I never called the police until midnight. By the time an officer got here, it had stopped. That was one o'clock."

"Did you talk to any of the occupants of the house?"

"I tried," she snapped. "I phoned Miss Lilly, but I couldn't get her on the line. Her creepy driver said she was 'indisposed.' Believe me, I gave him a piece of my mind. Pasty-faced little fuck!"

I was so stunned by the "little fuck" coming out of her mouth that it took me a second to take in the rest of what she'd said.

"Pasty-faced?"

"An albino," she snapped. "You know, white? Pasty-faced? Man gives me the creeps every time I see him."

"There's an albino working in that house?"

"That's what I said, young man. Are you going deaf?"

"No, ma'am."

"Well, we're done here. My Manhattan's getting warm." She stopped and squinted at me. "You're smiling like an idiot," she barked, and slammed the door in my face.

I guess I was, too.

Chapter Thirty-Three

"Lilith, darling. How lovely to see you," I lied.

A ghostly shape moved in the gloom behind Lilith, and Ghul the ghoul appeared. I'm not sure what Ghul is—I know he's not full-blooded human. He's been with Lilith for millennia, so there must be some vampyre in there somewhere. But he doesn't claim any clan and he's enough of an aberration that none of the clans claim him. Only Lilith. She keeps him by her side constantly. Whether he's her servant, her son, or her lover, no one knows. Perhaps he's all three.

I do know he is a genuine graveyard-haunting, flesh-eating ghoul, though, and there are probably no more than a handful still on this earth.

"Why have you come here?" Lilith demanded. She was wearing some sort of black Vivienne Westwood number, a cross between a Goth wedding dress and a dominatrix nightgown.

"I've come to see you, Lilith."

"You've seen me, now go."

"You've moved things around since I was last here," I said, looking at the living room, which was empty, save for two more chandeliers. "Are you going into hibernation or is this just your minimalist period?"

"You know what I love about actresses, Ghul?" Lilith said, turning away from me. "They have an opinion on everything. Fashion, politics, art, world peace—as if anyone cares." She tilted her head to look up at him. "These are the same people who make their living parroting words written by others, who move where they are told to move and dress the way they're told to dress. They can't even take care of their own business affairs, but they can tell people how to vote."

Ghul said nothing. He rarely spoke.

I wandered toward the window, keeping as far from the mismatched couple as I could. I was under no illusions: individually they were deadly; together they were unstoppable. The danger in the room was palpable.

"What do you want?" Lilith demanded.

"I have some questions for you. I'd like some answers." I moved closer to the rear door. Four ancient vampyres prowled in the darkness, hideous misshapen shadows.

"I have nothing to say to you," Lilith snapped. "You forget yourself, Ovsanna Hovannes Garabedian. You are my subject. You answer to me!"

"Not in this country I don't," I snapped back, deliberately raising my voice, hoping the Ancients would hear me and start paying attention. "That is not the tradition." The Ancients were very keen on tradition. "I came here first, Lilith. I staked my claim and therefore this is my fiefdom—and in my kingdom you answer to me."

Lilith waddled forward. She'd put on a little weight since I last saw her, and I didn't even want to think about what she might have been eating. I could smell the acrid rage coming off her in waves. She was shivering with it. If I'd had a gag reflex, I'd have been bent over; she smelled of sulfur and sour milk. "I am Lilith, the First, Everlasting, Immortal. Mother of the Vampyre and the Were. You owe me fealty."

Lilith had other names—the Night Hag, the Night Monster—but I wasn't about to remind her of those at the moment. I wiped flecks of her hot spittle from my cheek. "I am Clan Dakhanavar of the First Bloodline, Chatelaine of Hollywood. There is none above me on the West Coast of America. Not even you, Lilith. You know the tradition!" I yelled my last words at her, drawing in more and more of the Ancients.

Some of them had gathered in the foyer and someone had lit the chandelier. Most of the bulbs were broken, however, and the few that remained threw a dull yellow glow down on the Ancients, revealing cracked, black leather skin, misshapen molted wings, split talons and claws—a genuine Nightmare before Christmas. God help me if I get that old. Of course, Lilith could put paid to that concern in the next few minutes if I wasn't careful.

Behind Lilith and Ghul, I saw others move into the room, her army of Bobhan Sith and Dearg Due, the *dhampirs* and the were.

"What do you want, Chatelaine?" Lilith whispered, her face turned down and to the side.

She wanted to keep the conversation unheard by the others, but I wouldn't allow it. "I want answers, Lilith," I repeated, so all could hear me. "I want to know who is responsible for the deaths of my kin."

"I have no answers for you," Lilith said, turning away. "It would be better if you left now."

"That sounds like a threat."

Lilith turned to face me and, in that moment, no longer looked like a grotesque old woman in too much makeup. There was no humanity in this face, nothing human at all. This was evil—ancient and implacable. "I have killed vampyre before, you know. Feasted off their flesh, sucked the marrow from their bones, eaten their brains raw from the bowls of their skulls." She no longer made an attempt to keep our conversation quiet. Lilith stepped closer and her cloying ancient mustiness enfolded me. "Do you know what vampyre tastes like, Ovsanna?" she asked.

"Chicken?"

"Memories."

A tongue, short and black, darted out from between her painted lips. "Everything they have ever done, every place they've been, all that they've seen, is there, wrapped in flesh and sinew, bone and marrow. A vampyre is a feast indeed. I can make one last for days."

Lilith was now so close that I could touch her. What I had thought at first was caked-on Baby Jane makeup wasn't makeup at all; it was her skin. Pale yellow and cracked and mottled, like a desic-cated grapefruit. Her teeth were little more than stubs barely pro-truding above her gums. Worn down by millennia of eating human bones, no doubt. In contrast, her eyes were bright and impossibly blue.

"Is that something you want to be saying in the present com-pany?" I asked, indicating the Ancients gathered behind me.

"They are in no danger, Ovsanna," Lilith said loudly, walking around me. "You are."

I turned to follow her.

"A danger to yourself and to others. The police are investigating you, Ovsanna. How long will it be before your somewhat nebulous past comes to light? The police will shine a light on you, actress. The press will turn that into a spotlight you cannot escape from. Your very existence endangers all the vampyres of America, Ovsanna Ho-vannes Garabedian."

I turned again, trying to face Lilith and keep an eye on Ghul at the same time. I did not want him at my back. "A Hunter is de-stroying my clan, killing them in the old ways, the traditional ways, ensuring that there will be no regeneration. Now, he's started killing humans around me."

"Sending you a message." Ghul spoke, his voice dead, devoid of expression, his mouth shaping the words with difficulty. "But what is the message, vampyre? Do you understand it?"

"This Hunter seems determined that this spotlight will only illuminate me and my world."

"You Dakhanavar always were paranoid."

"Kept us alive," I reminded him. I turned quickly, aware that Lilith was behind me. She was standing at the door leading out to the pool, talking quietly with a saurian creature. Something was wrong here, horribly wrong. I was beginning to believe I'd made a terrible mistake coming here.

I turned to face the ghoul. Tall, unnaturally thin, with pink-white skin and a pale oval face split by blood-red eyes and the thin red line of his lips. I doubt he had ever been handsome, but now he looked like a dissipated walking corpse in a tuxedo that might have been in fashion when Capone was paying taxes.

If the Hunter was another vampyre, then he would have needed the blessing of the most senior vampyres in the country . . . and no one was more senior than Lilith. I also had little doubt that if someone was looking to usurp me, he would have Lilith's blessing. She'd always hated me for claiming Hollywood before her, and I think she secretly wanted to be an actress. Val Lewton gave her a small part in the original *Cat People*—they were sleeping together—but she must not have been very good; by the time he produced *The Body Snatcher,* she was playing a corpse. She couldn't even do that properly. They had to do six takes on one scene. I mean, how hard is it to hold your breath?

And I had walked right into her bestial arms.

Lilith was standing at the door to the garden, surrounded by her *dhampirs* and weres. More Ancients had gathered in the gloom. It was impossible to guess their numbers, but there must have been dozens.

In my entire lifetime, I'd only encountered a handful and never more than one at a time. The last time the Ancients had gathered in any great number, in September 1666, the Great Fire of London had claimed hundreds of vampyre lives. Many believed the fire had been set deliberately, probably by agents of the Church Militant, though there had been rumors at the time that a Rogue vampyre had been responsible.

I moved across the room, purposely ending up near the huge fireplace. Perhaps I could effect a change into something small and birdlike and escape up the chimney. With the cool marble protecting my back, I folded my arms across my chest and confronted Lilith. "I believe you have authorized a Hunt against me."

She was staring at me. According to legend, when the world was newly formed she had been beautiful beyond compare, but that was before she had been cast out of Eden and consorted with demons. The Night Hag had not been beautiful in millennia. But now, with the evening gloom blurring the lines of her face, leaving only her blue eyes clearly visible, bright and almost innocent, I could understand how Adam had been seduced by her.

And then she laughed. It was the most terrifying sound I have ever heard. If evil had a voice, then this was it. When the laugh trailed off, she stepped closer to me, put her hands on her hips, and snarled. "No, Ovsanna, I have not authorized a Hunt against you. It is *I* who have declared war on you! *I* have been hunting you!"

She slashed out with her right hand and her claws raked across my face, shredding the flesh on my cheek. My fangs unsheathed, my talons extended, I went for her throat, but her creatures were on me before I got to her flesh.

I am Dakhanavar, vampyre elite, trained from the moment of my birth as a killer. I fought back. I kicked and slashed, tore flesh with my teeth, sliced through bodies with my claws, ripped through *dhampirs* and were-creatures. I could see Lilith standing back, arms folded across her chest, her bizarre wedding dress splashed with my dark blood. She was urging on her female vampyres. I fell back under the onslaught, leaving Dearg Due and Bobhan Sith writhing on the floor in pools of their own blood and intestines.

There was a moment when I thought I was going to make it, when the door was in sight, and then the Ancients attacked. . . .

CHAPTER THIRTY-FOUR

PALM SPRINGS
5:00 P.M.

Pasty-faced little fuck.

Not the most politically correct way to describe someone suffering from albinism. But in this case, probably accurate.

Eva Casale, the special effects woman at Anticipation, had been seen with an albino. Milla Taylor, currently in two parts on the coroner's table, was also seen in the company of an albino.

And now Ovsanna Moore had come to Palm Springs to visit the same albino.

I have to admit that I was disappointed. I didn't want Ovsanna to be guilty, but the evidence never lies, as the guy on *CSI* says all the time, and then goes on to prove how it does. Someone with a lot more common sense would have waited for backup, but I was still working on the assumption that Ovsanna trusted me enough to talk face-to-face. I needed to ask her why and how and all those other good questions a nosy detective likes to put to a suspect.

I wandered back to the Bobs, careful to keep my excitement under control. "We're going to need a search warrant for the Eden property and the grounds where the SUV is parked. Don't look," I added quickly.

The two Bobs swiveled in their seats to look at the house up the road. Montoya looked at me like I was speaking a foreign language. "Do we have just cause?" he asked.

"Witness statement," I said vaguely. "How fast can you get it?"

"Are you kidding? This is Palm Springs and it's five o'clock. Every judge in town is either playing tennis or on his second martini. It's gonna take a while."

"Well then, here's what I want you to do. It's a private road, right? No exit past the house? Get as many units as you can and seal off this end of the road. But tell them to come in with their lights off. It's dark enough out here and we're far enough away, they may not be visible from the house. Then get Captain Barton in BHPD. Tell him I believe the occupants of the house are directly involved in the Cinema Slayer crimes and that we're going to need a SWAT team just to get into the building, Let him take it from there. Now go; get the roadblocks set up."

"Where are you going?"

I nodded up the road toward the house. "Going to knock on a door."

"Is that wise?" Montoya asked, peering shortsightedly at the house.

"Probably not."

I wanted ten minutes alone with Ovsanna. I needed to look her in the eye and hear what she had to say one more time. I was sure now she'd lied to me about the threatening phone calls, but I still didn't have a clue what her part was in the multiple murders. All my instincts told me she wasn't a killer. But my instincts wanted to throw her down on a bed and climb inside her, too, so it seemed pretty obvious my instincts couldn't be trusted.

And if she was guilty, I wanted to make the arrest myself. In part, because I wanted to protect her—from the treatment she'd get without me around and from the media. And in part, because I'm no fool. I knew how this would look in my file. Maybe Dominick Dunne would write my story for *Vanity Fair.* "The Final Curtain: Capturing the Cinema Slayer." Give me something else to tape up in my locker and remind myself sometimes that I know what I'm doing.

If Ovsanna weren't involved, she could have bought the movie rights for Anticipation. Get Viggo Mortensen to play me. Johnny Depp isn't tall enough.

The wall around the house was fifteen feet high, at least; big double doors were set into the center of the wall, with a smaller arched door to one side. The intercom was set into the wall beside the smaller arched door. I unsnapped the restraining strap and loosened the Glock in its holster. Maral had said Ovsanna had gone inside. With the car where it was, I figured she was still in there, maybe with the albino. And where the fuck was Maral?

I was just about to press the intercom button when I spotted something sparkling on the ground. I knelt and, shielding my penlight from above, flashed it over the dirt. Grains of glass twinkled back at me. I picked up a handful of glass and dirt and let the dirt sift through my fingers. The glass was safety glass. Some of the pieces had dried blood on them. Still crouching, I turned my head and aimed the light back toward the SUV. From this low angle, I could see a trail of fragments leading from the black SUV driver's door— right to where I was standing.

I unholstered the Glock and released the safeties. I always keep a round chambered—not necessarily good weapon craft but really good police craft. You don't want to pull a gun in a gunfight and then have to chamber a round. Besides, even though I didn't have them on, the Glock 17L has three safeties.

I could now justifiably claim that I was following a witness statement and a trail of evidence leading from the SUV to the house where I believed Maral McKenzie had been taken following her abduction. I pressed the flat of my hand against the steel door and pushed. In any good movie, it would have clicked open. This one didn't. Short of ringing the bell or using a SWAT team with an explosive charge, I wasn't going to get in that way. I set off around the side of the house, keeping close to the wall, watching out for cameras or alarms. If there were any, I didn't see them.

There were no streetlights and no moonlight. I couldn't see two feet in front of me. I kept my left hand on the stone wall, the Glock in my right, rounded a corner, and stopped, the gun snapping up, breath catching in my throat. I thought I was facing a person, but when my heart stopped hammering I realized it was nothing more than one of the countless palm trees that gave the city its name. This one was listing sharply to the left, its top directly across the wall of the estate. Shoving the gun back in its holster, I did my best to mount the tree and half climbed, half dragged myself up the trunk. Two humongous rats darted out at me from their nest in the palm fronds. I knocked one of them off the trunk and watched him land on the top of the wall. There was a loud buzzing, a small arc of light, and the damn rat's fur burst into flames. So . . . electric wires embedded in the top of the wall. Whoever owned this house took their security very seriously indeed. Well, better the rat than me.

I climbed farther up the trunk to a point where I was leaning over the wall. There was water directly below me, not a swimming pool, a moat, for God's sake. A moat surrounding the entire house with a bridge leading from the short steel door to the house itself. It was too dark to make out anything in the water, but it sounded like there were huge fish swimming down there. I could hear their tails breaking water. There was thick vegetation on the other side of the moat, all the way up to the house. From the shadows they threw on the wall, I'd say cactus and agave, nothing you'd want to get too close to. From what I could see of the house, I was looking at several million dollars' worth of amazing architecture in stone, glass, and steel, a real fortress.

Most of the house was in darkness, but there was dim light in one huge room on the middle floor, probably the living room. From this angle, almost directly across from the room and with no sun to activate the privacy glass, I could see inside.

Ovsanna was there.

I could only see her profile. She was talking to a tall man in a tuxedo and a short girl in some punk-looking fancy gown. There was no furniture in the room, and I could barely make out other shapes standing in the darkness against the far wall. Human shapes. I pushed myself as far up the tree as I could, ignoring its ominous creaking, keeping an eye out for more rats and my feet away from the buzzing wires. Running a lethal dose of electricity through the wires was illegal, but there was probably enough to fry my nervous system and blow me off the tree. I doubted anyone inside would care if I broke my neck in the process.

Ovsanna moved and the guy in the tux turned just enough for me to see his face—white blond hair and pale skin. The albino. The short girl reminded me of someone. Then she turned toward me and I realized she wasn't a girl at all; she was an old woman dressed like a teenage Goth . . . looking astonishingly like Bette Davis in *What Ever Happened to Baby Jane?*

I couldn't tell what was going on. Ovsanna looked angry. Was she giving them orders? Yelling at them? She walked toward a floor-to-ceiling marble fireplace, turned her back to it, and stood there with her arms crossed over her chest.

There was no sign of Maral.

More people were crowding into the room but no one was speaking. They just seemed to be standing in silent rows watching Ovsanna and the older woman. There were flame-haired women to the fore, but I couldn't make out the details of any of the people standing in the background. They all seemed to be wrapped in black cloaks.

Maybe it was time to get that eye test I'd been putting off.

What the hell was going on here? And who were all these people? There were certainly enough for a party, but there was no party atmosphere: no waiters circulating with food, no streamers or balloons. No lights.

Maybe it was a cult. Some sort of devil-worshipping coven. Now that would make great press! This was California, home of the Church of Satan and the Temple of Set, as well as a host of smaller covens. A devil-worshipping cult would just be the icing on the publicity cake: I could see the USA Today headline: "Ovsanna Moore, High Priestess of Horror."

Then I had a sudden horrible thought: what if it was a horror movie convention? SuzieQ had dragged me along to a convention in San Diego once. I had a good time looking at the women in costume—SuzieQ had gone dressed as Vampirella. She'd made a fortune selling eight-by-ten glossies and posing for photos and I'd spent a busy afternoon keeping fans in order. Some of the fans had been terrifying in their intensity. Looking into the room below, I thought I saw some of that same behavior. The remnants of my mother's exceptional steak pizzaiolla soured in my stomach. Had I just closed off a road and called in Chief Barton for a horror convention? I felt a bead of cold sweat gather in my hairline, run down my forehead, and gather on the tip of my nose. I could almost feel my pension disappearing.

Ovsanna said something and the old woman threw her head back and laughed. Then she moved closer to Ovsanna and struck her across the face. Ovsanna grabbed her by the hair, her lips curled back and she looked like she was going for the old lady's throat with her teeth. Now the other people in the room were moving—fast.

A woman with flaming red hair stepped right in front of her. I didn't even see Ovsanna's hands move, but the woman lifted right off the ground in an explosion of bright red blood and crashed into the others standing behind her. I got the briefest glimpse of the body as it hit the ground: there wasn't a lot left of her head.

Ovsanna fought like a wild woman, kicking, punching, and biting. I guessed she must have had knives in both hands, because every time she struck out at one of the figures I could see her slicing them open. Arterial blood sprayed everywhere.

It wasn't hard to see what had happened to the bodies in Rough Trade, and I guessed I knew now who killed those movie stars.

There's a whole lot I should have done. Getting off the tree trunk would have been a good start. Drawing my gun and firing a shot through the window was an option. But for the first time in my life I was frozen with shock and absolute terror.

I watched Ovsanna slice her way through the people pressing in on her. And then I realized that I couldn't see the knives she was using . . . because there were none.

She was shredding people with her bare hands.

A hulking hairy bodybuilder stepped into her path: I saw her plunge her hand right into his chest and rip out his still-beating heart. I watched as a another hairy man leapt onto her back, saw her bend backward at an impossible angle and snap him right over her head, slamming him into the floor with enough force to shatter the floorboards. Then she grabbed his legs—for a moment I even thought she was holding a tail—and swung him around like a cudgel, using his broken body to batter the others.

What I was seeing couldn't be real . . . it couldn't be. Were they shooting a movie? Was that what this was—a location shoot for one of Ovsanna's horror flicks? Just special effects and Eva Casale's fake prop blood? Except . . . except there were no cameras . . . no lights . . . no makeup . . . no costumes . . . and definitely no director to call "cut."

This was no movie.

Two women—one red haired, the other dark—leapt at Ovsanna

from either side. Moving unbelievably fast, she caught both their heads and slammed them together with a crack I could hear through the window. Blood, brain, and bone geysered up across the ceiling.

A naked man who looked more simian than human wrapped unnaturally long arms around her. Ovsanna drove her booted heel into his bare toes, crushing them to a pulp, and as he opened his mouth to scream she reached in and wrenched out his tongue with her right hand. She kicked a second man so hard between the legs that I swear I saw his testicles stuck to the toe of her boot.

It was a massacre and I had to do something. I had to stop her before she killed any more people. She was obviously high on something, crystal meth or PCP. Gripping the trunk of the palm tree between my thighs, I drew my gun and tried to get a bead on her. She was pinned to the floor, but she was writhing and flailing and I couldn't get a clear shot. There were more and more people crowding into the room, pressing in on her, trying—and failing—to prevent her from lashing out with whatever killer kung fu/jujitsu shit she was using.

I was just about to fire a warning shot into a wall when something else stepped into the room.

Something that had no right to exist outside a nightmare. Something tall and leathery, with wings and honest-to-god horns. And a fucking tail! I was hoping that it was someone in costume when a second creature crawled into the room. On the ceiling. Ovsanna had risen and was moving toward the door when the first *thing* slashed at her. The blow staggered her, driving her to her knees, and suddenly the red-haired women and the hairy men were all over her, pinning her to the ground, covering her with their bodies. She managed to heave some of them off, but more and more of the leathery monsters crawled or slithered or flew into the room, and I realized then that what I'd seen standing in the shadows hadn't been people in cloaks at all.

I lowered the gun.

Adrenaline was pounding through my body. My hand was shaking so hard I couldn't aim the gun, but that didn't matter because I didn't know what to shoot at. I didn't even know what I was looking at.

The albino waded into the heaving mass of bodies and started pulling them off Ovsanna and tossing them aside. It was clear that some were dead and others were terribly injured. When he finally got to Ovsanna, she wasn't moving. He raised her over his head in both hands like some sort of trophy; then he turned, knelt before the old woman, and laid Ovsanna at her feet.

I was at least two hundred yards away, separated from the room by a wall of glass, but even so, I could hear the old lady's hideous cackling as she kicked the unmoving body again and again and again. . . .

CHAPTER THIRTY-FIVE

I realized something profound before the Ancients descended upon me.

I realized that I hadn't felt this alive in a century. It is our nature to kill. To rip and rend, to tear and break . . . and to revel in that destruction. My clan, of all clans, the Dakhanavar, are trained to guard and attack. Tonight, I'd killed a score of Bobhan Sith, Dearg Due, *dhampirs,* and were-creatures. I think I may have killed an Ancient, too—I certainly injured one. Its stinking blood had splashed on my face, and I had a long moment of disorientation as memories of times and places that had never been inhabited by humans crashed into my consciousness.

Well, if I was going to die—and that seemed likely—then at least I'd go out fighting.

I opened my eyes and the pain came, flowing along my outstretched arms and up my legs like hot metal. A misguided sense of pride was all that kept me from crying out; I didn't want to give those bastards the satisfaction. I was in a basement, dank, musty, and echoing. It stank of old wood and mould, of rotting flesh and decaying meat, of tainted blood.

And pain.

It smelled of pain.

A single bare low-wattage bulb cast yellow light over a ghastly scene. I had been crucified to a stone wall, solid silver rail spikes driven through the bones of my wrists and ankles to pin me to the solid brickwork.

And I wasn't alone.

All around me, similarly crucified to the basement walls, were the Vampyres of Hollywood.

One by one they raised their heads to look at me—Douglas Fairbanks and Orson, Peter Lorre and Theda Bara, her husband, Charles Brabin, and James Whale, Olive Thomas, Mary Pickford and Pola, even Tod Browning, and the always elusive Charlie Chaplin. Only Rudy was missing.

"Now you mustn't blame yourself," Orson said immediately. I had been nailed to the end wall and he was on the wall to my right. He even managed a ghastly smile.

"Who else do we blame?" Theda snarled.

Olive nodded, then grimaced as her weight shifted on her outstretched arms. "It's because of her we're here."

"Ladies, ladies," Douglas murmured, as cultured and urbane as always. "This is no time for arguments and apportioning blame."

"Besides," Peter hissed, "we all know who is to blame!"

"Enough," I gasped. "Enough." I turned to Douglas, who was hanging on the wall to my left. "Tell me what happened?" I asked. I tried to wrench my arm away from the wall, quite willing to pull my flesh out over the nail if necessary, but my vampyre metabolism conspired against me. My flesh kept healing around the wound, sealing the silver spike deep within my arm. The same process prevented me from Changing—but even if I had succeeded in a transformation, I would still have been pinned to the wall.

"Save your strength," Charlie advised.

Tod nodded in agreement. "We tried."

"Douglas? What happened?"

"Lilith," he said simply. "Lilith happened."

"And Rudy. Lilith and Rudy," Orson added. Although he'd lost some weight, his great bulk pulled him forward, stretching his arms back at a frightening angle.

"The shrew and the slime," lisped Peter.

Rudy. I should have known.

"Rudy betrayed us," Douglas said. "We're sure of it. We've talked about it over the past few hours," he said, nodding to Hollywood's elite pinned to the basement walls, like so many butterflies. "The attacks on your clan and then your staff were all designed with one end in mind: to bring each of us out of hiding and gather us all together in one place, your home."

"But you called the meeting, Douglas," I said.

"Yes, I did, but I realize now it was Rudy who put the suggestion to me. He was adamant that we should all come together to confront you. I remember now that he grew angry when Tod and Charlie refused to come. I didn't think anything of it at the time, just Rudy being his manipulative self."

"I wouldn't go anywhere for that egotistical deviant," Tod croaked, voice perpetually raw from the Lucky Strikes he never quite gave up.

"Why was it necessary to bring you all together?" I wondered. The pain was making me woozy and slow.

"Do you know where each of us lives?" Douglas asked.

I shook my head, then winced as the effort strained my shoulders. I looked around the room. I knew that Tod had stayed in Malibu and I knew Theda and Charles were in Manhattan, but I'd no idea where the others lived. Only Solgar knew how to contact all the Vampyres—

"Solgar," I snapped. "Solgar knows."

"Solgar is Clan Obour," Peter lisped. "He is above reproach. He would never have betrayed us."

"I issued the order for Solgar to gather the clan; Rudy kept insisting upon it," Douglas said. Even though he was in as much pain as the rest of us, his voice was even, perfectly controlled.

"This . . . all of the . . . the killings were done so Lilith and Rudy could discover the whereabouts of the Vampyres of Hollywood? Why?" I demanded.

"You're not old enough to remember when Philip IV moved against the Templars in 1307," Douglas said. "He knew if he captured some and left others free, then they would attack him, so he sent out sealed secret orders to every bailiff, deputy, and officer in his kingdom with instructions that they were not to be opened until the night of October 12, under penalty of death. On Friday, October 13, five thousand Templars were captured and imprisoned. Only twenty escaped. Philip wasn't creative enough to conceive of that plan on his own . . . his mistress at the time was Lilith."

I closed my eyes and tried to rise above the constant pain and concentrate on what Douglas was telling me. Everything that had happened—the deaths of my clan and my staff—was nothing more than a ploy to rouse the elusive Vampyres of Hollywood from their hiding places. Obviously they had been tracked from my home back to their lairs. My eyes snapped open. "And the Ancients?"

Douglas nodded. "She needs the Ancients. No ordinary vampyre, *dhampir,* or were-creature is strong enough to stand against us alone. But the Ancients . . . the Ancients, especially banded together, have the power to destroy us."

"Three came to my house in Silver Lake," Peter Lorre whispered; then his lips twisted into an ugly smile. "I may have killed one—"

Pola nodded. "Two came for me." She shuddered. "I swear I will never grow that old, that ugly. I will destroy myself first."

A thought struggled through my pain. "Why wasn't I taken with the rest?"

"I had an altogether more fitting end for you, my dear." Rudolph Valentino came down the stairs. He stepped into the basement and walked slowly down the middle of the room, his dark eyes lingering on each crucified vampyre. Gone was any vestige of Rolph Valenti; no pretense that he was a theatrical agent. He hadn't shaved and he was wearing his costume from *The Son of the Sheik:* high black boots over flowing pants, a brocaded blouse and vest, a cummerbund, a cloak, a scimitar, and a headdress. He looked like he'd lost his mind.

Pola screeched and struggled against the spikes as he walked past her with barely a second glance. A ghost of a Change briefly warped her face into something feline, before the pain of the spikes in her arms brought her back to her human form.

When I first met Rodolfo Alfonzo Raffaelo Pierre Filiberto Guglielmi di Valentina in 1918, he'd just arrived from New York, where he'd been working as a gardener, a dishwasher, and a dancer. It took three years in Hollywood before he got his first break in *The Four Horsemen of the Apocalypse* and his nickname Tango Legs. When *The Sheik* appeared later that same year, "Tango Legs" gave way to "Latin Lover." He was handsome, charming, a wonderful actor . . . and completely self-absorbed. Along with millions of other women across the globe, I fell instantly in love with him. And I believe he loved me. Briefly. As much as Rudy could love anyone. I Turned him, made him vampyre to preserve his beauty and, in truth, to keep him for myself. That didn't work. What can I say? I was young; I was in love.

Calling upon all my reserves and more than a century of acting skills, I kept the pain out of my face. "How long have you been plotting this, Rodolfo?" I knew he hated being called Rodolfo; it reminded him of his middle-class Italian upbringing.

"Decades, Ovsanna, decades."

Rudy stopped directly in front of me. I was pinned two feet off the floor, so he had to look up into my face. He had looked dissolute yesterday, but today he was even worse. The bruises beneath his eyes and his black tongue suggested that he was overindulging in blood, and probably tainted blood at that. I could smell its rancid stink.

"Once Hollywood belonged to me." Rudy tossed his headdress off his face with a carefully practiced gesture. All he needed was a camera. "I was the most famous actor of my day."

Douglas and Charlie both stirred and opened their mouths to respond, but Rudy pressed on, lost in his own private fantasy.

"My career should have spanned decades. But you convinced me otherwise."

"I told you if you died, then you would become immortal," I said through gritted teeth. "You needed to disappear, Rodolfo. You had made too many enemies, both mortal and immortal."

Rudy spun away, cloak swirling behind him. "You became jealous of me. All of you. I was a threat to your egos. You made me die too young."

"It was a beautiful funeral, though, much grander than mine," Olive observed.

"I'm sure you all enjoyed it," Rudy snarled, glancing sidelong at Pola. "Walking those eleven blocks jammed with eighty thousand of my distraught fans, I realized then what a mistake I had made."

"You could have come back," Charlie suggested, his British accent still clear after all these years. He nodded towards me. "You could have done as Ovsanna has done: come back as a son or grandson. Valentino's son would have worked."

"You killed me," he snarled, no longer pretty. "Wrote me out of Hollywood history."

"Hardly," Orson protested.

Rudy ignored him. "So I decided to destroy you . . . but more, much more than that, I decided to reclaim my city."

"It was never your city," I reminded him.

"It should have been." He returned to stand before me. "I once asked you to marry me."

"August 1925," I said.

He blinked slowly, perhaps taken aback that I remembered. His black tongue curled across his lips. "You should have said yes."

"Rodolfo, you didn't love me. You wanted to make Natasha angry. I loved you once, Rudy, when I Turned you, but not then. Then, I knew who you were, what you were really capable of."

"You should have said yes," he repeated, eyes glazed and distant. "We could have ruled Hollywood. Chatelain and Chatelaine, Master and Mistress of the most powerful city on earth. Think of what we could have created, Ovsanna! We could have made an empire." For a moment, emotion overtook him and I watched the Change flicker across his face: his features turned lupine and vicious. He shrugged and his face resumed its human form. "But no matter. It was you who taught me the value of time, Ovsanna. So I waited. I spent decades tracking Lilith's whereabouts and then invited her to Hollywood as my guest."

So the mystery of Lilith's sudden appearance in California in the late sixties was finally explained. I'd always thought Manson had something to do with it.

"So tonight the old order changes." He spun back down the room and drew the scimitar. This was no movie prop; the edge glittered in the light of the basement's single bulb. "Tonight the Vampyres of Hollywood die the One True Death. At sunrise, Lilith and I will claim Los Angeles as our own, Master and Mistress of the City of Dreams."

"And the rest of my clan?"

"Why, they will swear fealty to the new chatelaines. They're actors, Ovsanna, most of them. They don't care who represents them as long as they get work. My London agency will open an office in Hollywood; maybe I'll take yours. And Anticipation will need a new studio boss. I can do what you've been doing and I can do it so much better. Perhaps it's time for . . . *The Return of the Sheik,* time to introduce the world to the 'new Valentino.' "

Pola spat at him, "What's happened to you, Rudy? We are your friends, your admirers, your family in blood. You can't destroy us. You can't."

"You are all nothing to me. I can destroy you, all of you, and I will. The Ancients will do it for me; they worship Lilith."

"But not you," I reminded him.

"They will," he said confidently. He gestured around the room with the sword. "Tonight we dine on vampyre flesh, we sup vampyre blood. The youngest of you is nearly half a millennium, the oldest close to a thousand years old. Lilith has promised me that eating your flesh will grant me a lifetime of memories, knowledge, and experiences. No single vampyre has ever drunk the blood of eleven of the most powerful vampyres in the world. I will experience all the lives you have lived, and all that you have done. That will make me the equal of Lilith."

Chaplin stirred. "There are twelve of us here. Who escapes your Last Supper?"

"Ah, yes, the lucky one," Rudy whispered. He walked down the basement to stand below me again. "Lilith has a special treat in store for you." His voice was rising, bloody black spittle flying from his lips. "You could have made me the ruler of Hollywood, you could have saved me, but no . . . no, you refused me; you forced me to die, destroyed my career, my life, cast me out into the shadows, where I watched lesser talents claim my throne."

"Steady on," Orson muttered. "You were a pretty face, Rudy. You were never that good."

"It is not enough that I kill you, Ovsanna Hovannes Garabedian; I must destroy you, ruin your name and your reputation, ensure that you are written out of the annals of Hollywood."

My senses flared and I knew what was about to happen even before Ghul appeared at the other end of the basement holding the limp body of Maral in his arms.

Rudy drove his sword into the floor and took Maral from the ghoul's white hands. Then he turned and held her up to me like an offering. I smelled her sweet perfume and the bitterness of fresh blood on her flesh. There was a bruise over her right eye, a thin cut above her eyebrow.

"I'm going to kill her myself, right here, right now in front of you."

I howled and shrieked, struggled against the metal spikes, wrenched hard enough to shift the stones in the wall. Blood, thick and black, flowed from my wounds, and I wept pale ichor. A dozen Changes warped my body, but to no effect: I remained pinned to the stones.

Rudy dropped Maral at my feet. "Tomorrow morning, her butchered body will be found in your home. There will be evidence of drugs, pornography, probably even cannibalism, and any other perversion I can think of. There will be items linking the previous murders to you, trophies from the scenes of each crime. It will be the biggest scandal ever to hit Hollywood and when it is over, your name will be a curse. You, of course, will be missing, and I doubt a world-wide search will ever find you: the Jimmy Hoffa of the entertainment industry."

Ghul stepped forward and his thin lips cracked into a hideous smile. "Lilith has reserved you for herself as is her right. It will take her a month to devour you, and I will ensure that you survive till the last mouthful."

Rudy laughed, the sound high-pitched and hysterical. "What do you have to say to that, Ovsanna Hovannes Garabedian, Chatelaine of Hollywood?"

CHAPTER THIRTY-SIX

PALM SPRINGS
5:50 P.M.

I was numb with horror and working purely on automatic. Breaking through the garden, I'd seen creatures beyond description. If I were still Catholic, I would have said that I'd seen devils from hell itself.

After that thing had taken Ovsanna, the rest of the monsters, the humans, and the peculiar beast people remained in the abattoir that was the living room. Gathered in a circle around the old Baby Jane woman in her weird, blood-spattered dress, they were eating the dead. The remains of my mother's pizzaiolla were spattered on the trunk of the palm tree. I'd heaved until there was nothing left but clear bile.

My mind had shut down. I had only one thought: to rescue Ovsanna. I'd watched her almost fight her way out; I'd seen the others take her down and then the albino carry out her unconscious body. Whatever they had in mind for her, it certainly wasn't good. I tracked the albino through the windows as he moved through the house, following his progress into what must have been a kitchen, except there was neither stove nor refrigerator there. These people ate their meat raw and bloody. The albino pulled open a door and disappeared down a flight of stairs. Seconds later, he turned on a dim light on the first floor and then disappeared again, down another flight of stairs. Whatever room he was going to, there were no windows; it was belowground. Basement, probably. He reappeared on the second floor a few minutes later and tossed a bloody hammer on the kitchen table. Something inside me twisted and I swore that if I found Ovsanna's corpse down there, I was going to put a bullet into the pasty-faced fuck, but only after I had messed him up with the hammer. Petty, I know, but I was in a petty frame of mind.

I got as far to the end of the palm as I could, held the Glock above my head, and dropped feetfirst into the moat. It wasn't deep, but it was stocked with things I was glad I couldn't see in the dark. Something slimy, with rubbery suckers, wrapped around my leg. I pounded on it with the handle of the Glock and it let loose just as a fucking fish bit into my ankle. I could hear more of them swimming toward me as I got my feet on land. I was missing a two-inch chunk of flesh from the back of my foot.

I kept my eyes fixed on the second-floor living room while I used my gun to hack through some of the cactus. The feast—there was no other way to describe it—was a scene by Hieronymus Bosch: women coupling with the leather-skinned beasts; animal-like creatures mounting one another in the midst of the blood, bones, and gore. In the middle sat the Bette Davis look-alike—cackling with glee.

I'm not the brightest, I know that. Sometimes it's been my saving grace. I didn't dwell on the implications of what I was seeing, didn't try to make sense of it. I ignored the scene in the room because I could do nothing about it; I just broke it down into its simplest components. All I knew for a certainty was that a woman was being held hostage and I needed to rescue her. I'd work out the details later. If there was a later.

I'd made it past the Spanish dagger and prickly pear and was climbing up the base of the bridge when the steel gate opened and a cloaked figure came through. I had the Glock ready to fire, but as it got closer I discovered I wasn't looking at another beast. If I hadn't been so terrified and sickened, I'd have laughed out loud. He looked liked Rudolph Valentino in those Sheik movies he did in the twenties. He was wearing a costume that was a cross between an Arab sheik and a Spanish bullfighter. The whole ensemble came complete with a sword and cape. He brushed past above me, close enough to touch, and disappeared through the front door.

I pulled myself up on the bridge and followed him into a dimly lit foyer just in time to see him go down the stairs to the ground floor.

The orgy in the living room had reached a crescendo. No one was paying attention to anything they weren't eating or screwing, and the old lady seemed mesmerized at the sight of it all. I dropped down to the ground on my belly and inched to the stairway door near the kitchen. The hall below me was empty. Bloody boot prints tracked across the tile floor and disappeared down another set of stairs.

I was at the top of the first set of stairs, just about to continue down, when the albino came out of a room below and stepped into the hallway there. Seen close up, he was an ugly misshapen son of a bitch, with tiny red eyes and skin the color of dead fish. He was carrying a limp Maral McKenzie in his arms. As he walked below me, I caught the stink of something foul, and I clenched my teeth to keep down what little bile I had left: he smelled like dead fish, too. He disappeared down the second set of stairs.

I needed to get down there. Holding the Glock close to my chest, I slipped from my hiding place and darted into the kitchen. Pressing flat against the wall, I risked a quick look downstairs. There was the hint of light from below and I could hear the murmur of voices. Snatching the hammer from the kitchen table, I shoved it into my belt and took the first step on the stairs, keeping close to the edges, hoping that none of them squeaked.

I could hear the indistinct drone of a voice and then someone started screaming.

The noise was the most terrifying sound I had ever heard. It was pain personified, overlain with a howl of raw anger, rage, and terror, and it was coming from Ovsanna. It took an enormous effort of will not to rush down the steps. In a way I was grateful for the sound, because it meant that she was still alive.

I heard a second voice, a man's voice, gloating, arrogant. "Tomorrow morning, her butchered body will be found in your home."

I was guessing it was the Valentino knockoff. And he could only be talking to Ovsanna.

Four steps from the bottom, I crouched down and peered into the basement. From my position on the stairs, I could only see a segment of the room, a length of dirt floor and about a foot of the wall. Standing five feet in front of me was the albino in his tuxedo. Directly in front of him, I could see the booted legs of the costumed Sheik. Maral's unmoving body was lying on the ground before him. There was no sign of Ovsanna.

The Sheik continued his ranting, and I realized I was listening to a confession. "There will be evidence of drugs, pornography, probably even cannibalism, and any other perversion I can think of. There will be items linking the previous murders to you, trophies from the scenes of each crime. It will be the biggest scandal ever to hit Hollywood and when it is over, your name will be a curse. You, of course, will be missing, and I doubt a worldwide search will ever find you: the Jimmy Hoffa of the entertainment industry."

I padded down the last few steps and pressed myself flat against the wall, my gun ready to fire. There was a second voice, the accent unlike any I had ever heard before, the sound cracked and broken, and I knew immediately it was the albino. "Lilith has reserved you for herself as is her right," he grated. "It will take her a month to devour you, and I will ensure that you survive till the last mouthful."

My stomach flipped. After everything I had just witnessed, I had no doubts these people were serious. And then the Sheik laughed and the sound was pure insanity. "What do you have to say to that, Ovsanna Hovannes Garabedian, Chatelaine of Hollywood?"

I'd heard enough. Holding the Glock in both hands, I stepped into the basement. "Put your hands up, you murdering little fucker!"

There were probably two seconds of absolute shocked silence, and I needed them to make sense out of what I was seeing: The walls of the basement were hung with men and women, arms outstretched, crucified with spikes through their wrists and ankles. Ovsanna was hanging on the end wall, facing me. Appallingly, they were all still alive and their heads turned as one in my direction.

The albino spun and lurched toward me, arms outstretched, mouth opening wide to reveal a circular maw of triangular teeth that never belonged in a human mouth. I pulled the trigger on the Glock and kept pulling, starting low and letting the recoil bring the gun up along his body. I load the Glock with Cor-Bon 115-grain HJP +P rounds. One round will take the average person down and make sure they don't get up. It took five rounds at almost point-blank range to even slow the albino. I watched huge gobbets of white flesh and stringy black blood erupt from his back. His giant hands fell on my shoulders, almost driving me to my knees. I knew if I went down, I was dead. He opened his mouth wide and dipped his head toward my face. Ramming the long, square barrel of the gun into his open mouth, snapping some of the ragged teeth, I pulled the trigger. Twice.

The shots lifted him off the ground and the top of his bald head popped off like a busted cantaloupe as he went tumbling away. He hit the ground five feet away from me—and exploded into black molasses-like sludge.

Everyone in the room, including the people nailed to the wall, exhaled in disgust.

The Sheik came at me with his sword, his eyes wide and utterly mad. There was something wrong with his face; in the light of the single bulb, which was now dripping black gore, it looked as if he were changing into some sort of dog.

"Who . . . who . . . who . . . ," he panted like a marathon runner.

"Peter," Ovsanna said, her voice calm and controlled, despite the excruciating pain she must have been in. "The others will be here. Shoot him and free us."

The Sheik turned and slashed at her with the sword, opening a wound across her belly and down onto her thighs.

I shot him in the right kneecap, sending him crashing to the ground. Then I shot him in the left for good measure. At this range the 115-grain round practically tore his legs off. He flapped on the ground, howling, clutching his shattered legs.

"Peter," Ovsanna said evenly, "you must sever his spine to complete his death."

I was about to protest when the thrashing man suddenly went silent and started to change. Something terrible was happening to his body, something that snapped bones and rent flesh. I heard muscles tear and cartilage grind.

"Young man?" Numbed, I turned to look at the man with the pencil-thin moustache nailed to the wall beside Ovsanna. He was another movie star look-alike, but I couldn't think who. "Kill him now and free us quickly." He tilted his chin. "We're about to have company. I can hear them coming."

The Sheik abruptly lurched upward, and he was no longer human. A wolf's jaws snapped at me. I shot it through the top of the skull, then, mindful of Ovsanna's advice, pressed the gun barrel against his spine and fired again, severing his neck. The creature folded in on itself and started to melt. I swear to God, I will never eat Jell-O again.

I took a step toward Ovsanna, but she shook her head. "Free Orson and Douglas first," she said, nodding to the two men on either side. "They'll be of more use to you."

I turned to the big man and pulled the hammer from my belt. "This is going to hurt."

"Believe me, it's certainly better than the alternative," he said in a powerful voice.

"What's the alternative?" I asked, inserting the end of the claw hammer into the spike driven into his wrist. Somehow his flesh had started to cover the head of the nail.

"Being eaten," he said, and continued to smile, as I tried to pull the spike out of the wall and his flesh. Gripping the hammer with both hands, bracing my legs on the wall, I levered. The pain must have been excruciating, but the man never cried out, even when the spike ripped out of his arm with the sound of crunching bones. "Good boy," he said, then took the hammer from my shaking hands and reached over to lever the spike out of his left wrist. "Keep an eye on the door, there's a good lad."

Working purely on instinct, I released the clip and my training took over. I had fired eleven rounds, and although there were still six in the gun, I didn't want to have to change clips mid-fight. Taking up a position at the bottom of the stairs, I pointed the gun up and waited.

I kept glancing over my shoulder, watching as the man Ovsanna called Orson used the hammer to lever the spike from his feet and drop flat on the ground with a groan. Then he clambered to his feet. "If you'll excuse me," he said to Ovsanna, as he quickly wrenched the nails from the flesh of the man she'd called Douglas.

Douglas dropped lightly to the floor and snatched up the Sheik's sword. Then he joined me at the door, slashing the sword to and fro, smiling a too-perfect smile. He looked like he knew what he was doing. I looked down at his bare feet. I could clearly see the holes in them. And they weren't bleeding.

"When this is over, I'm going to be asking some questions," I said, proud that I managed to keep my voice composed.

"When this is over, you will deserve some answers." He grinned, eyes sparkling. There was something so damned familiar about him.

"Do I know you? Have you been in the movies?"

"Once upon a time, dear boy. Once upon a time."

And then a monster dropped down the stairs. It reared up on two huge legs, massive claws slashing. It looked like a cross between a wolverine and a rabid bear. Before I even had time to react, Douglas slashed a *Z* across its stomach, and coils of greasy intestines spurted out of its body and wrapped around its legs. "Slows them down, every time," he said delightedly.

Just to make sure, I shot the thing in the head. Gore sprayed across the others that were shoving into the room: some human, some beasts, some I couldn't even describe. Douglas was extraordinary, handling the sword as if it was an extension of his arm. Each movement was precise: he sliced jugulars, cut tendons, blinded eyes, disemboweled and severed arteries to leave his victims helpless before me. I executed them without a second thought.

Suddenly the big man Ovsanna had called Orson was beside me. I hadn't even seen him move. Seconds ago, he'd been pinned to the wall with a one-inch spike through his wrist. Now the ugly hole was little more than a ragged tear and closing up even as I watched it. There were talons where his nails should have been. "Ovsanna needs you," he said. "Give me the gun and spare clips."

"Can you shoot?" I asked automatically.

"Can I shoot! Dear boy, my mother—rest her soul—was a crack shot. She taught me everything I know. I could shoot before I could walk."

Like every cop, I've been trained never to give up my weapon, but I handed over the gun without a second thought. "You've got four rounds left in this clip, one full clip of seventeen, and a third with six rounds in it."

"I'll make every bullet count." Then he took up a position beside Douglas. "Just like old times," he said.

"The old times were never like this," Douglas said with a grin, as he decapitated a beautiful young red-haired woman with the jaws of a shark. Her head, green eyes blinking in surprise, mouth working silently, rolled between his legs. He kicked it back into the fray. "I haven't had so much fun in years."

Orson had freed most of the men and women from the wall, and a black-suited man who looked astonishingly like Peter Lorre was working on the few who remained. Ovsanna sat on the ground at the back of the basement, beneath where she had been hung, cradling Maral's head in her lap, gently stroking her hair. Two women stood behind her and there was something frighteningly familiar about them. I felt I knew them from somewhere: they both looked like daytime soap stars.

I crouched in front of Ovsanna, unable to keep my eyes off the terrible wounds in her flesh. I could see right through the hole in her wrist . . . and again, there was no blood. I looked around quickly: the walls should have been running red with blood where arms and legs had been nailed. They were dry. And Ovsanna hadn't bled when the Sheik sliced her.

Ovsanna lifted her head from Maral's limp body and stared at me and I saw something in her black eyes. "Thank you," she said simply. "We are in your debt, Peter King," she said formally, "a debt we will honour and repay a hundredfold."

Everyone murmured what might have been an "aye."

She pressed her hand against my cheek. I turned it to look at the wound in her wrist. A flap of skin had appeared over the hole; it was throbbing with veins.

"If I was to ask you what you are, would you tell me?" My mouth was dry; I could barely get the words out.

"If you were to ask," she said very quietly.

"What are you, Ovsanna? Who are you? Who are these people?"

"I am Ovsanna Hovannes Garabedian, Chatelaine of the Clan Dakhanavar of the First Bloodline, and we . . . why, we are the Vampyres of Hollywood."

Chapter Thirty-Seven

"I need you to do something for me, Peter."

He looked at me numbly and nodded. I was surprised he was still functioning. I had a good idea what he might have seen; I had left the living room in a bit of a mess, and Lilith and her followers were never ones to let a meal go uneaten.

Bizarrely, the first thought I'd had, when he stepped into the basement and yelled at Rudy, was that he really knew how to make an entrance. He could be the next Kurt Russell. One moment we'd been hanging on the wall, waiting—though never ready—for death, and then Peter was there and suddenly Ghul the ghoul was so much soup. After countless millennia, shot down by a BHPD cop. And then Rudy. I didn't even feel him cut me with the sword, but I watched Peter shoot the legs out from under him and then follow my instructions and hit his spine. And Rudy was dead. Just like that.

Everything changed.

As Peter and Douglas fought Lilith's beasts, Orson freed me and set about releasing the others. I sat on the ground and gathered Maral into my arms, holding her tight, relishing her strong heartbeat and her steady breathing. Brushing the blood off her forehead, I brought my fingers to my lips and sucked, drawing sustenance from the stickiness. Mary and Pola came to stand beside me, old enmities forgotten for the moment.

"What do we do?" Pola asked.

I opened my mouth to respond, but it was Orson who answered for me. "We go to war," he boomed.

"But the Ancients?" Mary protested.

I raised a hand for silence. "It is Lilith we must concern ourselves with." I looked into Orson's bright eyes. "I know what I must do. Ask Peter to join me."

When Peter came and crouched before me, his eyes locked onto mine, looking for answers to the nightmare he'd landed in.

And when he asked me who we were, I told him.

I watched his eyes widen, saw recognition in them as he looked at the members of my clan. I saw him look at Mary and recognize her; then his head snapped around to look at Douglas, who was laughing delightedly as he slashed with the sword, every inch the hero, Zorro, Robin Hood, and the Black Pirate all over again. Peter suddenly realized who Charlie and Peter were and his mouth opened even wider. I saw questions forming and I pressed my finger to his lips to silence them. "I swear to you I will answer every question you have, but not now. Not now. I need you to do something for me."

He nodded.

"I need some of your blood."

I could have taken it by force and he would have been powerless to resist, but after all he had done for us, I couldn't do that to him. I waited, watching the confusion in his eyes, and then the decision. He pulled up the sleeve of his jacket and presented me with his left wrist. "How much?"

"About a pint."

"Will it hurt?"

Taking the proffered wrist, I pressed it to my lips. "Not too much," I promised as my teeth lengthened. "Just a little prick."

"Not the first time someone has said that to me." He smiled and I locked on.

His blood was rich and heady. Memories and impressions flooded my system, fragments of the terrible images he had witnessed. I was concentrating hard on preventing the Change from completely altering my features when he turned to Mary and asked, "Why do you do this?"

"The Chatelaine needs to replenish her strength before she fights again. We cannot fight the Ancients without her to lead us."

"The monsters, the leathery black things: what are they?" Peter asked.

"The Ancients. Very, very old vampyres."

"And you are all like them?"

"Not at all." Pola sounded affronted. "There's no one here over nine hundred years old. The Ancients are a thousand years and more."

"And the crazy woman in black?"

I raised my bloody face from Peter's arm and saw him blanch. His blood, hot, sweet and incredibly powerful, surged through me, leaving me gasping. "That is Lilith," I snarled, this time unable to prevent a Change from warping my features into something saurian. "The mother of us all." I dipped my head to lick his wrist, my saliva closing and healing the wounds. "Before Eve, there was Lilith, the equal of Man. When she was thrown out of the Garden of Eden, she consorted with another race, an ancient serpent race that pre-dated mankind. In time she gave birth to new hybrid creatures, the vampyre and the were-folk." Laying Maral gently to one side, covering her in my torn jacket, I rose to my full height, and sought a Change I'd not used in three centuries. With Peter's blood fueling me, black batlike leathery wings unfurled out of my rear ribs and rose over my shoulders. "Hear me."

The Vampyres of Hollywood and the sole human, Peter King, looked at me.

"I am your Chatelaine. I could command your obedience if I so wished, but I will not command. Not this night. It is time to choose." My voice was altering as the Change warped my body. "Tonight, Lilith and Rudy sought to destroy us all. Tonight, we have a choice: we can flee and hide, as we have done for some many centuries, or we can take the fight to Lilith."

"And what if you slay Lilith?" James asked me. "If she dies, do we not all die with her?"

"James, you fool," Tod hissed. "You forget we created that myth."

"Oh! So we did."

"So choose: flee now and spend the rest of your lives starting at every shadow, or stand and fight with me." The Change was nearly complete, rendering my voice almost unintelligible.

Surprisingly, it was Charlie Chaplin who stepped forward first. "I helped make this town," he said simply, "I'll not let Lilith destroy it." Hollywood had treated him abominably, and yet here he was volunteering to defend the town that had once abandoned him. And one by one the others stepped forward, except Douglas and Orson, who were still defending the stairs. I knew what their response was.

I crouched awkwardly before Peter. I was as much a monster now as the creatures outside, but I saw no fear, no loathing in his eyes. "When we leave here, take Maral and flee. And whatever you do, don't return until there are no more sounds."

"There are police on the way. SWAT, too."

"It would be better if you kept them away."

"I was thinking, it might be better if this place burned to the ground," he suggested. "Fewer questions that way. With answers I couldn't even begin to give."

I think I fell in love with him then.

I turned and walked away, striding past my army. The Vampyres of Hollywood had *Changed,* taking on the shapes that had inspired mankind's darkest myths. Theda's kohl-rimmed eyes turned blood-red as she morphed into a sleek black jaguar, twice its natural size. Olive's curly hair filled with snakes writhing out of the skinless bones of her skull, her body nude and full breasted, with the haunches of a goat. Orson, my beloved Orson, grew even more bloated, hair covering his giant girth, a were-bull with huge, curling horns. One by one, Mary and Charles, Peter and Pola, and Tod and James and Charlie transformed into werewolves and gargoyles, grotesqueries with falcons' wings and bat faces, scales and snakes' skins. Only Douglas chose to remain in his human form, though it was subtly altered to make him taller, broader, more heroic.

I paused at the door and turned to look back at Peter King. He was standing at the back wall looking at me, and for a moment I saw myself through his eyes. I had allowed my body to adopt the ancient and original form of the Clan Dakhanavar: that of the dragul, the dragon. Peter raised his hand in farewell. The claw I raised was tipped with six-inch-long nails.

CHAPTER THIRTY-EIGHT

PALM SPRINGS
6:30 P.M.

After everything else I'd witnessed this evening, discovering that Hollywood's classic actors were still alive didn't faze me. As I put names to faces, the one thought uppermost in my mind was that I had to get some autographs for my mother. I guess I was in shock. Probably the same shock that allowed me to watch Ovsanna drink my blood and then begin to change into a dragon. Not some cuddly Disney creation, either. She wasn't Barney. She was something that looked like it belonged on the side of a Gothic cathedral, complete with claws, teeth, tail, wings, and crocodile skin. Only her eyes remained unchanged. I'd almost said "human," but I knew then that Ovsanna and the rest of the people in the basement—indeed the whole house—were not humans. A massive bull-headed man, looking like something off a Greek urn, handed me back my gun. I think he said, "You've six rounds left"; then he turned and stamped down the room on proper cloven hooves.

And suddenly they were gone and the basement was empty.

I found myself completely disorientated and the room suddenly shifted and spun around me. Had I just imagined everything? For just a moment I wondered if I were tripping; had the cactus outside been smeared with acid or something, some toxic hallucinogen that poisoned me through my cut skin? But there was a bruised bite mark on my wrist and the black, sticky shape on the floor that had just been the tuxedoed albino. And Rudolph Valentino's Jell-Oed remains were bubbling in the dirt. That hadn't been a look-alike and this wasn't an hallucination. Shit. I'd just shot the real Rudolph Valentino.

I was gathering Maral into my arms when she opened her gray eyes, then her mouth. I pressed my hand over it. "It's Peter," I said urgently. "Police." Her eyes focused, then narrowed as she recognized me. "What's the last thing you remember?"

"Talking to you on the phone . . . and then there was someone at the window . . . and then . . ." She trailed away and shook her head. "You wouldn't believe the dreams I've had."

"Nightmares?"

She nodded.

"I've seen them," I said grimly. "Can you stand?"

Maral McKenzie came shakily to her feet. "Ovsanna . . . ?"

"Is fine. She told me to get you out of here."

"Where is she?"

"Upstairs."

"Doing what?"

"You wouldn't believe me if I told you." I checked the clip on the Glock, then pulled my backup piece, a .32 S&W, from my belt. "Can you shoot?"

"I'm from Louisiana," she said, her accent suddenly pronounced. She slipped off the safety, flipped open the cylinder, checked the loads, and snapped it closed, all in one smooth movement. "Is there anything you want to tell me?" she asked.

"Like what?"

She lifted a booted foot. "Like what the fuck I just stepped in?"

"Believe me," I said sincerely, "you really don't want to know."

The stairs were awash with blood and body parts. Ovsanna's Vampyres had cleared the bodies from the stairwell as they'd fought their way upstairs. I stepped onto what might have been a brain and promised myself, when this was over, that I was going to burn every stitch of clothing I was wearing. Maral, to her credit, kept her mouth shut and her eyes fixed firmly ahead. Looking down at the floor was definitely not a good idea.

The house was eerily quiet.

I had expected screams and shouts, but there was nothing. When we reached the kitchen windows, I realized why. They were all out-side: the Vampyres of Hollywood, the monstrous Ancients, and Lilith's "people," whatever they were. They were standing in a circle on the mountain side of the house and they were completely silent. In the center of the circle stood Lilith and the dragon Ovsanna. Lilith didn't look like Baby Jane anymore; she was slowly changing, elongating, transforming into a huge yellow snake.

Maral stopped, widemouthed at the bestiary, and I caught her arm and dragged her away. She put her mouth close to my ear and pointed with her chin at the dragon. "Ovsanna?"

I nodded.

"Impressive. I didn't know she could do that," she muttered.

"You knew she was a vampyre!"

"Yes. Of course."

"We'll talk about that later," I promised. "Let's go."

With everyone gathered on the mountain, we made our way through the house. I'm sure that it had once been beautiful, but it was never going to make the pages of *Palm Springs Life* again. There were bodies everywhere, stacked like cordwood in the corners, propped up against the walls, shoved into side rooms, hanging from above over the exposed beams. All of the bodies were pale and bloodless, and most had parts missing.

"They're so young," Maral whispered.

I nodded; I'd already noticed that. "Runaways," I said softly. "Some of the thousands who come to Hollywood looking to be famous."

"It could have been me," Maral muttered.

We stopped outside the door to the dining room. Neither of us wanted to step inside. What remained scattered across the floor was indescribable. "I want to burn this place to the ground."

"Amen to that," Maral said sincerely. "I have an idea," she added, turning and darting back through the house. "Help me find the garage."

The triple-door garage was at the far end of the house. I hadn't followed the stone wall that far in the dark or I would have come to it. Probably could have saved myself the swim in the moat if I had. We got to it through another flight of stairs from the kitchen. It was huge, but I guess it had to be—everything from the empty rooms upstairs had been dumped into it. Antique chairs stacked on top of cut velvet sofas, all of them shredded and broken. A long, ornate cherrywood dining table was scratched by the computers, VCRs, TVs, clock radios, and a microwave piled on top of it. Broken beds in a corner, covered with torn blankets and stained pillows. Lilith should fire her decorator.

There were three cars in the garage, a classic 1940 Studebaker Champion, a modern BMW 7 series, and an enormous black Hummer.

"Check the tanks," Maral snapped.

"They'll be full," I promised, and they were, ready for a quick getaway, no doubt. The doors were unlocked, keys in the ignition. I tried the three buttons on the Hummer's dash; the middle one worked the garage door. I climbed out of the car to find Maral stuffing the fuel tanks with lengths of cloth torn from a blanket. I could smell the gas.

"My granddad taught me this trick," she explained.

There was a storage cupboard at the back of the garage, filled with an assortment of cleaning supplies that had obviously never been used. Most of them bore the legend "Inflammable." Carrying out a handful, I emptied them over the blankets and pillows, dumped more onto the velvet sofa and a stack of books lying on the floor. I returned to the cupboard and filled my arms.

And when I turned around, a red-haired, fang-toothed woman was looking at me. My gun was on the shelf behind me and I knew, even as her fingers sprouted daggerlike claws and lunged at me, that I was not going to make it.

The axe caught her in the side of the head and slammed her into the wall. She stood looking at me, blinking slowly until both eyes popped out of their sockets and she slid wetly to the floor, leaving a sluglike trail on the wall.

"Your granddad teach you that, too?" I asked Maral, shakily.

"Sure did."

I emptied the remainder of the cleaning supplies around the rest of the room and turned around to find Maral pulling the microwave off the table. She heaved it up onto a workbench and plugged it in. The clock started blinking on and off. "Are we cooking?"

"You feel like eating after all we've seen?" she demanded, lifting the microwave off the bench and putting it on the floor beside the rag hanging from the Hummer's tank.

I shook my head. I didn't think I'd ever eat again. I wondered if Mom would buy my explanation.

Maral popped a jar of varnish and a pot of paint into the microwave, spun the dial to full, and set the clock for three minutes. She pressed the start button and the plate started to turn. "We should go," she said.

I looked at her stupidly.

"There are certain things you don't put in a microwave unless you want a big fiery explosion." She grinned, catching my hand and dragging from me from the room.

"Learned that from Granddad, too?"

"Nope, I worked that one out for myself."

CHAPTER THIRTY-NINE

Lilith became the serpent.

Standing in the center of the circle behind the house in Palm Springs, surrounded by her followers while I was backed up by the Vampyres of Hollywood, she began the appalling transformation into a shape that is forbidden to my kind. Once Changed into a serpent, a vampyre can never change back; it is impossible to return to oneself. But Lilith is not one of us. The creature that had tempted Adam and Eve in the Garden had been no devil, no demon: it had been Lilith.

When I led my vampyres up from the basement, destroying all in our path, I had expected to find the Ancients arrayed against us. But when they saw us burst from the house, led by a dragul, I watched them melt back into the shadows. The Dearg Due, the Bobhan Sith, the *dhampirs* and were-creatures threw themselves at us, but we easily brushed them aside, reveling in their destruction, relishing the taste of their blood.

Douglas fought at my side. "Why aren't the Ancients attacking?" he shouted.

I answered him in Armenian, finding it easier to shape the words using a throat never meant for human speech. "They know what happened to Rudy and Ghul. Suddenly Lilith is not so powerful as she would have them believe. The Ancients are fearful, they do not want to die—and they know if they go up against us, at least some of them will perish."

"As old as time and still afraid to die," Douglas said, a note of genuine wonder in his voice.

Bull-headed Orson strode up beside me, plucked a pair of *dhampirs* off the ground and flung them at the cowering Ancients. The broken half vampyres crashed to the ground at their feet and the Ancients fell snarling upon them. "Let's kill the *dhampirs* and the were-creatures, then feed them to the Ancients," he rasped. "They'll feast upon them until they are too stuffed to move and then we'll take them."

"Enough!"

The voice, low and subsonic, rolled across the mountain. Stones and gravel tumbled down the hill and the water in the moat roiled.

"Enough!"

Lilith had appeared, standing in the living room door. Immediately the surviving *dhampirs* and were-creatures fell back.

"Enough."

In the sudden and absolute silence, the tiny woman-child in her hideous makeup made her way outside. I was wearing the dragul form, impenetrable to sword or spear, strong enough to tear steel and pulverize stone, and even I felt the sour tendrils of fear at the back of my throat.

And as she approached, she changed.

Before humanity claimed this earth, the snake people ruled. Lilith bred with the last of them and created us and, in doing so, she became one with them. Now her features elongated: nose pushing forward, chin sliding back, eyes shrinking, moving higher on her head. Her wig slid away, revealing a scabrous scalp. I watched her arms shrivel up her sleeves, and then the filthy dress slid away. She was briefly—horrifyingly—naked and then she was no longer human.

"Ghul is dead," I said. "Rudy, too."

A black forked tongue flickered in her mouth. "Dear, sweet Ghul," she hissed, sounding genuinely upset. She didn't seemed too put out about Rudy, I noted. "You have no idea what he was. He was glorious, my Morningstar. Ah, the flesh he has eaten, the blood he has drunk. The meat of generations." Her legs had fused, and her body was elongating and changing color as she moved closer.

I was aware that a circle had formed around us, the Ancients and the surviving *dhampirs* and were behind Lilith, the Vampyres of Hollywood behind me.

Lilith was almost completely serpentine now: huge and hideous, her yellow-veined body rippling with muscle, her mouth filled with enormous upper and lower fangs. If she wrapped those coils around me, dragul or not, I was just so much paste, and I was sure her fangs could penetrate my armored hide.

"We could all rush her?" Douglas suggested. "She might get some of us, but not all—"

I shook my massive head. "This is my fight. I must do it alone. If I defeat her, then the Ancients and the surviving *dhampirs* will owe me fealty."

"And if she defeats you? And eats you?" Douglas said grimly. "Your flesh and blood alone would make her immeasurably more powerful."

"If that happens, Douglas, then I suggest you run!"

Even as I was speaking, Lilith lunged. She was fifteen feet away, then she twisted and coiled and suddenly she was airborne above me. I threw myself down and forward and passed beneath her, feeling her stinking skin brush my wings. The serpent hit the ground hard enough to shatter the stones beneath. Without pausing she turned and spat at me—a huge gobbet of luminescent phlegm-colored slime. I spun away and most of it splashed onto an unfortunate *dhampir*. The venom ate through her flesh, revealing muscle, sinews, then bone. The unfortunate creature was still alive as it started to eat away at her internal organs. An Ancient put her out of her misery by snapping off her head. And eating it.

Lilith moved again, the upper part of her body turning in one direction, the lower half in another. I dodged her lunging, snapping teeth, but her armored tail caught me across the chest, driving me back into the arms of a tall, chitinous Ancient. His claws grabbed my arms, holding me, but I drove my head back and up and my pointed horns caught him in the soft flesh under the chin, penetrating mouth and tongue and driving up into his brain. He was dead before he hit the ground.

But the moment's distraction was enough for Lilith. Her tail coiled around my ankles, slithering between my feet, and suddenly she was on top of me. I caught her massive throat in both hands before her fangs bit into my face, my six-inch-long claws digging deep into the thick skin. I felt her throat work in my hands and barely managed to turn her head to one side as she spat again. An Ancient fell writhing as the venom ate away its slablike face. A single drop caught the edge of my wing and hissed like acid through the skin. The pain was indescribable. I brought my wings around, encasing her serpent body in their leathery folds, using their hooks to rip and tear her yellow flesh.

"Too late, dragul Dakhanavar, too late." Lilith's voice was a foul whisper.

The coils of flesh around my legs tightened. If I fell, it was all over. My hands were still locked around her throat, keeping her teeth and spit away from my face. Drool was running down her chin, and even the diluted venom was burning my talons. It was only a matter of moments before she broke free and spat full in my face. Or bit it off.

So I bit her.

Opening my dragul jaws wide, I clamped down on the flesh of her neck and bit hard. The taste of her flesh in my mouth was disgusting, the feel abhorrent. The sudden burst of images, memories, and sensations overwhelmed me and I loosened my grip. Lilith erupted into a frenzy and flung me from her. I crashed onto the ground, shattering the flagstones, tearing my wings to paper on the cacti. Shakily, I got to my feet, spitting Lilith's meat from my mouth. A stringy spray of phlegmy venom arched through the air towards me. I turned sharply, and then the ground shifted beneath my feet, and suddenly I was surrounded by huge fish in the filthy water of the moat.

Water is not the natural habitat of the dragul. We cannot swim.

Terror and Lilith's abhorrent blood in my mouth gave me the strength to Change. There were a dozen shapes I could have taken if I'd thought about it, but I couldn't think, so when I rose from the water I was Ovsanna Moore. Piranhas were tearing at me.

I scrambled out of the pool and stood up. I had fought as a dragul, but I would die as a human; there was something fitting about that.

And suddenly Lilith was towering over me and around me, jaws gaping. She wouldn't use her venom on me this time, I knew. She'd want to taste my flesh and drink my blood. Maybe I could choke her on the way down. I was certainly determined to try. Her mouth opened, wider, wider, wider still as the bottom jaw unhinged.

"I am going to swallow you whole."

I heard a pop and smelled the stink of gasoline, and the next instant a wash of superheated air detonated out from the center of the house. Half the house vaporized in the massive explosion. Huge stones rained down in lethal shrapnel. And then, in what seemed like slow motion, the front end of a Hummer hit Lilith full in the teeth and drove her head back into the ground.

"Swallow that, bitch."

It took Lilith's body mere seconds to liquefy and dribble into the pool.

CHAPTER FORTY

PALM SPRINGS
6:50 P.M.

I'd just opened the front gate when the massive explosion ripped the heart out of the house. Maral and I stopped, then as one turned and ran back through the chaos. The house looked like the antechamber of hell. Piles of dead bodies burned like flaming torches; floorboards were warping and snapping in the intense heat. Huge swaths of the ceiling had bellied inward. Rooms had disappeared.

We raced through the dining room—I'll never eat barbecue again—and burst out into the backyard. Flaming stones were falling like rockets, exploding all over the garden, cacti were alight, and flames shot up the palms, while ribbons of burning cloth spiraled slowly downward.

I'd expected to find monsters and the Vampyres of Hollywood, but instead the garden was deserted . . . save for the lone figure of a bloody and battered Ovsanna Moore leaning against the rear end of the Hummer. Its front was buried nose deep in the ground. Ovsanna turned. She had a slight smile on her face as we both came running up.

"When you said we ought to burn it to the ground, you really meant it, didn't you."

"I had some expert help," I said, looking at Maral.

Ovsanna brought Maral's hand to her lips and kissed it. Then she brought my lips to hers and kissed me. I wondered if there was a message there.

"Where's Lilith?" I asked.

"I guess the whole thing was just too much to swallow," Ovsanna said.

I was sitting on the side of the road, one arm around Ovsanna Moore, the other around Maral McKenzie, watching a prime example of Palm Springs real estate burn to the ground, when the first of the fire trucks arrived. Then the PSPD, Chief Barton, the paramedics, and the press. Lots and lots of press.

"What happened to the Ancients and the were-creatures?" I asked quickly, before they had a chance to descend on us.

"Fled into the desert. I think they've had enough to eat for a while."

"And the Vampyres of Hollywood?"

Ovsanna turned her head and tilted her chin toward a long line of crows perched on the roof directly behind us, looking like something out of *The Jungle Book*. "A little singed about the feathers, but safe."

After everything I'd seen, I didn't even question her. "Say, do you think you can get me some autographs for my mother?"

"I think I can manage that." Ovsanna smiled. "You rescued us, Peter," she continued. "I think we were kidnapped by some sort of cannibal cult, don't you? Doesn't that sound like something the press will buy?"

"Sounds like a movie," Maral drawled.

"Oh, it will be," Ovsanna promised, leaning into me, putting her head on my shoulder. "This is going to make you a hero, Peter," she added.

"I've been a hero before. It has its downside. The last person I rescued bit me on the ass. At least you haven't done that."

Ovsanna raised her head and smiled. I swear I saw fangs.

"Well . . . not yet anyway," she said. And then she kissed me.